Select praise for the
New York Times b...
Rachel Vincent

"Readers who haven't read *Blood Bound*
will have no problem getting into this story."
—*RT Book Reviews* on *Shadow Bound*

"*Blood Bound* offers a little something for everyone:
a convincing magical system for urban fantasy fans;
for romance readers, a love that time and distance
can't break; and a twist-and-turn plot for
mystery buffs.... A gritty, dangerous world of
sorcerous bindings and forbidden love."
—*Shelf Awareness*

"With *Blood Bound*, Vincent has created an original,
new paranormal universe full of interesting characters
with awesome powers or Skills, as they are called in
the book. Readers will enjoy getting to know Liv,
an exciting heroine with a complicated past."
—*RT Book Reviews*

"*Blood Bound* is a strong, cohesive work
founded on a unique paranormal premise
and will lead nicely to the rest of the trilogy."
—*Fresh Fiction*

"Action-packed, clever and full of twists…
a series into which everyone interested in
the paranormal genre can sink their teeth.
—*The Romance Reader Reviews*

Also by
New York Times **bestselling author**
Rachel Vincent

From
HARLEQUIN MIRA

The Shifters

STRAY
ROGUE
PRIDE
PREY
SHIFT
ALPHA

Unbound

BLOOD BOUND
SHADOW BOUND

From
HARLEQUIN TEEN

Soul Screamers

Soul Screamers Volume One
"My Soul to Lose"
MY SOUL TO TAKE
MY SOUL TO SAVE

Soul Screamers Volume Two
MY SOUL TO KEEP
MY SOUL TO STEAL
"Reaper"

Soul Screamers Volume Three
IF I DIE
"Never to Sleep"
BEFORE I WAKE

WITH ALL MY SOUL

RACHEL VINCENT

OATH BOUND

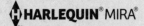

HARLEQUIN® MIRA®

If you purchased this book without a cover you should be aware
that this book is stolen property. It was reported as "unsold and
destroyed" to the publisher, and neither the author nor the
publisher has received any payment for this "stripped book."

Recycling programs
for this product may
not exist in your area.

ISBN-13: 978-0-7783-1430-1

OATH BOUND

Copyright © 2013 by Rachel Vincent

All rights reserved. Except for use in any review, the reproduction or
utilization of this work in whole or in part in any form by any electronic,
mechanical or other means, now known or hereafter invented, including
xerography, photocopying and recording, or in any information storage or
retrieval system, is forbidden without the written permission of the publisher,
Harlequin MIRA, 225 Duncan Mill Road, Don Mills, Ontario M3B 3K9,
Canada.

This is a work of fiction. Names, characters, places and incidents are
either the product of the author's imagination or are used fictitiously, and
any resemblance to actual persons, living or dead, business establishments,
events or locales is entirely coincidental.

® and TM are trademarks of Harlequin Enterprises Limited or its corporate
affiliates. Trademarks indicated with ® are registered in the United States Patent
and Trademark Office, the Canadian Trade Marks Office and in other countries.

For questions and comments about the quality of this book, please contact us
at CustomerService@Harlequin.com.

Printed in U.S.A.

To the readers who traveled with me
into this dark, twisted world.
I promise there is light at the end of the tunnel…

One

Sera

I've never been very good with the word *no*. I have trouble saying it. I have more trouble hearing it. And accepting it…well, I find that damn near impossible. Always have. Which is why, when the guard at the gate in front of Jake Tower's house—his *estate*—refused to let me in, I kind of wanted to pound his teeth into his throat, then out the back of his head.

Instead, I took a deep breath and counted to ten. "Let's try this again." I laid my left arm across the open window in my car door and glanced through my windshield at the huge house beyond the closed gate. The road actually ended in front of the Tower estate in a cul-de-sac of its own, so that drivers, rebuffed by the locked gate, could turn their cars around and skulk back the way they'd come, properly intimidated by a wealth and power most could never even touch.

I don't skulk.

"Sera Brandt, to see Julia Tower," I repeated, my voice firm with the kind of self-appointed authority only colossal loss and boundless rage can produce.

"I told you, miss." The guard sounded exasperated this time. "Ms. Tower isn't seeing anyone else today. She's suffered a recent family tragedy, and—"

"She'll see me. Just get on your little radio and tell her I'm here."

"You don't have an appointment, and she's not—" My left arm shot out the open window and I grabbed the front of his black shirt. Before he could do more than grunt in surprise, I jerked him down and forward, smashing the front of his face into the top of my car.

Dazed, he backed away on wobbly legs when I let him go, blood dripping from his nose and down his chin, and before he could think clearly enough to go for his gun, I shoved my car door open, knocking him off his feet entirely. He landed flat on his back, his head inches from the guard booth, arms splayed out at his sides.

If his partner had been there, I'd have been in big trouble. But I'd waited until his partner left for the bathroom, or coffee, or a cigarette, or whatever the Tower estate guards spent their free time on, specifically to avoid that snag.

While the man on the ground moaned and held both hands to his bloody face, I unsnapped the holster exposed by his open jacket and pulled the gun out. I wasn't sure what kind it was—I'd never shot one—but it was big, so I set it on the desk through the window of the guard booth, to keep it out of his immediate reach.

If I'd known how to get the bullets out of it, I would have taken them.

Then I pulled his radio free from the other side of his belt and pressed the button.

And that's when I realized where I'd messed up. I'd introduced myself by the wrong name. The guard didn't give a shit who Sera Brandt was, and Julia Tower—Lia, to those who knew her personally—certainly wouldn't. So when I pressed the radio button and the soft hum of static was replaced with an even silence, I looked straight into the camera attached to the roof of the guard booth and gave them my real name.

"This is Sera Tower. Open the fucking gate."

For a moment, radio silence followed my announcement while the camera whirred, zooming in on my face, and I wondered if my message would even get through to Lia, who surely had better things to do than listen in on the guards' radio frequency.

According to the internet, both the official news sites and the often more reliable gossip pages, Lia Tower had taken over her brother Jake's business affairs when he'd died four months before, and I could only assume she'd taken over most of his personal affairs, too. But that was truly just a guess. Until the guard refused to let me see her, I didn't even know for sure that she still lived in his house—according to the obituary, Jake Tower also left behind a wife and two small children, who had surely inherited the property.

"Sera…*Tower?*" a faceless voice asked over the radio a second later. His skepticism was clear. He'd never heard of me. I'd never wanted to be heard of, until then.

I'd never even said it out loud before—my real last name. I'd never claimed my connection to the family I'd never met. The family my mother had hidden me from, for most of my life. But there was no other way through that gate, and I couldn't get what I'd come for without the resources locked away in the fortress of a house behind it.

"Do you have an appointment?" However, I could tell by his uncertain tone that the question felt as ridiculous to him as it sounded to me. I was a *Tower,* after all, if I were telling the truth. But protocol is protocol.

"I don't need one. Just tell her Sera is here. Jake Tower's love child has come home."

The first-floor study they stuck me in could well have been called a library. Hardback books lined floor-to-ceiling shelves covering three walls. The center of the room held two couches and several small tables, but I sat on the window seat built into the fourth wall, so I could see the entire room.

A glance at my cell phone told me I'd been there for nearly forty minutes—8:00 p.m. had come and gone, without even the offer of a drink. No wonder my butt was going numb. But they'd stationed a guard outside the door and told me to stay put, and now that I'd already gotten Lia's attention, creating another scene didn't seem very likely to work in my favor.

Making me wait was a strategic move on Lia's part. It had to be. To show me how unimportant I was. The internet was virtually void of information about the Towers' personal lives, and my mother hadn't been much more forthcoming, but I remembered every single thing she *had* told me over the years.

They are master manipulators.

Everything they do has a purpose—sometimes several purposes—whether you can see that or not.

Don't think that being one of them makes you safe. They won't hesitate to spill their own blood from your veins, if you become a threat.

With that in mind, I suddenly wondered if I was being watched. Studied. Or had I moved beyond simple caution and into paranoia? Either way, I couldn't resist a couple of casual glances at the ceiling to look for cameras. But if they were there, they were hidden. Like I'd been for years.

On the first day of kindergarten I'd discovered that the dad I'd grown up with wasn't actually my father, genetically speaking. My dad—he was Daddy, back then—was still waving goodbye to me through the classroom window when this little girl with curly pigtails asked me how come my dad was dark and I was light.

I'd never really thought about that before. I'd always assumed that I matched my mom for the same reason my little sister matched our dad. Just because. The same reason the ocean matched the sky, but the grass matched the trees. But before I could explain about how we each matched a different parent, a little boy with a smear of chocolate across one cheek poked his head into our conversation with an unsolicited bit of vicious commentary.

"That's 'cause he's not her real dad. She's pro'ly adopted."

I punched him in the nose, and then his cheek was smeared with chocolate *and* blood.

That was the very first punch I threw. It was followed, in rapid succession, by my first trip to the principal's office, my first expulsion and my first visit with a child psychologist.

In retrospect, I can see that I overreacted. Pigtails and Bloody Nose were just naturally curious. They probably didn't mean to throw my entire life into chaos and make me question my own existence at the tender age of five.

It took nearly an hour for the principal, guidance counselor, and my parents to calm me down enough to buckle me into my seat in the car. It then took another hour for my parents to explain that I wasn't adopted. I was simply conceived out of wedlock, fathered by a man my mother knew before she ever met my dad.

That's a lot for a kindergartner to absorb, but my parents seemed confident that I could handle it. My dad reassured me that he loved me more than I could possibly imagine, and that he would always be my dad. And that was that.

But my temper failed to improve.

When I was about fifteen, I overheard Mom tell Dad that I might have gotten my temper from my father, but my sharp tongue had come from Aunt Lia. Eight years later, as I stood waiting impatiently for an audience with her, nerves and anger buzzing just beneath the surface of my skin, that was still virtually all I knew about the aunt I'd never met.

That, and that Aunt Lia was perfectly willing to let her own niece stew in isolation. Obviously this wasn't the hugs-and-kisses kind of family. But it was the only kind I had left.

My dad had been a mechanic and an amateur musician who smiled with his eyes, even when his mouth took a firm stand. My biological father had been the head of one of the largest, most dangerous Skilled crime families in the country who, according to my mom, probably smiled as he ordered people hunted down and executed.

I hadn't come into the Tower house with blinders on.

Finally out of patience and buzzing with nerves, I crossed the room and pulled the study door open.

"I'm sorry, ma'am, but you'll have to wait inside," the guard posted in the foyer said.

"Or what?" I propped my hands on my hips. "You'll shoot me?"

His hesitation and confusion told me two things. First, he was accustomed to intimidating people with his size and his gun. Second, he wasn't actually prepared to shoot me in broad daylight, in the middle of his boss's formal entryway—an admirable trait in a human being, but quite possibly a liability in a syndicate muscleman.

"Fine. Shoot me," I called over my shoulder as I marched past him on the marble tile, headed for an office whose blurry occupants I could see through the frosted-glass door. I was halfway there, irritated guard on my heels, when something small and mechanical raced across the tile in front of me, and I stopped inches short of tripping over it.

I bent to pick up the remote control car just as two small children stumbled to a stop in front of me.

"Sorry." The little girl pushed tangled brown hair from her face and stared up at me through huge, bright blue eyes. "Ms. George says Kevin drives like a maniac."

"She also says you suck your thumb like a baby." The boy—Kevin, evidently—snatched the toy car from my hand. I started to tell him exactly how rude he was being, but then I saw his face and the words froze on my lips. It was like staring at a younger version of me, with shorter hair. He had my pale skin and ruddy cheeks, and those greenish eyes no one else in my family had. And based on the utter disdain for adults that shone in his eyes, our similarities went far beyond the physical. I'd never met an authority figure I hadn't challenged.

If my mother hadn't had the patience of a saint, life would have been very difficult for us both.

"Where is Ms. George?" The voice—feminine, but completely lacking in warmth—was accompanied by the click of heels on the marble floor. I looked up to find Julia Tower, the aunt I knew only from my mother's description and photos found online, crossing the foyer toward us, looking not at me, but at the children.

The little girl clasped her hands at her back and stared up at her—our—aunt. "She fell asleep during *Charlotte's Web*."

"She lost interest when I told her the spider dies," Kevin added. "I shoulda told her they'd butcher the pig."

Julia exhaled slowly, as if clinging to her patience, then frowned at the guard coming to a stop behind us. "Take them back upstairs and wake up that worthless nanny."

"Should I tell Mrs. Tower—"

"No." Julia's features scrunched up with the word as though she found the thought revolting. "There's no reason to bother Lynn."

As the guard herded the children back upstairs, my aunt finally looked at me for the first time. The weight of her gaze made me want to squirm, but I knew better. Show the wolf a weakness, and it'll rip out your throat. Stare it down, and it might back off.

But Julia Tower didn't back off. She didn't rip my throat out, either, but I couldn't dismiss the certainty that she was holding that option in reserve.

"You're Sera?" She studied my face as intently as I studied hers. In person, her eyes were bluer than they'd appeared online, but the real-life version lacked the warm, approachable quality she'd evidently worn like a costume at various social and political gatherings.

In person, her eyes were more of an ice-blue, as if I were looking into the soul of a glacier, rather than that of a warm-blooded human being.

When she'd finished her silent assessment of me, she gestured stiffly toward the office I'd been headed for in the first place. Two large men dressed in black followed us inside, and I wondered what it said about her that she employed not one but two personal guards to protect her in her own home.

Just how many people currently wanted my aunt dead?

"I asked you to wait in the study," Lia said as one of the men at her back closed the office door and lowered blinds to cover the frosted glass, effectively isolating us from the rest of the house. I blinked at him, and my pulse tripped a little faster. Were they closing the blinds for a private conversation, or so they could shoot me without witnesses?

Did that kind of thing really happen?

"Yeah. I'm not very patient."

Julia's brows rose. "Well, you certainly *sound* like my brother." From the liquor cart to the right of her huge dark wood desk, she poured an inch of amber liquid into a glass, then sipped from it while she examined me from across the room. Without offering me any.

Finally Lia set her glass on the desk blotter, but before she could speak the office door opened behind me and another man in black stuck his head into the room. "Sorry to interrupt, Ms. Tower," he said without even a glance at me. "But they're ready. Just waiting on your authorization."

"Do it," Lia said. "And let me know the moment it's done." The man nodded once, then backed into the hall and pulled the door shut.

I wondered what order she'd just given, and whose life it would ruin. Just because the Tower syndicate knew nothing about me didn't mean I knew nothing about it. I hadn't been able to find many day-to-day specifics online, but the overtones of greed, violence and corruption came through loud and clear, even in vague articles citing anonymous sources, who may or may not have disappeared shortly after they were interviewed.

My birth family was dangerous and evidently unburdened by scruples. I'd come to the right place.

My aunt focused on me again, as if she'd never been interrupted. "What do you want?"

"Couldn't I just have come to meet the rest of my family?"

"Of course you could have." Still standing behind her desk, she stared straight into my eyes without a hint of doubt. "But you didn't."

That's when I realized I was being tested. My mother was right; Liā Tower never did anything without a reason. Lying to a Reader—someone who could scent dishonesty in the air, the way the rest of us might smell meat on the grill—wasn't going to get me anywhere.

"No. I need a favor."

"Of course you do." Her slow smile made my skin crawl. "Let's sit and chat." She gestured toward a chair in front of the desk and when I sat, she sat behind the desk, clearly establishing our roles—my aunt and I would begin our relationship on opposing sides.

"First of all, who are you?" she said, and I realized that our chat would actually be an interrogation.

"I'm Sera Tower. Your niece."

When she glanced at the open laptop on her desk, I wondered if she'd spent the past half hour researching me. Or maybe she had some faster, Skill-based method of finding information.

Lia waved one hand, dismissing my reply. "Your full name."

Right. Like I was going to give her that kind of power over me. My mother had been unSkilled, but well-informed, and she'd taught me well. With my full name, Julia could have me tracked. Or bound against my will. At least, she could try.

I shrugged and tried on a lighthearted smile. "I'll tell you mine, if you tell me yours."

Her forehead wrinkled in a frown. "Fine. Your full first name, at least. What is Sera short for?"

"Serenity."

Lia's brows rose in surprise. "I'd guessed Seraphine. And Cecily actually gave you my brother's surname?"

My chest ached at the memory of my mother, and at Julia's acknowledgment that they'd once known each other. The truth was that they'd been friends back in high school, before Lia's brother had come between them. My mother hadn't gone into detail beyond that, but I'd gathered that the end of their friendship was neither swift nor painless. At least, not for my mom.

If Julia'd suffered from the loss, I saw no sign of it twenty-three years after the fact. However, I *could* see one small truth behind her eyes, but only because my mother had warned me of it. Lia had said my mother's name on purpose, hoping to draw more information out of me than she'd actually asked for. More than I should be willing to give.

She wanted to know how much my mother had told me about her. About Jake. About the family and their business.

But I was desperate, not stupid.

"Yes," I said, holding her gaze. "It's not on my birth certificate or anything, but I'm officially a Tower."

What many people—mostly the unSkilled—didn't know was that it doesn't matter what's written on some stupid form a new mother fills out, while she's still high on painkillers. It's what she names the baby in her heart and head that counts. And for some reason, the day I was born my mother was thinking of me as Jake Tower's daughter.

"Why would she do that?" Lia looked privately puz-
zled for a second, then she directed her confusion toward me.

"My guess is because I'm a Tower."

"And you're willing to submit to a blood test?"

"Hell, no." She could do more damage with my blood
than she could with my full name. "But I'll take the
cheek-swab DNA test. From a disinterested third party."

Her brows rose again. "It's adorable that you think
there's any such thing."

I wasn't sure how to respond to that.

Lia folded her arms on her desk. "Needless to say, I
won't be doing anything for you until I have proof of our
alleged genetic connection." She set her drink on her desk
blotter again, then leaned back in her chair, arms now
crossed over her chest. "But for the sake of expediency,
what is this favor you want?"

I glanced at each of the guards, one of whom stood
behind Lia and to her left, while the other was posted at
the closed door behind me. Their short sleeves covered
their upper arms, hiding their binding marks so that I
couldn't tell whether or not they were Skilled, and if so,
what those Skills were. But they obviously had ears and
mouths. "Will you ask the gentlemen to step outside?"

Lia shook her head slowly. "I can't do that. What if
you're an assassin sent here to kill me?"

"Why would an assassin walk through the front door?"

"That would be a very good question for the man who
killed my brother," she said. "He did that very thing."

Right. But he wasn't an assassin, at least, not according to the newspapers. The official story was that Jake
Tower and several of his men had been killed by an angry,
mentally unstable employee, who'd also died in the tragic
shooting.

"Why would I want to assassinate you?" I asked, but she only watched me, waiting for me to draw my own conclusions. "I don't want to hurt anyone here. I just need a favor. A private favor. Can't you hear the truth in my words?"

Something fierce flickered behind her eyes, and I realized the game had changed. I'd changed it, by admitting I knew her Skill.

"Out," she said, and at first I thought she was kicking me out of the office, or maybe off the property. But then her bodyguards silently filed into the foyer, and I realized the order wasn't aimed at me.

When the door closed behind them she studied me again through narrowed eyes. "What is your Skill, Serenity Tower?" She said my name with a special emphasis, as if it was the punch line of some joke I would never understand.

"I don't have one." I'd been saying that for so long I almost believed it myself, and it didn't occur to me until the words were already hanging in the air between us that a Reader would be able to hear the truth, even in such a tiny lie.

Her brows rose again, and she seemed to be tasting my words on the air, and for a moment I couldn't breathe, certain she'd caught me in a fib I'd been living for so long it felt like a part of me.

But my lie was practically true, which must have made it *taste* true, because when she met my gaze again, hers was much less guarded. She was no longer threatened by me. "You're a long way from home for a little girl with no Skill."

"And you're hiding out *in* your home *behind* your Skill," I shot back, bolstered by my small, secret victory. I enjoyed the anger that settled into the thin lines of her forehead. What was she hiding *from?*

"I'm not hiding. I'm in mourning," she insisted, but I didn't have to be a Reader to see that there wasn't a single note of truth in those words. "So, why I should do this favor for you?"

I hesitated, momentarily stumped. I'd expected a yes or a no, but I hadn't expected a why. "Out of respect for your dead brother?"

Julia's frown deepened. "I fail to see the connection between his death and your brazen, opportunistic grasp at a branch of the family tree you've never even acknowledged before."

Right. Like my "acknowledgment" of their blood in my veins would have been welcomed in the house Jake Tower had shared with his wife and two legitimate children.

Take two. "Because we're family, and I need your help."

"And what will you do for me in return?"

"If I have to pay for it, it isn't a favor," I pointed out, and that time she laughed out loud, looking genuinely amused for the first time since we'd met. "You should help me because we're family. Doesn't that mean anything to you?"

Julia sipped from her glass, looking at me in some odd combination of pity and delight. "The big city is going to swallow you whole, country mouse."

I wouldn't be around long enough for that. "Are you going to help me or not?"

"Assuming your DNA test comes back as you say it will? Yes. We're going to help each other. Tell me what you want, so I can determine what this favor is worth, Serenity Tower." She set her glass on the desk blotter, then gave me a humorless little smile. "That sounds like the name of a building. A sweet, pretty little building where flowers grow in the front yard. So what is it you want from me, Serenity?"

"I want you to kill someone."

The slight narrowing of her eyes was the only sign that she'd heard me, and after that, she only watched me, waiting for more. Making me uncomfortable with every second of the silence that stretched between us, until I had to speak, or risk losing my mind.

"It doesn't have to be you personally." I was just prattling by then, but I couldn't help it. I'd never ordered a hit before, and suddenly I wondered if I was doing it all wrong. Was I supposed to use some kind of special code to avoid incriminating us both? *Too late now...* "I just need you to...coordinate. And pay." No sense hedging about that part. If I'd had the money, I might have tried another...contractor. One who didn't share my DNA.

Julia didn't even blink. If she'd ever been flustered in her entire life, I couldn't tell. "And what makes you think I would be able to help you with something like that?"

My pulse whooshed in my ears, but I was in too deep to turn back now. So I sucked in another breath, then forged ahead, full steam.

"I know who you are. Who you *really* are." Which is why I'd never been closer than eight hours from the Tower estate in my life. Until now. "I know what kind of people you employ, and I know how you keep them loyal." They were bound in service, their oaths sealed in blood-laced tattoos that would not fade until the day the bindings expired. *If* they expired. "And you're not surprised that I know, because everyone knows. Your business comes from word of mouth. It *has* to come from word of mouth, because...well it's not like you can advertise."

"Is that so?" Julia was a statue. A living, breathing statue, her expression frozen in an almost convincing mask of disinterest.

My temper flared. "Help me or don't help me. Either way, stop wasting my time."

Julia exhaled slowly and this time when she met my gaze, hers was stripped of all pretense. "You get that impatient streak from your father," she said, and I almost sagged with relief. "I assume the prospective target is the human-refuse pile who slaughtered your mother and the rest of your surrogate family?"

I blinked at her in surprise. "How did you…"

Her gaze flicked toward the laptop open on the desk between us, then returned to me. "Sera, there's nothing about you that I don't know or can't find out."

"Good." I shrugged, refusing to be intimidated. I may not have grown up in a Skilled cartel family, but I'd faced scarier things than a woman with high-speed internet and cold eyes. "Then you shouldn't have any trouble figuring out who that 'human-refuse pile' is. I have a description, and the police may have some of his DNA from the crime scene." Easily the most difficult sentence I'd ever had to say aloud. "But that's all I know."

A short moment of silence followed, but I sensed that was less respect for my slain family than an opportunity for Lia to gather her thoughts.

"First of all, I'm very sorry for your loss." Yet she sounded distinctly disinterested. "However, it sounds like what you really want is more complicated than simple closure on a family tragedy. You're asking me to identify this killer, track him down and deal with him in some permanent manner. Right?"

I couldn't help noticing that she hadn't once said anything incriminating. Which made me wonder if we were being recorded. Or if she *thought* we were being recorded.

"Yeah, I guess. Some *painful* permanent manner." No sense in playing coy when I'd already said what I wanted, in front of whatever cameras may have been recording.

"Well, those complications raise the price."

"I don't have any money." Not enough to pay what she was likely to charge, anyway. What little life insurance there'd been had barely paid for the funerals. Three of them.

"I would never charge my own niece for such a service," Lia said, and I couldn't tell whether or not the irony was intentional. "However, I do require something from you in return."

"And that would be..." I shifted in my chair. It took every bit of willpower I possessed to keep from promising her whatever she wanted, right then and there. The price didn't matter. I just wanted the bastard dead, my family's deaths avenged with blood and pain, so that I could mourn them, then start to let them go. So I could gather the shattered remains of my life and try to piece them back together.

So that they would be avenged.

But the price *did* matter, the voice in my head insisted, sounding just like my mother. *She'll demand service,* that voice insisted. *She'll make you sign on the line, and you'll work for her forever to pay off this debt. His life for yours, Sera. It's not worth it.*

But I wouldn't be dead, and he *would* be. That bastard's death was worth a few years stuck in a less than ideal job. Worth whatever they made me do. And it wouldn't be forever. It would just be for a few years, right? Service terms had limits, didn't they?

People survive working for the syndicates. It happens all the time. Right?

I was already resigning myself to life under Julia Tower's thumb when she leaned back in her chair again, watching me for a moment before she spoke. "I want you to disappear."

"Excuse me?" Surprise made my voice squeak, but Lia only waited for my answer like she might if she'd asked for the last fry from my plate. But I didn't know *how* to answer.

"If I do this favor for you, Sera, I want you to disappear. Forever. My brother's wife and children are devastated with grief," she said, and I frowned, picturing the children who'd nearly bowled me over in the foyer. Were they laughing and chasing butterflies over their father's no doubt overpriced grave? No. But they weren't crying and ripping their hair out, either.

"They don't deserve this," Lia continued. "I won't put them through the additional pain and humiliation of finding out he sired a bastard with some slut he knew in high school."

She said it with no visible emotion, her words just as cold now as her condolences had been minutes earlier.

My cheeks flamed. I shouldn't have cared what she thought of me. Jake Tower may have been my father, but he was never my dad—that title would always go to the man my mother married, who'd loved me and my sister more than he'd loved his own life. And who would never have called me a bastard or insulted my mother.

But Lia's insult hit its mark, and I knew that if I wanted to avenge my mother's death, I would have to let the insult against her stand. And I would have to leave the Tower estate, so the Towers could continue to live in blissful ignorance of my existence, and the messy circumstances of my conception and birth.

No problem. After fewer than ten minutes spent with Julia, I never wanted to see her again.

"So, if I promise to go away after it's done, you'll… take care of this for me?"

"I'll need more than a simple promise, but yes."

"What does that mean?" But I was pretty sure I already knew.

"I need your word in writing. Sealed in blood." She wanted to bind me to my oath, which would physically prevent me from ever going back on it.

My heart dropped into my stomach. I had no intention of going back on my word, but the thought of letting someone bind me to anything made me sick to my stomach. My mom had preached against that the way most mothers warn their kids not to talk to strangers, or run in the house.

Or jump off a cliff.

"Why? You have my word that I don't want anything else from you, but someday I might want to get to know my…half siblings." Just saying that felt strange. My real sister was dead, and she was the only sister I would ever have. Surely the only one I'd ever want. But…I'd just lost the only family I'd ever known. I wasn't about to give up the right to *ever* get to know what few relatives I had left, even if they couldn't replace what I'd lost. Even if they were rich, and spoiled, and quite possibly as vicious as our father and aunt.

My mother was an only child and her parents were dead. Jake Tower's children were the last blood-based connection I would ever have to another human being. There was always the chance that one of those kids— probably not Kevin—would grow up to be a decent human being and parent to the only nieces and nephews I'd ever have.

I shrugged. "Or they might want to know me."

"Sera, it's those children I'm thinking about." Lia pushed her laptop aside and folded her arms on her massive desk, meeting my gaze with an intense one of her own, like we'd suddenly become confidantes. "Lynn, their mother, is a sweet, beautiful woman, but between the two of us, she's never been the brightest bulb in the chandelier, and right now she's too blinded by grief to think clearly. But someone has to look out for the children. I'm not going to help you unless you're willing to give up any claim to their inheritance."

"Money?" I gaped at her. "You think I want your brother's *money?*"

"I don't know what you really want, Sera. I know your net worth, your college GPA and how much you paid for the heap of metal parked in front of my house, but I don't know anything about you as a person, because you evidently felt no desire to connect with this side of your family until you needed something from us." Her accusation was as sharp as her gaze, and I couldn't really argue, though I felt my cheeks flame again. "But I will do whatever needs to be done to protect those children. If you really aren't trying to steal their inheritance, you should have no problem swearing to that."

"I don't," I snapped, struggling to think through the anger swelling rapidly to fill both my head and heart. The bitch was appealing to my morals on behalf of two half-orphaned children. I didn't for a second believe that was her only interest in the matter, but I didn't want anything from the dead father I'd never met, and I certainly didn't want anything from *her*. Except this one favor. "Write it. I'll sign it, and you'll never see me again. I don't want anything but the slow, painful death of the bastard who killed my family."

"Wonderful." Lia shifted in her chair and folded her hands in her lap. "And, of course, you'll be willing to give up the Tower name."

"My name?"

"My brother's name," she corrected. "His children's name. *My* name. You've never even used it, have you?" I shook my head, and she shrugged as if what she was asking was no big deal. "Then why would you mind giving it up?"

Why *would* I mind?

I started speaking before my thoughts had fully formed, fueled by anger, unburdened by forethought. "Because it's my *name.* It belongs to me every bit as much as it belongs to you. Because for whatever reason, my mother wanted me to have it. Because whether you like it or not—hell, whether *I* like it or not—that name is part of who I am, and I don't even know what that *means* yet, other than the fact that the aunt I share it with is a *real bitch.*"

Julia blinked, and I relished the glimpse of surprise that flickered across her expression, the first I'd seen so far. "You're not thinking this through. There's nothing that can be done about the fact that it belongs to you, so in that sense, it can never be taken from you. But you'd be safer *using* another name. Your stepfather's? Or even your mother's. You'll be infinitely harder to Track if no one knows your real surname, Sera."

Yet we both knew she wasn't thinking of my well-being.

But that wasn't the point. The point was that which-ever last name I used was *my* decision. Mine. And no snotty rich bitch with a chip on her shoulder and blood on her hands was going to tell me what I could or couldn't call myself.

But Julia Tower had yet to come to that conclusion. So I helped her along. "No."

She stood and leaned forward, both palms flat on the surface of her desk. "I am the only person *in the world* who will do what you want done without asking for a dime in return. My price is simple. You will sign over your right to anything Kevin and Aria stand to inherit. Including their surname. Or I will have you removed from this property immediately, and you can hunt down this killer yourself, then spend the balance of your life behind bars, paying your debt to society. You have three minutes to make a decision."

But there was no decision to be made. And Lia damn well knew it.

While I sat glaring up at her, resisting the urge to stand and start yelling, the office door opened behind me and Lia gestured for someone to come in.

I twisted in my chair to see a woman in her thirties carrying a manila folder. My aunt held out her hand and the woman marched past me to give her the folder. "That's the best I could do, on short notice, but if you have another hour…"

Julia waved dismissively, and the woman's sentence faded into a tense silence while my aunt read whatever the folder held. After several seconds, she lifted the top sheet of paper and scanned the next one. Then she flipped the pages back into order and closed the folder. "Sometimes simpler is better. Unnecessary language leaves room for loopholes. This will do. Send in the Binder." She motioned toward the door, and the woman in brown headed for the foyer as though she was being physically pulled in that direction. As though she couldn't wait to leave.

I knew exactly how she felt.

Julia sat, then slid the folder across the desk toward me. "Sign."

"Now?" I could practically feel the blood drain from my face as I stared at the newly drafted binding document—the real reason she'd kept me waiting so long. She expected me to sign it right then and there, and the Binder she'd called for would seal my promise in blood—either his or mine. Or both.

I hesitated, my hand flat on the closed folder.

"Sign, or get out," Julia said, and there wasn't a hint of doubt in her voice. She'd already figured out that I wasn't going to leave without getting what I came for. No matter what it cost.

I opened the folder, my hand shaking with rage. *It doesn't matter,* I told myself, as I picked up the pen she slid toward me. *You don't need them. You've never needed them.*

But what if those kids needed me someday? What if Kevin or Aria needed help from a relative who *didn't* have a chunk of ice in place of her heart or *wasn't* the dim bulb in the proverbial chandelier? Was there anyone in this cesspool of corrupt power they could count on? Could money buy friendship or trust?

The only thing I knew for sure was that if I didn't sign, the man who killed my entire family would never see justice. The police can't catch a Skilled criminal, much less convict him.

I scanned the first page, only half reading my own promise to forfeit any and all birthrights, including the Tower surname. I'd scribbled the first three letters of my name on the line at the bottom of the second page when the door flew open behind me and slammed into the wall.

"Sera?"

Startled, I turned so fast the pen left a long black line across the bottom of the page. Gwendolyn Tower stood in the doorway, as perfectly put together as any picture of her I'd ever seen, except for the puffy, pink flesh around her eyes.

She blinked at me and I wondered what she was seeing. Did I look like her husband? Why didn't she look surprised? Lia had implied that Lynn and her children knew nothing about me.

Then Gwendolyn's gaze slid past me. "Julia, what the hell are you doing? Did you tell her?"

My pulse spiked. *Tell me what?*

Lia stepped around the corner of her desk, ready to intercept her sister-in-law. "This is business. It's none of your concern."

"Tell her!" Lynn Tower shouted, and the guard standing behind her flinched, then looked to my aunt for some instruction.

"Go back to your room." Julia took Lynn's arm while I watched in stunned silence. "I'll explain everything when we're finished here."

Lynn turned to me then, her eyes damp, her gaze strong. "It's yours, Sera. All of it. Jake's personal property and assets went to me, but his business holdings go to his oldest child. Don't let her cut you out."

"Gwendolyn, *out!*" Julia shouted as I fell backward into my chair, my legs numb from shock. The guards guided Lynn, gently but firmly, toward the door at about the same moment I realized I still held the pen Lia had given me.

Business holdings? What did that even mean? Properties? Companies? Buildings? Cash?

It's yours, Sera. All of it.

Lynn's words played over in my head as I watched the guards escort her forcibly out of the office.

The truth hit me in that moment, like a burst of light in front of my eyes—painful, disorienting and nearly blinding.

I'd just inherited Jake Tower's criminal empire.

Two

Kris

"So, how many is that, Kris?" My sister Korinne perched on the arm of the couch, one knee drawn up to her chest, thick hair tucked behind her ear. We'd both inherited our dad's blond hair, but hers was several shades paler than my own. "How many poor, unfortunate souls have we freed from the corrupt clutches of the Tower machine?"

"As of today?" I did a quick tally of the names listed in the notepad on my lap. "Twelve. With three more strong possibilities."

"Only twelve?" Kenley, my youngest sister, groaned from an armchair in the corner. If she were a couple of inches taller, she and Kori could have been twins. "It feels like a hundred." Kenni looked exhausted, yet much younger than her twenty-six years, as if trauma had somehow left her more innocent than it had found her. More fragile.

Vanessa handed Kenni a cool rag, still damp from the kitchen faucet. "We knew breaking the bindings would be tough, but that last one was easier, right?"

"Yeah. If by easier, you mean just as hard as the eleven before."

Van stood and wedged herself into the oversize chair behind Kenley, who scooted forward to make room for her. Kenni leaned back with her head against her girl-friend's shoulder, and Van laid the cool rag over her forehead, offering wordless comfort in the face of the enormous task we'd all undertaken. A task that felt more impossible by the day.

A binding is like a metaphorical—and metaphysical—rope, tying one person to another. Or one person to his oath. Or one person into obedience or employment. My sister Kenley was one of the most powerful Binders in the world, but she would gladly have given up her Skill, if that meant escaping the notice of syndicate leaders who wanted to "hire" her for her ability.

The problem with syndicate employment is that it isn't just a job, it's an existence. Worse. It's indentured servi-tude, wherein the employee is obligated to do whatever the employer requires, within the bounds of the contract they signed and sealed, usually in blood. For however long that contract lasts.

A five-year term is the standard. Five years in syndi-cate service feels like an eternity.

Kenley and Kori each served six and a half.

Before Jake Tower died, Kenley was the most impor-tant cog in the Tower syndicate machine—the gear that kept the engine running. Tower'd had administrators, accountants, clerical staff and laborers to do the day-to-day work. He'd had muscle—like Kori—to enforce the rules. He'd even had a pool of highly specialized law-yers on-staff to write iron-clad employment contracts.

And he'd had Kenley to seal those contracts, locking

people into his service in bindings so strong that only she could break them.

Of course, the terms of her own contract had prevented her from freeing anyone she'd bound into service, but now that she was no longer a Tower employee, she was trying to do the right thing. To free all the people she'd enslaved by breaking the bindings she'd sealed for Jake Tower, which had transferred to his sister, Julia, upon his death.

We were all trying to help her, but the process was slow. And difficult. And dangerous, because Julia Tower didn't want those bindings broken. Each one Kenley psychically severed robbed Julia of another employee, eroding the source of her inherited wealth and power.

"I know this sucks, Kenni, and I hate being stuck here as much as anyone." Kori glanced around at the house where we'd spent almost every waking moment of the past three months, hiding from Julia Tower and her henchmen. I could practically see cabin fever raging behind her eyes. "But it could be worse, right? At least there's no resistance pain."

The binding enslaving Kenley to the Tower syndicate had been broken when I'd killed the Binder who'd sealed it. Okay, there *may* have been some doubt about whose bullet actually hit him first, but the point is that since the Binder was dead, breaking the bindings *she'd* sealed was no longer in violation of Kenni's oath. Which is good, because when you resist a sealed oath, your body starts to shut down one organ at a time until you give in and keep your word.

Or you die.

But even without the resistance pain, breaking each binding one at a time was still long, mentally exhausting work for Kenley, even with the rest of us pitching in to identify and contact those who wanted out of their oaths to Tower and to coordinate the secure, clandestine meetings.

The project had taken over our lives, and it was as much a survival effort on our part as an effort to liberate those who wanted freedom. As long as Julia Tower had employees bound into her service, she'd have the resources and power to eventually hunt us down and eliminate the threat we represented.

"So, who's next?" Ian Holt sank onto the couch next to Kori, and she leaned into him, a display of trust and affection I'd rarely seen from her. I don't know how he got through her mile-thick outer shell, but I do know that I've never seen her happier. And I know that Ian helped free Kori, Kenni and Vanessa from that bastard Jake Tower, and that he'd stuck around to help us free everyone else Kenley had been forced to bind. As far as we were all concerned, Ian was part of the family, even if Kori never got around to putting a ring on his finger.

"Um…" I checked my list again. "Rick Wallace." I glanced at Kori. "What do we know about him?"

She shrugged. "He's a Silencer. Average strength. Mid-thirties. He's also a world-class asshole who's literally never heard 'no' from a woman, because he sucks the sound right out of the word every time one tries to say it. I'm not surprised he wants out from under Julia Tower, but I'm kind of surprised he'd contact us, considering how many times I've threatened to cut his tongue out and serve it to his latest 'date' on a toasted hot-dog bun."

Ian made a face. "That's disgusting,"

Kori nodded solemnly. "So is Rick Wallace."

"Agreed. But no one deserves to be tied to Julia Tower," Kenley insisted, and Kori kept her mouth shut, though she obviously wanted to argue. "When and where is the meeting?"

"Meghan's parents' house," Ian said. His sister-in-law had offered to let us use the house when she and his twin brother left town.

"Olivia's already securing the site," Kori added. "We're supposed to meet her there in half an hour. If you're sure you feel like it."

"I'm fine." Kenley squared her shoulders and sat straighter. "Let's just get it over with."

"Eat something first," Vanessa insisted, and before Kenley could object, Van was halfway to the kitchen in search of food.

I followed her, headed for the coffeepot, and my grandmother looked up from the stove when she saw me. "Kristopher, the knobs are missing."

"Really?" I frowned down at the stove. "That's weird." We'd had to take the knobs off the day before, when she lit the fire under one gas burner, but forgot to put a pot over the flame and nearly caught the whole damn house on fire.

"What happened to them?"

"I dunno, Gran. Maybe Liv or Cam will track them for us." Olivia and her boyfriend were both Trackers, but he worked mainly with names, while she worked with blood.

"Don't get smart with me, Kristopher Daniels," Gran snapped. "I'll ground you till you're twenty-five years old, and you can forget the senior prom."

She'd lit the candles on my thirtieth birthday cake six months earlier, and I couldn't even remember most of my senior prom. Which is how I know I probably enjoyed the hell out of it. Or maybe that was the after-party…

"I'm not getting smart, Gran."

"Well, *that's* the truth…" Kori mumbled beneath her

breath as she walked past on her way to the fridge, and I ignored her.

"I'll look into the missing knobs, I swear."

"Do it now. I want to make some—" Gran's scowl morphed into an instant smile when she noticed Vanessa taking the lid off a plastic container of cookies. "You two make such a cute couple."

"Gran…" I started, but she slapped my arm, which was only a minor improvement over the way she used to slap the back of my head when I was twelve and the occasional—okay, frequent—profanity slipped out.

She'd given up smacking Kori for cussing when my sister was ten.

"Don't give up on him just because he pretends to be emotionally unavailable, Vanessa," Gran said, and I realized for the first time that she'd never forgotten Van's name. Not even once. "He's a slob and he leaves his towel on the bathroom floor, but he's a pretty good boy."

"No, I'm not." I shook my head at Van. "I'm very, very bad."

Vanessa laughed as she wrapped two cookies in a paper towel, then took them into the living room for Kenley, leaving me to explain things to my grandmother on my own. Again.

"Vanessa's not my girlfriend, Gran. She's with Kenley, remember?"

"Oh, please." Gran huffed in exasperation. "Anyone can see how much she likes you."

No one else could see any such thing. But trying to explain to Gran that Kenni and Vanessa were more than friends was like trying to explain…well, like trying to explain *anything* to Gran. Futile. We'd had a few temporary victories in the battle against Alzheimer's but the backslides all but killed any real hope.

While Gran searched the kitchen drawers and cabinets for the missing stove knobs, Vanessa joined me again at the coffeepot with an empty mug of her own. "I've been meaning to ask you…" she said as she filled her mug. "Does your grandmother have a Skill? I've never seen her use it."

"No, thank goodness." I pulled the sugar bowl closer and stirred a spoonful into my coffee. "Alzheimer's and Skills don't mix well." You can't just take the knobs off a Skill to make sure it isn't accidentally left running when the user forgets what year it is.

"I'm ready," Kenni called from the living room, and I looked up to find her brushing cookie crumbs from her shirt while Kori slid a 9 mm into the holster beneath her left arm. Ian handed her a light jacket to hide the gun, just in case. His jacket was already in place, and if I didn't already know where his own weapons were hidden, I'd never have known he had any.

"I'll go." I set my coffee on the counter, untouched. "You and Ian can stay."

Kori frowned, always unhappy to be taken out of the action. "Why?"

"Because I'm sick of watching the two of you actively hate the rest of the world for interrupting your privacy. And because I don't trust you not to kill Rick Wallace before Kenni has a chance to break his bindings."

"I wasn't gonna do any permanent damage," Kori mumbled.

"It's my turn anyway." I grabbed my own jacket from the back of a chair at the kitchen table.

When she started to protest, Ian pulled her close. "Shut up before he changes his mind." Then he turned to me. "Go on. We'll hold down the fort."

"And I'll pretend I don't know what you're about to

do with my sister. Ready, Kenni?" But when I turned, I found her kissing Vanessa goodbye. "Damn it, people," I groaned. "This is a hideout, not a couples retreat!"

"Jealous?" Van teased, sinking into the chair Kenley had just vacated.

Was I jealous?

I might have been jealous of all the sex they were having, in their respective pairs, if each of those pairs didn't involve one of my sisters. But because my sisters *were* involved, envy of their physical relationships wasn't really…relevant. In fact, the very thought was vaguely nauseating.

As for the rest of it—the casual touches, intense looks and the feeling that the world would stop spinning if intimate eye contact was broken—I'd gone down that route once. The curves in the road were unpredictable, the speed bumps were more like small mountains, and the sudden roadblock thrown into my path had resulted in a collision I'd barely limped away from.

Since then, I stuck to the highway, with the other casual drivers. Regular shifts in the scenery, no stop-and-go traffic and the freedom to change lanes whenever I got bored.

"Let me get my stuff." I jogged up the stairs and into the center bedroom, where I'd been sleeping for most of the three months we'd spent finding and contacting Tower's remaining disgruntled employees and arranging clandestine meetings. Three months hiding from Julia in her own city while we slowly chipped away at the bedrock of indentured servants forming the foundation of the empire she'd inherited.

Eventually, that foundation would crumble, and its queen would plummet to the ground. And as with the fall of any corrupt dynasty, the peasants would rejoice.

I sat on the edge of my unmade bed and pulled open the nightstand drawer, and while my hand went straight for my gun, my gaze found something else instead.

What the hell?

My notebook. The indecipherable roadmap from my one disastrous trip down lover's lane.

What the hell was it doing in the hideout house? In my bedroom? In my bedside drawer?

I lifted the notebook and flipped back the red cardboard cover. I hadn't seen it in more than a year, but I still knew the curve of every *G* and the slanted cross of every *T*. I used to keep a yellow No. 2 pencil in the spiral, for when I needed to jot something down in the middle of the night.

But that was years ago...

The notebook was all I had left of Noelle. Twenty-three pages of dates and phrases—a visible reminder of the hardest lesson I'd ever learned, like an alcoholic's sobriety chip or a junkie's faded track marks. In the beginning, I'd read it so many times that now the cardboard cover had started falling apart and the entries in pencil had started to fade. Most of them, in retrospect, made no more sense than they had when I'd written them in the first place.

But...how the hell had the notebook gotten into my nightstand? It should have been in storage with everything else Gran and I hadn't brought with us to the hideout house.

Kenley and Olivia were ready to go, so the notebook mystery would have to wait. I shook my head, trying to dislodge Noelle from my brain, then shoved the notebook back into the drawer and grabbed my .45. I popped the clip free and counted the rounds, then slid it back into place with a satisfying click. On my way down the stairs,

I shrugged into my holster and jacket, then dropped the gun into place beneath my left arm.

"Ready, Kenni?" I said from the landing.

"Liv should be there waiting for you." Kori sipped from my coffee mug. Without asking permission. "Call me if you need anything. I can be there in an instant."

"I know." Kori and I were Travelers—shadow-walkers—able to step into one shadow and out of another, anywhere within our range. When she was twenty-two, Kori got roped into using her Skill on behalf of the Tower syndicate to protect Kenley, who was already trapped in the same organization.

Tower signed Kori more for her skills with a knife and gun—and so he could use her to manipulate Kenni—than for her strength and range as a Traveler, which is mediocre at best.

My strength and range as a Traveler are better than most people know. Definitely better than Tower knew. And I'd like to keep it that way.

"We're sure this guy's for real?" I stepped into the hall closet with Kenley as she turned off the light.

"He's an asshole, but he's legit," Kori said from the hall. "Anne listened in on the original call."

As a Reader—a human lie detector—Kori's friend Annika was less helpful on the front lines than Olivia was, with her gun and her Tracker abilities. Liv had helped us find those interested in breaking their bindings to Julia Tower, and she'd been my backup on more than one occasion. But Anne was invaluable behind the scenes. She helped keep us from walking into traps.

"Thanks for doing this," Kenley whispered in the dark as her small hand slid into my grip. "I know your work is important, and you didn't have to uproot yourself and Gran, and—"

"This is important, too, Kenni."

I knew much more about her work—and our work to undo her work—than she knew about what I'd been doing while she and Kori were slaves to Jake Tower's every whim. While they were bound to the syndicate, there was so much I couldn't tell them. So much I couldn't show them. So much I couldn't do for them, without putting them in greater danger and risking the lives of everyone else counting on me.

Knowing that didn't ease my guilt over the years they'd spent bound to Tower, out of my reach. But finally, all that had changed. Now I could stand with them. Fight for them. Protect them.

Now I could help them take down the organization that had broken Kenley's spirit bit by bit, with every binding Tower had made her seal. The criminal underworld that had heaped unspeakable abuse on Kori, left her scarred physically and psychologically.

Julia Tower was the brain at the center of her late brother's operation, and with him gone, there was no one to apply the brakes to her ambition or restrain her psychotic enthusiasm for backstage world domination, or whatever evil scheme was currently sparking across her synapses.

"No one deserves to be tied to Julia Tower. Not even the assholes." And if we actually managed to take down the Tower syndicate, one human brick at a time, no one would benefit more than the people I worked with. "So let's go make this asshole a free man."

Kenni squeezed my hand—as good as a smile in the dark—and I tugged her forward one step. Two.

Then the room around us changed.

The air tasted different at Meghan's childhood home. Cleaner, with an antiseptic aftertaste that told me she was a much better housekeeper than anyone living at our hideout.

Meghan's bathroom was colder, too, and the tiles sounded different beneath my boots—harder, and more echoey than the linoleum in the house we were renting under a false name.

Kenley released my hand and flipped a switch on her side of the wall, and soft light from one of those old-fashioned round bulbs lit the bathroom with a yellowish glow. Everything here was a little older. The tub was porcelain, standing on claw feet, and the rest of the house had real hardwood floors. Tongue and groove. Not that we could see much it from the bathroom, because the rest of the house was dark.

Unease crawled across my back. Why was the rest of the house dark?

Stay here, I mouthed to Kenley, and she nodded, eyes wide. She could feel the wrongness, too.

I stepped into the hall and the floor creaked beneath my feet.

"Kris?" Olivia called, and the pain in her voice triggered alarms like bolts of electricity shooting through me.

"Liv!" Kenley cried, and I was so busy trying to hold her back that my brain didn't process what else Olivia had said until it was too late. Until Kenley had already pulled free from my grasp and was halfway down the hall, her shoes squeaking on those hardwood floors.

"Run!" Olivia's frantic shout ended abruptly, then echoed in my head as a hand shot out from a bedroom on the left side of the hall.

Kenley screamed as the hand dragged her into the room, pulling her right off her feet. I charged into the bedroom an instant later, my gun drawn, and nearly ripped the light switch out of the wall as I flipped it.

Bright light flooded the unused bedroom, but I was too late. They were already gone.

"Kenley!" I shouted as I threw open the closet door and checked under the bed, just in case. But no amount of screaming my little sister's name would bring her back.

Furious, and more scared than I could ever remember being, I raced out of the room and down the hall in the direction of Olivia's shout, but my footsteps went silent the moment I stepped into the living room.

I froze, trying to puzzle out the problem. Trying to hear around the sudden, unnatural silence.

"Wallace."

I said his name aloud as the realization sank in, but though I could feel the rumble of air being forced over my vocal chords, they made no sound. Or, rather, the sound they made was swallowed before it could be heard.

That same silence swallowed my roar of frustration.

The lights were off in the living room, just like in the rest of the house, but the drapes were open and the light shining in from the street was enough to illuminate Olivia, hunched on the floor with one hand pressed against her bloody temple. A man knelt behind her, the barrel of his gun pressed into the back of her head.

Olivia was saying something. No, she was *shouting* something, but I couldn't hear her. Wallace—the human Silencer—wouldn't *let* me hear her. But her point was obvious.

This was a trap.

My teeth ground together and my finger tensed on the trigger of my gun.

"Where is she?" I shouted, but no sound came out. "Where the hell is my sister?"

Wallace only smiled at me, one half of his face shrouded in shadow.

I aimed at his head, and my gun made no sound as I clicked off the safety.

Olivia shouted harder, shaking her head, her face red with the effort, but Wallace didn't look worried. He wasn't prepared to actually shoot Olivia, because he didn't think I'd pull the trigger. He kept not-thinking that until the moment I shot him in the forehead, and his brains sprayed the wall at his back.

The first thing I heard was the thunk of his body hitting the floor.

Olivia gasped, and the sound was as sharp as a scream after such heavy, unnatural silence. She scrambled away from the dead man and stood, gaping at me. "You could have hit me, you asshole!"

"Give me a little credit, Liv." I hadn't missed anything I'd aimed at in the past decade. "Kori learned to shoot from *me*. Remember?"

"Kenley?" Liv grabbed a dusty white doily from the nearest end table and pressed it to her bleeding forehead.

"They got her. Dragged her out through the shadows, right in front of me." My baby sister was gone, and I felt her absence like a gaping hole in my own heart. I'd lost her, but I would damn well get her back. "Was it the Tower bitch?"

"That's my guess." She stomped into the kitchen and started rooting around under the sink, presumably looking for bleach, or something else that would destroy the blood she'd spilled to keep it from being used against her.

I popped the clip from the grip of my gun and replaced the spent round with an extra from my pocket. Something told me I was going to need them all. "Where would they take her?"

"No idea. Cam might know. Or Kori." Because they'd both served in the Tower syndicate.

Olivia already had her phone out, but she looked up when I pulled the drapes closed in the living room, blood boiling in my veins. "Where are you going?" she demanded a second before I would have stepped into the darkness.

"To get Kenley." I wasn't sure what the Towers had done to Kori when she was locked up, but I could *not* let that happen to Kenni. "Tell the others I'll be right back." Then I stepped into the shadows, leaving Olivia gaping at the space I'd just vacated.

A single step later, my foot hit the floor in Jake Tower's darkroom. Only now it was *Julia* Tower's darkroom. I'd never been there before—the one time I'd been in Tower's house, I'd come in through the basement, after Kori shot a hole in the infrared grid built into the ceiling—but I'd mentally scouted it out a million times in the past six years. Every time I'd briefly considered simply charging into the heart of Tower's empire and demanding my sisters' freedom.

I'd never been stupid enough to actually go through with such an asinine plan.

Until now.

For the span of four heartbeats, I stood alone in the enemy's darkroom, breathing. Thinking. Steeling myself. If I pressed the intercom button, the man in the security control room would see me with the infrared camera mounted in one corner of the ceiling. Then he'd press a button, and toxic gas would be pumped in through one of the vents overhead. I'd die in a pool of my own blood. Or vomit. Or both.

So instead, I felt for the light switch by the door—thank you, Kori, for the inside information—and flipped it up. Light flooded the tiny room from a fluorescent strip overhead.

The monitor built into the wall buzzed to life and a man's face appeared on the screen, frowning at me.

I shot the monitor.

I shot the camera in the corner of the ceiling.

Then I turned away from the door without compromising my aim and shot the door lock—absent knob—once, twice. On the third try, as the hiss of air overhead told me my extermination had begun, the lock exploded and shrapnel sprayed my jacket, but the lack of pain told me none of the metal pieces had penetrated the leather. The door swung open two inches.

The alarm sounded as I stepped into the hall, scraping the insides of my skull raw while I tried to remember everything Kori had ever told me about the layout of Tower's house.

Second floor. Employee's wing. To the left are unused bedrooms and the path to the family wing.

I turned left, just as two men rounded the corner toward me, guns drawn. I squeezed off two shots, and both men went down with blood roses blooming on their abdomens. I could have shot again, but they were no threat, bleeding on the floor, and I'd probably need all my ammo.

To the right, the stairs lead to the foyer, my sister said in my memory.

I turned right and jogged down the stairs while the alarm repeatedly skewered my brain, and I took out two more guards on my way down. I'd aimed to disable, not kill, but I had no time to check my accuracy. By the time I hit the floor, doors were flying open. People were pouring into the two-story foyer.

My heart thumping in my ears, and on the lookout for more guards, I scanned the shocked, growing crowd, but didn't find the face I was looking for. Julia's.

"Everyone over there!" I shouted over the alarm, directing Tower's confused employees away from the front door, toward the atrium at the center of the house, its entrance nestled between the two mirror-image staircases.

Startled men and women in suits followed my directions, but most of them didn't look truly scared. They saw guns on a daily basis, and once the rest of the security team arrived, I would be both outnumbered and outgunned.

"Where's Julia Tower?" I demanded. No one answered, but several people glanced at a frosted-glass door to my left. The only one that hadn't opened when the alarm went off.

I backed toward the closed door, adrenaline pumping through my veins, still aiming at the small crowd, but before I could reach for the knob, the door swung open on its own.

Inside, three women stared out at me in various stages of shock, fear and anger. I recognized Lynn Tower immediately, her hand still on the doorknob, and I dismissed her almost as quickly. She wasn't a threat, nor would she have the information I needed.

Julia stood behind the desk, telephone in hand, halfway to her ear.

I aimed at her, and she froze.

"Where's my sister?" I shouted, still competing with the alarm, but Julia only smiled. She knew I couldn't kill her until I had the information I'd come for.

Then the third woman turned in front of the desk to look at me, blocking my aim at Julia. Her eyes were wide and green, her features delicate. She held her hands out at her sides, showing me she was unarmed.

"What's the problem?" She rounded the chair slowly to stand in front of me and the yellow scarf draped loosely over her shoulders caught my gaze and refused to let go. "Who are you looking for?"

I could hardly hear her over the alarm, and my brain didn't process a single thing she'd said, because in my mind, I heard another voice, speaking to me from my own past.

Take the woman in the yellow scarf.

Someone, somewhere pressed a button, and the alarm died, though it still echoed deep inside my head.

"Why don't you put the gun down, and we can work this out," the woman in the scarf said, slowly walking toward me. She looked scared, but calm. Determined.

"Sera…" Lynn Tower backed away as the woman in the scarf approached.

Sera. The woman in the yellow scarf.

"It's okay," Sera said, and I backed away from her in shock, one step for each of hers, my gun aimed right at her. But I wouldn't shoot her. I couldn't. I *needed* her, though I wasn't sure why. Was she supposed to help me get Kenley back? Was she a hostage? An informant? A lieutenant in the Tower army?

Was that even possible for someone so young?

"Freeze!" someone shouted, and I looked up to find three of Tower's guards aiming large guns at me from the center of the foyer.

My guts twisted into knots while I waited for gunfire, and there was nothing for me to do but hold my aim. This was a fool's errand from the beginning, but I wasn't fool enough to let go of my gun.

"Stop!" Sera yelled, and the men hesitated, confused. "He's looking for someone. There's no reason for this to get any bloodier."

I recognized her tone. Gentle and patronizing. That

was the voice you'd use to talk a man down from a ledge. A crazy man.

"Shoot him!" Julia yelled from inside her office, heedless of the fact that I was still aiming at Sera, and the men raised their weapons.

"No!" Sera turned on Julia. "Tell them to drop their weapons. Please!"

Julia scowled, and her anger was like black clouds rolling over the sun—I felt like I should duck before I got struck by lightning. Julia Tower didn't take orders— she *gave* them.

But then she spoke, clearly enough for everyone to hear. "Put down your guns!"

The men obeyed instantly—so fast it was almost comical—squatting to set M16s on the ground at their feet, their faces fixed in identical masks of confusion.

Sera turned back to me. "Give me your gun, and you can go home."

Surely she lacked the authority to back up a promise like that. Julia held all the power in Tower's territory. But if that was true, why had Julia ordered her men to stand down at the request of a woman little more than half her age?

The girl in the scarf had guts—I had to give her that.

Or maybe she was just trying to disarm me, so I couldn't shoot her when they shot me.

Sera held out her hand for my gun.

I glanced at the disarmed guards. Then I glanced at Julia and Lynn Tower, watching us both from inside the office, one nervous, one furious. Then I glanced to my right, and saw the open storage closet a few feet away, where a housekeeper had been digging for supplies when I'd come down the stairs waving my gun.

Instead of giving Sera my pistol, I grabbed her hand and pulled her with me into the closet.

She screamed, and I threw the door shut.

"Kill him!" Julia shouted.

"No!" Lynn screeched.

I fired twice into the ceiling, killing both the visible and the infrared lights at once. Then, as the first bullets ripped through the closet door, I pulled Sera into the shadows with me.

I took the woman in the yellow scarf.

Three

Sera

His eyes were a pale bluish gray. They were the first things I noticed after Lynn Tower opened the office door over my aunt's protest.

The next thing I noticed was his weapon, and the two men bleeding on the marble tile in the foyer. Bile rose to my throat at the sight of so much blood pooling on the floor, and brutal memories tried to surface, but I shook them off. None of the bystanders were hurt. He'd only shot people who'd aimed guns at him.

This man may have been a killer, but he was no murderer. The distinction was small, but important.

The man aiming his gun at me looked furious, pale brows furrowed, jaw clenched, aim unwavering. He was looking for someone—I'd missed the specifics, thanks to the alarm—and was obviously willing to do whatever it took to find…whomever. He looked desperate.

But not crazy.

Those blue-gray eyes seemed to see everything all at once—every guard aiming a gun at him, every witness watching, and every possible escape route. He was too calm to be crazy. And if he was sane, he could be reasoned with.

He *had* to be reasoned with, because if Julia had him shot and his finger twitched on his own trigger, he'd blow a hole right through me, and no one other than Gwendolyn Tower seemed particularly concerned by that possibility.

My heart thudding in my ears, I held my hand out for his weapon, demanding focus and calm from myself as I mentally counted the shots I'd heard. But I couldn't be sure of the number, thanks to the alarm.

He glanced at my scarf, then at my hand, and for a moment I thought he was actually going to give me his gun.

Instead, he grabbed my hand and dragged me into a supply closet, nearly hauling me off my feet. Startled, I screamed when he kicked the door shut, but then he raised his gun and shot into the ceiling, once, twice.

The closet went dark and glass rained down on us from the broken fixtures. Too shocked to speak, I tried to jerk my hand from his grip, but he pulled me again, and I stumbled after him, one step, then two.

The last thing I heard was gunfire coming from the foyer. They shot at us. They *knew* I was with him, and they'd fired anyway! On Julia's command!

That *bitch!*

Then there was silence, except for the sound of my own panicked breathing—too fast and too hard.

The darkness was absolute, and I couldn't see a thing. I couldn't feel a thing, except for his hand tight around mine, and the body heat that told me this room was smaller than the last, and that he was standing much too close.

I opened my mouth to scream again and he dropped my hand. A door opened and he stepped out of what

I could now identify as an empty coat closet, his gun aimed at the floor.

That blue-gray gaze found mine again from a narrow hallway outside the closet. He was staring, as if something about my face made no sense.

"What the hell just happened?" I demanded, torn between the need to know exactly where I was and reluctance to venture beyond the closet into unknown territory.

"Traveling. Colloquially known as shadow-walking."

"I *know* what it means. Where are we? Who are you?"

"I'm the man who just saved your life." He holstered his gun. "You're welcome." Then he turned left and marched down the hall. "You want a drink? I'm having one."

"Wait!" I wrapped one hand around the door frame and leaned into the hall as he turned to face me from a living room full of dated furniture. "Are you *damaged*? You didn't save my life. You nearly got me killed!"

He crossed his arms over a well-defined chest put on display by a snug blue T-shirt. "I pulled you out of the line of fire."

"I wouldn't have been *in* the line of fire, if it weren't for you. And if it weren't for *me,* they would have killed you!"

"They tried. They shot at us both." His wary focus narrowed on me until it felt invasive. "Sera, right?" he said, and I declined to answer. "Why were they willing to kill you, Sera?"

I blinked, scrambling for a response that wouldn't actually tell him anything about me. "Where are we?" I demanded when I couldn't come up with any answers of my own. "What am I doing here? Who *are* you?"

"Who am *I?*" Anger hardened his features and furrowed his brows. "Who the hell are *you,* and where's Kenley?"

"Who's Kenley?"

His anger visibly swelled in response to my question and he marched toward me, fists clenched at his sides, warning echoing in every step as his heavy boots clomped on the wood floor.

My heart lurched into my throat. I backed into the closet, peering through deep shadows for something to use as a weapon, but there was nothing. The closet was completely empty.

He was two steps away when I pulled the door shut, my pulse whooshing in my ears, then held the knob, using all of my weight to keep the door closed. What the hell was I thinking, jumping in the middle of syndicate business? I should have let Julia kill him....

The man growled, then the door was ripped from my grasp so fast I stumbled into the hall after it. He caught me before I could fall, but I shoved him off so quickly I almost missed the change in his expression.

"You're not a Traveler." He exhaled and the relief lining his features echoed within the sound. "I thought you'd disappeared through the shadows."

If I could have, I would have, but even without having grown up in the Skilled subculture, I knew better than to confirm or deny my own abilities.

I backed away from him, past the open closet door, hands open and ready to grab the first potential weapon I came across. "Let's try this again. Who are you?"

Anger resurfaced behind his eyes, but was quickly replaced with confusion. "You really don't know?"

"Why should I?"

He shrugged, and his jacket rose to reveal his holstered gun. "Well, if you work for Julia Tower—"

"I don't."

"Then what were you doing in her office?"

"That's none of your business." Being related to Jake Tower was dangerous, and having that fact known could be deadly. My mother had made sure I understood that, and Julia had just reinforced that lesson with a lethal spray of bullets.

His gaze narrowed. "Why would she tell her men to drop their guns at your request?"

Shit. So much for revealing nothing about myself.

New plan: reveal as little as possible.

"Because she wants something from me."

"What does she want?"

She wanted me to sign away my rights to the Tower legacy, not to protect her niece's and nephew's interests, but so that the wealth and power would remain under her fist, at least until they came of age. But… "Again, that's none of your business. Who is—"

He reached for me, and before I realized he wanted to brush aside a strand of hair caught on my scarf, I knocked his hand away and took another step back. My fists rose automatically. He glanced at me in surprise. "I'm not going to hurt you."

"That's a true statement." I was ready to fight.

He blinked, startled, then looked kind of disappointed. "No, I mean, I don't *want* to hurt you. You don't need to defend yourself from me."

"Right. You just shot several people and hauled a strange woman into a strange house against her will. Naturally I should assume you mean me no harm."

"Okay, I know how that sounds." He held both hands up, showing me he was unarmed, yet his gun still peeked out at me from its holster. "But I promise this is not that kind of abduction. If you don't believe me, look behind you." He gestured to something over my shoulder, and my need to know what was behind me warred with my need to keep him in sight.

I turned and pressed my back against the hallway wall so I could see both him and…the old woman asleep in a recliner in the room next to the closet I'd just stepped out of. Her ample chest rose and fell silently. Several melting ice cubes floated in a glass of watered-down tea on the small table next to her.

"Who's that?"

"My grandmother. She's a pretty deep sleeper, thanks to her medication, but she *will* wake up if you keep shouting, and I'd appreciate it if you'd let her sleep."

"You're serious?" What kind of armed killer kidnapped strange women and took them home to *Grandma?* What kind of family *was* this?

Although, considering the branch of my own family I'd just met, I didn't really have room to criticize.

He shrugged again and shoved his hands into his pockets, trying to look harmless; but even with his grandmother asleep in the next room, that was impossible to believe. He'd taken down at least four of my aunt's guards in just a couple of minutes, and his aim at me had never wavered, even with half a dozen guns pointed at him. The man had nerves of steel. He may have been many things—including a devoted grandson—but harmless was not one of them.

Yet he hadn't laid a hand on me.

"Why am I here? Who are you?" Why would he shoot to wound men who would readily have killed him? Why would he kidnap me at gunpoint, then claim to have no violent motive? Why would he think I knew his name, then refuse to give it to me?

Normally I'd assume I understood the destructive, violent nature of a home invasion. I'd become an unwilling expert on the subject when I'd lost my entire family a few months before, and getting caught in the middle of this one should have sent me over the edge.

But the Tower estate was no ordinary home, and the man in front of me was no ordinary invader. He hadn't broken in to kill someone, he'd broken in to *find* someone, and I was inexplicably fixated on the differences between his crime and the one that had shattered my entire reality.

Or maybe I just really needed those differences to exist. Maybe I needed him to have a good reason for what he'd done—what he was *still* doing—because I hadn't seen one damn thing in the world worth living for since I'd become an orphan and an only child, well into adulthood.

This man, whoever he was, had something worth living for. Something worth fighting for. Something worth *dying* for. And I really wanted to know what that was.

"Who were you looking for?" My voice was barely a whisper, but he heard me. In fact, he seemed to hear the need behind the question.

For several seconds he only watched me. Studying me, as if he was trying to decide whether or not he could trust me—an irony, considering that *he'd* just dragged *me* through the shadows. Finally he exhaled slowly and met my gaze with a heavy one of his own. "Julia Tower took my little sister, so I broke into the Tower residence to get her back."

I closed my eyes and an ache radiated from the center of my chest as my own sister's smile haunted my memory. My next inhalation hurt. I'd never seen his sister and I still didn't even know his name, but I understood his pain. I would do anything to get Nadia back, if that were possible, but…

"You broke into the Tower estate." It sounded just as crazy when I said it as when he'd said it. "There are easier ways to kill yourself, you know." Yet hadn't I done the same thing—minus all the gunfire?

Another shrug from the man with no name. "I figured that was the last thing they'd expect, thus the thing they'd be least prepared to defend against. Turns out I was right."

"No, you were lucky." As was I, but I'd known going in that they'd want to talk to me.

He scowled. "I make my own luck."

"You nearly made yourself a used-bullet receptacle. When did your sister go missing?" *Please, please don't let his sister be an actual child.* Surely he was too old for that. But then again, I'd just met two young siblings of my own…

"She didn't just 'go missing.'" He leaned with one shoulder against the wall, two feet from the end of the hallway. "Someone pulled her through the shadows a few minutes before I…met you."

"Well, then it couldn't have been Julia. She's—" At the last second I realized she wouldn't want me telling strangers what her Skill was. Not that I cared what she wanted, but pissing her off wouldn't make her any easier to deal with. "She's not a shadow-walker. Anyway, I was with her when your sister disappeared. It wasn't Julia."

"It wasn't her personally," he agreed. "She doesn't do her own dirty work. But my sister was taken on her orders, and Julia knows where she is."

There wasn't a single glimmer of doubt in him. Not in his unflinching gaze, his steady voice or the confidence in every word he spoke. And when I considered the bullets flying through that storage closet and Julia's apparent willingness to slaughter me in cold blood to keep me from inheriting her fortune, it wasn't hard for me to believe my aunt capable of abduction.

But then, obviously so was the man who'd *kidnapped* me.

Anger flamed up my spine with the sudden realization of where I fit into his storm-the-castle routine. "So, what, when you couldn't find your sister, you took me instead? What am I? A hostage?"

"No, I…" His cheeks flushed, and for the first time since he'd dragged me through the shadows, he seemed unsure of what to say. "It's more complicated than that."

"It's *complicated?*" Unless he'd just discovered he'd inherited millions in ill-gotten gains from a crime-boss father he'd never met, making him the target of a crime-boss aunt he *wished* he'd never met, he couldn't possibly understand the meaning of the word *complicated.* Not the way I understood it, anyway.

"Look, I'm the last person Julia Tower would be willing to trade your sister for." Though she might strike a bargain for my corpse—not that I had any intention of admitting that to a man desperate to rescue his sibling. "So, I need you to take me back. But I swear if I hear anything about your sister, I'll let you know what building you should break into next. So why don't you just give me your name and number, and I'll—"

"Sera, I can't take you back there." He held my gaze, and his statement had the grave finality of some indisputable truth. "They tried to kill you."

I crossed my arms over my chest, reeling from the irony. "You can't let someone else kill me, but you're fine with the fact that you kidnapped me?" What kind of weird-ass moral code was he following?

"I didn't really kidnap you." He glanced over my shoulder into the bedroom where his grandmother was now snoring loudly in her recliner. "I just…removed you from a dangerous situation. You're welcome." He mustered up a grin, obviously trying to diffuse my mounting anger and frustration, but it didn't work.

"For the last time, it wasn't dangerous until you got there, and I didn't ask to be removed."

Still, he had a point. I didn't want my father's dirty money, but would Julia even listen long enough to let me say that, or would she shoot me on sight?

I exhaled through clenched teeth. "Fine. Take me somewhere else then. Drop me off downtown." Where I could regroup and decide how best to proceed with my homicidally estranged aunt. And get my car back.

"I can't." He rubbed his forehead with one hand. "I'm sorry, but you have to stay here until I figure out what to do with you. So…make yourself comfortable." He twisted to wave one hand at the living room, and indignation began to smolder deep in my gut. "I'm guessing you're about ready for that drink now?"

"You can't be serious." I followed him into the tiny living room, where a couch and several armchairs surrounded a worn coffee table, all facing a small television.

"I am," he called over one shoulder as he crossed the living room toward the kitchen. "And could you be quiet for a minute? I need to think…"

"No I can't be quiet!" That smolder deep inside me burst into a blaze, and I felt as though I could breathe fire. "I'll tell the whole damn neighborhood I've been kidnapped if you don't take me someplace public, right now!"

"There's no neighborhood." He turned to face me from the kitchen doorway, infuriatingly calm, and gestured to the sidelights flanking the front door.

I glanced through the glass and groaned. No other

houses. No other buildings. No traffic. Nothing but star-light and a narrow gravel road, illuminated by the porch light. Where the hell were we?

"And you're not kidnapped," he continued when I turned, ready to roast him alive with the power of my rage. "You're just…borrowed. I'm gonna put you back." He frowned and his gaze dropped to the floor for a second. "Well, probably not back where I found you, but… My point is that you won't have to stay here forever."

"I don't have to stay here at *all*. You can't just *borrow* people!"

He glanced around the empty room, as if expecting someone to agree with me. "Kinda looks like I can. You want some coffee? Or are you thinking something stronger? I'm thinking something stronger."

"What is *wrong* with you?" I demanded when anger defeated my attempt at something more articulate.

"My sister's missing, my grandmother has Alzheimer's, Julia Tower wants me dead and you're turning out to be kind of a pain in the ass."

"Then *maybe* you shouldn't have *kidnapped* me!"

He rubbed his forehead, then raked one hand through his blond waves. "Well, hindsight is worthless, so could you just shut up so I can figure a few things out?"

"What things?" I demanded, but then I figured that out for myself. He'd broken into Julia's house, guns ablaze—surely an unforgivable insult to the head of a Skilled crime syndicate—but she had yet to return the favor. Which surely meant she didn't know where he was. "If you're worried that I'll tell Julia where you are, or something like that, you can relax. I don't know who you are, or where we are, and she hasn't exactly inspired my loyalty today."

"Loyalty is compulsory when you're bound." He hesitated, but just for a second. "*Are* you bound to her?"

"No. I'm not bound to anyone."

"And I'm just supposed to take your word for it?" His frown deepened and he glanced at my left arm, covered by my long-sleeved shirt. "I...um...need to see your arm."

But even if I'd felt obligated to show him my unmarked arm—and I didn't—I couldn't have complied without taking my shirt off. And that wasn't gonna happen.

"No." Was this what my mother's obsessive caution had spared me? A lifetime of suspicion, and dangerous loyalties, and lives defined by the color of the marks on my skin? By the constant need to prove I had no syndicate marks and served no one but myself?

"I'm asking nicely," he said, but there was a warning threaded through his voice.

"And if I refuse nicely?" I backed up several steps, blindly aiming for the front door while my heart pounded in my throat. "Are you going to get less nice?"

Was *I* going to have to get less nice? He was bigger and stronger, but I had no problem fighting dirty, and I had nothing left to lose.

"No." He exhaled in frustration. "Look, you don't have to take anything off. We can cut your sleeve, or you can change into something of my sister's. I just need to know that when I let you—" He stopped, then started over. "That when you *leave,* you won't be obligated to go back and tell Julia everything you saw and heard here today."

My heart thumped painfully. "Can't you just take my word for it?"

He looked kind of sad. "I wish we lived in the kind of world where I could, but we don't. Can't you just show me? If you don't have a mark, why is this such a big deal?"

That question cut straight to the heart of the matter, and suddenly everything seemed really clear. "Because I don't have to. Because you don't get to see anything I don't want to show you. Because you don't have the right to keep me here and make demands. Because the fact that I *don't* have a mark means I don't have to take orders from anyone. Including *you!*"

He blinked at me in surprise. Then he nodded. "All valid points. And in a perfect world, they'd matter, but here, they don't. I can't take you anywhere until I know you pose no threat to me and mine." With that, he turned and stepped into the kitchen while I fumed from the middle of the living room floor.

"Fine." My jaw already ached from grinding my teeth. "I'm guessing your range is no more than a few miles, so we can't have gone too far." I had some cash, my only credit card and my phone. No reason I couldn't walk back to civilization on my own.

"Why do women always err on the side of *under*estimation?" he mumbled, pulling a bottle from an overhead cabinet as I headed for the front door. "My Skill could be *huge,* for all you know." He had his back to me. He wasn't even watching.

A second later, as I twisted and pulled on the front doorknob to no avail, I saw why.

"The door's nailed shut!" Furious, I bent to examine the nails and my teeth ground together when I noticed the tiny crosshairs. "Those aren't nails, they're screws!"

And half of them had been countersunk. No one was getting through that door without an electric drill, a Phillips head bit and a spare half hour.

"Did that myself," my kidnapper called from the

kitchen. "Of course, we can probably kiss the security deposit goodbye. Ironic, isn't it, considering that I actually made the house *more* secure."

I stood to glare at him through the kitchen doorway, fingering my phone in my pocket. If I didn't dread explaining the circumstances of my abduction, I'd have already dialed 911. "Look, I don't recognize your particular psychosis, but trust me when I say this is a very special kind of crazy. Why the hell would you screw the front door shut?"

He shrugged, leaning with one hip against the counter, a half-empty bottle of whiskey in one hand. "We don't use that exit."

My focus found the door behind him, which presumably led to the backyard, and before I could decide whether or not to make a break for it—which would involve running right past him—he shook his head. "We don't use that one, either."

Both exits were screwed shut because he and his grandmother had no *use* for them? *Bullshit.*

He was prepared to house a prisoner, which meant this was premeditated. How could I have misread him so drastically? The fact that he cared about his sister didn't make him less dangerous; it made him *more* dangerous. If his rash invasion of the Tower estate was any indication, he'd do anything to get her back. He'd gone in *planning* to take a hostage. The bastard wasn't going to let me go until he got his sister back!

But…that didn't make any sense. Why trade me, if he didn't *want* me to go back to Julia? Was that just an act? Or had he planned to kidnap someone she valued—someone she would bargain for—but got stuck with me instead? If so, what was the new plan? What good was a hostage who couldn't be traded?

No good at all.

Panic raced through me like fire in my veins. This was real. The psycho with nice eyes had taken me, but had no use for me. Even if he truly had no plans for violence—and his grandmother's presence seemed to confirm that—he had no intentions of letting me go, either.

Knowing the doors didn't function made my skin crawl, as if I were trapped not just by this house, but by my own body. My own mind.

I needed fresh air. Space. *Now.*

Logically, I knew that was the panic talking. There was plenty of air, and the house wasn't that small—the foot of the staircase in one corner of the living room meant there was an entire second story I had yet to see. And the hum of the air conditioner told me the ventilation was fine. Being locked up wasn't going to kill me.

But being stupid might.

Think.

Assuming he truly loved his grandmother—and I'd seen no reason to doubt that—he wouldn't leave her alone if she couldn't get out of the house. What if there was a fire?

There had to be a functioning exit.

I took a deep breath and swallowed my panic. "Fine. If you don't use the doors, how do you get out of here?"

He didn't even look up from the soda he was pouring into a short glass, over an inch of whiskey. "The same way I brought you in."

Damn it. "You're both shadow-walkers?"

"Not all of us. But enough."

All of us? How many were there? "And I assume the windows are…"

"Screwed shut. Which is overkill in some cases, because about half of them were already painted shut. This place is pretty old."

Great. No one could get in or out of whatever weird-ass house he'd dragged me into without the ability to travel. Or something to throw through a window, and a good head start.

I'd call that Plan B.

Plan A needed to be smarter, and a little more tech-savvy. While my kidnapper rattled pots and pans in the kitchen, I dug my cell from my pocket and sank onto the couch. I opened the GPS function on my phone and waited while the map loaded, slowly, slowly, slowly narrowing down my location.

Cell phone reception in his stupid, screwed-shut house sucked.

"You still alive in there?" he called from the kitchen, after about a minute of silence from me.

I considered not answering, but then he'd come looking for me.

"Alive and pissed off!" I called back.

"I'm sorry about that. I didn't plan this, but now we're kind of stuck with each other for a bit."

Yeah, right. And finally, the GPS centered on my location.

I didn't recognize any of the street names, but that was no surprise, considering I'd never been to the city before and I'd let my car's GPS navigate the whole way to the Tower estate.

I zoomed out on the map, searching for familiar landmarks, and when I couldn't find any, I zoomed in again, hoping to narrow my location down to a street address. Or at least a close cross-street. Then I'd call the police and have this grandma's-boy, kidnapping son of a bitch arrested.

I didn't have to press charges, or even explain how I'd wound up in the House of Crazy. I just needed the cops to come open a door.

But there didn't seem to be any cross-streets. We were truly in the middle of nowhere.

The loading icon spun and spun as the map tried to refresh, and I stared at it in mounting frustration and anger. My hand clenched around the phone so hard the plastic case groaned and my knuckles turned white, but finally the new map loaded, and—

My cell was ripped from my grasp.

"Hey!" I stood and reached for my phone, but he stepped back and my nails clawed his forearm instead, drawing four white lines, but no blood.

"Sorry. Can't let you do that." Then the bastard dropped my phone and *stomped* on it, grinding with the heel of his hiking boot until shards of metal and plastic were hopelessly embedded into the worn carpet.

Fury sparked the length of my spine and my right hand curled into a fist. I swung before I even realized what I'd intended, and my fist slammed into his jaw. "You owe me a phone!"

He stumbled back in surprise, rubbing his face, and I ignored the ache in my hand as I knelt to scrape up the remains of my cell, just in case. But it was *trashed*.

"This isn't funny!" I shouted.

"Agreed." He stomped into the kitchen and a second later I heard ice rattle.

"You can't keep me here. If you think I'm going to twiddle my thumbs as your hostage, you kidnapped the wrong damn woman."

"Would you please calm down?" He appeared in the living room again, this time holding an ice-filled plastic sandwich bag to his jaw. "I'm the one with everything to lose here, and you're the one throwing punches. You're not a hostage, and you're not in any danger. In fact, you're safer here than you were with Julia Tower, so please sit down and *shut up!*"

I heard his words, but I couldn't process them. I wasn't a hostage? I was in no danger? The facts didn't support those statements—he'd dragged me through the shadows and locked me up in a strange house. My *entire family* died in a locked house. Their *own* locked house.

No exits, no neighbors and no phone. I was *screwed.* Unless...

Maybe there was a landline. Some people still had those.

When a glance around the living room revealed no phone, I stomped into the kitchen, and he only watched me, still icing his jaw. "What are you doing?"

There was a phone on the wall by the fridge. A really *old* phone, connected to the handset by a long, curly, yellow cord. I picked up the handset and started to dial—until I noticed there was no dial tone.

"We never hooked it up." He picked up his drink, drained it, then set the empty glass on the counter next to an open box of macaroni and cheese. "No need, with cell phones, right?"

*Speaking of which...*I could see the outline of his in his back pocket. Maybe I could hit him with something, then take his phone and lock myself in another room long enough to call for help...

"It's passcode protected," he said when he turned and caught me staring at the seat of his jeans. "More useful as a paperweight than as a phone, if you don't have the code. Or were you just staring at my butt?"

"I wasn't..." I stopped, angered anew by how flustered I was. "Unless your phone is ancient, it'll still make emergency calls."

"True." My kidnapper pulled the phone from his pocket and held it up. "Do I need to smash mine, too?" He looked reluctant, but willing. I shook my head because I couldn't steal it later if he busted it now.

He pulled a clean rag from a drawer and wrapped his ice pack in it, then pressed it to his jaw again. "You throw one hell of a punch."

"You smashed my phone."

"Sorry. I couldn't let you call Julia."

"Julia?" I scowled and backed slowly toward a microwave cart on the other side of the room, where several steak knives were spread out on a folded towel, evidently set out to dry. "I told you I don't work for her. I was calling the police."

He shrugged. "Well, that's almost as bad. I'm sorry about your phone, though."

"What kind of kidnapper apologizes? And lives with his grandmother? And forgets to take away the victim's phone?" My spine hit the cart and I slid one hand behind my back, feeling for the handle of a knife. "You're the worst kidnapper *ever*."

He watched me closely, but stayed back. "I'm not a kidnapper."

"My unwilling presence in your home says otherwise."

"Okay, yes." He acknowledged my point with another shrug. "But there are extenuating circumstances. Why don't we sit and discuss this over a drink? Or are you hungry? I'm not much of a cook, but I can handle boxed mac and cheese, if you're interested."

I wouldn't eat or drink a damn thing he gave me, but...

"What happened to the stove?" I glanced pointedly at the front of the ancient appliance, where all four of the burner-control knobs were missing. Was *nothing* normal in his house?

"Oh. Gran nearly burned the house down yesterday, so we had to take the knobs off the stove, and now I can't remember where Ian hid them…" He turned and took a cookie jar from the top of the fridge, and when he peered inside, I let my fingers skim the cart at my back, searching for the knives.

My kidnapper huffed in frustration and put the jar back. "They were in here yesterday, but now they're gone…"

My fingers closed around the handle of a knife and my stomach roiled when I brandished it at him, trying not to think about the damage a different blade had done behind my parents' locked doors. Could I do to my kidnapper what was done to my entire family? Even though he hadn't laid a hand on me?

Yet.

He hadn't laid a hand on me *yet.* And he claimed not to want me to return to Julia Tower, but hadn't he already proved he'd do anything to get his sister back? Why wouldn't he trade me for her? I'd do it in a heartbeat, if our situations were reversed.

"Give me your phone, or I swear I will gut you." By some miracle, my hand was steady. The same could not be said for my stomach. I *hate* knives.

His pale brows rose and he crossed his arms over his shirt. "Then how will you get out of here? You don't know where you are, and it'll take the police forever to trace a cell phone. My grandmother doesn't have one. And she's not a Traveler."

I frowned and glanced at the kitchen window, mentally working on a Plan C.

"You could break the glass and shout for help," he

suggested. "But I can't let you go, and even if you tried, you'd cut yourself trying to climb out." Only an idiot would leave her blood lying around for anyone with the requisite Skill to use against her. "And there's no one around to hear you scream for help. The nearest neighbor is more than a mile away."

More than a mile between houses? Either he was lying—though the lack of traffic noise said he wasn't—or his range was much better than I'd guessed.

Either way, I had to get out, and I had to do it before his friends came back and my odds got even worse.

"Why don't you calm down and have a seat?" He glanced at the kitchen table and the four chairs around it. "If I put my gun down, will you put your knife down?"

"Hell, no! I'm not going to put the knife down, I'm not going to sit, and I don't want to talk to you. So you can either let me out of here, or you can get ready to bleed."

I scanned the kitchen, looking for something light enough to lift, but heavy enough to break glass.

"Sera…" His tone resonated with warning as he set the ice pack on the counter, tense now, as if he might pounce if I made one wrong move. "Whatever you're thinking…don't."

My gaze landed on a ceramic napkin holder shaped like two halves of a pineapple, sitting on top of the microwave. The kidnapper took one step toward me, arms out at his sides, as if I might rush him at any moment.

Instead, I grabbed the napkin holder and hurled it at the nearest window.

Glass shattered and a jagged hole appeared in the pane. Both halves of the pineapple landed on the dark grass outside, about a foot apart.

"Damn it," he swore.

"Kris?" a woman's shaky voice called from the other

end of the house, and recliner springs groaned as his grandmother sat up in her chair.

"It's okay, Gran. Go back to sleep," Kris—finally the kidnapper had a name!—said without taking his gaze from me. "You shouldn't have done that," he whispered, and anger flickered across his expression.

"I probably shouldn't do this either, then, right?" I grabbed a wooden rolling pin from a stainless steel canister of large utensils and swung it at what was left of the window. Glass exploded outward, onto the grass.

"What the hell are you doing in there?" his grandmother demanded, and the chair groaned again. "If one of you hellions put another pool cue through my—"

"It's fine, Gran," he called back. "Stay in your room."

I kept swinging and glass kept breaking. I knocked as much of it out as I could, to make the window safe to crawl through, and he only watched me, his eyes narrowed in irritation, a red blotch growing on his chin where I'd punched him.

When the glass was gone, I met his gaze, trying to decide whether to relinquish the bludgeoning weapon or the stabbing weapon—I'd need at least one free hand to climb through the window.

"Please don't do this," he said, and the earnest note in his voice actually made me hesitate. For about a second.

Then I threw the rolling pin at him and lunged for the window while he ducked.

I was halfway out when he wrapped one arm around my waist and tried to drag me back in. My heart beat so hard my chest almost hurt. I clutched the window frame and swung the knife behind me. The serrated blade caught on material and when I jerked it free from the snag, he swore again. But he didn't let go or stop pulling, and I wasn't strong enough to keep him from hauling me back into the house. At least, not without the use of both hands.

In the kitchen once again, he pinned my left arm to my side with his other arm wrapped around my waist. I shoved the knife in my right hand backward, hoping to catch a vital organ, but he caught my wrist before the blade made contact.

"Please drop the knife, Sera. I don't want to hurt you."

"Sorry I can't say the same." I tried to twist my arm free, but his grip was relentless and I couldn't reach anything with the blade.

"Kristopher, what the hell is going on?"

My shoes brushed the floor when he spun with me still in his grip, evidently as startled as I was to find his grandmother standing in the kitchen doorway, her stern frown aimed at us both.

"Call the police," I demanded, tossing hair out of my face. He grunted when my skull smashed into his… something. "I'm a hostage being held against my will."

Her frown bled into a sympathetic smile. "Oh, hon, you're not being held, you're being *moved.* We're the good guys. But I need you to hold it down, so you don't wake up the rest of the kids."

"The rest…" Fresh panic made my pulse trip faster. "How many other hostages do you have?"

"None." Kris groaned in frustration. "She's not a kid, Gran. We don't have any kids right now, remember?" He shifted, and his next words were softer, spoken near my ear. "You're not a hostage. She's confused."

The old woman propped wrinkled fists on ample hips. "Kristopher, let her go. That's no way to earn her trust."

"I can't let her go. She has a knife."

"Good. I hope she skewers you with it." His grandmother marched past us both, glanced in obvious irritation at the stove with no knobs, then pulled a mug from the cabinet above the coffeemaker. "You can't keep bringing them in with no notice, Kris. We don't have a bed for her right now. One of the boys will have to sleep on the couch until we find someplace safe to send her."

Boys?

Kris groaned again. "She's not a kid, Gran. She's *fully* grown." His declaration carried equal parts appreciation and frustration over that fact, and I wasn't sure how to feel about that. "And we're not sending her anywhere."

"What the *hell* are you people talking about? I haven't been rescued, I've been kidnapped."

Kris's grandmother shot him a questioning look over her mug, as if *I* were the one who made no sense.

"I didn't kidnap her. Exactly," he said. "But if I let her go now, she'll stab me. Again."

Again? Was he already bleeding?

The grandmother pulled the full carafe from the coffee machine. "Is this decaf? You know I hate decaf."

"It's fully leaded," he said, his mouth inches from my ear, his grip on me unrelenting.

"What is *wrong* with this family?" I demanded when the hard kick I landed on his shin did no good, and she made no move to help me.

Gran gave me a stern frown and poured coffee into her mug. "We have a strict no-weapons policy for the residents. He'll let you go as soon as you put the knife down, but not a moment sooner."

My grip on the knife tightened. "Who *are* you people?"

"Don't tell her anything," Kris said, hauling me backward when I tried to kick the nearest cabinet. "I think she works for the Towers."

Gran's eyes widened. Then she blinked and gave her

head a little shake, as if she'd just woken up and needed to clear the cobwebs.

I kicked backward again, and again I caught Kris's leg. He grunted, but didn't let go. "I don't work for anyone," I insisted, but no one was listening.

His grandmother looked up from her mug, scowling fiercely, and everything about her was suddenly different, from the harder edge to her voice to the stiffness of her posture. "Kristopher Daniels, tell me you did *not* bring a Tower employee into this house."

Kris groaned into my ear. "Gran, my *name* is top on the list of things you weren't supposed to tell her!"

"Take her back." Gran blew calmly over the surface of her coffee as I kicked her grandson over and over again, growing angrier each time he only grunted and squeezed me tighter. "If she works for the Towers, she's dangerous."

"Taking her back won't make her any less dangerous. And anyway, I can't take her back." Kris *oofed* when I threw my head back and my skull caught his...chin? But his grip around my waist never loosened. "They tried to shoot her. Right now, I can't really blame them."

"Why would they shoot their own employee?" Gran asked.

"I don't work for them! And they weren't shooting at me, they were shooting at *him*." Though they were clearly willing to count me as collateral damage. *"Let me go!"* I shouted when my anger crested, and I shoved the knife back with all the strength I had.

The blade snagged on material again, and Kris gasped, then grunted in frustration. *"Damn it,* Sera!" He let go of my waist, but before I could do anything with my freed left arm, he spun me around and slammed me against the front of the refrigerator.

Air burst from my lungs, then his forearm pressed into my collarbone through my sister's yellow scarf, pinning my shoulders to the fridge. Panic tightened every muscle in my body. I fought blindly as memory obscured reality and it became hard to focus on his face.

His free hand curled around my right one, which still gripped the blade. His angry blue-gray gaze bored into me, his legs pinning mine so that I couldn't kick. "*Please* drop the knife, Sera! You got me. I'm bleeding. You win."

"Open the door and let me out," I growled through clenched teeth.

He exhaled heavily. "I can't. I'm sorry you can't see that, but I can't let you leave yet, for your safety and for ours. I have to ask you some questions, and you *have* to answer them. But it doesn't have to be this hard. Please, please, please let's do this the easy way."

"Fuck you." I glared into his eyes from inches away. "I don't owe you anything."

His expression hardened. "Fine. We'll do it the hard way. Just keep in mind that that was your choice." He squeezed my left wrist, but I gripped the knife in spite of the growing pressure and pain until I actually lost control of my own fingers.

The knife slipped from my failed grip and clattered on the floor. He kicked it across the linoleum and it *thunked* into something I couldn't see. In the second my left leg was free, I tried to knee him in the groin, but he deflected the blow with the outside of one very solid thigh.

He was just plain too big to fight, unless I was willing to fight dirty—and I was—or I could catch him by surprise. Which became the new Plan D.

His eyes narrowed, his gaze cautious. "If I let go, are you going to play nice and show me your arm?"

I stared back at him. "Are you going to hand over your phone and power tools?"

His grandmother laughed from the kitchen table, and I realized she'd been watching us the whole time. Sipping her coffee.

Kris groaned. "Are you this much of a pain in the ass every time someone asks to see your marks?"

"No one's ever asked to see my marks. And again, *I don't have any.*"

"How have you never been asked to prove that? What, are you from Mars?"

"Worse," his grandmother said, and I saw her watching us over his shoulder, a shrewd gleam in her eye. "Suburbia. There isn't much syndicate activity in the outskirts, Kris. You know that better than most."

He did? What did that mean?

"Yeah, I do." His grip on me loosened and his gaze softened, but he didn't let me go. "Okay, I get that you're out of your element, and you're obviously clueless about the way this city operates. So let me give you some survival advice. Stay out of the east side unless you want to deal with Cavazos. Stay out of the west side unless you want to deal with Tower—which you evidently do." His disgusted expression told me exactly how dumb he thought that decision was, and I bristled beneath his judgment. "And when someone asks to see your arm, you show them your damn arm, so they know whether or not they're allowed to fuck with you. They won't all be as nice about it as I've been."

"You call this nice?" I snapped.

He stared at me for a second, apparently gauging the sincerity of my question, while his grandmother shook her head slowly at the table. My naïveté was evidently confounding.

"This is the kid-glove treatment," Kris said. "There are people out there who would have cut your clothes off the first time you refused."

"My shirt," I corrected, and he shook his head.

"The left arm is the most common place people are marked, but it's not the *only* place."

Chills raced up my spine, then down into my hands, which began to shake. I glanced at his grandmother for confirmation, and she nodded solemnly.

Kris's gaze narrowed on me again, and he seemed to be studying me from a new perspective. "What the hell are you doing here, Sera? Girls like you don't belong in the city."

"No one belongs here," Gran said, and I let her answer stand for me.

"Now, I'm going to let you go, and you're going to turn around and pull your left arm out of your shirt and show it to me. You can keep everything else covered, but your left arm is non-negotiable. Got it?"

"How am I supposed to prove I'm not marked anywhere else? I'm not taking anything off."

"No need." Gran chuckled into her coffee, and I couldn't believe the change in her from a few minutes earlier. "A whore would never be so hard to undress."

"Whore?" I blinked at Kris in incomprehension.

"Cavazos marks his prostitutes with a red ring on the inner thigh." He chuckled a little at my shocked expression. "Don't worry. I've never met anyone less likely to bear a red mark in my life."

I wasn't sure whether or not that was a compliment.

"I'm going to let go and back up, and you're going to show me your arm. Ready?"

"If I do, you'll open the front door?"

He frowned. "No, but showing me your arm will put you one step closer to that. Here goes..."

He let go of my right hand and removed his left arm from my shoulders. Then he backed up several steps, still watching me.

My heart thumped in my ears as I turned slowly, reluctant to put him at my back, even with his grandmother in the room. My focus raked the counter next to the fridge in search of a weapon. But there was nothing within easy reach.

I would have shown him my arm, if that would have gotten me released. But since it wouldn't, I couldn't see the point in capitulating. In letting him think I could be pushed around.

Instead of pulling my arm free from my sleeve, I spun and launched myself at Kris. I rammed him in the chest with my shoulder, just like my dad had taught me when I was twelve.

Air burst from his lungs and he stumbled backward into the table, which slid across the floor and into the far wall without even spilling his grandmother's coffee.

Gran cackled as he tried to stand, holding his spine where it had hit the table, and I ran for freedom. I had both hands wrapped around the window frame when he grabbed my arms from behind.

I lost my balance when he jerked my arms behind me and would have fallen headfirst out the window if he hadn't hauled me back in, pinning my wrists in one of his hands.

"Let go!" I twisted and kicked backward, but a second later something cold and hard wrapped around my wrists. A soft zipping sound froze me in place, and the plastic around my wrists got tighter. "Are you serious?

A zip tie?" Why would he even *have* those if he wasn't planning to take a hostage?

He spun me around to face him again, anger drawn in every line of his face, and when I tried to pull free, his grip on my arm tightened. "Just FYI, this is *not* the easy way."

He pulled me into the living room. When I refused to sit on the couch, he gave my left shoulder a small shove, and I fell onto the center cushion, my hands trapped behind me.

He sat on the coffee table facing me, at eye-height again, and that's when I saw where he was bleeding. My blade had sliced across his right forearm in two different places.

"Has anyone ever told you you're a total pain in the ass?" He rolled back his sleeve and flinched with one look at the long, shallow cuts. "I'm sorry about the zip tie. I don't usually tie women up, but I don't know what else to do with you."

"Don't apologize because I'm a woman. Apologize because you're an asshole!" I shouted.

His grandmother laughed out loud from the kitchen doorway, holding her still-steaming mug of coffee. "I like her, Kris. I doubt Vanessa will, though."

Who the hell was Vanessa?

Kris's jaw clenched, but he didn't even glance at his grandmother. "Just so we're clear, the zip tie isn't the only equipment at my disposal. I'm also *fully* prepared to tape your mouth shut."

In reply, I leaned back on the couch and kicked him off the coffee table.

Four

Kris

The closet door opened down the hall as I was rinsing my cuts in the bathroom. I went for my gun out of habit, trailing water across the floor and blood across my arm.

"Kris?" Kori called, and I slid my gun back into its holster and stepped out of the bathroom with a clean white towel pressed to my arm. "What happened? Liv said you went after Kenley, but she lost your scent."

She meant my psychic scent—the personal energy signature given off by my blood, which blood Trackers, like Olivia and Cam, could use to find people.

"No surprise there. The Towers' nanny is a Jammer, right?" Being near a Jammer is like being in a psychic dead zone—you can't be tracked, either by name or by blood. That's a benefit those who can afford it will gladly pay for, but it comes with a couple of obvious disadvantages, as well.

"You went to Jake's house?" She lifted the towel from my arm and her pale brows furrowed over eyes as deep a brown as our mother's had been. "What the hell were you thinking? It's a miracle you walked out of there with only—"

"Hey!" Sera shouted from Gran's bedroom—the only one on the first floor.

I groaned. There was no good way to tell Kori about our new guest, but letting Sera deliver the news herself was number one on a long list of bad ways to get the job done.

Kori's focus shifted from my wounds to the closed bedroom door. She dropped the rag into place on my arm and her hand found the grip of the gun holstered beneath her jacket. "Who the *fuck* is that?"

Gran chuckled from the living room, where she was sipping iced tea in front of the muted television. She'd refused to help me with Sera on the grounds that I deserved whatever I got for bringing a stranger back to our hideout, even though she only remembered who we were hiding from about half the time.

"Hey!" Sera shouted again, while I actively regretted not gagging her when I'd had the chance. "Whoever's out there, if you're even *marginally* sane, *please* consider calling the police. But if you're as psychologically damaged as Kris and his grandmother, then by all means, carry on with whatever the descendants of Norman Bates do for fun on the weekend. I'm sure I'll still be here whenever you get around to stabbing me and laughing maniacally over my cooling corpse."

"That's Sera." I pressed the rag tighter against the cuts on my arm. "She's rational and calm, and just generally pleasant to be around. I think you're gonna like her."

"I like her!" Gran called over the wooden creak of her rocker.

Kori took a single, cautious step back and slowly pushed the bedroom door open.

Sera sat in Gran's rolling desk chair, kind of tilted to the side because I'd used a leather belt to secure her bound arms to the back of the chair.

Kori made a noise deep in her throat. It sounded like an angry mutation of my name. "Who the fuck is that, and where the hell is Kenley?"

"The short version?" I said, and she nodded without taking her focus from Sera. "I went to Tower's looking for Kenni, but Julia was more interested in having me shot than in answering my questions, and I didn't have time for a leisurely search of the compound." Not that I'd expected her to actually be there. I'd hoped Julia might value her own life enough to order my sister's return. Or at least tell me where to find her. "I didn't find Kenley, but I did find Sera, and they seemed willing to shoot through her to get to me, so I figured she wouldn't mind being removed from immediate danger." I shrugged. "Turns out they might have had the right idea."

"Fuck you." If Sera's eyes could have shot flames, I would have been nothing but a pile of ash. "Untie me."

Kori turned to me, both brows raised. "Wait. Julia took our sister, and your brilliant plan was to break into her house and return the favor?"

"No, my intent was to get Kenni back. But Sera was there, and she got between my gun and Julia." *And she was wearing a yellow scarf...* "Then they started shooting at us—at *both* of us—so I had to take her with me."

"You *had* to take her?" Kori pushed pale hair back from her face, then crossed her arms over her chest. "Fine. What are you planning to do with her? She's a bargaining chip? A trade?"

"I'm a *hostage,*" Sera said.

Kori turned on me, but the anger I expected to find in her eyes was backlit by something more bitter. More personal. "We don't take hostages, Kris. And we damn sure don't take prisoners. That's not how we operate."

"I'm aware. She's neither prisoner nor hostage," I insisted as I lost the battle not to stare at Sera some more. At her scarf. At her eyes. At the tension in her frame, telling me she would fight until the very last breath was forced from her body, if that's what it took. She didn't need a reason to fight—she just needed an excuse.

I didn't want to be her reason *or* her excuse. Or her jailer. In spite of her sharp knife and her even sharper tongue, I was captivated by the fire inside her and curious about the fuel that fed it.

And I *needed* to know why Sera had shown up in my notebook, nearly a decade before I met her.

"She's a guest," I continued, watching Sera while I spoke to my sister. "She's a *reluctant* guest who really shouldn't be thrown out in the cold until we know whether or not she's bound to tell Julia Tower about everything she's said and heard here."

"Agreed. Although she wouldn't have seen or heard anything if you hadn't brought her here." Kori exhaled and crossed her arms over her shirt. "So...who is she?"

A pang of disappointment unfurled in my chest. "I was hoping you could tell me that."

"I don't recognize her. But she could have signed on with Julia after I left the organization."

Understatement of the decade. Kori hadn't just "left" the Tower syndicate. She'd fought her way out in an elegant clusterfuck of a showdown, in which Ian, Olivia and I all kicked ass and fired guns on her behalf.

They say combat is a bonding experience for those who survive. They're right.

Kori eyed our guest's awkward tilt. "Why is she tied up?"

"Because he's psychotic," Sera spat.

"Because she's a flight risk," I corrected, and I got the distinct impression that she was flipping me off behind her back. "Did I mention she's feisty? Because she's also stubborn."

"Fascinating." Kori glanced at the long sleeve covering Sera's left arm. "Does she have marks?"

Sera groaned, still glaring up at me. "I told you, I don't work for Julia Tower!"

I could only shrug. "She keeps saying that, but she won't prove it."

"You have to prove it. That's the way the world works." Kori studied Sera's scowl. "Either you know that, and you're refusing because you're marked, or you're naive enough to think you actually have a choice in the matter. That's adorable, but completely erroneous."

"She's not from around here," I said, while Sera shot rage daggers at us both.

"No shit. Did you ask her nicely?"

"I said please and everything, but remember how I told you she was gentle and pleasant? I lied."

"So what's the plan?"

I leaned against the door frame and eyed Kori expectantly. "I was hoping my sweet, gentle little sister could use her charms to verify that our guest doesn't have any marks."

Kori huffed, still eyeing Sera as if she were a puzzle she didn't have the patience to solve. "Kenley's unavailable at the moment."

"Then I guess you'll have to do."

Kori turned on me. "She's your problem. *You* check her for marks."

I groaned, then tugged Kori into the hall after me, where I lowered my voice. "I've already had to catch her, restrain her, catch her again, then tie her up, and after all that, cutting her shirt open just feels like crossing a line."

Sera huffed from the bedroom, where she could obviously still hear us. "So you're saying there *is* a limit to the cruelty and unreasonable demands you're willing to inflict on the woman who saved you from a future as a human sieve?"

Gran laughed from the living room. "I like her! I think we should keep her!"

"We can't keep her, Gran. She's not a kitten!" Kori shouted.

I tried to not to dwell on the fact that way too many of the women in my life communicated at top volume and maximum ridicule. Then I lowered my voice even further. "Wasn't checking for marks part of your job description? Aren't you supposed to be good at this?"

My sister shrugged. "I know seven different ways to get a look at her bare arm in the next thirty seconds, but none of them are gentle, and a couple of them would obligate me to marry her in several third-world cultures." She slapped me on the arm. "You're on your own. But I will give you a little advice."

I groaned. "Don't you need wisdom in order to dispense advice?"

"Nah, just experience. Listen up." Kori tugged me farther from the half-closed bedroom door. "Don't force her into showing you her arm. *Talk* her into it. Otherwise, she'll never forgive you."

"What makes you think I want her forgiveness?"

My sister's eyes narrowed, but the real censure was in the contempt behind them. "Don't be an asshole, Kris. We both know you care what she thinks of you."

"And you've drawn that unlikely conclusion based on…"

"Oh, please. You took one of Julia's pretty young women instead of one of the *many* fat, balding men bound to her. Though I hope it's obvious now that you've bitten off more than you can chew."

"You think I took her because I *wanted* her? What am I, a caveman?"

"In her opinion?" Kori shrugged. "Probably."

"I took her because they were going to kill her to get to me." And because she was wearing the yellow scarf. But I couldn't tell my sister that. She didn't know about the notebook. She didn't even know about Noelle. "I couldn't just leave her there."

Kori rolled her eyes. "Julia would have killed anyone to get to you, or to any one of us, but you will never convince me that you'd have pulled one of her meathead laborers through the shadows to 'protect' him."

There was no use arguing with her when I couldn't explain myself without mentioning the notebook, and I couldn't tell her about that because I'd never told *anyone* about the notebook or about how I'd filled it. About how, for the first time, one of those indecipherable lines had made sense, and I'd pulled Sera through the shadows just in time to prevent us both from being killed.

If the woman in the yellow scarf was real, then everything else I'd written down could be real, too. What had I missed in that notebook? What had I ignored? What other horrible things could I have *prevented?*

"Go talk to her, Kris. We can't keep her tied up, but we can't afford to let her go, and the only other option isn't going to sit well on my conscience."

"You have a conscience?" I went for the obvious joke, so I wouldn't have to think about what she was really saying, because if I thought about that, Kori and I would fight.

I hadn't fought with Kori in a very long time. For a very good reason.

"I have a conscience and you have a brain, and I suspect they're both getting rusty, so let's put them to use. Kenley needs us, and your Sera's getting in the way."

"I know." But if Sera *did* work for the Towers, she might be able to help us find Kenley. "Did Liv catch Kenni's scent?"

"Not a trace." Kori didn't look surprised. When the Towers wanted someone to disappear, that someone disappeared.

"They won't kill her," I whispered, trying to reassure us both. Killing Kenley would release Julia's remaining employees from their bonds of servitude and obedience, and that was the last thing Julia wanted.

"I know. But the Towers are capable of far worse than death." Kori shook her head, jarring loose memories I could almost see floating beneath her carefully controlled expression. She nodded once, curtly, then headed back into the bedroom, where she studied Sera's face again with no sign of recognition. "She's definitely not one of Jake's, but if she's Julia's, you can't trust a word she says without third-party verification."

"You knew him?" Sera's eyes widened and a little of her hostility melted beneath the curiosity she couldn't quite hide. It looked genuine, and I was as fascinated by what she didn't know as I was by what she might be able to tell us. "You actually knew Jake Tower?"

Kori sank onto the bed, which put her at eye level with Sera. "I knew him very well." She shrugged out of her jacket and pushed up her short left sleeve to reveal two chain links tattooed on her upper arm, now the faded gray of dead marks. "I served him for six years— most of that spent under his direct supervision—which is how I can say with absolute confidence that he was one of the cruelest, most recreationally sadistic men to ever walk this earth."

Sera shifted uncomfortably in her chair, but didn't break Kori's gaze. She looked the way I felt every time a pill I had to swallow got stuck in my throat.

"I knew his brother, too, until I had the privilege of ending the bastard's cold-blooded existence," Kori continued. "I know Julia Tower better than anyone should ever have to know Julia Tower, and with every single breath I take, I regret my decision to let her live. Instead of cursing my own foot when I stub my toe, I've taken to cursing the foul womb that produced all three of the Tower siblings. Their family tree is rotten all the way to its decayed-ass roots, and I don't see how Jake's kids—as innocent as they look now—can possibly rise above the malice and brutality that is their birthright."

Sera flinched as though she'd been slapped, and Kori frowned.

"You never met him, did you?" she asked. Sera shook her head. "But you know Julia?"

"I just met her today. You…" She blinked and shrugged, as if her shoulders were sore. "You killed Jonah? Jake's brother?"

"Yes." Kori's eyes glittered with the memory, but her gaze was unflinching. "I stabbed him in the throat with a chunk of porcelain from a smashed toilet, and the only regret I have about killing him is that so many people were denied the opportunity to see him die."

"Damn, Kori," I said, and my sister glanced up at me for a second, then returned her attention to an obviously shell-shocked Sera.

"Does that bother you?"

Sera stared at her lap, evidently considering the question, and when she finally looked up, her gaze was so sharp it could have drawn blood. "Did he deserve it?"

"Jonah Tower was a rapist, torturer and murderer." Kori spoke as if the words meant nothing to her, hiding the truth behind a battered stoicism that made my chest ache. "He was a sadist son of a bitch who deserved a much longer, more painful death than he got."

"Then may he rot in hell for all of eternity." Sera's voice hinted at everything my sister's hid. There was a perilous depth to her conviction, and I wondered just how closely to the edge she was teetering. How little would it take to send her tumbling over the edge? Why did I want so badly to pull her back from that abyss?

I knew nothing about her—not even her last name— but I recognized so much of what I saw in her. There was pain behind her anger. A lot of pain. I may have been a convenient target—I *had* locked her up in a strange house—but I wasn't the true cause of either her pain or her anger.

"How did Jake…die?" Sera asked.

"Ian shot him," I said.

Kori nodded. "It was a clean death. Fast. Better than he deserved."

"Ian is…" Sera glanced at both of us, in turn.

"He is the other half of my soul. The good half."

It was amazing to see the change in my sister when she talked about Ian. She was still fierce and dangerous— Korinne would never be anything less. But with his name on her tongue, she looked as if she may not hate the world after all. Not the *whole* world, anyway.

"But you didn't kill Julia?"

Kori shook her head slowly, looking as if she was remembering that day, and I remembered it with her. Though the Towers were a huge obstacle in my life's

work, I'd never been in their house before that day. I'd
never dealt with any of them face-to-face. "I wanted Julia
to suffer. She *deserved* to suffer," Kori said. "I changed
my mind a second later, when I realized that leaving her
alive would really mean making the rest of the world suffer, but by then I'd lost my chance."

"Why did you hate them?" Sera asked. "I mean, other
than the whole 'birthed from an evil womb' thing. What
did they do to you?"

For a minute, I thought Kori might actually answer.
That she might finally talk to someone other than Ian
about what woke her up screaming in the middle of most
nights. Kenley knew part of it. I think even Vanessa knew
more than I did. I'd started to ask, once, but Gran, in a
rare moment of absolute lucidity, told me to leave it alone.

I did, because when she's thinking clearly, Gran is
never wrong.

But after nearly half a minute of considering, Kori
only stood and glanced at me on her way to the door.
"You got this?" she asked, and when I nodded, she disappeared into the hall and pulled the door shut behind her.

"Is she okay?" Sera asked as I sank onto the bed,
where my sister had been seconds earlier.

"Kori's always okay." Even when she isn't. "All right.
Here's what I need you to understand. I don't know
you—"

"I understand that."

I resisted the urge to growl at her. The woman was as
infuriating as she was fascinating. "I wasn't finished.
My point is that since I don't know you, I have no idea
whether you're telling the truth or just acting. I'm trying
to give you the benefit of the doubt, and I'd appreciate it
if you'd return the favor. I'm not asking to see your arm
out of any testosterone-driven need to boss you around

or make you do something you obviously don't want to do. I'm asking to see your arm because that's what I have to do to protect my friends and family."

Sera lifted one brow and tossed her head in the direction of the door Kori had just closed. "I don't think she needs your protection."

I shrugged. "Maybe she doesn't, but that doesn't mean I don't want to protect her. Either way, Gran and Kenley *do* need protection, and frankly, I care more about keeping them safe than I do about respecting the modesty of your covered arm. I care more about keeping them safe than I care about anything else in the world. I wish that was something you could understand, but even if it's not—"

Her eyes widened in surprise, and I realized something I'd said had gotten through to her. "I do understand that."

"Then give me a look at your arm, Sera. A couple of inches below your shoulder. I won't touch you. You don't have to take anything off. Just give me a reason to trust you enough to untie you and let you be in the same room with my family. Okay?"

She frowned. "*You* don't trust *me?* You kidnapped me."

"Okay, we're going to have to agree to disagree about that particular descriptor, but I'm very sorry for dragging you out of there. There were guns aimed at us both and I didn't have time to think it through, but that was my mistake. If I could do it over, I'd do it differently." Though I wasn't sure how… "But since I can't, we have to deal with the situation as it currently stands. That would be a lot easier for me if you'd show me your arm, and it'd be a lot easier for you if you weren't tied to a chair. You can make both of those things happen. It's your choice."

"Are you patronizing me?"

"No. I'm asking you to play nice and I'm giving you my word that I'll do the same. I'd like to take knives and zip ties out of the equation."

"After I show you my arm, then what?"

"If it's unmarked, I'll let you out of that chair and out of this room. Then we're going to have a civil drink or a cup of coffee—your choice—while we wait for a friend of Kori's."

"What friend?"

"She's a Reader." Annika, the human lie detector, who would always owe Kori a favor and would always be owed one from her in return, because of Kenley's binding. "She's going to listen while we ask you some questions, and if she likes your answers, we're going to take you home and you can go on with your life. Which, incidentally, will last much longer if you stay away from Julia Tower."

The door opened behind me, and Kori appeared in the doorway. "I'll go get her in a minute," my sister said, and I realized she'd been listening through the door. And that she'd already called Anne.

Sera frowned. "And if your friend doesn't like my answers?"

Kori shrugged. "Well, then we'll all have some difficult decisions to make. But I promise that if we have to kill you, it'll be a quick death."

Sera turned to me, suddenly pale. "Is she serious? Is that supposed to be comforting?"

I held her gaze, because that was the least I owed her. "Coming from Kori? Yes."

"You people are *so* screwed up!"

Before I could reassure Sera that I wouldn't let my sister deliver a mercy killing, Kori leaned against the door frame and made a thoughtful sound. "I think the problem here is that you don't understand the alternative."

"The alternative, wherein you open the door and I walk out, and we never have to see one another again?"

"Um, no. The alternative that actually bears some resemblance to reality." Kori looked poised to continue with her typical colorful, disturbing delivery, so I cut her off and stepped into Sera's line of sight before my sister could make things worse.

"*We* hope to convince you to talk to us by giving you coffee and deploying a Reader. The Towers would substitute an experienced torturer for our cup of dark roast."

"Seriously?"

Before I could answer, Kori turned and pulled up the back of her shirt to reveal a canvas of scars I'd only seen once, myself. Thick welts. Mottled burns. And at least two complete sets of bite marks.

Sera gasped and Kori lowered her shirt, then turned, her expression as empty as I'd ever seen it. "They didn't even want information."

"What did they want?" Sera whispered.

"To hear me scream."

Sera looked queasy, and I knew how she felt. The evidence of Kori's suffering made me sick to my stomach, and the empty way she spoke about it made me want to kill someone. But she'd already taken out one of the men responsible. Ian had killed the other.

Kori had nothing left to battle but her own memories.

"They *will* want information from Kenley," I said. "They'll want to know where we are, and how many of us there are, and how easy it would be to erase us from existence. If we let you go and you *are* obligated to report to Julia, she won't have to torture you to get that information. But they *will* have to torture Kenni for it, and we won't let that happen."

Kori continued with the part I didn't want to verbalize. "If you know anything that could help us get her back, you have to tell us. And if you're obligated to do or say anything to Julia Tower that would put Kenni in greater danger than she's already in, I'll have to kill you to stop that from happening. I'm not going to bullshit you about that. But I promise it won't hurt, because the difference between us and Julia Tower is that if we kill you, it'll be a mercy."

But that wasn't going to happen. I wasn't sure how I could justify letting her live if she was a threat, but I was determined to do it.

"This is *so* fucked up," Sera mumbled, staring at the floor in shock, and I couldn't help but believe her. She was horrified by what she was hearing and what Kori had shown her. If she was bound to Julia, she was so newly bound that she hadn't yet discovered the horrors of syndicate service for herself.

Surely she wasn't a good enough actress to make us believe such a convincing display of naïveté. Surely no one was *that* good....

Kori huffed. "You have no idea. You gonna show us your arm?"

Sera tossed her head, throwing long, brown hair back from her face. "Let me up and I'll show you. I'm not one of them. I'll *never* be one of them." There was something new behind her eyes. Something strong and resolute. "But I'm not convinced you're much better than they are, so let's let your Reader friend do her thing, so I can get the hell out of here."

"We're not like them," I insisted as I unbuckled the

belt securing her to the chair. "I know you have no reason to believe me, but we're *nothing* like them."

"Right. You kidnapped me and tied me up, and now you're ready to kill me. From my perspective, the distinction between you psychos and the Tower psychos isn't exactly glaringly clear."

"We're not *ready* to kill you," Kori said. "We're *willing* to kill you. There's a big difference."

Sera sat straighter when I pulled the belt loose and laid it on the bed behind me. "And that difference would be?"

I slid my pocketknife between her wrists and the zip tie, and she stiffened the moment the metal touched her skin. I used my free hand to brace hers, so she wouldn't get cut.

Her skin was soft and warm. I hesitated for just a second, so I'd have a reason to keep touching her. Then I severed the plastic with my blade and let the cut zip tie fall to the floor. I closed my knife and slid it into my pocket, and when I spun the chair around so that she faced me, she was rubbing the red marks on her wrists. And waiting for my answer.

I gripped the chair seat on either side of her legs and rolled her closer. My gaze met hers from inches away and she gasped at whatever she saw in mine, then bit her lip. "The difference is that if the Towers think you're a threat, they will have you beaten, raped and tortured in front of an audience—they'll call it an object lesson—before they finally give you conflicting orders and watch your body tear itself apart trying to follow both commands at once."

She'd stopped breathing, but her gaze had only intensified. Sharpened. "You're trying to scare me."

"Yes. But I'm scaring you with the truth." I tried not to think about how close she was and how badly I wanted to touch her. And how much she would hate that.

I hated knowing she'd recoil from my touch.

"They are bad people who do bad things for sport and for profit. *We* are good people who do bad things to protect people who can't protect themselves from the Julia Towers of the world." I should have let her go. I should have pushed her chair back so she could stand, but I didn't *want* to let her go, and I didn't feel particularly guilty about that.

"You'll do bad things, too, eventually," I said, and when she shifted in the chair, her jeans brushed my thumb. "In our world, there's no way around that, and the fact that I met you in Julia Tower's office tells me that you're in that world now, for better or worse. The only thing you have left to decide is which side you want to fight for. Because you will fight, or you will die."

Kori shrugged. "Or maybe you'll fight, *then* you'll die. That happens here, too."

Neither of us acknowledged her. Sera's gaze was locked in mine. At least, that's what I thought until I tried to look away and discovered I was as trapped by the look in her eyes as she was by the doors I'd screwed shut.

The difference was that I didn't want to escape.

I should have moved my hand, but Sera hadn't moved her leg, so I left my hand where it was and let the heat bleeding through her denim warm one side of my thumb. "Take off your scarf," I said, and my voice was lower than I'd meant for it to be. Deeper. I didn't think she'd comply, but her gaze held mine while she unwound the thin material from her neck and shoulders. She handed it to me and I held it for a second, stunned by the realization that the yellow scarf from my notebook weighed nothing.

And that it smelled just like her. Clean, and vaguely sweet and enticing, in a way I could never have put into words, but would never, ever forget.

Kori cleared her throat and I blinked in surprise, then realized I was still staring at Sera from less than a foot away, and now I was fingering her silk scarf like some kind of pervert with an accessories fetish.

I rocked back onto my heels and draped her scarf over the foot of my grandmother's bed, hoping my face wasn't as red as it felt.

"We still need to see your arm." I stood and Sera stared up at me, and I wished I knew her well enough to understand the intense blend of strength, fear and anger warring behind her eyes. "You want me to step outside?"

Her fingers found the hem of her shirt and her gaze hardened. "I don't care what you do."

But that was a lie. Women who don't care what you do have no reason to tell you that.

I started to turn, to give her some privacy, but she turned faster. She pulled her left arm out of its long sleeve, then lifted that side of her shirt to her shoulder, revealing half of a slim, almost delicate waist above the denim clinging to the swell of her hip.

My throat felt tight. I tried not to stare. When that didn't work, I tried not to *look* like I was staring. If Kori noticed, I couldn't tell. She was fixated on Sera's arm, as I should have been.

With the front of her shirt clutched to her chest, Sera twisted to show us her left arm, and I exhaled in relief before I realized she would hear that, and that she might understand how badly I'd wanted her to be unaffiliated with the Towers, and not just for her own sake. Not just for Kenley's sake.

For my sake.

Her arm was smooth and pale, and completely unmarked. She was free from obligation not just to the Towers, but to any of the other syndicates who routinely marked their employees in the same spot. And that was most of them.

Sera was unbound.

Based on the lack of dead marks, she'd *never* been bound, which would explain her incomprehension of just how vile the syndicates really were. But if that was the case—if she didn't work for Julia Tower—why had my notebook told me to take her? How was she supposed to help us get Kenley back?

Maybe she wasn't. My head spun with that possibility. Maybe Sera wasn't supposed to help me. Maybe *I* was supposed to help *her*.

Kori shrugged, arms folded over her chest, while Sera slid her arm back into its sleeve. "Well, assuming the rest of her is as spotless as her arm, I'm good with letting her walk around unfettered until Anne gets here."

"Me, too." I hadn't planned to tie her up at all until she tried to climb out the window.

"The rest of me is fine, but I'm not showing you anything else." When Sera turned to face us, I saw that her resolution was just as firmly back in place as her shirt. "I'm not a prostitute."

"We know," I assured her.

Kori shrugged again. "I believe you, but what I believe doesn't matter. You have to make Anne believe." She turned to me, already reaching for the doorknob. "I'll go get her." Then she stepped into the hall and left the door open behind her back.

"She's…interesting." Sera glanced at the bed, as if she was considering sitting, then she sat in the chair instead. "Kinda scary."

"Yeah. I'd like to say that's Tower's fault, but the truth is that Kori's always been a little scary. I think that's why he liked her." Until suddenly he didn't like her.

"She really worked for him?"

"Yup." I knew better than to give her any new information, but I could verify what Kori had already said. "And she hated every minute of it."

"She seemed legitimately surprised to see me."

I sat on the edge of my grandmother's desk, trying to look casual, as if I weren't dying to interrogate her, to figure out how and why she fit into my notebook. And by extension, into my life. "As opposed to what?" Then I understood. "You still think I planned this."

She shrugged and glanced at the nails I'd driven into the window frame. "You sealed all the exits. It's kind of hard to believe you didn't go to the Tower estate intending to take a prisoner."

"Okay, I know that looks bad, but the doors and windows have been nailed shut for weeks," I insisted, shoving my hands in my pockets. "I did that to keep everyone else out, not to keep you in."

She looked like she wanted to believe me, but...

"If you can't take my word for it, ask Kori when she gets back." Or any of the others. I'd tell her to ask Gran, but I could never be sure what decade Gran was currently living in.

"If that's the truth, why do you have such easy access to restraints?" She bent to pick up the severed zip tie.

"Those are for my job."

"Are you a cop?" She studied me closer, as if that thought made her rethink her original assessment.

I actually laughed. "No. I...um...retrieve things." That was half the truth. I couldn't trust her with the other half. Not yet. Although if Gran kept slipping into the past, Sera would figure it out for herself.

"Things?" Sera may have been young, but she was a born skeptic. Not that I'd given her any reason to trust me.

"People, usually," I admitted, and she opened her mouth to start shouting something that probably included a lot of I-told-you-so's, so I spoke before she could interrupt. "I know how that sounds, but it's legit." *Mostly.* "I work part-time for a bail bondsman, doing the jobs his unSkilled employees can't handle."

Olivia had hooked me up with Adam Rawlinson, the man she'd worked for before Ruben Cavazos—the Towers' biggest rival for control of the city—had snared her exclusive services via extortion and blood binding. Rawlinson served neither syndicate, and his clientele was mostly those who also wanted to avoid syndicate tangles. And could afford to pay.

"Bail bondsman?" Sera seemed to think about that. "So, you find runaway criminals?"

"No. His Trackers find them. I go get them and turn them in. Thus the zip ties." I glanced at the one she still held. "But I also do odd jobs for private collectors." *Very* odd jobs. For *very* private collectors.

Her gaze narrowed. "What kind of collectors?"

"Not people collectors, if that's what you're thinking." Not anymore. Not since Micah, and the realization of just what I'd been aiding and abetting. "Just stuff the rich are willing to pay for, but can't get their hands on through other means."

"And that's legal?"

I shrugged. "Not always. But it pays, and it doesn't hurt anyone, and someone has to keep the lights on and the water flowing around here."

"What, no one else here works?"

"*Everyone* here works. But most of that work goes toward accomplishing our higher purpose, rather than actually paying the bills."

Ian helped me out when he could—the man could

make darkness appear in broad daylight—and Kori had taken a couple of Rawlinson's jobs, but they were both more useful to Kenley's efforts than I was, so it was my mostly steady, mostly legit income that paid to rent and heat our hideout house while we slowly chipped away at the foundation of Julia Tower's inherited power.

Sera looked as though she wanted to say something, and as if whatever she wanted to say might not be an insult to my moral fiber; but before she could do more than open her mouth, Ian called out from the hall as the floorboard in front of the empty closet creaked.

"Kori?"

"She went to get Anne," I said, and a moment later Vanessa appeared in the bedroom doorway, with Ian at her back.

"Kenley?" Van's forehead was lined in worry. She hardly even glanced at Sera.

"We haven't found her yet," I said, and I could see from Van's wince that she hated hearing the words as badly as I hated saying them. "But we will. They won't kill her."

"I'm not worried about them killing her." Vanessa frowned at our guest. "Who's this?"

"This is Sera…um…" I shrugged with a glance at her. "That's all I know so far, except that she almost certainly doesn't work for the Towers."

"I don't," Sera said.

"And that she may be able to help us find Kenley."

Sera sighed and slouched in her chair as Van sank onto the bed next to her. "I would if I could, but I honestly know nothing about your sister."

"What happened?" Ian said with a pointed glance at my arm.

I removed the towel and Vanessa gasped. "Those are going to need stitches. Or a Healer."

I glanced at the neat line of horizontal scars on her right forearm and I remembered that she spoke from experience.

Sera scowled at my cuts, but she looked more guilty than angry. "I'm sorry, but you brought it on yourself."

Ian blinked. "You did that?"

She leaned back in her chair and crossed her arms over her chest. "He kidnapped me."

Ian and Vanessa turned to me with matching arched brows.

I glared at Sera. "It's not like it sounds."

She snorted. "It's exactly like it sounds."

"It's complicated," I insisted.

She shrugged. "He may be right about that."

"I'm sorry, who are you?" Van eyed the severed zip tie on the floor, then the blood finally seeping through the towel on my arm. "Did I miss that part?"

"She blocked my aim at Julia Tower when I went looking for Kenni."

"But I don't work for Julia," Sera repeated. "Or for anyone else."

Ian lifted the towel for another look at my cuts, then dropped it into place again and turned to Sera. "Then why would you stand between her and a well-deserved bullet?"

She blinked, evidently surprised by the question. "He wasn't really going to shoot her." Sera turned to me with a frown. "You weren't, were you?"

"Not before she told me where Kenni is. But you didn't know that. Why would you shield her from a bullet, if you're not bound to her?" Nearly everyone who'd worked for Jake Tower had been contractually obligated to take a bullet for him, but I couldn't think of anyone who would have done that voluntarily.

"Because I'm a decent person," Sera said, and I believed that. But I also believed there was more to it. "Beyond that, it's really none of your business."

I folded the rag and set it on the desk next to me, then met her gaze again. "You're actually wrong about that, but you're welcome to wait for Anne before you start answering questions, unless you want to repeat everything."

Sera groaned. "Why is everything such a pain in the ass here? And who are you two?"

"Oh, sorry." Ian stepped forward and offered her his hand. "I'm Ian."

"Kori's Ian?"

He chuckled. "Um…yeah. You met her?"

Sera paled. "She offered to kill me, for my own good."

His grin broke into a full-fledged smile. "Well, then, she must like you."

"Kori's an acquired taste." Vanessa offered her hand next. "I'm Van."

"And how do you fit in here?"

"Kenley and I are…" Vanessa's eyes watered, and Ian lightly wrapped one arm around her. When she didn't object—Van usually didn't like to be touched—he squeezed her shoulders, and her tears fell.

"She's part of the family," I finished for her. Van had spilled blood for us in Tower's basement, just like Kori had, and that would have made her family even if she and Kenni weren't in love.

"We have a little time. Julia needs Kenley alive," I reminded Vanessa, and she finally nodded stiffly.

Sera frowned. "Why? Why does Julia need your sister?"

Van turned to me, brows arched in question. "How much are we telling her?"

"Nothing, until Anne's had a chance to—"

"Motherfucker!" my grandmother shouted from the kitchen, and I was up in an instant, my bloody towel forgotten. I pulled the bedroom door open farther, and the scent of cooking beef rolled over me, eliciting dueling waves of dread and hunger.

Gran had found the stove knobs.

I raced down the hall and through the living room into the kitchen, expecting to find flames engulfing the room. Instead, I found my grandmother standing in a crimson pool, in her house shoes.

"What happened? Where are you cut?"

Gran scowled at me. "I'm not cut, I'm just old and clumsy."

Several sets of footsteps slowed to a stop at my back and Sera laughed as she brushed past me and took the open can my grandmother held. Thin red liquid dripped down the side of the label, over her fingers. "It's tomato sauce." She set the can on the counter next to three others lined up there, and took my grandmother's hand. "Here, let me help you out of that mess."

Gran stepped out of her house shoes and onto a clean spot on the floor, clutching Sera's hand for balance. "Thank you, hon." She shook her head. "I guess that's what I get for using marinara out of a can, but you don't leave me much choice when you buy the wrong tomatoes and lose all the chopping knives, Kristopher."

I'd "lost" all the chopping knives just like I'd "misplaced" the stove knobs. Life and work had both gotten much harder when senility had started to affect Gran's everyday function, instead of just her perception of time.

"Gran, that's way too much sauce. There are only five of us now." Six if I counted Kenley. Or Sera.

Sera shot me a questioning look, but I couldn't figure out how to explain what reality Gran was living in at that moment without telling her about the kids. And I could *not* afford to tell her about the kids.

She turned back to my grandmother. "Here, you have a seat, and I'll get that cleaned up." She pulled out a chair at the table for my grandmother, then turned toward the mess on the floor and grabbed a roll of paper towels.

"Don't worry about that, hon. You're a guest. Kristopher will get it. Kristopher?" Gran glanced at me expectantly and I held up my arm, silently pleading my bloody hardship.

Gran rolled her eyes. "Oh, fine, bring me my sewing kit, and I'll stitch you up."

Ian noticed my panic as I tried to come up with a reason to refuse my grandmother's offer—some reason other than the fact that she could no longer see well enough to cross-stitch, much less repair my open, bleeding wounds—and he stepped in.

"I got it, Gran." Everyone called her Gran. That's the only way she'd have it. "I need the practice, but maybe you wouldn't mind giving me some pointers while I work?" Ian pulled out a chair for me and I sank into it, grateful both for the rescue and for his tact.

"Be glad to, hon." Gran scowled at me as she spoke. "Anything for a man not ashamed to admit when he needs help."

I rolled my eyes. "I don't need help. I need stitches."

Ian chuckled as he pulled the first aid kit from the top of the fridge.

Sera turned off the stove, then knelt to help Vanessa clean up the spilled sauce. When she gasped, I turned to find her staring at the series of straight, thin scars climbing Vanessa's bare forearm. "What happened?"

Van scooped up a sloppy handful of sauce with a paper towel, then dropped it into the trash can. "Jake Tower had me tortured to get to Kenley." She shrugged as if the memory meant nothing to her. And maybe it didn't. She'd certainly been through worse. "It happens."

Sauce dripped from the napkin Sera clutched. She looked sick. "No, it doesn't. Torture doesn't just *happen.*"

Vanessa blinked at her with round, sad eyes, as if she pitied Sera's naïveté. But I remembered the warring pain and anger I'd seen in in her earlier, and I wondered if we weren't seeing naïveté at all, but the memory of some trauma of her own.

"Let's see that arm." Ian sat on the edge of the chair next to mine and opened the first aid kit on the tabletop, while I laid my forearm on a clean white dish towel.

Sera stood and dropped her soggy napkin into the trash, then plucked a bottle of rubbing alcohol from the kit and handed it to Ian, who burst out laughing. Too stubborn to ask for the hydrogen peroxide instead, I glared at her and clenched my teeth while he poured alcohol over my forearm.

"Clean and shallow," he said after a close look at the cuts, while they continued to sizzle in sterile liquid. "How did this happen?"

"She sliced my arm open."

"I was going for something lower," Sera said, and my own grandmother laughed out loud.

"That would have made this moment much more awkward." Ian popped the cap from a tube of liquid bandage. "You want this, or sutures?"

I studied the two two-inch cuts. Then the wickedly curved suture needle. "Liquid bandage."

He sealed my cuts while Sera and Van mopped up the spilled sauce, and my grandmother made a production of directing both operations. As Ian was packing up the first aid kit, the closet door opened once again.

I stood so quickly my chair scraped the floor, and Sera backed away in surprise. Ian put one hand on the butt of his gun and Vanessa grabbed a knife from the butcher block beside the stove. Gran's knuckles went white as she grasped the edge of the table.

We had no reason to suspect that Julia had found our hideout yet, so we kept the closet dark, for ease of use. But there was no stopping that moment of tense silence, waiting to see who would step out into the hall. Especially since Julia had sprung a trap for us at Meghan's house.

"It's us," Kori called as the door creaked open.

Gran exhaled softly, Van put her knife back and Ian let go of his gun and stood.

"Hey." Kori glanced at Sera, then went straight into the arms Ian held open. Behind her, Annika and her daughter, Hadley, stood in the living room. Only Hadley wasn't really Annika's. She was Noelle's.

For a while, when we were young, and stupid, and unfettered by the bitter obligations of our adult realities, I'd loved Noelle, and she'd been mine. But her baby was not.

Hadley *could* have been mine, if the cards had fallen another way, and maybe that would have changed Elle's fate. I'd never really thought about being a parent, but I would have done it for Elle. There was a time when I would have done anything for her, if she'd asked. Anything.

Instead, she carried, delivered and let herself die to protect Ruben Cavazos's secret baby.

There were days I still hated her for that. Though, mostly I hated her for not telling me. For never *once* telling me that she was pregnant, and that the father was the head of a fucking Skilled mafia family. The *married* head of the Skilled mafia.

I'd found out about Hadley less than six months earlier, when Anne was finally forced to admit that her child wasn't really hers and Olivia figured out who the father was.

The child looked like Cavazos, in a certain light. But mostly, she looked like Noelle.

"Hey, Hadley!" Vanessa called as my grandmother wrapped the little girl in a hug and Ian scruffed her hair. Everyone loved Hadley the same way everyone had loved Elle. And not just because—like her mother—she was beautiful.

Hadley harvested love like it was a plant in her garden. She tended it with hugs and watered it with sweet smiles, and I, too, loved her, even though looking at her hurt.

She had no idea I'd ever known her birth mother beyond the occasional hello.

There were days when that still broke my heart.

I could have helped Noelle. I could have protected her. I could have *saved* her, and kept her little family together. If I'd been able to interpret the lines scribbled in that damned notebook.

But I'd failed Noelle, and although I didn't know it at the time, I'd failed Hadley. And I'd put my notebook away, convinced after Noelle's disappearance that I would never be able to interpret enough of fate's Rosetta stone in time to truly make a difference for anyone referenced in it.

I'd remained convinced of that until the moment I saw Sera and recognized her scarf from a line written with my own hand.

In the kitchen, I ran one finger over my sealed cuts,

then I looked up and found Sera watching while everyone else fussed over Hadley. A ghost of a smile haunted her lips—her mouth was beautiful, now that she'd stopped scowling—and some private pain shone in her damp eyes.

The window she'd broken hadn't been repaired, yet she wasn't running. Maybe she knew there were more than enough of us to stop her. Maybe she finally understood that she was safer with us than on her own, if Julia Tower was willing to kill her.

But ultimately, she was there because she was *supposed* to be with us. Sera was there to help us get Kenley back. Or maybe I was supposed to help her with whatever accounted for that battered determination—that visceral need to fight—that echoed in every word she said. Or maybe both.

Either way, in the hour since I'd met her, Sera had frightened, fascinated and fought me. She'd drawn my grandmother's amusement, Kori's compassion and my blood. Even if I'd wanted to let her go, deep down I knew it was too late. Like Van and Ian, she'd already been caught by the Daniels' family snare, snagged not just by my interest, but by everyone else's, as well.

And like the Towers—perhaps the only thing our families had in common—once the Daniels get a good grip, they don't let go.

Five

Sera

"Okay, here's how this works." Kori Daniels dropped into the chair on my right, and it took most of my concentration to avoid looking as on-guard as I felt. She was serious about giving me a quick death if I turned out to be a threat to her sister, and the scary part was that she truly seemed to think she'd be doing me a personal favor. "Kris and I are going to ask you some questions and you're going to answer them. Anne's going to let us know whether or not you're telling the truth."

I crossed my arms on the table, hoping my anger came across as confidence. "So this little game is predicated on the fact that you all already think I'm a liar? Doesn't that mean the deck is stacked against me?"

Across the table, Kris scooted forward in his chair and my gaze was drawn to his as if the man had his own gravitational pull. Why was it so easy for me to look into his eyes, yet so hard to do…everything else in the world? "We don't think you're a liar," he said, and I didn't get a chance to point out the irony of him saying that in the company of a Reader because Kori opened her big mouth. Again.

"Yes, we do," she said. "Everyone lies. I don't give a shit about most of your lies. I just need to know you're telling the truth about a few things."

I glanced at the little girl seated to my left, contentedly munching on spaghetti I'd helped make. No one seemed concerned about her picking up bad language. Or hearing something that might scare her.

Maybe that was all par for the course with Skilled children—surely she was Skilled, if her mother was a Reader. Unless her father was unSkilled. With only one Skilled parent—as in my case—a child had a slightly less than fifty-percent chance of inheriting a Skill. At least, according to what I'd read online.

"Ready?" Kori glanced over her shoulder at Anne, the Reader, who leaned against the kitchen counter near the stove. Anne nodded. Ian, Gran and Vanessa all watched as they ate from bowls of sauce-drenched noodles.

I felt as if I was on trial. In Wonderland.

Kori started to ask the first question, but Kris beat her to it. "Who *are* you?"

I exhaled slowly, reminding myself for the millionth time that losing my temper in a room full of armed and hair-trigger people would be a very bad idea. "I told you, my name is Sera. And that's all you're going to get out of me until you're ready to reciprocate." But even then I couldn't tell them the whole truth. These were the last people in the world I wanted to tell about my connection to Jake Tower.

Fortunately, I already knew more about them than they knew about me. Than *anyone* still living knew about me. Gran had given me Kris's last name and after learning that Kori had worked for Jake Tower, I'd made the connection. She wasn't just your average former Tower employee, assuming there was any such thing. She was Korinne Daniels, the most visible member of Jake's personal security team for years—her face was in the background of nearly every photo I'd found of him online.

Shortly before his death, however—which I now knew she'd had a hand in—she'd disappeared from the photos.

Unfortunately, once I'd made the connection, I couldn't unmake it. At the very least, Kori Daniels was a murderer. Who knew what else she'd done for my biological father—she'd clearly been on the receiving end of the Tower brutality, but I found it hard to believe she hadn't also dished it out. How could she *not* have, working for Jake Tower?

Did Kris and his sister have that in common? I hadn't seen his bare arms or back, but I'd seen his gun and his proficiency with a zip tie, which didn't quite fit with the quiet but intense way his gaze held mine or the protective anger that emanated from him when he thought about his missing sister. If they didn't like my answers— if they thought I was a threat to Kenley—would I even have a chance to fight, considering all those weapons in the room?

Would they kill me in front of the little girl?

"Sera *what?*" Kris folded his arms, watching me as if there was no one else in the room. As if my name was the most important piece of information he'd ever lacked. "You said you'd play nice if we untied you. Please don't give us a reason not to trust you."

"I said I'd tell you what you need to know, but you don't need to know my last name to know if I work for Tower." I leaned forward, looking right into his blue-gray eyes. "I don't work for Julia Tower. If you don't believe me, consult your pet Reader."

Anne bristled at being called a pet, but she nodded, confirming the truth in my statement.

Kori only rolled her eyes and leaned back in her chair.

"That's not specific enough. Do you now, or have you *ever* worked for the Tower syndicate in any capacity?"

"No." I held Kris's steady gaze, glad his sister's question gave me no reason to be nervous.

Readers don't function like so-called lie-detector tests. They don't read changes in body temperature and blood pressure; they taste or scent the truth in a statement. Some are better than others. Some can tell you're lying, but not what about. Some can tell you *thought* about lying. Some can tell that you're hiding something, even if you never technically lied about it.

I had no idea how good Anne was. I hoped I wouldn't have to find out.

Anne nodded, confirming my honesty again, and every gaze in the room centered on me once more.

"What were you doing there?" Kris asked, and I realized he hadn't even glanced at Anne after my previous answer. Did he think he could read the truth for himself? Was he looking for a specific reaction from me? "Why were you in Julia Tower's office?"

I hesitated.

I hesitated so long that people started looking at Anne again, even though I hadn't said anything. But they didn't need a Reader to tell them I was considering lying; my silence said that clearly enough.

Finally, I exhaled slowly and decided to tell them the truth. Most of it, anyway.

"I was trying to hire her. Well, her people, anyway."

Kori leaned forward, obviously skeptical now. "Hire them to do what?"

It took me a second to understand her suspicion. I

wasn't the typical Tower client. I didn't drive an expensive car or wear fancy clothes. I had no obvious wealth, power or authority. I had no discernible means with which to hire the Towers, other than a service agreement.

I met her gaze and held it. "The kind of thing the Towers do. You'd know that better than I would."

She glanced at Anne, who shrugged. "Nothing yet."

Their Reader wouldn't scent any untruth from me. I couldn't afford to let that happen.

"And you can pay for something like that?" Ian quietly voiced the question they were all thinking. No one looked at him. They were too busy watching me.

"I…" *Don't tell them more than they need to know.* My strategy for dealing with Julia Tower had turned out to be just as useful with the Daniels family. Which did nothing to set me at ease. "Yes, I can pay."

Anne frowned. "She's not lying, but she's not being straightforward, either. I don't think she planned to pay in cash."

"Blood?" Kori asked, and I understood that she didn't mean my blood. People often paid with the blood of— and thus the means to control—someone else. Someone more important.

"Service?" From Vanessa.

"Information?" Kris held my gaze with an intense one of his own. "Do you have information Julia wants?"

"Not that I know of."

"Are you going to sign with them?" Vanessa repeated, her forehead deeply lined. Kori hadn't asked me if I *would* work for the Towers—only if I *had.* "Don't sign with them."

Before I could answer, Hadley spoke around a mouthful of noodles. "Sera won't work for them." The child chewed and swallowed, while every head in the room turned toward her. "She'll work for herself."

"What, she's a Reader, too?" I couldn't tear my gaze from the little girl, who seemed completely unaware of the seven sets of eyes staring at her. "What is she, five?" How could a child that young already have a Skill?

"Seven…" Anne mumbled. "But she's not reading you." The mother sank into a squat next to her daughter's chair, one hand on the little girl's denim-clad knee. "Hadley, honey, how do you know that?"

Hadley shrugged, digging another spoonful from her bowl. "Dunno."

"Are you sure?" Anne asked, while everyone else seemed to be holding their breath, and I wasn't sure if she was asking whether the child was sure about what she'd said, or about not knowing how she knew.

"Yeah." Hadley looked up from her bowl. "Can I have some cheese? The sprinkle kind?"

Ian opened the refrigerator door and pulled out a green canister of Parmesan, then set it on the table in front of Hadley, who immediately opened it and dumped what must have been a quarter of the canister into her bowl.

"Do you know anything else interesting?" Anne said, while her daughter stirred dried cheese into her noodles.

"About her?" Hadley glanced at me, and my stomach started to twist.

"Sure." Kris had given his full attention to the child. "Or about anything else."

The little girl blinked at me, apparently considering the question. "She'll go back to that house. And she's gonna tell you she's not really Sera."

"What?" The unease in the bottom of my stomach spread until my entire body felt tense. "What the hell is she talking about?"

"Holy shit, she got Elle's Skill," Kris half whispered, and my confusion thickened.

Kori shook her head. "No way. She's too young."

Kris shrugged. "Elle was young, too."

"Who's Elle?" Vanessa glanced from one face to the next expectantly, and I was relieved to see that someone else seemed as lost as I felt.

"Not *that* young," Kori insisted, and it was clear the Daniels siblings were holding their own conversation.

Anne stroked her daughter's hair. "We don't know when Elle's Skill manifested. It was before any of us met her. That's all we can be sure of."

"Okay, who the hell is Elle, why would Hadley have her Skill and what does she mean I'm not really Sera?" I demanded, hands flat on the table. "Is there another Sera I should know about?"

"Noelle was Hadley's biological mother," Kori said, but I think she was explaining more for Vanessa's benefit than for mine. "She died six years ago. She was a Seer."

"Seriously?" Vanessa's eyes were huge. I shared her surprise. According to my mom, Seers were *very* rare. They were also notoriously ambiguous.

"You're telling me that *first grader* is a Seer?" I studied Hadley, searching for some sign that she knew more than she should about…anything, but she seemed completely oblivious not just of the future, but of the present. She sat there scooping the last cheese-coated bits of noodle from the bottom of her bowl, evidently unaware that everyone in the room was either scared of her or in awe.

"We're as new to this particular party as you are." Kori scooted her chair closer to the child's, but before she could ask another question, Kris spoke over her again.

"Hadley, what else can you tell us about Sera?" Kori glared at him, and I joined her, but Kris only shrugged.

"What? That's what they're here for, right? To find out why Sera was with Julia? To see if we can trust her?"

"That's not..." Kori started, and this time it was the child who interrupted.

She was staring straight at me.

"He'll bleed for you." Hadley's words sent chill bumps marching over my skin like troops on the battlefield. "He will cry for you, and he will lie for you, and he will kill for you. And you will leave him on the floor, like she left him in the bed, and he will never forgive either of you."

Stunned silence settled over the room and we all stared at her. Then, as if she hadn't heard a word she'd just said, Hadley pushed her empty bowl toward the center of the table. "Can I watch TV? Do you have *The Little Mermaid?*"

Vanessa practically jumped at the chance to park the child in front of a movie. "I don't think we have that one, but there are several kids' channels on cable." She escorted Hadley out of the kitchen and a moment later a children's laugh track bubbled out from the television in the living room.

"That's a creepy little girl you've got there, Anne Lawson." Gran set her bowl of pasta in the sink, almost untouched.

"Gran!" Kris scolded.

"What? It's true." She ran water into her bowl. "The earlier she knows how screwed up her life's going to be, the better."

I heard their whispered argument, and vaguely noticed Vanessa come back into the kitchen, but I didn't process any of it. I saw nothing but the child's eyes, staring into mine. I heard nothing but her voice, and the ominous pronouncements rolling off her tongue to sit heavy in my heart. And in my gut.

"Is she ever wrong?" I wasn't surprised when no one heard me. My voice hardly carried any sound. "Hey. Has she ever been wrong?" But I realized on the tail of my own question that no one could answer. They'd just found out about Hadley's Skill, along with me.

My mom said it was something special, to see a child discover his or her Skill. But this didn't feel special. And it didn't feel like a discovery—at least to Hadley. Had she already known what she could do? Or was she still oblivious, after sending all seven of the adults into shock?

"Who was she talking about?" Kris's question drew me out of my own head, and his intense gaze prevented my mental retreat. "Who's going to bleed for you?"

"I have no idea. She's probably wrong about that, like she's wrong about my name. I'm Sera. I've only ever been Sera." Ironically, that and my maternal middle name were the only parts of my identity I *was* sure about—the only parts not thrown into question by my illegitimate, criminal bloodline. "If she's a Seer, she's not a very good one. Not yet, anyway." But even I could hear the note of doubt in my voice.

Prophesies have a way of making sense only in hindsight.

"She will be." Anne sank into her daughter's seat and gripped the edge of the table, knuckles white with stress. "Noelle was never wrong."

No one argued.

"Okay, look, I've answered all your questions and this place just keeps getting weirder." I stood, glancing around at them all. "Could someone please let me out of here now? I've been more than patient with your assorted paranoia, psychoses and obsessive barring of all exits."

"If we let you out, will you go back to the Tower estate?" Kris asked, and suddenly my chest ached. I seriously considered lying—I probably could have gotten away with it, with Anne still in shock over the manifestation of her daughter's Skill.

"Yes," I said instead, because there were some things I'd *have* to lie to them about, at some point. They deserved what truth I could give them. "Eventually. I still need their help."

Kris scowled. "But they tried to kill you."

"They tried to kill you, too, but you'll still go back, won't you, if that's what it takes to find your sister?"

He nodded, jaw clenched in determination.

"Same here." But the Towers couldn't give me back my sister. The best they could do was help me avenge her death, along with my parents' deaths.

"Then she's right." Anne glanced into the living room at her daughter. "Hadley said you'd go back, and you confirmed it."

I considered pointing out that Hadley could have been talking about any house, but no one would have bought that. The house on everyone's mind was the Towers'. Not that it mattered. Anne was more interested in her daughter's emerging Skill than my relationship with Julia Tower.

The same could not be said for Kris Daniels.

"What do you want Julia's help with?" he asked, and the topic shifted back to my interrogation.

"That's private." I sat again, but on the edge of my chair this time, silently reminding them I had no intention of getting comfortable. "But I will tell you it has nothing to do with any of you, or your missing sister."

Anne nodded silently, without even looking at me. She was still watching her daughter.

Kris scooted closer to the table and his chair scraped the floor. "Do you know where you are right now?"

"In the kitchen of a very strange house full of very strange people. Beyond that? No. Nor do I care."

Anne nodded again and my irritation swelled. I was already tired of having my every statement analyzed by a truth-reader—if that was what I'd missed growing up in an unSkilled family, I was more grateful than ever for my plain old parents. And I was sick of being the only one answering questions.

"Do you intend to provide the Tower syndicate with information about any of us, as payment for whatever you need done, or for any other reason?"

"No. Considering that your sister used to work for them—" I glanced at Kori "—I suspect they know far more about you all than I do." Which was more than I ever wanted to know.

"Valid point," Vanessa mumbled.

"What *do* you know about us?" Kris asked. He was digging for information no one else seemed to care about, as if he had an agenda they didn't share. As soon as I'd had that thought, I realized it was true. But no one else seemed to have figured it out yet.

Hmmm...

"I know nothing about any of you, except what you've shown and told me. And that Kori used to be security for Jake Tower. That's it."

His gaze narrowed on me in suspicion. "She never said she worked security. How did you know that?"

"Because after being locked up with you nutcases for the past couple of hours, I finally realized where I've seen her. In nearly every photograph of Jake Tower ever taken. As his bodyguard."

"Why were you looking at pictures of Jake?" Kori asked.

I exhaled heavily and folded my hands on the table.

"Research. I wasn't about to walk into the Tower estate and ask for a favor without already knowing everything I could possibly find out. No matter what you might think about me, I'm not an idiot." But I'd evidently said something wrong. Kris had been staring at me for the past ten minutes, which was unnerving enough on its own. But now his gaze looked feverish. Eager, like a cat who'd just caught a mouse.

"Favor? You went to ask them a *favor?* Not to hire them? Why would the Towers owe you a favor?"

Shit. But it was too late to backtrack. "They don't *owe* me a favor. I just thought it was worth a shot."

No one bought that. Hell, *I* didn't even buy it.

A second earlier, Vanessa and Gran had looked ready to curtail his line of questioning, and maybe even let me go. But that all changed in a single heartbeat. And too late, I realized I'd forgotten to be careful around the Reader.

"She's lying." Anne sat up straight in her chair. "They *do* owe her a favor. She believes they do, anyway." And suddenly everyone was looking at me as if I'd grown a second head.

Damn, I hate Readers.

"Why would the Towers owe you?" Kris demanded, and I could feel their interest like a living thing, ready to burrow deep inside me and feast on my secrets.

"They don't." My mind raced as I tried to decide what I could say to make them let me go. "I was totally over the line, asking them for a favor. I never met any of them before this afternoon. I swear on my full name." Which—with any luck—they would never know.

"Anne?" Kori said.

The Reader frowned without taking her gaze from me. "I don't taste anything false, but that doesn't make sense.

Why would you ask the Towers for a favor, if you don't have any connection to them? That takes one hell of a set of balls." Yet she looked less impressed than incredulous.

"How did you even get in to see Julia?" Kori asked. "Kris said you were in her office, with just her and Lynn?" She glanced at her brother for confirmation and he nodded. "Jake didn't meet with strangers in his home. Not even prospective clients. That's too much of a security risk. I can't see Julia veering from that policy, especially considering that we're not the only ones who want her dead, thanks to rumors that she was involved in her brother's murder."

"Rumors?" I couldn't help but ask. The Towers were my business now, at least until I figured out what I'd actually inherited from my biological father. "Does that mean they're not true?"

"Oh, those rumors are one hundred percent true," Ian said, and I glanced at him in surprise. "She asked me— in a circumspect, but very obvious kind of way—to kill Jake. I was happy to oblige. For my own reasons." His smile was for Kori, and Kori alone, and for one short moment I envied the intimacy the smile demonstrated, even in a room full of people.

But then his point sank in.

"That's right. You killed Jake Tower." Kori had told me that, but I hadn't yet mentally connected the gun that had fired the bullet with the trigger finger of the man sitting in front of me. The man who'd killed my biological father, who—by all accounts—had received a much better death than he'd deserved.

How could I have known so little about the man who contributed half my DNA? How was it possible that I knew more about him now, three months after his death, than I'd ever known in life?

But I felt guilty about that thought as soon as I'd had it. I hadn't known much about Jake Tower because he hadn't mattered. My real father was my mother's husband. My sister's father. They were all the family I'd wanted, and if I'd never lost them, I wouldn't *need* to know the family that didn't want me. I wouldn't care about what the Towers owed me, because I wouldn't need that favor.

Anne was right about that. The Towers *did* owe me. They owed my mother for the years she'd spent hiding me. For the nights she'd spent worrying that I would turn out to be like my biological father, in spite of the happy, healthy life she'd made damn sure I had. And they were going to pay what they owed, even if that meant pressing whatever advantage my inheritance—Money? Property? Companies?—gave me.

"Yes," Ian said, answering a question I'd almost forgotten I'd asked. "I shot Jake Tower with his own gun. He died quickly, but in a great deal of pain."

"Well, the general consensus seems to be that he deserved that." I stood and wiped my hands on the front of my jeans. "So...who's taking me out of here? You can drop me off anywhere. Seriously. The front lawn is fine." Just as long as I was on the other side of those counter-sunk screws.

Kris looked at Kori, whose gaze flitted from Ian to Anne to Vanessa, without once straying to Gran, who seemed to have forgotten we were there at all, while she rinsed dishes and lined them up in the dishwasher.

"I have one more question." Vanessa met my gaze boldly. "Is there *anything* you can do to help us get Kenley back? Anything at all?"

I exhaled slowly, pretending I was actually considering the question, when I was really trying to figure out how best to get away with a lie. The safest approach seemed to be avoiding lies altogether, in favor of a marginally relevant truth. "I told you, I never met any of the Towers until today. And they shot at me," I said. "Ask Kris if you don't believe me."

"Technically, they shot at *me,* but they made no particular effort to avoid her," he verified. "But that doesn't mean anything," he added, and I wanted to smack him for the reversal. "She met with Julia Tower in her home office. And when she told the guards to put their guns down, they did."

But that wasn't quite right. "They weren't obeying *my* order, they were obeying Julia's." And I had no idea why she'd complied when I'd asked her to give it, but I wasn't going to say that. Everyone was already staring at me as if an alien might burst out of my stomach at any second. "And she was only trying to keep you from shooting any more of her people."

Kris shook his head. "Julia doesn't care who gets shot, as long as it's not her."

"Her people mean nothing to her as individuals. One gunman is as good as the next," Kori verified. "Except me. I'm better than the rest. But I'm not theirs anymore."

"Is that why they took your sister? Are they using her to get you back?"

Kris choked on a bitter laugh, as if the sound got wedged in his throat. "They don't want Kori back. They want her dead."

I couldn't imagine growing up in their world. Playing a lifelong, lethal game of hide-and-seek, where those who were found were either enslaved or killed. Who could you trust? When could you let your guard down?

And just like that, with a sudden devastating clarity, I understood Kris's paranoia and reluctance to set me free. He'd tried to tell me, but I'd refused to understand;

he truly couldn't afford to let me go if I was bound to Julia Tower.

"If they want you two dead, why are you so sure Kenley's alive?"

"Kenley isn't muscle," Vanessa said. "She's special. Julia needs her. But I need her more." And that's all she seemed inclined to reveal. "If there's anything you can do to help…"

"I wish I could." Evidently that sounded like the truth—and it was—because no one even looked at Anne. "But I don't even know how to make Julia do what I need done. In fact, she tried to kill me, as Kris seems to enjoy pointing out." I stood again and shoved my chair back, newly determined to avenge my sister after hearing about theirs. "Now, you either get me out of here or I'm climbing out the window. And the only way you're going to stop me is by killing me."

And, *man,* did I hope they recognized hyperbole.

Silence descended as gazes flitted all over the room, as if they were taking a psychic vote. In the end, it came down to a stubborn stare-down between Kris and his sister. "Huddle?" he suggested, and she nodded. Then they left the room without a word.

I started to follow—if they were gonna argue about me, I had a right to hear—but Vanessa put a hand on my arm. "I wouldn't," she said.

"Well, *I* would. They don't need a private powwow to decide what to do with me, because it's not their decision. I'm leaving."

"No, you aren't," Hadley said from the living room, and Vanessa tried to hide a smile.

"The hell I'm not. Unless personal liberty was suspended while I wasn't watching, you can't hold me here against my will."

Vanessa laughed, and I turned to glare at her. "I'm sorry." She made an obvious struggle to banish her smile. "It's just painfully obvious that you've never spent any time in a Skilled syndicate. Or even near one." Van turned to Ian. "She's no threat. She's more clueless than we ever were."

I frowned, one hand on the back of the chair I'd just vacated. "I feel like I should be offended by that, but you seem to be the only one seeing reason. Kind of."

"Sera," Ian said, and I turned to look at him, surprised all over again by the quiet dignity he embodied, in contrast to Kris and Kori, and the explosive nature of their sibling relationship. "I know you have no reason to trust me yet, but please believe me when I tell you that no one in the city has less desire to hold you prisoner than Kori."

There was more to that, but I knew better than to ask. "What about Kris?"

"Kris is acting weird," Anne admitted, pouring coffee from the pot into a clean mug. "He usually returns people to wherever they belong. You may be the first he's kept."

Before I could figure out what to say to that, Gran sank into the chair Kori had vacated, wiping her hands on a dish towel, and smiled up at me. "Hello, hon," she said as if she'd just noticed me for the first time. "Are you a friend of Nikki's?"

"Who's Nikki?" How many more people could they possibly fit into the House of Crazy?

Ian sat in Kris's chair. "Nikki was her daughter. Kori, Kenley and Kris's mother." He turned to her. "Gran, Nikki died a long time ago. Remember? And you raised her children?"

"Yes, of course I know that," she snapped, though the confusion never cleared from her eyes. "Kenley gets straight A's. Kori gets suspended."

"What about Kris?" I wasn't sure why I cared, and I only realized after the fact that I was probably contributing to her confusion.

"Kris is a good boy. Spends too much time in his room alone, though. Gonna give himself carpal tunnel, and I don't mean from typing."

Ian tried to hide a chuckle, but I laughed out loud. I couldn't help it. And I *really* hoped she was remembering the past, rather than the present.

The past. I sat up straight, surprised by the sudden realization that Gran wasn't living in some fantasy world, she was living in her own past, when her daughter was alive. So, who were the kids she'd mentioned when I'd first met her? If Nikki was real, surely they were real, too. Did Kris, Kori and Kenley have other siblings they hadn't mentioned? Cousins? Could I piece together an understanding of their lives by filling in the blanks in their grandmother's memory?

As bad as I felt for Gran and her dementia, it was good to know I wasn't the only one unsure of who I really was and what I was doing in that house. I was starting to believe the Daniels family and their friends were almost as messed up as I was.

Six

Kris

"What the hell is wrong with you?" Kori shoved pale blond hair back from her face as I closed my bedroom door behind us. "She's not a threat. We have to let her go."

"Not yet. She may know something about Kenley."

"She doesn't." My sister sank onto the end of my un-made bed, her eyes even darker than usual with exhaustion. And fear for Kenley. And probably anger at me. "Sera was just in the wrong place at the wrong time, and that got her kidnapped by some jackass who follows his dick as if it points true north."

"It's not like that—"

Kori rolled her eyes. "Don't even try it. I see the way you look at her, but you can't keep her just because you want her, and the longer you try, the more she'll hate you."

"I'm not looking at her in any particular way." I wasn't going to deny that Sera was beautiful. But… "This isn't about sex. She's not even my type."

"Oh, please. Your type is 'conscious.'"

My type was Noelle. Since I was eighteen years old,

I'd never wanted more than a single night with anyone but her, and that hadn't changed when I'd realized she was gone. Losing Elle didn't make me want someone else. Losing her made me want to push everyone else away.

But Sera was different. I'd known that from the moment I first saw her. Noelle was dead, and Sera was the first clue I'd found to the secrets that were born on Elle's lips and died in my notebook. But beyond that, Sera was important in her own right. She needed us. We needed her. I wasn't clear on the hows and whys, but I *knew* the answers were there. Sera had them.

I could have them, if I could earn her trust. But I couldn't do that if Kori sent her away.

"You said it yourself, Kor." I pulled out my desk chair and sat backward in it, facing my sister. The room was so small I could have reached out and touched her— I'd given the larger rooms to the couples. "Julia never would have let her in the house if she wasn't important, but if she's important, they wouldn't have been willing to kill her. Something's going on there. We're missing something."

Kori shook her head. "I said *Jake* never would have let her in the house, and I assumed Julia would do the same. But I could be wrong. Maybe she's taking all her meetings at home, so she can control the venue, to minimize risks." I started to argue, but my sister talked over me. "And maybe it's not Sera who's important—maybe it's killing her that's important." She shrugged. "Maybe Julia was just hoping to kill two birds with one bullet."

"They used way more than one bullet…" I mumbled. But I couldn't find fault in her logic. "Fine. Maybe they want to kill Sera. But if that's the case, don't we have an obligation to protect her? You know, the whole enemy-of-an-enemy thing?"

"Do I look like a Boy Scout to you?" Kori scooted back to sit yoga-style on my rumpled blue comforter. "I only give a shit about three things right now. Getting Kenley back, unharmed." She ticked off the points on her fingers. "Breaking every binding keeping Julia Tower in power. And protecting the people I care about. And I don't care about Sera-whatever-her-last-name-is. I don't even know her. And neither do you." Her gaze narrowed on me. "She's not going to sleep with you, Kris. You fucking kidnapped her."

"I'm not trying to…" Not that I'd turn her down. But that wasn't the point. "And I didn't kidnap her. I—"

"Save it. We're letting her go." She stood and headed for the door, and I stepped into her path.

"Sit back down. We're not done here."

Kori blinked at me, more curious than truly angry. "What the hell is going on with this girl, Kris?"

"We can't let her go." When I was sure she wouldn't stomp out of the room without hearing me out, I sank onto the end of the bed facing her. "I think she's important. We might need her."

Kori frowned and sank into the chair I'd vacated. "Need her for what?"

"I don't know. I just know that I was supposed to take her, so I took her."

She crossed both arms over the back of the chair. "Kris, what the hell are you talking about?"

I hesitated. I hesitated so long my sister started to look at me funny. "Okay," I said finally. "I'll tell you what I know, but you have to promise not to—" *call the men in white lab coats* "—laugh."

"No way. That's a sister's most sacred birthright."

"Shut up and come here." I scooted to the front of the unmade bed, next to the nightstand. My hands started to sweat as I pulled open the drawer and lifted out the notebook.

"What's that?" Kori tried to take it as if we were still kids arguing over a new toy, but I pulled it away from her, just like I always had as a child.

"This is Noelle. What's left of her, anyway."

"What does that even mean?" She sank onto the mattress next to me.

"Don't get mad." Another deep breath. "I know she was your best friend, but when you guys were sixteen… we started…seeing each other. Like, *all* of each other. Privately."

Kori laughed.

"Why is that funny? I'm serious. Elle and I were a thing." A top secret, middle of the night, swear-on-your-life-you'll-never-tell kind of thing.

Her smile had taken on a life of its own. "It's funny that you think I didn't know."

"You *knew?*" I couldn't process that. Surely if she'd known, Elle and I would never have heard the end of it.

She shrugged. "I figured there had to be a reason she wanted all the sleepovers to be at our house, and that it had nothing to do with Gran's winning personality." Another shrug. "Also, I woke up in the middle of the night a few times, and she was gone. The first time I freaked out—until I heard the two of you down the hall." Kori shuddered at the memory. "It was disgusting. It was also none of my business."

Disgusting? "Yeah, well, now my room is between the one you share with Ian and the one Kenni shares with Van. I think we're even." But the mention of Kenley had sobered us both.

"So…what's with the notebook?"

I flipped it open and gave her a look at the first page

full of dates and broken phrases—whatever I could understand of Noelle's night mumblings. "Elle talked in her sleep."

"Holy shit." Kori grabbed the notebook. Her focus scrolled left to right, up and down as she read. "You wrote all this down in the middle of the night? Are they predictions?"

"Some of them." I fought the urge to snatch the notebook back. Those handwritten lines were all I had left of the girl I'd loved more than the world itself, from the first time I saw her until the day she'd died. Then long after. They'd been mine that whole time. Private memories. Abandoned potential. And—when I realized I couldn't interpret any of the lines—my secret shame. "I don't know how many are predictions and how many were just dream fodder. For all I know, they're all both. Maybe her dreams *were* predictions."

She flipped through the pages, scanning words too fast to be absorbing any of them. "What made you start... I mean, how did you know to write them down?"

"I didn't at first. But do you remember the day that school bus driver fell asleep and drove through a crosswalk? The crossing guard died?"

"Yeah." She nodded slowly, her gaze unfocused with the memory. "After that, we started driving Kenley to school, so she wouldn't have to take the bus."

"Yeah." That had made sense at the time. If one bus driver was a Nyquil guzzling lunatic, they all could be. "You had a sleepover the weekend before. Noelle snuck into my room when you, Liv and Anne passed out, and afterward, we fell asleep. A couple of hours later, I rolled over to tell her she had to get back to your room before anyone woke up, and she was talking. Kind of... whispering. But her eyes were closed. She was asleep."

"What'd she say?" Kori's eyes were huge.

"I can't remember, exactly, but it was something about a crosswalk, then, 'Wake him up!' It made no sense at the time, but then that Monday, there was the bus accident, and I made the connection. I wrote everything down after that. See the dates?" I pointed out the first one, and Kori stared at it, fascinated. "I know it sounds stupid now, but at the time, all I could think was that if I'd known what she was talking about, I could have stopped it. I could have saved that crossing guard. She had kids, you know. It was in the paper."

My sister stared into my eyes as if she could see through them into my soul. "So you thought that if you wrote it all down, you could…what? Play superhero? Snatch women from railroad tracks before the train even leaves the station?"

I could only shrug. "I told you it sounds dumb."

"Yeah, it does." Yet there was a smile lurking at the corners of her mouth. "But only because prophesies are notoriously ambiguous, and *you* are notoriously ambitious. So…did it work?"

"Not even once." I could feel my shoulders slump and wondered if I looked as guilty and frustrated as I felt. "I stopped sleeping when she came over, so I wouldn't miss a word. I kept a flashlight in my nightstand—"

"Next to the condoms, right?" Kori said, and it took me a second to realize she was teasing.

"Yeah, actually. Anyway, writing it down was easy. Figuring it out was hard." Impossible, really. "Every now and then something would happen, and a line or two from the notebook would suddenly make sense. But by then, it was too late. I never figured any of it out in time to actually make a difference, until today."

"Sera?" Kori had made the connection, but she couldn't understand it yet. But then, neither could I.

"Here." I took the notebook and flipped through the pages, looking for the familiar entry. I'd read them all a million times, but that one had always stood out, because of the directive.

"Damn, Kris," she mumbled as I scanned page after page. "How long were you two…a thing?"

"Six years." I didn't realize my sister was staring at me until I found the right entry and looked up. "Off and on," I amended, with one glance at her stunned expression. "Mostly off, for the last two, when… Cavazos. Then Hadley."

It hurt to think those thoughts, but it hurt even more to speak them.

"Oh, shit." She covered her mouth with one hand. "So, you and Elle were still together when she met Ruben?"

"We were never really together. Not like that. Not exclusively." I'd *tried* for exclusivity, but Noelle was the kind of bird that dies in captivity. She'd needed the freedom to soar wherever the wind took her, and it took her away from me as often as it brought her back.

But in the end, freedom killed her faster than captivity ever could have, surely. And maybe I would have seen it coming, if I could have interpreted that damn notebook.

When I found my way out of my own head, Kori was still staring at me, waiting for more information. For the glimpse into a side of Elle's life she'd never seen.

"She left after high school, like everyone else." Anne and Liv had gone to college. Kori had attended the school of life and nearly flunked that the way she'd nearly flunked high school, because she refused to play by the rules. I'd had no better college prospects than she'd had, so I'd stayed with Gran and Kenley, working for anyone who needed a shadow-walker. I hadn't been picky about the jobs, then. I hadn't understood that not all of the syndicates' recruits were volunteers.

I hadn't realized I'd become a subcontractor helping them fill quotas until something that went very wrong turned out to be very right. I'd spent most of the decade after high school trying to make up for what I'd done the year I was nineteen, but Noelle had…

Well, no one really knew *where* Noelle went after graduation. She just kind of disappeared about the same time I was turning my life around. But…

"Elle came back more often than the rest of you," I told Kori as I turned the pages of my notebook. "And when she was in town, we'd just pick up where we'd left off."

That was all my sister needed to know. She didn't need to hear about ice cream in bed, and all-night Abbot and Costello marathons, and the conversations we'd had when Elle was awake.

She didn't need to know that every time Elle left town again, she'd sneak out of my bed in the middle of the night, with no note. No goodbye. It might be months before I saw her again. Once, it was years. And she'd arrive just as suddenly as she'd left. With no warning.

Until she stopped arriving.

"You found it?" Kori's voice brought me back to the present, as if time was a rubber band being snapped against my skin.

It stung.

"Yeah. Here."

She followed my finger to a passage written in blue ink, nearly eight years earlier. Noelle had been twenty. I'd been twenty-two. "Take the girl in the yellow scarf." Kori looked up at me again. "That's it? Just, 'Take the girl in the yellow scarf'?"

"Yeah. It meant nothing until today, when I saw Sera standing there in that yellow scarf."

Fresh skepticism swam in my sister's eyes. "How do you know she meant *this* girl? *This* yellow scarf? Is she seriously the only girl in a yellow scarf you've ever seen?"

I thought about that for a second. "Yeah, actually, I think she is." The only one I remembered, anyway. And that had to mean something, right? If I'd seen another girl in a yellow scarf, I hadn't noticed her, and that had to mean something, too, right? "Anyway, I know because the moment I saw her, I thought of this. And not just my handwriting, blue ink on white lines. I thought of the night Noelle *said* this. The night I wrote it down. It just felt…" *Right.* "It felt like this is the girl Noelle wanted me to take. So I took her. And as bad as I feel keeping her here when she wants to leave, I can't let her go until she's done whatever she's supposed to do, or I've done whatever *I'm* supposed to do. Or until I know whatever Elle wanted me to know."

But Kori clearly thought I'd lost my mind. "Kris…"

"Don't. I'm not crazy. Do you have any idea how many people have died because I couldn't figure this out?" I closed the notebook and laid one hand on its ratty cover. "Because I don't. I have no idea how many people I've failed to save, like I failed to save that crossing guard." Like I'd failed to save Noelle. "I don't know, because I can't figure most of these out. This is the first time I've even come close to seeing what she wanted me to see, and I'm not going to give up on that." I wasn't going to give up on *her*.

"Is this about that boy? Micah?"

An old, bitter pain rang through me at the mention of his name. I hadn't consciously thought about him in years, but his face was never far from my memory. "No. This has nothing to do with him."

"Because you know, you can't punish yourself forever, and no matter how many kids you shield, you can't bring Micah back."

No. I couldn't. But I could stop it from happening to the others. To the kids most in danger of being headhunted by the Skilled mafia. Kids like Kenley, who'd barely been in college when she was extorted into joining the Tower syndicate. Kids like Micah, who'd been delivered into their own personal hell by people like me, who didn't ask enough questions—who didn't *care* enough to ask the right questions—and became unwitting, unbound cogs in the very machine I wanted to destroy.

But for once this wasn't about Micah.

"This is about Noelle, and the things she saw, and the things I'm supposed to do. There's a reason she said those things in my bed. There *has* to be. Destiny doesn't deal in coincidences."

"But Kris…Noelle didn't say these things to you." Kori spoke with a firm voice, as if that might make her assertion easier to believe. "She said them to no one. In her sleep. We don't know if Elle ever remembered a word of this." She took the notebook from me and flipped through it aimlessly. "She wasn't trying to saddle you with some kind of heroic mandate. She was just… sleeping."

I'd thought about that possibility over and over since Noelle died, and every time, I came to the same conclusion. "Did you ever hear her talk in her sleep?"

Kori shrugged. "I don't know. Maybe a couple of times."

"Exactly. You didn't hear much of it because even when she came for your sleepover, she slept in *my* bed.

I think she fell asleep with me on purpose." She started to object, but I spoke over her. "Think about it, Kor. She could have snuck back to the sleepover as soon as she had what she'd come for. But she didn't. She stayed with me—she *slept in my bed*—for a reason."

Kori looked as if she didn't know what to say.

Then, she looked as if she had *too* much to say.

"You're telling me—with a straight face—that you think Noelle slept with you off and on for six years so that you'd record her prophesies in a notebook she didn't even know you had, then drive yourself nuts for the rest of your life, trying to figure out what she was talking about, when *she* didn't even know she was speaking? Seriously?"

Well, when you put it like that… "Yes."

"Kris…"

"*Think* about it, Kori!" I set the notebook on the nightstand and turned to face her more directly. "No one knows what Elle knew, and most of what she said only makes sense years after the fact. Maybe she *did* know about the notebook. Maybe she wanted me to keep it. Maybe she knew I was going to write in it before *I* knew I was going to write in it. Hell, maybe she knew she wasn't going to be around long enough to do anything about all the stuff she saw, and this was her way of asking me to take over for her."

Kori exhaled slowly, apparently struggling for patience. "Fine. Let's assume you're right. Why on *earth* would she have wanted you to kidnap Sera?"

"Maybe she wanted you to trade her for Kenley?"

Kori and I both glanced up to find Anne standing in my bedroom doorway. We hadn't even heard her open the door.

"No." I stood to pull her into the room, then closed

the door behind her. I wanted to know how much she'd heard, but I didn't want to ask, in case that led to more questions from her. "Elle wouldn't want me to use her as a hostage. Or to give her back to people willing to kill her."

"You don't know that." Anne brushed long red hair over her shoulder and leaned against the closed door with her arms crossed over her shirt. "Elle would do whatever it takes to protect the people she loves, the rest of the world be damned. Look what she did to us to protect Hadley."

I frowned, and Anne clarified: "Don't misunderstand. I love Hadley, and I wouldn't give her up for anything in the world. But Noelle never asked me if I wanted to be a mother. She never asked me if I wanted my husband to be murdered. Or if Liv wanted to be bound to that abusive bastard Ruben Cavazos. Or if Kori wanted to be put in the middle of the whole thing, then shot and locked up. Noelle didn't give any of us a choice about any of that. She just stacked the deck, content to let the cards fall as they may, so long as Hadley was protected. Who says she wouldn't be willing to sacrifice Sera—some stranger none of us even knows—to help Kenley?"

"She wouldn't." I refused to believe it. I *couldn't* believe it. "She was just doing the best she could with what she had. She never asked to be a Seer."

"None of us asked to be what we are." Kori pushed pale hair back from her face. She looked tired. "And a large part of what and who we are now is because of Elle plucking strings and pushing buttons behind the scenes."

Anne nodded. "Besides, Kris, you have no idea what Elle knew about Sera. Maybe Hadley's right. Maybe she's not who she says she is."

"She hasn't told us anything but her first name," Kori pointed out.

I turned to the Reader. "But you said she was telling the truth about that, right?"

Anne frowned and her gaze lost focus, as if she were seeing the kitchen from twenty minutes earlier, rather than my bedroom from the present. "I didn't read any untruth from her, other than about the favor she thinks the Towers owe her. But I didn't really read much truth in the rest of it, either. It was more like... Well, it was like most of the time I got no reading at all. Normally I would assume that means the speaker is telling the truth. But in this case...there's just something weird about her."

I grasped at the straw she'd unintentionally handed me. "Okay, Anne doesn't trust her, so we shouldn't let her go yet." I turned to Kori. "That's two against one."

Anne rolled her eyes. "You realize you're now supporting both sides of the argument, right?"

I shrugged. "Whatever it takes. I need her. *We* need her."

The Reader exhaled heavily. "If we're voting, we should include Ian and Van."

Kori shook her head. "We're not voting. We're letting her go."

"You're not in charge, Kor." I stepped in front of the door again. "I can't let her go. Not yet."

Kori glared up at me, something dangerous shining in her dark eyes. "Then kill her."

I blinked at my sister, waiting for the punch line. Because surely that was a joke. We only kill those who pose a threat.

But no punch line came.

"Kori, I'm not going to kill her."

She shrugged, looking up at me. "Then let her go. Those are your options. You kidnapped her, scared the crap out of her, bound her hands, then tied her to a chair.

There's a very good reason she doesn't want to be here. So put her out of her misery. Release her, one way or another."

And that's when I understood. Kori had spent six weeks locked up in Tower's basement. She doesn't talk about it, but we all know she was tortured. Of *course* she would be in favor of letting the prisoner go, regardless of the extenuating circumstances. Even if the prisoner wasn't really a prisoner.

"I'm trying to *help* her, Kori. And I'm trying to let her help us." Even if I didn't understand the specifics of either scenario yet.

"Listen to me." My sister stood on her toes and leaned closer so that I couldn't possibly misunderstand. "We. Don't. Lock. People. Up."

"I'm not—"

But before I could figure out how to finish that sentence, Kori's phone buzzed. She pulled it from her pocket and frowned. "Olivia's freaking out about something. I'll be right back." She reached past me for the doorknob, and I only let her through because getting her out of the house for a while seemed like a good idea. "While I'm gone, you either let Sera go, put her out of her misery, or convince her to stay of her own volition. If you can't get the job done, I'll do it myself."

I glanced at Anne, who could only shrug while Kori stomped down the hall, then down the stairs. "She's right."

I groaned. "Why do you always take her side?"

"I don't." Anne crossed her arms over her chest. "As you might recall, she once kidnapped my daughter. But this time, she's right, and if you don't make a call, she'll fight you for it."

"I know." I sank into my desk chair again and glanced

up at Anne. "My very earliest memories is the day my mom went into labor with Kori. As they were leaving for the hospital, I *begged* them to bring home a baby brother for me. Life's been screwing me ever since."

Seven

Sera

After the Reader went upstairs to find Kris and Kori, her daughter sat next to me on the couch with a glass of chocolate milk. I tried to ignore her, not because I didn't know how to talk to children, but because I didn't know how to talk to that particular child. And because, honestly, I agreed with Gran—she was more than a little creepy.

For several minutes, Hadley sipped from her bendy straw and watched cartoons while I tried to puzzle out my next move. I'd decided there had to be an emergency exit, aside from the one I'd created from a broken kitchen window, which Ian was patching with a sheet of plywood. As far as I could tell, Kris and Kori were the only shadow-walkers in the house, so there had to be an easy way out for the rest of them. What if there was a burglary? Or a fire?

There *was* another way out. I just had to find it.

"Where's the baby?" Hadley said from my left, but she had to repeat the question with a tug on my sleeve before I realized she was talking to me.

"I'm sorry?" Surely I'd heard her wrong.

Her big, round eyes blinked up at me. "Can I hold it?" When I couldn't figure out how to respond, she continued. "Is it a girl baby or a boy baby? I love babies, but I like girl babies better."

"Um…I don't have a baby." My foot began to tap. My knee jiggled on the lower edge of my vision.

"Then who is the cradle for?"

"What cradle?" My chest felt tight. I had to open my mouth to suck in more oxygen than my nose could handle at one time.

"The wooden one, on rockers." Hadley frowned up at me, as if I were being intentionally obtuse. "You know. In the striped room."

My stomach tried to launch itself through my torso and out my throat. I had to swallow convulsively to keep my lunch down. There was only one cradle she could possibly have assumed was mine. I twisted on the couch to face her fully. "You saw the cradle?" That last word cracked in half and fell from my lips in jagged pieces.

Hadley nodded.

"What color were the stripes on the walls?" I demanded, my voice both fragile and sharp, like a thin sliver of glass.

"Green and yellow." Hadley frowned, as though she was trying to remember. "And purple. Light purple," she said, and my next breath escaped on a sob.

My dad had been so thrilled to find out he was going to be a grandfather, despite the circumstances, that he'd given up his home office to make room for the baby, even though it wasn't due for five more months. He'd painted the walls himself. He'd even gotten the cradle down from the attic, where it had been since Nadia outgrew it. That cradle had been in his family for generations. He was so excited by the thought of using it again.

"Where's the baby?" Hadley's question ripped me out of my own memories and back into the cruel new reality that had become my life.

"The baby…died." In its mother's womb. The day my sister and parents were murdered in their own home.

Hadley blinked at me in confusion, and for a second I envied her the shattered misconception that babies couldn't die. Too late, I realized I'd probably ruined that for her.

Then the implication of what she'd just said hit me like a sledgehammer to the chest, and I leaned back on the couch, breathing through the pain.

Hadley had seen my house. She'd seen the baby's room. For whatever reason, and despite the questionable accuracy of her earlier prediction, she seemed to be tuned into my psychic frequency. Or something like that.

Which meant that she might have more visions, or prophesies, or whatever. She might be able to tell me the name of the man who killed them. She might even be able to help me find him.

I might not need Julia Tower after all.

"What else did you see?" I demanded so suddenly that she gave a startled little yip and sloshed chocolate milk onto her lap. "Did you see a man in hiking boots? Do you know his name?" All the police had been able to tell me was that boots like his—he'd left bloody footprints all over the house—had been sold at hundreds of stores, all over the country. Ballistics found no match for the bullets he'd fired. He'd left DNA, but it didn't match anything in the database.

They had suspects, but no smoking gun. My family's killer was a ghost.

When the child only blinked her startled, teary eyes at me, I made myself take another deep breath and calm down. She had no idea what I was talking about. She probably didn't even understand her own Skill yet. She was *so* young. We'd have to start with something more basic.

"Hadley, I'm sorry. I didn't mean to scare you. Here." I took her milk and set it on the coffee table, suddenly glad that Ian's hammering obscured our conversation. "I just want to ask you a few questions. Is that okay?"

She nodded hesitantly.

"Great. Thanks. Hadley, how did you know that the cradle and the striped room were in my house?" It was actually my parents' house, but that was close enough. She'd somehow associated me with what she'd seen.

Hadley only shrugged.

"Okay. Did you see anything else…about me?" She shook her head. "Anything else about the house?" I was scaring her again. My voice was too intense. My grip on her hand too desperate. "Did you see any of the other rooms?"

"Just…" She squeezed her eyes shut as if she was trying to see it all again in her head. "I saw the living room. There was a guitar—a wooden one—on this metal stand. By a chair. The kind that you can lean back and put your feet up on." She opened her eyes and met my gaze, and seemed pleased by whatever she found there.

My heart ached with every beat. "That's my dad's guitar. And his chair."

Except that guitar was gone. *Destroyed.* A bullet shattered it the night my parents died. The police believed my father was actually playing it when the attack started.

I'd buried him with what was left of it. Other than his family, it was what he'd loved most in the world.

So how the hell could that guitar be in Hadley's vision of the future?

It couldn't.

Maybe she'd seen another guitar. Maybe even another room. But that was too much of a coincidence, wasn't it? An acoustic guitar on a metal stand and an old-fashioned wooden cradle in a green, yellow and purple striped room?

I could only think of one other possibility, but before I could give it voice, footsteps thumped on the stairs. A second later, Kori jogged into sight on the landing, then headed straight through the living room and into the dark hall closet without a glance at anyone else. When she didn't come back out a second later, I realized she was gone.

Kris and Anne, the Reader, came down a minute later. "Okay, I think we've come to a compromise about…what to do with you." He sat on the arm of a chair across the room.

Distantly, I realized I should have been furious about that. None of them had the right to do *anything* with me, but that fact was hard to focus on, with the new possibility now taking up most of my attention.

"If you're willing to—"

"Has she ever done this before?" I asked Anne after a brief glance at Kris. When the Reader only frowned at me, I nodded toward her daughter. "Has she ever had a premonition before today, or am I actually witnessing the birth of a Skill?" A very extraordinary Skill, if my hunch was right.

"As far as I know, this is the beginning of it." Anne sank onto the couch on Hadley's other side. "Why?"

"She…knows things. Things about me." I took another deep breath. "About my family."

"What kind of things?" Anne glanced at her daughter, but Hadley was watching cartoons again, ignoring the adults.

"She's always been creepy, Anne," Gran said from the doorway, and when I twisted to see her, I realized that she might have been listening the whole time. "But she seems to have taken that to new heights today."

"Gran!" Anne snapped.

Gran shrugged, wiping her hands on a dish towel. "If that girl's anything like Elle, she's more conscious of how strange she is than any of us ever will be." Then she turned and headed back into the kitchen, where Ian was still hammering at the window I'd broken and Vanessa was keeping him company.

"What did she say?" Kris slid from the arm of his chair onto the cushion, glancing from me to Hadley, then back to me.

"She described some things in my house. Things she's obviously never seen. But that's not the weird part—"

"Could you all please *stop* that!" Anne said, exasperation riding every syllable. "She's not weird. If anything, she's *gifted*."

"You're right." I nodded. "In fact, I think she's more gifted than any of you realize—"

The hall closet door flew open so hard it slammed into the wall, and the entire house fell into silence. Kris stood, one hand on his gun. Ian and Vanessa appeared in the kitchen doorway, also armed, with Gran peeking over their shoulders. Only Hadley seemed completely at ease with the possibility of invasion.

Maybe she already knew who was there.

"See?" Kori stepped into the living room and everyone relaxed. "They're all here. Alive and well. Plus one." Me, evidently.

I'd never seen the woman who stepped into the room behind her, brown hair pulled back into a ponytail, blue eyes narrowed in confusion. "I'm telling you, none of you is emitting a psychic signature right now. Or else, they're all being…swallowed."

Uh-oh.

After a quick scan of the living room and what she could see of the kitchen, her gaze fell on me and lingered. "It's her. It has to be."

"What's me?" I said, but I was pretty sure she'd figured out something no one else ever had, other than my mother.

"What's going on Liv?" Kris sat on the arm of his chair again, but Kori and the new woman—Liv—remained standing. Staring at me.

"She's a Jammer. She has to be. She's jamming every one of your signatures. It's like you don't even *exist,* from a tracking perspective. Who are you?" she demanded. "I know every Jammer in the city, by name and face at least, but I don't know you."

Kris's eyes widened. "What the hell is she talking about?"

Liv crossed her arms over her chest, and I noticed a slight bulge beneath her jacket. Were they *all* toting guns? "I tried to track you, to make sure you made it back from wherever you went."

"The dumb-ass broke into Jake's house," Kori added with an irritated glance at her brother.

"But I couldn't find any of you. Anywhere. I got nothing from this house, and couldn't pick you up at Anne's, or Meghan's, either. And there's no way you could have gotten out of my range that quickly. I thought…" She shrugged, and we could all see what she'd thought.

She'd thought they were dead.

152   *Rachel Vincent*

"Then Anne and Hadley disappeared, too. I had Cam double-check for me, and he couldn't find any of you either."

"We're fine." Kori gestured to the room full of people. "Safe and sound."

"Safer and more sound than ever, evidently," Kris said, and I looked up to find him staring at me. "You're a Jammer?"

I nodded reluctantly. No use denying it.

Anne pulled Hadley closer, as if my omission had put the child in some kind of danger, when in fact, the opposite was true. "Why didn't you tell us?"

"Because it's none of your business."

"You scared the *shit* out of me!" Liv snapped, and my own temper flared. "You should have told them, so they could tell me."

I stood, furious now. "Five minutes ago, I didn't even know you existed, much less that you'd freak out about not being able to find your friends. A situation that could've been remedied with a simple phone call, FYI."

Liv's eyes widened, and Kris seemed to be…grinning.

"And considering that I didn't choose to be here and I can't exactly turn off the jamming—" which didn't work like most other Skills "—as far as I'm concerned, you can all go stick your heads up each other's asses for all I care." I glanced at Hadley and flinched when I saw her staring up at me, evidently unfazed by the profanity. "Or, you could just let me go."

"Let her go?" Liv glanced around at her friends, waiting for an explanation.

"Kris kidnapped her from Tower's house," Kori said.

Her brother groaned. "I didn't kidnap her. I just…" He shrugged. "She needed to come with me, but I didn't have time for her to reach that conclusion on her own."

"Yeah," I snapped. "They call that *kidnapping*."

"You kidnapped Julia Tower's Jammer?" Liv looked impressed.

"No!" Kris and I said at the same time. Then I continued. "I'm not her Jammer. She doesn't even *know* I'm a Jammer. No one does, except you bunch of psychos. Thanks for that, by the way." I hoped they all choked on my sarcasm.

Everyone stared at me. Then Liv turned back to Kris. "What the hell were you thinking, breaking into Tower's house? Kidnapping someone? Who *is* she?" She turned to me again. "Who are you?"

"Sera," I said. "And for the thousandth time, that's all any of you are getting from me until you give up some private information about yourselves."

Looks flew across the room. Ian, Vanessa and Gran had joined us by then, and everyone seemed to come to the same conclusion.

"Fair enough." Liv stepped forward and extended one hand for me to shake, over the coffee table. "Olivia Warren. I'm a Tracker. Bloodhound, specifically, but I can also use names when I have to. In the spirit of disclosure, and because you can't hang out in this crowd for long without finding out anyway, I technically work for Ruben Cavazos."

"Technically?" I wasn't very familiar with syndicate bindings, but I knew who Cavazos was. *Everyone* knew who Cavazos was.

"Not by choice. But one of these days, he's going to cross the line, and I'm going to have to…renegotiate." She glanced at Hadley and forced a smile.

"Cavazos will never cross the line," Kori mumbled. "Because you keep pushing the line back. When Cam gets tired of that, he'll renegotiate *for* you. He may even survive."

I glanced from Kori to Olivia. "And Cam would be?"

"Cam's her boyfriend," Hadley said, and I looked down to see her smiling up at Olivia. "He works for my biological father, too."

"Your biological father?" That struck a little too close to home.

The child nodded, and brown hair fell over her forehead. "Ruben. He lives in a big house, and there's a *huge* TV in my room there." She glanced at her mother and frowned at Anne's stiff expression. "But I still like it better at home."

"Your dad is Ruben Cavazos?"

"Not her dad," Anne corrected. "Her father."

Damn, could I ever identify with *that* statement.

I already knew about Kris and Kori Daniels, and their missing sister, Kenley, who was a Binder. Ian introduced himself as Ian Holt, a Blinder—he could pull darkness from…wherever and make shadows wherever he wanted. He and Kori kind of seemed made for each other.

Vanessa was unSkilled. She was also Kenley's girlfriend, though it didn't take long for me to realize that Gran seemed to think Van and Kris were an item.

"Your turn," Kris said when everyone else was done making formal introductions. "Who are you? Who are you *really?*" he added for emphasis.

"Sera Brandt."

"And…" Liv prompted.

I sighed and sank on the edge of the couch cushion behind me. "And…I'm a Jammer. But I don't tell people that." Then I told them what my mother had told me when I was eighteen and we'd finally figured out that I was, indeed, Skilled, even though she wasn't. "I'm fortunate enough to have escaped syndicate notice so far, both because I live as far from organized syndicate activity as I can, and because I'm naturally hard to find. That's part of being a Jammer." The very *best* part of being a Jammer, and the only reason my mother had been able to hide me as well as she had. I shrugged. "That's it. All that's worth telling, anyway."

Anne shook her head. "There's more," she said and they all turned to me expectantly. Again.

"What, you think I'm just going to bare my soul to a room full of strangers? Not gonna happen. The interrogation's over. We're either going to have a civil discussion, or none at all."

"I'm fine with that," Kris said with a shrug, and I glanced at him in surprise.

"Good. But to be clear, in a legitimate conversation, both sides get to ask questions and no one monitors the truth in their answers." I shot a pointed glance at Anne, who shrugged, and I wondered if her ability was impossible to turn off, like mine. If so, was it even realistic of me to expect her to keep a perfect stranger's secrets?

"I think we can all respect that," Kris said. "What do you want to know?"

"What are you all doing here? Why are you hiding out in a house locked up from the inside? What is the 'higher purpose' you mentioned earlier? Why does Julia Tower need your sister?" I hadn't realized I had so many questions for them, until the words tumbled from my mouth.

"Okay." Kris took a deep breath. "Every one of those questions has a complicated answer, and when you put them together…the explanation is pretty involved. But the short version is this—we're trying to take the Towers down."

"Take them down? Like, kill them?" I wasn't sure

whether to be thrilled by the prospect—considering Julia's willingness to take *me* down—or horrified.

"Put them out of business," Ian clarified. "We're trying to end their syndicate."

"Which will mean killing some of them," Kori added. "Most notably, Julia."

Olivia sank into the chair where Kris still perched on the arm. "Kenley's an important part of the effort. Julia took her to stop her from working against the syndicate."

"But you're sure she won't kill Kenley?"

Kris gave me a grim nod. "She can't afford to, at least for the moment."

"Okay." I stared at the floor, still processing most of what I'd just heard. "Your turn."

"What do you want from Julia?" Ian asked. "What could possibly be worth putting yourself on their radar?"

"I need her to do something for me. Something personal and very important, that I can't do for myself. But you don't have to worry about them recruiting me. She doesn't know I'm a Jammer." *And she wants me as far away from her borrowed empire as possible.* "So I think I'm safe in that respect."

"Some people are never safe," Vanessa whispered. "Even when they legitimately have no Skill."

"Anyway, she'll figure it out if you wind up working with her." Kris shrugged. "She's a Reader. She'll know if you lie."

So they knew her Skill. But they hadn't yet realized I knew ways around the truth.

"What did you want from her?" Kori asked. But instead of answering, I stood and wiped my sweaty palms on my jeans.

"That's all I can afford to tell you, and I don't want to insult you with a lie." *Again.* Though, if they were smart, they'd search for my name online the moment I was gone, and from there it would be easy to guess what I'd wanted from Julia. But at least if they found the information themselves, I wouldn't have to say the words. I wouldn't have to remember it again for them, like I'd remembered it for Julia. "I need to go now. Please. That's as nice as I'm gonna ask."

Now that I knew Anne's last name, I could contact her on my own. Later. Maybe she'd actually let me talk to her daughter again.

"Wait, Sera." Kris stepped forward, and his eyes seemed to see nothing else. Nothing but me. "Please. I have a proposition for you."

Anne's brows rose.

"What proposition?" Kori asked, scowling, but her brother didn't even glance at her.

"Work with us. Please. Work *for* us, if you need to see this as a real job. We'll pay you. We need you."

Olivia frowned. "Do you really think that's a good idea?"

"I don't want your money," I said before he could answer her. "I don't want anything from you, except for an *open door.*" And another chat with Hadley, when I was ready. When I'd had time to prepare myself for what I might hear.

"Fine. Then let us work for *you.* As payment." Kris stepped closer, and his gaze intensified. This meant something to him. "An exchange of services."

I have to admit, I was curious. "Work for me...how?"

"However you need us. Whatever you wanted Julia to do for you. We'll do it, and you won't be indebted to the fucking mafia."

"We don't even know what she wants done," Ian pointed out.

"We don't have time to work for her!" Vanessa insisted. "We have to find Kenley. That's top priority."

"Agreed," Kori said, and everyone else nodded.

"Of course." Kris never even looked at them. "And Sera can help us with that. In return we'll owe her."

I shook my head slowly, thoroughly confused. "I can't help you. For the last time, I don't know anything about the Towers. I can't find your sister."

"No, but you can keep us hidden while *we* find her. All you'd have to do is hang out with us. Just…stay, and come with us when we go out." He turned to the rest of them then, glancing from face to face. "Julia won't stop looking for us just because she has Kenley. She wants most of us dead." He aimed a pointed look at Kori and Ian, who—I remembered—had killed Julia's brothers. My biological father and uncle. "Sera can virtually hide us in plain sight."

They seemed to think about that for a moment.

"Then she could stay even after we find Kenni…" Kori glanced at me. "If you *would* stay, and hide Kenley while she finishes…her work."

I had no idea what that meant. I had no idea what Kenley's work was, but I could certainly hide her. However… "What makes you think you can do what I need done?"

Kris actually smiled. "You happen to be in the presence of a sort of Skilled syndicate microcosm. Kori is a former syndicate bodyguard/hit man."

"Not by choice," she muttered. "And it's hit *woman*. Though I prefer 'badass assassin.'"

"Whatever you call her, she's the best," Kris said, and his sister looked somewhat mollified. "Liv and Cam are currently syndicate Trackers, on the other side of the city. Ian is a former Marine—Special Forces. There's no skull he can't bust."

"It was a little more delicate of a job than *that*." Ian

looked insulted. "Though there was plenty of busting skulls."

"Also, he can practically make his own damn eclipse. Which dovetails nicely with the Skill Kori and I share. Once we get Kenley back, we'll have a Binder, and I—" He shrugged, not quite self-depreciatingly. "I'm good at finding things."

"And finding *people*..." I remembered what he'd told me earlier. A people-finder was exactly what I needed. Also, a people-executioner.

Kris was right. Together, they represented a nearly complete cross-section of the Skilled population. And if I agreed, they'd have a Jammer.

But if we were going to do this...

I took a deep breath, then glanced around the room. "If I'm going to seriously consider working with you guys, you should know what you're getting into."

Kori shrugged. "Whatever it is, we've probably done it before."

I hoped she was wrong. But then again, practical experience would come in handy.

I took another deep breath, but that one wasn't enough to calm me. To fill the hole in my chest that had been growing since that horrible night. "A few months ago, my family...died." I avoided the *M*-word at the last second, with a glance at Hadley. If she hadn't seen any specifics of their murder, I wasn't going to mentally lead her to the scene of the crime. "Unpleasantly. All of them." I could tell from the looks of empathy and comprehension that the adults had all heard the part I hadn't said. Even Gran. "I wanted Julia to find the man responsible. And end him."

I waited for the objections, or at least some shocked protests. But none came.

Kori glanced at Ian, who glanced at Liv, who glanced at Kris, and they all seemed to come to the same conclusion at the exact same time.

Kris nodded. "Okay."

I blinked at them. "That's it? Just like that? You're all okay with just…ending someone?"

"Just someone?" Kori met my gaze with a frank one of her own. "No. A cold-blooded murderer? Yeah. I'm good with it."

"Oh." I wasn't sure why that surprised me as much as it did. Obviously, I was okay with it, too. It was my idea. The driving force behind my existence for the past few months. But I'd never expected to find a squad of assassins ready and willing to help me carry such a task out.

I made a mental note not to look that particular gift horse in the mouth.

"Okay, then. You have yourself a Jammer. Just so we're clear, though, I'm free to leave whenever I want, right? This is no longer a hostage situation?"

Kris rolled his eyes. "It never was."

"Then…can someone take me to get my stuff?"

Kori stood, but Kris was faster. "Yeah. The sooner the better."

"Great." I headed straight for the closet door with Kris behind me, but I turned back when I remembered what I'd never gotten a chance to say earlier. "Oh, Anne?" I said, and she looked up. "Your daughter is no ordinary Seer."

"What do you mean?" She looked decidedly nervous.

"She doesn't just see the future. She can also see the past."

Eight

Kris

It was nearly midnight by the time we left the hideout house to go after Sera's things, which meant the outside world would still be one big den of shadows. Including most of the Tower property, except where the perimeter lights would render my shadow-walking ability null around the exterior of the entire property.

According to my sisters, motion sensors were scattered throughout the grounds and if triggered, they would activate floodlights, which would both highlight our position and prevent our escape. Fortunately, Kori remembered enough to mark the motion sensors for me on a hand-drawn map of the property. She didn't think Julia would have gotten around to changing the exterior security features, considering that so far, both of their breaches had originated from inside the house itself.

I held Sera's hand as we stepped through the dark hall closet and into the cool fall night. Thanks to the moon, stars and lights from the Tower house, nature's darkness wasn't as black as the closet, but it was more than dark enough to accommodate my Skill. As we took our first step on Tower's thick lawn, I had to remind myself to take my hand back. It didn't want to let go of hers.

I was on alert, my every nerve ending buzzing from the knowledge that we could be discovered at any moment and that even if we weren't shot on sight or imprisoned by light, Sera couldn't escape without me and my Skill. I stayed as close to her as possible and told myself it was for her safety.

We started in a patch of deep shadows to the left of the rounded front porch, not close enough to trigger sensors built into the walls, but not exposed enough to be easily seen in dark clothes. Sera's were borrowed from Kori. They clung to her in places they didn't cling to my sister—thank goodness—and I almost wished for normal, non-shadow-walker night vision, to render me immune to the distraction.

"It's gone," she whispered, staring at the broad, semi-circular driveway, and I had to refocus my thoughts to remember why we were there. Sera was like a mental magnet, constantly pulling my focus off true north. She set me spinning, like a compass needle with no direction. She was a dangerous distraction. A beautiful, enigmatic distraction…who was saying something I should listen to. "My car is gone."

I glanced at the front of the house. The driveway was empty. "They probably moved it around back." Where most of the employees parked, according to Kori.

Rather than walk around the huge house and risk triggering an alarm, I took us through the shadows once more. This time we stepped out onto an open patch of grass behind the small, half-empty parking lot.

"That's it." She pointed to a small blue four-door sedan, one of only five cars on the lot, which gave me hope that Julia ran a skeleton crew at night. Sera's car was parked next to the tall industrial lamp rising from the center of the lot. It was *completely* drenched in light. We couldn't get to it without risking being seen by anyone patrolling the grounds. Or simply looking out a rear-facing window.

"Is there anything in there that can't be replaced?" Shopping was much safer than sneaking around in Tower's backyard. And considering that they'd already moved her car, Julia's men could just as easily have taken her stuff to dig for private information. Middle names. Policy numbers. Receipts. Anything that could give them something to use against her.

"Pictures," she whispered. "I brought my mom's photo album. Those can't be replaced. I don't know if she even kept the negatives."

Shit. Her dead mother's photos. *Real* photos, with no digital footprint. "Okay. You have your key?" I asked, and she nodded, pulling the electronic key fob from her pocket. The gaze that met mine was scared, but steady. And intense. "When I say go, you're going to run for it. Stay hunched over, to make as small a target as possible. Keep the car between you and the house. I'll keep watch from here."

Sera frowned and glanced back at her car, and hair fell across her face. "There has to be a better way," she whispered. "I can't fight a bullet. Can't outrun one, either."

I brushed that strand of hair behind her ear and looked directly into her eyes. "You won't have to. I'm faster than anyone Julia has on staff, and more accurate than anyone she's ever met. Including Kori." I pulled back the side of my jacket to show her my gun, hoping the sight of it would reassure her the same way the feel of it reassured me.

She actually grinned, and something in my throat tightened at the sight. "Not exactly modest, are you?"

"Modesty is for the mediocre. Now, when you get there, use the key to unlock the car manually, so it doesn't beep. Is the album in the trunk?"

Sera shook her head, her gaze glued to me, and I realized I liked having her full attention. A lot. "No. It's in the backseat."

"Good. Go in through the rear door and close it as softly as you can. Make sure the interior lights go off. You should be able to see fine with just the parking lot light. Sit on the floorboard and gather what you need— as much as you can carry without hampering your ability to run. You good so far?"

She nodded, and, though she still looked noticeably nervous, her hands were steady and her jaw set. I was impressed, considering that she'd probably never done anything like this before.

"When you have what you can carry, get out, close the door and run back to me." I glanced around at the acres of shadowed lawn—my personal transit system. "I'll have you out of here in a single step. Questions?"

She glanced at my gun. "You sure you're not exaggerating your skill with that thing?"

"Anyone who so much as pokes his head out of that house before you get back here is going to get permanently ventilated. You have my word."

"The word of a kidnapper?" She seemed *way* more amused by that than the situation warranted.

"I didn't kidnap you. I—"

"I know. You liberated me from a den of evil. Or you anticipated my forthcoming desire to flee. Or maybe you released me from the burden of choice. Whatever it was, don't do it again. Got it?"

"Got it."

She still looked pissed off by the memory.

Pissed off looked good on her.

"You ready?" She looked scared, but she also looked determined. Sera wasn't fearless, by any means, but she wasn't going to let fear stop her. I could respect that.

In answer to her question, I drew my gun.

She turned and ran. With no warning. One second she was standing next to me in the shadow-drenched grass and in the next instant, she was racing across the lawn toward the parking lot, a glaring island of light, as if she were being chased by hounds from hell.

I scanned the night, alert for movement, but I saw none.

Sera's footsteps thumped softly from grass onto pavement and her speed increased. She was one hell of a sprinter—a black blur racing across the pale pavement, hunched over, just like I'd instructed.

When she reached her car, she dropped into a squat, shielded from view of the house. Sera fumbled with her keys for a second, then opened the front door and reached inside to unlock the back door. Then she closed the front door softly and climbed into the back of the car.

I lost sight of her then, but if I couldn't see her, neither could anyone else.

The soft click of her door closing had just rolled into the still night when a man dressed all in black turned the corner from the east side of the huge house. He carried an automatic rifle. I couldn't tell what kind from the shadow it cast against the wall, but it had a long barrel and a scope, which meant he could hit me—or Sera—from much farther away than we actually were.

Kori hadn't mentioned guards with rifles walking the grounds. So much for a skeleton crew. My home invasion must have really spooked Julia.

I stepped back slowly, carefully, fading deeper into the

darkness with one eye on the guard, the other on Sera's car, waiting for her head to appear above the backseat. Hoping he wouldn't notice her.

The guard walked slowly—too slowly—and with each of his steps, my blood pressure rose. My heart beat a little harder. I pulled my suppresser from my jacket pocket and quietly attached it to the end of my gun.

Halfway. The guard was almost halfway across the yard, crossing the large covered patio, headed toward a pool, surrounded by its own privacy fence and adjoining pool house.

Then Sera sat up inside the car.

For the span of several held breaths, neither saw the other. I was the only one who knew how close to disaster we all sat. Sera's head bobbed between the seats as she gathered her things, still oblivious. But her movement drew his eye.

The guard pulled a radio from his belt, swinging his rifle up with the other hand. But he couldn't aim one-handed, and since the intruder hadn't noticed him yet, policy dictated that he call for backup first.

I aimed.

I'm fast. But I'm not faster than the spoken word.

I could hear the static of his radio, but not what was said into it, or the reply that came back. I fired once. The gun *thwuped.* The guard tumbled backward and went down on the patio steps. I couldn't see his wound from where I stood, but I knew he was dead before he hit the ground, because I knew where I'd hit him. The middle of his forehead.

Sera still hadn't seen him, and more were surely on the way.

Shit! I glanced at the house. No activity yet. But that wouldn't last long.

Gun aimed at the ground to my left, I jogged across the grass and into the parking lot, where the light made me feel exposed. Naked. Vulnerable.

"Sera!" I hissed, but she didn't hear me. She was below seat-level again, doing something I couldn't see.

I scanned the back of the main house as I approached the car, then squatted next to the rear tire just as the back door of the house opened and two more guards came out. I pulled open the rear door of her car, and Sera's squeal of surprise was swallowed by the shouts of the guards as they discovered their coworker's body.

"It's me!" I hissed, and Sera exhaled. "We gotta go!"

"Okay, just let me…" she whispered, bending again to gather her things.

"Now!" I snapped, and she flinched. And that's when I realized what was taking her so long. She was gathering the photos that had fallen across the backseat and floorboard. Her mother's album was old and worn out. It had practically fallen apart in her hands.

They must have looked through it all the time. That thought nearly broke my heart.

But then there was more shouting. More footsteps. I peeked through the rear windshield to see that three guards had become five, and they were fanning out across the porch, handguns and rifles drawn, prepared to search the property. They wouldn't have to go far to find us.

"Sorry, Sera, but we have to go." I sank out of sight again. She peeked over the backseat, then dropped onto her heels in the floorboard, air wheezing in and out of her lungs.

"Shit!" she whispered. "Do you have another gun?"

"Can you shoot?"

She shook her head, but her hands were steady as she gathered the photos. "But I'm a fast learner."

"Good. I'll teach you—if we get out of here." I scooped the last of the loose photos into my left hand and dumped them into the computer bag she held open, then took it from her and slung the strap over my shoulder. I helped her out of the car—awkward, with us both squatting— then carefully, silently closed the door.

Then I peeked around the end of the car.

There were too many of them. They were all armed. Even if they were all horrible shots—and they wouldn't be—they were close enough that it would take more effort for them to avoid hitting us than to hit us.

"Change of plans. Give me your keys."

"What?" Her eyes were huge again. But her voice was steady. "We can't drive out of here!"

"We can't walk out, either, unless you've decided your body didn't come with enough holes in it." And that wasn't possible, because her body was *perfect*. My job was to keep it that way.

She peeked through the rear window again, then dropped into a squat with her back against the car, eyes wide. "What's the plan?"

"Give me your keys. Crawl into the backseat and stay down on the floorboard. I'll drive us into the dark, then we get out and shadow-walk into the closet."

She nodded. "Sounds easy enough."

"Except for the part where you lose your car to a storm of bullet holes."

"Can bullets penetrate a car?"

"*This* car? Yeah. So stay down. Ready?"

"No."

"Too bad." I plucked the keys from her hand and pulled open the back door. Three of the guards' heads swiveled in our direction, but they weren't at the right angle to see the open door.

Sera climbed onto the rear floorboard, then pulled the door mostly closed. I opened the front passenger door and crawled across the bucket seats, banging my knee on the center console. The interior light came on. And that's when the bullets began to fly.

Rifles are loud. So is the collision of bullet and car.

Bent almost in half, I stepped on the brake pedal and shoved Sera's key into the ignition. I turned the key, and when her engine growled to life, I shifted into Drive and stomped on the gas without even peeking through the windshield. It was a straight shot into the yard. The blissfully dark yard.

But I forgot about the curb. Tower's stupid backyard parking lot had a stupid fucking curb all the way around it.

The front tires slammed into the raised concrete then rolled over it. My chest hit the steering wheel and Sera hit the back of my seat.

She screamed as more bullets ripped through the trunk. Several shattered the rear windshield and lodged in the headrest of the driver's seat, and I hoped she'd stayed down and the bullets had all gone up.

I stomped the gas pedal again, and as soon as night washed over the windshield, I swerved sharply to the right and slammed the gearshift into Park. "Out!" I shouted as bullets ripped through the passenger side of the car. I dove out the driver's door and rolled onto the grass as Sera's door opened.

She crawled out onto the grass, shaking, and I pulled her up by one arm, pinning her computer bag between us when the strap fell off my shoulder. More bullets flew, but most of the guards were shooting handguns. Bigger bullets, but less power.

"Give me your hand!" I said, pulling her farther into the dark.

"What?"

"I have to be touching your skin." But all I could find was her sleeve.

She fumbled in the dark, but couldn't catch my hand, so I shoved the computer bag at her and picked her up as though giving her a bear hug, one hand sliding beneath the back of her shirt.

Two steps later, the air changed. Silence descended with the weight of my own conscience, and we collided with the closed closet door. Sera fumbled with the knob and the door flew open before I was ready. We fell to a heap on the hall floor. When I looked up, I found three different guns aimed at our heads.

Gazes focused on us. Tensed postures relaxed. Everyone seemed to exhale in relief all at once. Kori, Ian and Liv holstered their guns, and Liv bent to offer Sera a hand up. "I take it you didn't get the car."

I stood and brushed off my pants, then picked Sera's computer bag up from where it had fallen on the floor. "I'm just happy that we made it out unshot." I handed Sera's bag to her and her eyes widened. Instead of taking it, she unzipped it while I still held it and pulled out her laptop. Or, what remained of her laptop. A bullet had punctured the computer's case and lodged in some part of its electronic guts.

"Seriously?" Her forehead was deeply furrowed. "I've known you for all of four hours, and you've managed to destroy my phone, my car and now my computer. If I didn't know any better, I'd say you were still trying to cut me off from the outside world."

"Would it help to remind you that your computer died a noble death, in defense of both our lives?"

She snatched her bag from me, busted laptop and all. "No. That wouldn't help. If I'd never met you, my life wouldn't need defending." With that, she turned and marched into the living room where she sat next to Hadley, pretending to watch TV while silent tears rolled down her face.

Kori gave me a silent, brow-raised look as she pushed the closet door closed behind me.

"I don't think she likes me, Kor."

"Yeah, I can't figure that out. You're the friendliest kidnapper I've ever met." My sister shrugged. "She probably hates puppies, too."

That night, after Anne and Hadley had gone home, Vanessa loaned Sera something to sleep in and Kori dug out an extra toothbrush from the linen closet and told her to help herself to any toiletries she needed from the bathroom. While Sera showered, I sat backward in my sister's desk chair, conferring with Kori and Ian in their bedroom.

It was nearly twice the size of mine, and the bed looked all rumpled and…used. I tried not to think about that. At all. Ever.

"I asked Van to do a search for murdered families with a survivor named Sera," Kori whispered, even though we could all hear the shower running. "If she doesn't find anything in the immediate area, she'll widen the search."

"She won't find anything local." I laid my arms over the back of the chair, my voice almost as low as hers. "Sera's definitely not a city mouse."

"Or so she'd have us think." Kori's gaze narrowed on me. "Do you believe her?"

"About everything? No. About that? Yes. Anne says she's hiding something, and we have no reason not to trust Anne. But I believe Sera doesn't know the city and truly has no clue about the Towers."

Ian sank onto the love seat in front of a large window. My room had only one small window, and no couch. "Do you trust her?"

That was a more complicated question. "I don't know."

"That's kind of a 'no' by default." Kori shrugged. "Either you trust her, or you don't."

"I don't trust her *yet*." But I wanted to. And I wanted her to trust me.

Ian pulled Kori down with him on the couch. "Maybe we'll be able to once we figure out who the hell she is."

"Crossing my fingers for Vanessa on that account," I said, and Kori gave me that same I'm-laughing-at-you-but-you're-too-dumb-to-know-it grin she'd been using on me since the sixth grade.

"Cross your fingers for yourself." She glanced at Ian and he smiled. "If I had any money, I'd bet that you'll get her talking long before Van can dig up anything reliable."

"Kor, Sera hates me."

My sister's smile refused to die, and if it weren't so good to see her happy—even at my expense—I might have tried to rid her of it. "Maybe. But you're the only one she's really spoken to so far, other than Hadley. That has to mean something."

But I had my doubts.

Ian shrugged. "Either way, we're safer with her here, unless she's a mole planted by Julia Tower." But if that were the case, Anne would have known Sera was lying.

"We may be safer. But Kenley isn't," Kori said, and the mood in the room sobered instantly. We hadn't forgotten about her—not even for a second—but hearing her name brought all our anger, fear and frustration to the surface.

Ian put one arm around her. "We'll get her back, Kori. But there's nothing we can do for her tonight, and we won't be much good to her tomorrow without some rest. So kick your brother out of here, so we can all get some sleep."

"Get out, brother, so we can all get some sleep," Kori said, obviously struggling to maintain the illusion of optimism.

I stood, already backing toward the door. "You *have* to stop using 'sleep' as a euphemism."

I closed the door on their soft laughter and began my first-floor security scan, specifically checking on the window Ian had covered, which now felt safer than the ones that still held glass. Then I checked on Gran, who was snoring on her left side, and on the hall closet, which stood wide open, lit from within by a bare bulb hanging from the ceiling.

All the other rooms held a single infrared bulb in a floor lamp with no shade. We kept them on all the time as a security precaution. They shed no visible light, but kept the darkness too shallow for shadow-walkers to utilize.

Upstairs, Van was clicking away at her laptop in the room at the end of the hall, and I knew without asking that she wouldn't get much sleep, in spite of the late hour. Not with Kenley missing. But at least she'd found something constructive to do with the time.

When I was sure everything was secure and everyone was safe—except for Kenley—I headed into my own room. Then stopped cold with my hand still on the door-knob.

Sera stood naked in the middle of the floor with her back to me, a towel in her left hand, a T-shirt in her right.

For about half a second, I had a stunning, unimpeded view of one of the most beautiful sights I'd ever seen. She was slim, and soft and every curve on her body seemed designed to fit into my hand, or under my lips, or into my mouth…

Then she half-turned and saw me, and if she hadn't choked on surprise, she'd surely have screamed loud enough to break every pane of glass in the house. Fear flashed behind her eyes for just an instant, replaced almost immediately by blazing fury as she dropped the shirt and clutched the towel to her chest, its hem grazing her toes.

"Get out!" she screeched, and my confusion manifested as anger, which I probably had little right to express.

"This is my room."

"Oh, Kris?" Kori called from the room next door. "I forgot to tell you I gave Sera your room. Sorry!" But she wasn't sorry. That was *not* the tone of regret.

"You gave her…" Irritation burned in my cheeks and I turned to Sera, who'd wrapped the towel around herself and was tucking the loose corner between her breasts. I'd never wanted to be a towel so badly in my *life*. "So you're not…"

She rolled her eyes, one hand resting on the footboard of *my* bed. "You can't be serious. You thought I came up here to throw myself at you?"

I shrugged and leaned against the doorjamb, scrambling for composure to hide any sign that I'd liked what I'd seen. "It's happened before."

Her glare grew colder and she crossed both arms over the front of the towel, a secondary barrier between the two of us. "I promise, if I throw something at you, it's gonna hurt."

"Well, what was I supposed to think? There's a naked woman in my room."

"A woman you kidnapped, interrogated and conscripted into your mission, then dragged into the line of fire. Again. You're supposed to think, 'Gee, the least she deserves is a place to sleep and a little privacy.'"

I couldn't really argue with that. "So, what…" I asked, loud enough for Kori to hear. "I get the couch?" We all knew she was listening in anyway.

"Unless you think you can talk Gran out of her bed," my sister called back, and I could still hear repressed laughter in her voice.

"This is because I'm a guy, right?" I crossed the room and grabbed the duffel bag I'd been living out of for more than three months. "Girls never take the couch." And Ian and Kori wouldn't both fit on the one downstairs, which only left me…

"You're such a gentleman." Sarcasm dripped like venom from Sera's lips. "I'm *floored* by your hospitality. Now, would you please get the hell out of my room so I can put some clothes on?"

"No one's stopping you." And instead of leaving, I started loading my stuff into my bag. My stuff didn't amount to much—deodorant, a comb, a bag of unshelled peanuts I'd been munching from for two days.

I was halfway down the hall, the door already closed at my back, when I remembered Elle's sleep journal. *Shit.* If Sera found that, she'd think I was rude *and* crazy.

At the bedroom door again, I knocked twice. "Fair warning. I'm coming in."

"Just a second," she called. And that meant she was still naked. Or still partially naked. Maybe pulling her shirt over her head at that very moment.

My imagination was good and my memory was even

better, and I couldn't purge the mental image of her facing away from me, tugging a T-shirt over her bare back, where it hung down to hips that could make a man *weep*.

"Okay. Come in."

I opened the door. She was fully dressed in a T-shirt and shorts. *Damn*.

"What, one invasion of privacy wasn't enough?" She propped both hands on those hips, and my gaze stuck there for a second. "Three strikes and you're out."

"So, I get one more?" I was kidding. Trying to make light of the fact that my subconscious seemed determined to sabotage my efforts to not think about her naked by constantly showing me images of her naked. But she didn't look amused. "Sorry. I forgot something."

I stomped past her to the nightstand and quickly realized she wasn't going to look away while I removed the very private contents. But I guess I deserved that, considering how much of her I'd seen in the past five minutes alone.

Sera watched me shove the notebook into my bag, but didn't comment. "Night," I said as I closed the door behind me for the second time, and if she replied, I couldn't hear her.

For almost a minute, I stood outside the room, leaning against the door, fighting the urge to go back in. To say… something. Something brilliant, and funny, and without any kidnapper or peeping-perv overtone.

Whatever it took to make her stop hating me again.

I couldn't stand knowing that a couple of hours earlier, she'd smiled at me in the thick of enemy territory, yet here, where she was safe, fed, clothed and tucked into my bed without me, she hated me all over again.

But I was all out of brilliant and I'd never been very funny, so with a frustrated growl, I clutched Elle's notebook to my chest, pushed memories of both her and Sera from my mind, and stomped down the stairs to where the only arms waiting to hold me belonged to the cold, lumpy couch.

Nine

Sera

I slept like crap in the unfamiliar bed, and twice I woke up to the sound of someone crying, but I was too tired and disoriented to tell who it was.

Several hours later, I woke to find myself immersed in some kind of twisted Rockwellian family portrait. The kitchen table was crowded with stacks of pancakes, piles of bacon and three different kinds of syrup—none of them sugar-free. While Gran refilled mugs of coffee with a grease-stained apron tied around her waist, my new, heavily armed acquaintances loaded plates with fat and processed carbs, then headed into the living room to seats that seemed to have been assigned long before I'd joined the gang.

They spoke around full mouths, tossing out ideas about where to look for Kenley, speaking over one another, traipsing in and out of the kitchen to refill plates the whole time. I gave up trying to follow the conversation after a few minutes, and the second time a strip of bacon was snatched from the platter an instant before I would have taken it, I started guarding my breakfast with my elbow, like a basketball player.

"You have to be quick around here, if you wanna eat." Gran patted my shoulder, then tossed a grease-soaked paper plate into the trash. "A little aggression doesn't hurt, either. I swear, it's a miracle Kenley never starved to death, timid little thing. Not that they'd've let that happen. Kori always fixed her plate first, then ran her out of the kitchen so she wouldn't get trampled."

My family had been smaller. Quieter. Healthier eaters. Yet despite the differences, being surrounded by someone else's family made me miss mine *desperately*.

After breakfast, I helped wash the dishes, then settled into a chair at the deserted table with my ruined computer bag. I'd been sorting through the remains of my memories—my mother's photographs—for about ten minutes when Gran put a fresh mug of coffee on the table in front of me and asked me how long I'd known her daughter Nikki. Vanessa came to my rescue by distracting her, and I retreated back into my shell. Remembering. Mourning. Staring into the faces of my past around the bullet holes shot through several of the irreplaceable photographs and into my computer.

Vaguely, I heard life going on around me. Kris and Kori argued as if they were still in middle school and Ian played peacemaker as though he'd been born for the job. Vanessa alternately fretted over Kenley and raged at the bastards who would dare lay a hand on her, swearing vengeance with a furor I could never have imagined from the delicately grieving girlfriend the day before.

Olivia, the Tracker, stopped in for a bit to plot with the others, but then she was called away, either by Ruben Cavazos, her mafia-boss employer, or Cam Caballero, her mafia-employed boyfriend. I wasn't sure which. I didn't really care. All I could think about was that my vengeance had been put on hold while I sat there with nothing to do but remember, passively shielding the motley gang of violent do-gooders who'd promised to do violent good for me. Eventually.

My coffee had long since grown cold when Kris pulled out the chair next to mine and sat without asking or waiting for a welcome. "You okay? You don't have to sit in here by yourself, you know."

But I wasn't alone. I was with my family, the only way I could be now. When I didn't answer, he watched me in silence for a few minutes, and several times he took a deep breath, as if he might actually say whatever he'd come to say. But then he'd glance at the photographs and seem reluctant to invade my mourning ritual.

Then, after several more minutes and another glance at his watch, he started talking.

"Hey. I know this may not be a good time, but I have to ask you a couple of questions."

"I'm done answering questions." I sorted a picture of Nadia in her third-grade Halloween costume into a stack of others from that year.

"These aren't personal, I swear. They're work-related. Since you're working with us now."

I exhaled and picked up a picture of my dad playing his guitar. My eyes watered. "Fine."

"What's your range, approximately?"

"My range?" I looked up from my pictures to meet his gaze and discovered, now that the major light source was the incandescent bulb overhead, that his eyes were more blue than gray—the sun had long since stopped shining through the east windows. I'd been staring at pictures for half the day.

"Yeah. How far away from a person do you have to

be to...jam him? His signal, I mean." He closed his eyes and shook his head, then started over. "His psychic signal. How close do you have to be to a guy to make sure no one can Track him?"

I glanced at the single foot of space separating us. "Not this close."

Kris's cheeks actually flushed. Across the kitchen Kori laughed out loud and her brother glared at her. "I mean, assuming you're at the center of a vaguely spherical psychic dead zone, for lack of a better term, what's the diameter of your influence? How far can you spread your wings, so to speak?"

"I have no idea."

"Seriously?" Kori took the first bite of a candy bar, then spoke around it. "You seriously don't know the extent of your own abilities?"

"How is that possible?" Kris asked, and when I noticed Ian and Vanessa watching us from the kitchen doorway, I realized story-hour had commenced.

I shrugged. "My family wasn't Skilled. I didn't even know I was Skilled until I was nearly eighteen."

Kris whistled, looking impressed, though I wasn't sure why.

Ian crossed his arms over his chest. "Steven and I knew practically from birth. But then, our mom was pretty paranoid."

"Our parents didn't tell us until Kris started demonstrating Skills, but that was way earlier than eighteen," Kori said, and I wondered how old they'd been when their parents had died.

"That's the thing." I slid the photos back from the edge of the table so they wouldn't fall, unsure of who to look at as I addressed the entire room. "I'm a Jammer. I didn't accidentally walk through the shadows in my own room, or suddenly start calling my friends liars. Jamming is really a whole lot of nothing. Literally. I don't even do it on purpose. It just kind of...follows me."

"So you can't control it?" Vanessa's gaze flicked to Kori. "Didn't you say some Jammers can turn it off?"

Kori nodded, still watching me. "And some can restrict or expand their zone. You probably could, too, if you tried it."

"Maybe." But I'd never had any interest in narrowing my zone of influence, because I'd never wanted to be found.

"So, if your family isn't Skilled, how are *you* Skilled?" Van asked, and I remembered that she had no Skill. She probably knew less about the whole thing than I did. Though that hardly seemed possible.

I picked up a photo of me with Nadia and my parents, and handed it to Kris, who studied it for one long moment, then passed it around. "My mom had me before she met my dad. She and my dad are—were—unSkilled, but my biological father wasn't."

When everyone had had a look at my heartbreak, Van handed the photo back to me. Everyone was somber now, out of respect for my loss.

"So, what about him?" Kris seemed to be studying my eyes, like he could read more in them than I would say aloud. "Your biological dad?"

"I never met him." And since Anne was gone, I had no trouble leaving it at that—a technical truth hiding an even deeper one.

"Okay." Kris cleared his throat, bringing us back on task, whatever that task was—and there was now obviously a point to this line of questioning. Which had turned personal after all. "Since we don't know your range and we don't have time to figure it out now, we'll need you to come with us."

"Come with you where?"

"To get Kenley back." Vanessa said it as if it should have been obvious. "We think we know where they're keeping her."

"Why are they keeping her alive, exactly?" I regretted the question almost immediately. I'd just lost my whole family. I should have been more sensitive to their potential loss. "Sorry. I just… The Towers haven't demonstrated any particular respect for human life, that I've seen, and no one's actually explained why they need Kenley alive."

"They can't kill her." Kris glanced at Kori and Ian, who were leaning against the counter, side by side. They both nodded, so he continued. "Kenley sealed the contracts that bound Jake Tower's employees to him. The bindings Julia Tower inherited when he died."

Whoa…

I stared at the table, trying to hide my stunned reaction. "You can inherit someone else's bindings?"

Kris shrugged. "Only under certain circumstances."

"With very well-thought-out contracts," Kori added.

Ian took her hand. "And the strength of one of the world's best binders."

"So…what you're saying is that when Jake Tower died, his sister inherited all of the bindings that tied his employees to him? So they're now *her* employees?" I'd known she'd taken over the business, but I'd assumed any employees blood bound to her had taken the oath voluntarily, after Jake died. But if I understood what they were saying, none of those employees had been given any choice in the matter. Their contracts had been transferred *without their approval*.

"Yes," Kori said. "Which means she can't kill Kenley without losing nearly every employee she has."

But I hardly heard her. That made no sense. Why would Jake leave his employees to his sister, but his business assets—properties and capital, presumably—to his oldest living heir?

He wouldn't. He *wouldn't* leave the employees to Julia and the cash and infrastructure to…me. Those bindings were *part* of his business holdings. They had to be.

I sat back in my chair, stunned.

I hadn't just inherited money and buildings, and whatever dummy corporations they were shielded by. I'd inherited *people*. Dozens of them. Hundreds, maybe.

I'd inherited the fucking mafia!

With sudden, nearly blinding clarity, I understood why Julia had wanted me to sign away any claim to my inheritance and why, when that fell through, she'd been willing to kill me. As long as I lived, the Tower empire wouldn't truly be hers.

Kris saw the shock on my face and shifted uncomfortably in his chair. "I know. It's kind of creepy to think about." But he didn't know. Not what *I* knew, anyway. "But those bindings are the only thing keeping Kenley breathing, and that'll only last until Julia has a chance to rebind the employees to her directly, using another Binder. Cutting both Jake and Kenley out of the process. She's already started, and once she's finished, she won't need Kenley alive."

"Under normal circumstances, she wouldn't be able to rebind them," Vanessa said. "We all signed non-competition clauses from the start. But since she'd be rebinding them to the same organization, just under different leadership, the noncompetition clause doesn't seem to be functioning like we'd like it to." She shrugged thin shoulders. "Or at all. Fortunately, it'll take her a while to break all the bindings and institute new ones, making Kenley completely obsolete."

"Okay. Give me a minute." I gripped the edge of the table. My head was spinning. The whole damn *room* was spinning. "How sure are you that Julia Tower inherited all that from her brother?"

Kori and Kris glanced at one another and something unspoken passed between them, but it was his sister who answered. "Trust me—Jake's people would never follow orders from Julia unless they had to."

Okay, that made sense. But nothing else seemed to. I needed more information, but I couldn't outright ask for it. "Why would he leave everything to his sister instead of his wife? Or his kids?" What I really wanted to know was how Julia had wound up with what he'd intended to leave to his children.

"He left some stuff to Lynn," Kori said. "Personal stuff. The house is hers, but Julia gets to live and operate there, because it's always been the home base of the syndicate. But Jake would never have left business stuff to Lynn. She knows next to nothing about what he does, other than that it's illegal, immoral and pays very, very well."

"And technically, he did leave the business to his kids. The oldest, anyway." Kris looked disgusted by the mention of the little…rascal. "His name's Kevin. But he can't inherit until he's twenty-one, and until then, Julia has total control."

"Power of attorney?" That would explain her obvious authority.

"More like regent." Kris scooted his chair closer to the table and met my gaze with a solemn one of his own. "No one thinks either of Jake's kids will make it to twenty-one. Julia can't afford to let that happen. She's not allowed to hurt them, or outright ask anyone else to, but she had the same restrictions with Jake and still managed to have him assassinated."

Everyone glanced at Ian, who nodded solemnly—Julia had used him to kill her brother.

"How do you know all this?" Surely the Towers hadn't advertised the terms of Jake's will…

"Kenley." Kris smiled at the mention of her name. "She bound Julia as the executor of his will."

The executor. Not the beneficiary. So why were his guards still following her orders, if their bindings actually belonged to me? Because they hadn't been formally introduced to the true heir? Because the will hadn't yet been properly executed? Because I hadn't claimed my inheritance?

Whatever the reason, Julia couldn't afford for me to inherit. She'd keep trying to kill me—likely as collateral damage in the fight against the Daniels clan—until she succeeded.

If Kris hadn't kidnapped me, would I be dead already? Had I been minutes away from a bullet to the brain, that day in her office?

I wasn't sure enough of that to give him credit for saving my life, instead of nearly getting me killed. But I *was* sure that there was nowhere else in the city safer for me at that moment than with this band of heavily armed criminals—now that they'd decided not to kill me themselves.

But they would kill me in a heartbeat, if they found out I was the new head of the Tower syndicate.

Ten

Kris

On my way down from the upstairs bathroom, I glanced into the room that used to be mine and saw Sera staring at herself in the mirror. Just…staring.

"You okay?" I stopped in the doorway, hesitant to enter without permission, since a third strike would mean I was out. And whether or not I was ready to admit it, I very much wanted to be *in*.

She shrugged and met my gaze in the mirror. "I don't know what one wears on a covert mission. Not that I have many options." She held her arms out, inviting me to look. "Is this okay?"

"*Waaay* better than okay." The black top and dark jeans were Kori's, but Sera filled them out…better. So well, in fact, that I tried to forget they were my sister's clothes. "Doesn't matter, though. If this thing goes like we expect it to, it'll be less about stealth than about speed and brute force."

Still watching me in the mirror, she pulled her long brown hair into a high ponytail, and suddenly she looked eighteen years old. Young and vulnerable. Except for her eyes. The gaze that stared back at me in the mirror was ancient and war-wearied. Scarred. Which made a brutal kind of sense, now that I knew what had happened to her family.

She turned back to her own reflection. "So, what do you need me to do?"

"Just come with us." I stepped into the room, and when she didn't object, I took three more steps and half sat on the edge of the desk that had been mine a day and a half ago. "You don't even have to pick up a gun."

"In fact, we're not gonna give you one." My sister appeared in the doorway, and Sera turned to face us both. "Kris says you can't shoot."

"I said she can't shoot *yet*. But I'll teach her."

Kori shrugged, arms crossed over her chest. "If you're not planning to teach her in the next ten minutes, she's not getting a gun."

"Ten minutes?" Sera stepped into the boots she'd been wearing when I'd pulled her through the shadows in Tower's supply closet, and I made a mental note to take her shopping. She deserved clothes of her own. And for my own comfort, I really needed to see her in something my sisters had never worn.

"Yeah. Kori says they have fewer employees on hand after 6:00 p.m."

Sera's eyes widened and she glanced at the alarm clock on the nightstand. *My* nightstand. "How did it get so late? I think I forgot to eat lunch." Before I could offer her a snack, she sat on the bed to zip her boots and looked up at me. "Employees of what? Where are we going?"

"Well…" I glanced behind me, expecting Kori to answer, since she'd actually been where we were headed, but she was gone. "It's a pharmaceutical company. Of sorts. Only you don't want the kind of drugs they make."

* * *

"Why does a pharmaceutical company have a dark-room?" Sera whispered, still holding my hand in the dark. Kori and Ian stood less than a foot in front of us. I couldn't see them, but I could hear them breathing. Hell, I could practically feel their body heat in the cramped quarters.

"The drugs produced here are very…special," I whispered, fighting the urge to squeeze her hand, to run my thumb over the back of hers. Sera made me hungry for something I couldn't define—couldn't even understand—and each moment I spent with her made that craving worse. Yet the moments spent away from her didn't ease the urge.

I let go of Sera before I could embarrass myself, and for a second she let her hand hang between us, as if the release had caught her by surprise. Which is when I realized I hadn't done a damn thing right since the moment I'd met her.

"Keep in mind that 'special' doesn't imply legality or ethics," Kori added just as softly as I'd spoken.

Sera shifted her feet next to me. "So, how do we get out of the darkroom without alerting security?" Secure darkrooms have no interior doorknobs, as a precaution. Under normal circumstances, someone in the control room would have to buzz us into the building, but in this particular case, they were more likely to gas us through specialized vents in the ceiling.

We could shoot our way out, as I'd done at the Tower estate, but that would kill any hope of a stealthy entry.

"Have I mentioned that I'm a Blinder?" Ian's whisper was somehow even deeper than his normal voice.

Sera chuckled. "Yeah."

"Have we mentioned that he's the best in the country?" Kori added.

"Okay, we're all ready," Ian said before Sera could answer. A second later, he and my sister were gone, though in the absence of light, I felt, rather than saw them leave.

"What happened?" Sera's whisper held an edge of fear. In answer, I fumbled for her hand again—and got her hip instead. I thought she'd yell at me, but she just took my hand and held on tight, and I realized she'd figured out the plan. I tugged her forward, through the darkness Ian had produced, and two steps later, the echo of our soft footsteps changed when our boots hit the floor in the hall, which was just as dark as the adjacent darkroom had been.

That time, before I released her hand, I squeezed it in the intimate semi-privacy of near-total darkness.

The shadows around us faded completely in less than a second and a glance around revealed only a sterile white hallway, lined with doors. Sera turned and found the darkroom door behind us, marked and missing its exterior doorknob, as well, as only the most high-security rooms were.

"What the hell just happened?" she demanded, in spite of the finger I pressed against my lips, reminding her to keep it quiet. "I thought you were taking us into some other darkroom."

"There aren't any other darkrooms in the building. The whole place is fitted with an infrared grid." I gave her a smile. "Good thing we have Ian, huh?"

She glanced at him and nodded, and Kori leaned closer to whisper. "He can throw darkness through walls. Comes in handy."

Sera nodded, eyes wide.

Kori led the way, silently pointing out video cameras

as we went. Even unspoken, her point was clear. If someone was watching those monitors, we were screwed. But unless their alarm was the silent kind, so far, the coast was clear. Yet that put me even more on edge, because it made no sense. We'd expected to have to fight our way to Kenley.

Halfway down the next hall, I stepped closer to Kori and whispered into her ear. "Where is everyone? This is weird."

"I know. I expected the traffic to be light, but not nonexistent."

"We've walked into either a trap or a truly abandoned building."

She nodded solemnly. "We can either push forward or go home."

We weren't going home without Kenley. I gestured down the hall for her to lead on. "Just be prepared for anything."

She nodded again and stood on her toes to whisper in my ear. "Ian and I will take point. You watch out for Sera. A damsel in distress is always the weakest link."

Sera was far from helpless—the still-healing cuts on my arm were proof of that. But I would gladly watch out for her.

After several turns and an unlocked white door, then another Ian-assisted shadow-walk through a locked door, we came to a third door with a different, more complicated-looking finger-print pad/pass-code lock. "We'll go first and disable whoever's on duty, then open the door for you guys." Kori's shoulders were stiff with tension, her arms taut, her jaw clenched. My heart beat harder in response to her anxiety.

We were close.

In minutes, we could have Kenley, and she could be

just fine, and maybe she would forgive me for losing her in the first place.

"I'm sure she's okay," Sera whispered, and I looked up to find her watching me with big, worried eyes, her beautiful mouth turned down in what I first mistook for sympathy. But it was more than that. Deeper. I was seeing empathy. Sera had already been where Kori and I were, and her sister hadn't been okay.

I was so tense I could hardly breathe as Ian called up a small, precise cone of darkness. A second later, he, Kori and that darkness were all gone.

Sera and I waited, listening anxiously for the thud of impact or the *thwup* of a silenced gun. But the only sound was the click of the door lock as it disengaged. Kori pulled the door open with a scowl, then ushered us inside.

"What happened?"

In answer, she gestured toward the room they'd just broken into, which was empty except for a single long table scattered with loose sheets of paper. There were no employees. No other furniture. And no Kenley.

I was willing to bet that the papers they'd left behind held no useful information at all.

A glass panel in one wall overlooked another, much larger, even emptier space.

"This was the observation room." Then Kori pointed through the window, and I peered into the empty space, wondering if our sister had ever been there. Or had we been barking up the wrong tree from the beginning? "That's where they kept the vegetables."

"Vegetables?" Sera stared through the window, gripping the edge of the table so tightly her knuckles had gone white. "Why do I get the feeling you don't mean roots and tubers?"

"She's talking about human vegetables." The words

hurt to say. They hurt even worse to think about as my gaze caught on a length of medical tubing abandoned on the floor in the next room. "Only Tower wasn't growing them. He was bleeding them."

"Bleeding?" Sera's voice was brittle, as though it might actually break. "I'm not sure I want to know what that means."

"Jake collected people whose Skills he wanted and kept them in medically induced comas so he could take blood from them as often as possible, without actually killing them."

Sera blinked at me. "He collected...people?"

"And bled them." Kori pulled a string next to the windowsill and blinds dropped to cover the window, as if that could actually erase the memory of what she'd once seen through it. What I'd imagined. "Then he sold their blood as transfusions, intended to give the receiver temporary Skills. At significant cost."

I sank onto the edge of the table, struggling to breathe through my own disappointment. "Or for an equivalent investment of information."

Sera trailed her fingers down the closed blinds. The metallic rattle was loud after the eerie silence of the deserted building. "Information?"

"Tower also collected names and blood samples from anyone he might one day want to manipulate. Or blackmail. Or profit from."

Sera looked sick. Pale. Disgusted. And a little... guilty? Why would she feel guilty? I was the one who'd lost Kenley. "Is there any crime Jake Tower didn't commit as a matter of course?"

Kori shrugged. "I never saw him jaywalk."

"So, why did you think Kenley would be here?" Sera

picked up a sheet of paper, glanced at it, then dropped it on the table.

"Because Julia would have to keep her nearby and under close watch. The blood farm seemed like the ideal place," Kori said. "But it's gone." The devastation in her voice made my throat ache with every curse I held back. Every angry word I swallowed.

We'd thought we were close. We'd come determined to take out any- and everyone who stood between us and our baby sister, but there was no one to shoot.

Worse, there was no one to rescue.

"She moved the whole operation." Kori stared at the covered window in shock, and I realized she wasn't just stating the obvious. She was trying to *process* the obvious. Our failure. I'd been there over and over in the past six years, since Noelle died and my sisters were both conscripted into the Tower syndicate.

It never got any easier.

"We shouldn't be surprised," Ian said. "Julia's no idiot." He'd warned us from the beginning that Kenley might not be there. That the entire operation might have been moved, or she might have shut it down. But we'd had to try, and in my heart, I'd believed we'd find her.

I'd *needed* to find her.

"Okay, so let's find out where she moved them. There has to be something…." Kori picked up a sheet of paper from the table, scanned it, then tossed it aside and picked up another. She went through page after page, but most were blank and none of them held anything of meaning for her. The documents they'd left behind would only be useful as paper airplanes. A whole squadron of them.

"Kori," I said when she got to the end of the pages and started again, squatting to examine them on the floor. She didn't even acknowledge me.

"Kori." I knelt and put a hand on her shoulder, but she flinched and pulled away from me, and another crack widened in my heart. She didn't seem to recognize me. She seemed...scared of me.

I'd never seen Kori scared of *anything*.

I stood and gave her some space, because I didn't know what else to do, and Ian stepped into my place. He knelt in front of Kori and put one dark hand on the paper she was still clutching.

"Kori." He didn't try to touch her. He just waited for her to realize he was there. "Korinne. Look at me."

Finally, she looked up. She blinked, and there were tears in her eyes, and my chest ached as though someone had ripped my heart out and left the wound gaping open. "I lost her," Kori said. "I'm supposed to protect her, and I *lost* her."

"No, Kor, *I* lost her." I couldn't stand to see her like this. She looked so...hopeless. "But we're going to find her. And she's going to be fine."

"No, she won't." Kori turned on me, eyes blazing with anger, and Sera took a step back. "You have no idea what Julia will do to her if Kenley pisses her off. If *we* piss her off. She has to keep Kenni alive, but that doesn't mean she won't let them hurt her."

Them?

Kori ran one hand through her hair, then gripped a handful of it. "I know where she is," she whispered, and chill bumps popped up all over my arms. Ian shook his head, but she didn't even notice. "You know where."

"No." He was still shaking his head. "She's not in the basement, Kori. Julia's not stupid. She knows that's the first place we'd look."

"But it wasn't. *This* is the first place we looked. And we were wrong, because she's in the basement."

My hands curled into fists at my sides and my stomach started to churn. I felt helpless watching them. But I was *so* glad Ian could comfort my sister when I couldn't.

"No, we were wrong because Julia moved the whole operation. Kenley's not in the basement," Ian insisted.

"We have to check." Kori's eyes were narrowed, her jaw set in a firm line. Ian nodded, Sera shot me a confused look, but I couldn't explain, because I didn't fully understand Kori's mental shift, other than that it stemmed from whatever she'd suffered at Tower's hands, whatever she thought they were now doing to Kenley.

"We will. We'll look everywhere," Ian promised. "But for now, let's get out of here." He wrapped one arm around Kori, and as grateful as I was that he was able to comfort her, I felt that his gain was my loss. I didn't know how to be there for her anymore, and that realization resonated deep inside me, an ache I couldn't ease.

"What basement?" Sera whispered in my direction.

Kori's head snapped up and her sharp gaze found Sera. "Hell. The basement in *hell*. That's where she put Kenley. I know it is."

"Okay. Let's go." Ian held his hand out, then waited for her to take it. Finally she did, and there was a shift in her eyes. Behind her eyes. She blinked, then seemed to stand straighter, stronger, just from being close to him. Her focus returned, and she was with us again, back from whatever psychological detour had claimed her moments before.

I started to smile and welcome her back. Then something moved on my right. With a jolt of alarm, I turned just as two large hands aimed a silenced pistol through the doorway from the hall. I pulled my gun, but Sera was closer. And faster. She threw one arm up beneath his wrists, trying to raise his aim so he'd hit the ceiling.

It almost worked.

A flash of light came from the barrel an instant before the muted *thwup* echoed through the small room.

Ian crumpled to the ground. Kori and I fired at the same time—I hadn't even seen her draw. I have no idea whose bullet actually did the job, but the shooter stumbled backward into the hallway, then slid down the opposite wall, leaving a single wide red smear on the white paint.

Out bullets had struck so close together—over his heart—that I could only see one hole.

In the shocked silence that followed, no one moved for at least a second. Sera gaped at me. Then at Kori. Then at the dead guy. Then she started breathing really, really fast.

"Sera? You okay?"

"Fuck her!" Kori holstered her gun and dropped to the ground at Ian's side, where blood dribbled between the fingers of the hand he held to his own shoulder. "I need something to— Give me your shirt!"

But that was easier said than done. I handed Sera my gun, and she held it like it might explode and kill us all. I shrugged out of my jacket, ripped off my holster and pulled my T-shirt over my head, then tossed it to Kori.

While she wadded it up and pressed it to Ian's wound, I stepped into the hall, glanced in either direction, then squatted next to the downed man and checked his neck for a pulse.

"Dead," I announced, stepping back into the observation room.

"Of course he's dead," Kori snapped, still pressing my shirt against the hole in Ian's shoulder. "Are there any more?"

"Not yet. He's security. If the entire building's empty,

he may be the only one here, guarding the cemetery, so to speak. Or so he thought."

Kori brushed hair from Ian's forehead, and even in the dim light, I could see that his dark complexion looked strangely washed out. "I have to get him out of here, but I don't have enough bleach to clean this up."

"Go," Sera said. Her eyes were still wide, but her focus was steady. She was still with me. "We'll take care of it. They have to have a supply closet, or something."

"You sure?" Kori flinched when Ian grimaced.

"Go!" I shrugged into my holster, which felt weird against my bare skin, and took my gun back from Sera. "The longer you stay, the more blood there is to destroy."

Kori stood and fired her silenced pistol into the ceiling twice. Glass shattered, obliterating both sets of lights, and I pulled Sera close, tucking her head against my shoulder to shield it. When the glass settled, I glanced up to see Kori doing the same thing for Ian. He still looked pale. He was losing a lot of blood.

Kori helped him to his feet while he held my bloody shirt to his wound with his opposite hand. Then she pulled him through the darkest corner of the room.

The moment they were gone, I headed into the hallway, with another glance in both directions, just in case.

"Will he be okay?" Sera asked as I tried doorknob after doorknob. Most were unlocked, and all of the rooms were empty, which seemed to verify the fact that the building had been completely deserted.

"Ian?" I said, and she nodded, moving to the next door on her side of the hall. "Probably. Shoulder wound. Through-and-through, from the looks of the blood on the wall behind him. Gran will get him all patched up. But if we don't destroy his blood, Julia will be able to use it against him, and Ian will *wish* he were dead."

I threw open another door and found a break room with three card tables set up on the left, opposite a wall-length counter on the right, complete with two microwaves and a full-size fridge.

I headed straight for a package of napkins abandoned on the counter, and Sera started to follow me, probably to search the cabinets. But then she noticed an open door beyond the first table, which hadn't been visible from the hall. It was a bathroom.

She veered into the restroom and knelt to open the cabinet beneath the sink as I started opening cabinets in the kitchenette.

"Don't move."

I froze, the package of napkins tucked under one arm. My pulse raced, and I hoped he was talking to me, not Sera.

"Turn around slowly and put your hands on the back of your head. You even *look* like you're gonna go for your gun, and I'll blow your fucking head off."

Bittersweet relief took the edge from the stress of knowing a gun was aimed at my back. He *had* to be talking to me. Sera was unarmed.

I turned slowly and considered letting the napkins fall, so I could go for my gun at the first opportunity. But if the shooter was jumpy, he'd open a hole in my chest before they even hit the ground.

A man in a security guard's uniform—matching the dead man's—stood in the middle of the break room, aiming his silenced pistol at me with his back to the bathroom. He hadn't seen Sera yet.

He was one of Julia's, just like the last guy. Ordinary security guards don't carry suppressors.

At his back, Sera slowly, silently set a bottle of bleach on the floor, then stood without a sound. I couldn't look directly at her without exposing her, and my peripheral vision wasn't good enough to tell what she was up to. Which made me nervous. She had a history of confronting gunmen—she'd demanded my gun and foiled the aim of the dead man in the hall—and if she got herself killed trying to help me, I would never forgive myself.

"Unsnap the gun pocket from your holster and set it down, then kick it across the floor to me." The guard's aim held steady at my chest. Behind him, Sera glanced around the bathroom, and I had a horrible hunch that she was looking for a weapon.

I lifted both brows at the gunman as Sera knelt to pick up a bottle of spray cleaner, and I hoped she'd understand that my response was actually aimed at her. "This is a little ridiculous," I said. "I don't need a gun to kill you." That last part, obviously, was for the bad guy.

"Humor me," he said. "Hand over the gun."

Sera silently turned the end of the nozzle, opening the spray bottle, and my heart began to beat too hard. What the hell was she planning to do, shine his bald spot?

When she picked up a toilet plunger and hefted it, testing the weight, I nearly groaned. The handle was too light to pack a punch, and the rubber part on the end would do about as much damage as the proverbial wet noodle.

Her boots were silent on the tile, as the guard watched me unsnap my gun pocket. Her last step squeaked on the floor, and my heart nearly burst through my chest when he heard her and turned, his aim shifting with the movement.

Sera swung the plunger at his arms, driving his aim down as she sprayed the cleaner in his face.

The guard screamed.

I fumbled, trying to pull my pistol from the partly detached pocket.

The guard's gun went off with a *thwack*. A chunk of linoleum tile exploded to my left, and my heart leaped into my throat as I lurched out of the fire zone. The gunman abandoned his two-handed grip to rub his eyes, still screaming, and Sera shoved the stick end of the plunger into his stomach with a wild grunt of effort.

The guard oofed and swung the gun toward her. She ducked below his blind aim just before the *thwack,* and the bullet slammed into the wall at my back.

I let go of the gun pocket, and it dangled from my holster by one snap as I launched myself at the blinded guard, trying to pull his gun away before he could fire again. Sera circled us, struggling to stay out of the line of fire as we fought over the weapon.

The gun went off twice more, and my heart stopped with each muffled shot, certain I'd just met my own death. Shooting the guard would have been easier than wrestling his gun from him, but he had to live long enough to be interrogated.

Still trying to avoid the kill zone, Sera bumped into the countertop next to the fridge, then turned to pull it open. It was empty, as was every drawer she tried. The only thing that wasn't nailed down, other than the furniture and the microwaves, was…

She grabbed the cheap four-slice toaster and jerked so hard the cord pulled free from its plug. *Stay back,* I thought, as she circled us, avoiding the gun we still fought over, looking for her chance.

When I understood that she wasn't going to stop trying to help until I'd gotten the guard's gun, I realized I'd have to work *with* her, instead of silently cursing her dangerous involvement. I jerked hard on the guard's wrists, avoiding his trigger finger, and swung him around in a half circle.

Sera pulled the toaster over her head. The cord dangled against her back. When the moment was right, she swung the toaster down with another grunt of effort, straight into the guard's shiny, bald head.

The guard grunted, then crumpled to the floor. I ripped the gun from his grip and clicked the safety switch. I exhaled slowly and took a moment to celebrate the fact that we were both still alive. And whole. Then I turned to Sera, latent anger and intense relief coursing through me in a complicated storm of emotion.

"What the *hell* were you thinking? You could have been killed."

Her eyes widened and her triumphant smile faded. "I just saved your ass!"

"I didn't ask you to!" I couldn't make sense of the tight feeling in the pit of my stomach, as if I'd just survived some massive free fall that should have killed me, but my organs hadn't yet adjusted to the landing. "You could have been killed."

Sera frowned. "You already said that."

"Because it keeps bothering me." The words hurt coming out; the truth was still too raw. "Don't *ever* do that again." And suddenly I understood what was wrong with me. Why my heart was beating so hard I could almost hear it, even after the fight was over.

I wasn't scared of Sera dying because it would have meant I'd failed to protect someone else. I was scared of her dying because I didn't want her to die. Or leave. Or spill even a drop of blood. The thought of her getting hurt left me furious and terrified, just like the thought of Kenley in Julia Tower's cruel hands. Except Sera wasn't my sister, a fact I grew more grateful for with each passing second.

But her eyes still blazed with fury.

"Fine. Next time I'll let the bad guy shoot you! Don't cry to me when you're bleeding out on the floor!" She started to turn away, already bending for the spray cleaner she'd dropped in favor of the toaster.

"Sera," I said, and she stood slowly, mad at me again, for about the billionth time since we'd met. "Thank you for not letting the bad guy shoot me."

Then I kissed her. Because I couldn't fucking resist.

Eleven

Sera

Kris kissed me, and for a second, I forgot that we'd broken into one of Julia's buildings—or was it *my* building?—taken down two of her security guards and could be assailed by another at any time. I even forgot how pissed off I was at how ungrateful *he* was for the fact that I'd just saved his bare torso from certain lethal perforation.

And I was hyperaware of just how bare that torso was, framed only by his shoulder holster—the strappiest accessory I'd ever seen a man wear. And damn, did he wear it well.

Then everything that was wrong with that moment came roaring back, and I shoved him away, trying not to notice how firm his chest felt beneath my hands. "Why did you do that?"

His brows rose, and a smile lurked at the corners of his mouth. Which I was definitely *not* staring at. "Why did you bash that man on the head with a toaster?"

"Because you needed help with him."

"And now I need to be kissed. Wanna give it another shot?"

"No." I was extraglad there was no Reader around to call me on my lie. "This isn't the time or the place…"

His grin developed slowly, like a Polaroid from my mom's old camera. "So, it's not kissing me you object to—it's the time and place?"

"I object to this entire conversation. We told Kori we'd destroy Ian's blood."

Kris nodded, but his smile wouldn't fully retreat, and I didn't entirely hate that fact. He looked at the man on the floor and kicked him in the side once, to make sure he was really unconscious. "Oh, good. He's still breathing."

I exhaled in relief. I'd never killed anyone, and though I would have done it if I had to, to protect someone I cared about, I was immeasurably relieved to have avoided the worst-case scenario.

Kris's smile was back in full force. "He's also covered with bread crumbs. As are you." His gaze traveled south of my collarbone and I looked down to find that the front of my shirt—mostly the upper curve of my breasts—was indeed dusted with bread crumbs from the toaster I'd hefted. "I'm pretty sure I'm either supposed to drop you in a deep fryer or broil you on high for an hour."

I picked up the toaster from where I'd dropped it, then set it on the nearest table. "Like you know the difference."

Kris chuckled at his own expense. "Nice shot, by the way, with the spray bottle. You're like some kind of ninja housekeeper." He set the guard's gun on the table next to my toaster. "There's a joke in there somewhere. It involves a French maid's uniform and a wide selection of deadly weapons disguised as ordinary mops and brooms."

"Are you seriously making fun of me after I just saved your ass?"

"I'm not making fun of you. I'm just enjoying a little

humor at your expense." He knelt next to the guard's arm and pulled a folding knife from his own pocket. Before I could object to the cold-blooded murder of an unconscious man, Kris pulled the guard's sleeve away from his upper arm and sliced through the material.

I blinked in surprise as he folded the knife, then returned it to his pocket and ripped the man's sleeve open wider, revealing two interlocking rust-colored rings.

"Binding marks?" My mother had taught me that much, but she hadn't known the specifics, for good reason—she'd kept us too far away from the Tower syndicate to glean more than could be learned by watching the news and scouring the internet to make sure there was never any mention of Jake's older, illegitimate child. "What does the color mean?"

Kris's brows rose in surprise. "You really did just fall off the turnip truck, huh?" I frowned, but before I could come up with an insult of my own, he continued, "You truly don't know?"

"I told you, I don't work for the Towers. I never met any of them until two days ago." Two unbelievably long days ago.

"I'm actually starting to believe that." He let go of the man's sleeve, but left it gaping over the tattoos. "Okay, here's your Skilled syndicate primer. A term is five years long, and for each term you commit to, you get one ring, up front. The ink is usually mixed with the blood of either the Binder or the head of the syndicate—in this case, Jake Tower—to bind it in blood. This guy has two rings, so he's served his first five years and is somewhere in the middle of his second enlistment. When that term's over—or his binding is broken by other means—the marks will fade instantly to a dull gray. We call those dead marks."

"And the color?" I repeated, pleased to realize I'd followed his explanation with no trouble.

"Rust-colored rings, like this one, mean unSkilled labor, no matter what job the bearer holds. Secretaries, bodyguards, tech, clerks, lawyers, whatever. If you have no Skill, your mark is rust-colored. Except for those in the…um…oldest profession."

"Assassins?" I guessed, and he laughed out loud.

"Forget the turnip truck. You were *born* yesterday. I'm talking about prostitutes."

"Why on earth would prostitution be the oldest profession?"

His grin widened. "I don't know. That's just what they say. I guess sex is the universal currency. But my point is that those in the skin trade are all unSkilled also, but they have red marks. This guy—" he tossed an openhanded gesture at the guard "—is just a hired gun. No Skill."

"I can't believe I'm about to ask this, but…why didn't you just kill him? Because he didn't actually take a shot at you?"

Kris pulled a zip tie from the pocket of his jeans, then hauled the unconscious man toward the refrigerator by one arm. "That, and because dead men are notoriously difficult to interrogate." He propped the guard in a sitting position against the front of the fridge, then zip-tied the man's right hand to the refrigerator door handle, so that his arm stuck up at an odd angle. Then Kris patted him down until he found a cell phone, which he tossed into the drawer two down from the fridge—within reach, if the guard stretched far enough to strain his shoulder.

"Hand me a cup of water." Kris gestured toward a plastic cup sitting on the edge of the sink.

"What's the magic word?"

"Abracadabra. But I fail to see the relevance."

I crossed both arms over my chest. "Please. The magic word is *please.* Didn't your mother ever teach you that?"

"All my mother ever taught me was how to die in a car wreck. Gran taught me quite a few interesting words, but *please* was not among them. And, for the record, *please* is not a magic word. It has no supernatural properties at all that I can think of." He came one step closer, staring straight into my eyes with such intensity that I couldn't have looked away if I'd tried, and again, I was hyper-aware that he was half-naked. And that I wanted to know what that half felt like....

"Tequila's the magic drink. Everyone over the age of twenty-one and south of the Mason-Dixon line is familiar with its magical properties." Kris took another step, and I held my ground as my heart beat harder, wondering how close he would come. Or when I'd stop him. "Beans are the magical fruit, or so the boys in my third-grade class told me."

One more step, and we were less than a foot apart, and the very air seemed to sizzle between us. "Love is the international language, death is the great equalizer and *no* is the word most likely to turn a good man into just a friend, a drunk man into a jackass and misdemeanor-class asshole into a felon. But *please*..." He shrugged. "*Please* works no miracles at all."

With that, he reached past me for the cup, his arm brushing mine, his lips inches from my cheek. When he turned on the faucet and filled the cup with cold water, without ever breaking my gaze, I realized I was breathing too hard. As if I'd just run a marathon.

And in that moment, I became determined to pull the word *please* from Kris Daniels's mouth and show him just what kind of magic it could do.

"This is the fun part," he whispered, so close I could

practically feel his heartbeat through his bare skin and my shirt. My fingers skimmed his stomach before I even realized my own intention, and he exhaled against my neck, then just…*lingered.*

He was right. This *was* the fun part.

Then Kris pulled back and grinned at me. He dropped into a squat next to the unconscious man, his blue-eyed gaze sparkling with heat, and mischief, and beneath that, single-minded determination to do what had to be done.

Oh. *That* was the fun part. Interrogation. I felt my cheeks flush.

"Ready?"

It took me a second to realize he was talking to me. I nodded, still trying to puzzle my way through whatever had almost happened between us. Then Kris tossed water from the cup into the guard's face.

The man sputtered and blinked, and as soon as he was awake, he hissed in pain. "My eyes…" he moaned. "They burn. I can't see."

"That's too bad." Kris looked up at me and smiled one more time. "The view's amazing," he said, and my heart beat too fast. Then he pressed the barrel of his silenced gun into the hollow between the man's collarbones, and everything about him changed. Hardened. "Where the hell is my sister?"

"What?" The guard sputtered, then licked his lips, staring at nothing, the whites of his eyes an angry red color. "I don't know. Who's your sister? Who are you?"

"My sister is Kenley Daniels, and you motherfuckers took her. My sister is a part of me…" He glanced at the guard's name tag. "Ned. Losing her is like losing my own hand, and if I don't get her back, unharmed, poste fucking haste, you're gonna find out what it's like to lose one of *your* parts.…"

The guard swallowed, and his Adam's apple bobbed above the barrel of the gun. "I swear I don't know your sister, or where she is."

"He may be telling the truth," I said, and the man's unfocused, red-rimmed eyes rolled in my direction.

"I'm perfectly willing to believe that this idiot knows almost nothing, in the larger sense. But he was bound to Jake Tower, which means he knows more than he wants us to think he knows." Kris stared into the man's irritated eyes. "Isn't that right, Ned?"

"I swear, I don't—"

"The real problem will be making him tell us something he's been contractually prohibited from revealing. That's where this gets interesting." He turned back to Ned. "When did you reenlist? How long ago?"

"Three years." Ned answered quickly, and with no sign of resistance pain, and I realized that meant we hadn't yet hit the classified information. I'd never seen anyone suffering from serious resistance pain, and I have to admit, I was a little curious.

"Then you know my sister. She was Tower's top binder, and by the time you reenlisted for your second term, she would have been doing most of his bindings. Petite. Blonde. Answers to the name *Kenley Daniels*."

I saw recognition in his eyes, as if a light switch had been flipped behind them. "Yeah. I never heard her name, but that's her. Quiet thing. Kinda intense."

"Much better," Kris said. "Did you see her here? It would have been today. This afternoon."

"Kris," I said when the man shook his head, obviously confused. "She was never here. Julia wouldn't have had enough time to put her here, realize that was a mistake, then move the entire operation. There's no telling how long ago they moved the...project."

Kris frowned, thinking through what I'd said, and I shifted to face the guard. "Do you know what they did here, Ned?"

He didn't shake his head, but he didn't answer either, and when his entire body tensed, I realized he was waiting for pain—either from a blow from Kris or from resistance pain. Which surely meant we were very close to information he wasn't allowed to give us.

"Did you see any of it, before they moved everything?" I squatted next to Kris, and the guard nodded, but his mouth never opened. "You don't have to give us specifics," I said, and he looked marginally relieved. "We already know what Tower was doing. But here's the part you do have to answer."

He tensed again, immediately, and I paused to see if Kris wanted to take over, but he seemed content to let me ask the questions. Ned was obviously less intimidated by me. Maybe because I was a woman. Or maybe because I didn't have a gun pressed into his throat.

"What we really need to know is where they went. Do you know where the project has been relocated?" Because if Kenley was with the donors—even if they weren't actively bleeding her—she'd be wherever they were.

"I don't know. I swear that's the truth."

"He's lying." Kris's finger tightened on the trigger, and my heart thumped harder. "See how scared he looks?"

"He's scared because you're seconds away from shooting his head clean off his body. Shut up for a minute and let me talk to him."

Kris's eyes narrowed in irritation, but he didn't object.

I turned the man's head by his chin, so he was looking at me, though he didn't seem to actually see me. "Did you help them pack and load?"

"Yes!" Ned was obviously relieved to have an answer

in the affirmative for us. He looked like a man clinging to a life raft in the middle of the ocean. "There were vans, and—" His word ended abruptly in a groan of pain as his forehead wrinkled in a grimace. Resistance pain. He'd hit the silence barrier.

"Did you hear anything while you were loading? Did anyone say anything about where they were going? Anything at all?"

"I don't know." Ned shook his head. "I can't remember."

Kris pressed the gun harder into his throat. "Think. Think like your life depended on it."

Ned swallowed again and closed his eyes.

"Did they seem to be expecting lots of gas or bathroom breaks?" I asked. "Did anyone mention getting car sick on long trips or back roads? Were they worried about hitting rush-hour traffic? Anything like that?"

Kris glanced at me in surprise and—if I'm not mistaken—respect. Which irritated the hell out of me. Why was he surprised to find out I wasn't brain damaged?

"No. Nothing like that. But one of the nurses was complaining about warehouse bathrooms. Something about poor lighting."

"That's it?" Kris glared down at him. "That's all you've got? They moved to a warehouse? That could be anywhere. Tower must own dozens of them."

"What do you expect?" the guard demanded, suddenly almost bold in spite of the gun still pressed into the base of his throat. "I'm the guy they left behind to guard an empty building. How high would you expect that guy's security clearance to be?"

"He's got a point."

Kris groaned in frustration. "Fine." He withdrew his gun and backed away from the guard slowly, still aiming at the man's head. "The rest of this is up to you," he said, and it took me a minute to realize he was talking to me, because he was still looking at the guard zip-tied to the refrigerator.

"What's up to me?"

"Whether he lives or dies."

The guard stiffened again, and my heart slammed against my chest as I stood and backed away from them both. "Why? Why is that up to me?"

"Because you have the most to lose if we let him live. Julia already knows what I'm up to. Your participation in our mission to destroy her will be news, and not the kind of news she's going to take well. So...your call. Shoot him or leave him?"

As far as I knew, the guard didn't deserve death. He hadn't actually shot at Kris. He'd been cooperative to the best of his ability, in spite of restrictive bindings. But Kris was right. If we left him, he'd have no choice but to answer any question Julia asked, assuming my understanding of his bindings was anywhere near accurate. Then she'd know that I...

That I what? What could she learn from interrogating Ned? That I wasn't being held hostage anymore? That I was willingly working with the enemy? Those conclusions couldn't be hard for her to draw on her own, considering that she'd been willing to kill me not once, but twice—she *had* to know I was the one who'd snuck back in to raid my own car.

"Let him live."

Kris's aim didn't drop. "You sure?" he asked, and I nodded, but he only frowned. "Can I talk to you in the hall, please?"

I followed him out of the room reluctantly and pulled the door almost closed in the all-white hallway. "What?"

"I just want to make sure you understand how dangerous leaving him alive really is."

"Because I'm a simpleton, who can't be trusted to
make a decision without a man's guidance and supervision?" *Ass-hat.*

"Calm down, Wonder Woman. That's not what I'm
saying." He leaned against the door frame and crossed his
arms over his bare chest, lowering his voice to a whisper.
"I'm just saying that if you're new enough to the work-
ings of the Skilled syndicate to be unfamiliar with the
color-coding system, you may be even *less* familiar with
the level of cruelty and depravity that goes on within the
privacy of the Tower estate."

"Okay. Fair point. But I figure that—worst-case scenario—leaving him alive will give Julia Tower reason to
want me dead. Right?" I asked, and he nodded. "News
flash—that already appears to be the case. Which means
we have no legitimate reason to kill the poor asshole
bound into her service."

Into *my* service, if...

If what? What would it take to claim my inheritance?
If I could claim the bindings she had temporary control
of, could I then break them? Could I release the people
Kenley Daniels had bound into indentured servitude?

A new world of possibilities blossomed before me,
and my head swam as they swirled around me in a vor-
tex of blood, and oaths, and death, and freedom. Beneath
all that, Kori's insistence that sometimes freedom only
comes through death made me nervous, both for Ned
and for myself.

Kris's gaze narrowed on me, and I couldn't tell if he
approved of my logic. The part I'd explained aloud, anyway. And finally he nodded. "Okay. We'll let him live.

Let's find some bleach and clean up, so we can get out of here. I'll text Kori for an update on Ian."

"There's bleach in the bathroom," I said, already on my way back into the snack room to retrieve it. Kris was pressing Send on his phone when I handed him the jug of bleach and a roll of hand towels. "I'll stay here and keep an eye on Ned. Unless you're as bad at cleaning as Gran says you are at cooking."

His brows rose. "Trick question. Either I admit incompetence, or I get stuck with the dirty work."

"You catch on quick." I gave him a smile that felt like a lie on my lips, then gestured for him to hurry.

Once he'd disappeared into the room where Ian had been shot, stepping over the dead guy in his path, I quietly closed the break room door and knelt next to Ned, armed with his gun. He didn't need to know I had no idea how to use it.

Ned scowled at me. "What, you're going to shoot me now, after you talked that psycho into letting me live?"

"He's not a psycho. Though I understand the mistake. I thought the same thing when I first met him."

"Did he tie you to a refrigerator and hold a gun to your throat?"

"No. He kidnapped me and trapped me in a house with no exits. So I know he's an acquired taste. But this…" I waved the gun for emphasis, and he flinched as if it might go off in my hand, which made me suddenly nervous, even though the safety was engaged. "This has nothing to do with him. I just want to ask you a couple of questions."

"I'm guessing I have no choice but to answer?" he snapped with a glance at the gun, and I shrugged.

"That's what we're about to find out. Do you know who I am, Ned?"

He shook his head and tried to reposition his arm,

which was still zip-tied to the refrigerator handle over his head. "Why? Should I?"

"Do you know what happened at the Tower estate yesterday?"

"No. What happened?"

"Kris Daniels—the guy who just agreed to let you live—broke in through the darkroom and shot three of the guards. It was kind of—" *badass* "—a big deal. Julia didn't...send out a bulletin or something? Some kind of security alert? Isn't that the kind of thing she'd want people to be aware of?"

The guard shook his head slowly, his forehead furrowed as if he wasn't sure whether or not to believe me. "That's exactly the kind of thing she *wouldn't* want anyone else to know. Because it makes her look weak. Vulnerable. Something like that could never have happened when her brothers were alive."

But, of course, it had happened to them, too. Obviously Jake had stomped out any rumors before they could spread. Julia must have been taking notes.

"Assuming any of that actually happened..." Ned added.

"It did. I was there, and when he escaped through the shadows, he dragged me with him. Thus—" I shrugged "—the kidnapping."

Ned looked unconvinced, but I didn't have time to try to rectify that. So I pressed on. "If Julia were to tell you to...I don't know...sing the national anthem, would you have to do it?"

He nodded, obviously confused. "That, and anything else she wanted. Why? What's this about?"

I took a deep breath. *Let the great inheritance experiment begin....*

"Ned, my name is Sera Tower. My father was Jake Tower. I'm his oldest living…um…"

"Child" felt too familiar—I'd never known him as a father and I wouldn't change that for the world. But "descendant" felt too distant, as if Jake and I had lived in different time periods. So I went with…

"…offspring. I'm his oldest living offspring. And as such, your binding actually belongs to me, not to Julia Tower."

"Yeah. Right." Ned snorted, then shifted again, trying to take pressure off the arm tied to the refrigerator. "And I'm a midget in forty-eight-inch heels."

"It's true. That's what I was doing there yesterday. That's why Julia's trying to kill me—because if people find out she hasn't truly inherited her brother's kingdom, she'll be out on her ass."

Ned's focus narrowed on me, more in interest now than in skepticism. Everyone loves a scandal. "If you're Jake Tower's heir, why have I never heard of you?"

"Because I'm a secret. Probably an embarrassing one. Jake Tower, the family man, had an illegitimate child."

"Why the hell would he leave everything to an illegitimate child no one's ever heard of?"

"I don't think he meant to." I shifted on my heels. Squatting on the linoleum was getting uncomfortable. "In fact, I don't think he knew I existed. My mother spent most of my life hiding me from him, and I'm starting to think she was very, very good at that." No reason for him to know that I was even better at hiding myself— and anyone within my jamming zone. "This inheritance seems to be the result of a sloppily phrased last will and testament. But the only thing I'm really sure of is that Julia Tower wants me dead. If she gets her way, you may never be free of her." I was taking a gamble with my next statement—assuming he wasn't happy with his current state of employment. "If she doesn't…if I inherit the bindings…I'll let you all go."

Ned rolled his eyes and pushed himself into a straighter sitting position with his free hand. "Right. You're just going to break every binding your father ever had sealed. Dissolve his life's work. Give up unbelievable fortune."

I knew I had him when he called Jake my father.

"Yup." I nodded firmly. "I don't want to run the mafia."

His gaze narrowed until his eyes were mere slits, staring at me more in puzzlement than in disbelief now. "You're serious. You'd give it all up? Why?"

"Because I don't have any criminal inclination, nor do I have the right to control your life. But I am going to ask you to help me out with a little test."

"What kind of test?"

I stood and pulled open the last kitchenette drawer, where I'd found a box of plastic forks. They wouldn't have been much good as a weapon, when I'd needed one, but they'd be fine for the job I had in mind. I pulled one fork out and dropped it on his lap, careful to say out of reach of all three of Ned's unbound limbs. "Stab your right arm."

"What?"

"You heard me. Pick up the fork in your left hand and stab your right arm, between your elbow and your wrist." My theory was that in making him understand and believe that I truly was Jake Tower's heir, I'd taken his binding back from Julia Tower, without her even knowing it. But the only way I could think of to test that and be sure he wasn't faking—playing along, so he could report back to her—was to ask him to do something he'd never do, unless he really had no choice but to obey me.

No one who understood how much power blood truly

holds would ever willingly spill his own in front of a stranger.

"I'm not gonna—" Ned flinched, and his left hand flew to his forehead. Resistance pain; it was easy to recognize. Whether or not he was faking was harder to determine. "You're a bigger bitch than she is! Julia Tower never made me spill my own blood!" he insisted, still rubbing his forehead.

"Sorry about that. Can't be helped. Do it. Now."

His hand shook, hovering in the air between his forehead and the fork on his lap, and I watched, fascinated, as he silently weighed his options.

Then I heard faint footsteps in the hall, and my pulse raced so fast I got dizzy for a second. "Sera? You okay?"

"Yeah. Fine," I called through the door. Then I turned back to Ned. "I don't have time for you to think this through. Stab yourself in the fucking arm. Now!"

Ned groaned in pain, but his hand picked up the fork, squeezing it so tight his skin turned white from the pressure.

"Do it!" I repeated in a fierce whisper.

"Aaahh!" he shouted, resisting mentally, even as his body obeyed. Even as he stabbed himself in the arm, halfway between his elbow and the wrist lashed to the refrigerator door handle.

The fork stuck in his skin, standing up like a tower in the middle of his arm, blood welling slowly around the four buried tines.

"Sera!" Kris's footsteps grew faster and louder. "Sera!"

"I'm fine!" I shouted, staring in fascination as dark drops of blood dribbled down the side of Ned's arm and onto his pants. His breathing was ragged. Uneven. But that had to be from his efforts to resist—the fork hadn't penetrated deeply enough to do any real damage.

"Fucking *bitch!*" he growled through clenched teeth, and I almost shouted in triumph. He clearly hadn't wanted to stab himself. Which meant he'd had no choice. Which meant that his binding had transferred from Julia to me. "You *are* one of them."

I blinked at him in surprise. Then in horror. I *wasn't* one of them. Not in the way that he meant it.

"I'm sorry," I whispered, my words running together in my haste to say what had to be said before Kris got there. "Don't tell anyone what I've told you. Ever. Other than that, you are a free man. I release you from your binding."

Ned's eyes widened and he craned his neck, trying to see something on his arm, and as Kris threw the door open behind me, I saw what Ned couldn't. The marks on his arm had faded to a muted gray.

Shit! Kris would see. I lurched forward and pulled the flap of his sleeve over the mark as Kris's arm wrapped around my waist and hauled me away from Ned.

"Are you *trying* to give him back his gun?" Kris demanded, setting me on my feet out of the guard's reach, which is when I realized I still held the pistol. And that Ned had been reaching for it with his left hand when Kris pulled me out of reach.

The ungrateful bastard was going to shoot me! After I set him free!

But then, I *had* made him stab his own arm, then freed him of any restriction from hurting me. Maybe I hadn't thought that one through very well...

"What the hell happened?" Kris stared at the fork in Ned's arm.

"Ask your bitch," Ned snapped, and I was relieved to see that he was evidently still bound to silence, even though his employment binding had been broken.

Kris glanced at me, muttering something about how I wasn't anyone's bitch. Which almost made me smile. But I could only shrug in answer. "I don't know. He found a fork, and before I could take it away from him, he just… stabbed himself in the arm. It was weird."

Kris frowned as though he didn't believe me—go figure—but it took most of my concentration to keep from grinning in return. I'd done it. I'd figured it out. Now, if I could figure out how to do the same thing I'd done to Ned, only on a large scale, I could single-handedly put that bitch Julia Tower out of business for good.

Twelve

Kris

"How is he?" I leaned against the door frame in the threshold of Kori and Ian's room. Ian was asleep on the bed, shirtless, the thick bandage on his shoulder pale against his dark skin.

"He'll live." Kori closed her laptop without turning it off, then leaned back in the desk chair. "Gran got him all patched up and gave him something for the pain."

"I hope you double-checked the dosage." Gran only remembered what decade she was living in about half the time, and as much help as she was as a triage nurse—with forty years' real-world experience—on her bad days, she was as likely to overdose you as underdose you.

"I did." Kori waved one hand at the closed laptop. "Thank goodness for the internet, slow though the connection is. I wanted to call Meghan." Ian's sister-in-law was a Healer. "But he wouldn't let me. He says he can't drag Steve and Meg into any more danger, at least until his brother's fully healed."

"I can respect that." And Kori could, too. I could tell from how she was just frustrated, rather than actually angry. Ian's brother had hovered on the edge of death for weeks, resisting a binding that had been sealed using Kenley's blood without her knowledge. A few months earlier, Ian had been willing to kill Kenni to break the binding and save his brother. But then he met Kori, and now he was practically family. The brother I'd never had. He'd fought for my sisters when I couldn't be there.

I owed him more than I could ever possibly repay.

"Has Van had any luck ID-ing Sera's family?"

Kori shook her head. "I don't think she's actually looking anymore. Since the two of you came back with that scrap of intel, she's been exhausting every resource trying to figure out what warehouse Julia moved the blood farm into."

"At least that's keeping her mind occupied." Which was more than I'd managed for myself. "Try to get some sleep, Kor. We'll find Kenni tomorrow." *Or die trying.*

On my way down the hall, I stopped in front of the door to my former room out of habit and had one hand on the doorknob before I remembered it wasn't my room anymore. I stood there for a minute, thinking about Sera, and how much we still didn't know about her. About how badly I wanted to trust her. How badly I wanted her to trust me. But in the two days since we'd met, I'd nearly gotten her killed several times—it was a miracle she didn't run when she saw me coming.

But then, I had yet to see her run from anything.

She could have taken the coward's way out tonight. She could have told me to shoot Ned the guard, which would have kept her off of Julia's radar. Or, as close to off the radar as possible, for someone who'd survived being shot at by Tower's goons three times in less than two days.

Instead, she'd let Ned live and exposed herself as our ally, damning her to be hunted alongside us.

Why would she do that? We would have helped her hunt the bastard who'd killed her family either way.

When I finally lay down on the couch with the pillow I'd stolen from my own bed while she was in the shower, I couldn't get Sera out of my mind. Every time I closed my eyes, she was there, but the mental picture was never what I expected. Instead of a self-indulgent memory of her standing naked at the foot of my bed, I kept seeing her as she'd looked the day we met, in Tower's foyer, when her reckless bravery had nearly gotten us both killed.

After an hour and a half of staring at the muted television—any noise from the TV was guaranteed to wake Gran, even though she would have slept through World War III itself—I gave up and headed into the kitchen to nuke a cup of hot chocolate.

Armed with my steaming mug, I sat at the table with Elle's notebook and started flipping through the pages again, looking for new meaning in old words. Hoping that Ned's sliver of information would fit in with something I'd long ago forgotten I'd ever written.

"That stuff is crap in a mug," Sera said, and I thought I'd imagined her voice—wishful thinking—until I looked up to find her standing in the kitchen doorway, in Kori's robe.

"We have to get you some new clothes." I flipped the notebook shut. "Preferably something neither of my sisters ever wore."

"Why?" She glanced down at the robe, which hung open to reveal a snug tank top and shorts so short I didn't want to know which sister they belonged to. "Kori wants her clothes back?"

"Not that she's mentioned. But that's just creepy." I

waved a hand at her…whole body. "From my perspective."

"Your sister's clothes are creepy?"

I frowned. She was going to make me actually tell her how hot she was. "On you? Yes," I said, and her hurt expression clued me in to the fact that I'd just failed the Communicating With Women pop quiz. "That's not what I meant. You look…*so* good, in a way I don't want to associate with my sisters' clothes."

But that didn't do her justice. Sera looked practically *edible,* in that you'll-never-taste-anything-this-sweet-ever-again kind of way. In fact, all I'd had was a taste, and the thought of never tasting her again made me want to bite my own tongue off, to put it out of its misery. "Does that make sense?"

She gave me a mischievous smile. "I'm not sure. That almost sounded like a compliment."

"I'm only human, and you're…flaunting."

Her brows rose and she tied the robe closed. "Better?"

I had to swallow a groan. That wasn't better at *all*.

Instead of answering, which I wasn't sure I could do without begging for another peek, I kicked out the chair next to mine in wordless invitation.

Sera sat and picked up the empty hot-chocolate packet. Then she peeked into my mug and grimaced. "Seriously. How can you drink that crap? Hot chocolate is made with milk, and sugar, and cocoa. And a pot. On the stove."

I shrugged. "The microwave's easier."

She laughed. "Do you always make such little effort?"

I shook my head slowly, studying her, trying to decide whether I'd imagined smut behind likely innocent words. "No. The rest of my life is complicated. Food seems like the safest place to take a shortcut. We are still talking about food, aren't we?"

"Were we ever?" She stood before I could interpret either her tone or her expression and dropped the empty paper packet into the trash, then snatched my mug from my hands.

"Hey!" I protested as she dumped thin, chocolate-flavored water into the sink.

"I'll make cocoa. You tell me how you're going to kill the bastard who murdered my family."

"With a gun, almost certainly." I watched as she pulled a half-full jug of milk from the fridge, then started opening cabinets. "That's kind of my specialty."

"Are you armed right now?"

I took the .45 from my lap and set it on the table.

She frowned and pushed the last cabinet door closed. "I think you have a serious problem. Do you sleep with that thing?"

"Only when I sleep alone," I said, and either I was imagining things, or she blushed. A lot.

"Sugar?" Her brows rose in question, surely an attempt to cover her own…interest? Curiosity? Either way, I had sudden hope that she might not permanently hate me.

"Pantry. If we have cocoa powder, it'll be in there, too."

"I want to watch," Sera called over her shoulder as she dug in the small pantry, and for a second, I thought we were still talking about sleeping, and guns, and innuendo neither of us was likely to admit to. But that couldn't be right.

"Watch what?"

All noise from the pantry ceased, and her shoulders tensed. "I want to watch him die. I want to be there when the life fades from his eyes and he bleeds out on the floor."

"That might not be…" Healthy. It might not give her the closure she obviously needed. "Safe."

"Screw safe." She turned with an unopened bag of sugar tucked under her left arm and a yellow plastic canister of cocoa powder in her right hand. "My parents and my sister were 'safe' in their own home, behind locked doors, and look where that got them."

I didn't know what to say to that. Safety is an illusion, even in the best of times. The only true defense is vigilance, but that wasn't something a daughter/sister in mourning needed to hear. Yet I wasn't going to insult her with polite platitudes, either. Those hadn't helped me when my parents died.

"How are you going to find him?" She set the ingredients next to the stove, then pulled a pot from beneath the counter.

"Do the police have a description?"

Sera ripped open the bag of sugar, and thousands of tiny grains spilled onto the counter. "I can get you one."

"How? Was there a witness? Did the police take a statement? Because Van can get into their records, no problem, and you won't have to—"

"There was a witness, but her statement won't help." Sera lowered her head, and I *knew* her eyes were closed, though I couldn't see them with her back to me. "She told the police she couldn't remember anything. But that was a lie."

"How do you know?"

"I know." She pulled the blue plastic cap off the milk carton and set it in a scattering of sugar on the counter. "The witness lied because she was scared." Sera poured milk into the pot, but her hand shook, and some sloshed over the side. And that's when I made the connection.

"Oh, damn, Sera, I'm so sorry. I'm such an idiot." I

stood, but she wouldn't look at me. She just scooped sugar into a measuring cup she'd found in a drawer I'd never even noticed before. "You were there, weren't you? You saw what happened to them…." I reached for her because I'd never seen anyone in more desperate need of a hug, but she pulled away from me as if my hands were on fire, and that vicious ache was back in my chest, like it had been every time I'd failed to help someone I cared about.

"Do you like mint?" She dumped sugar into the pot, and it took me a second to make the mental jump. We were talking about cocoa again. "I saw some mint extract in the pantry…"

"Sera. Put down the whisk and talk to me. Please."

I didn't think she'd do it. But then Sera set the whisk in the pan and turned to stare up at me. She looked as if the world had just crumbled beneath her feet and a step in either direction would send her tumbling into that void along with everything else she'd ever cared about. With the life she'd lost when her family was murdered.

"Why didn't you tell us?" But what I really meant was, *Why didn't you tell* me?

"Why didn't I tell you?" Her voice was sharp, but her eyes were sad. "Why didn't I tell the guy who kidnapped me at gunpoint that I saw my parents and sister murdered in our own home?"

I closed my eyes and made a silent wish that would never come true, and when I opened them again, she'd turned back to the counter, measuring cocoa powder this time with stiff, precise movements. I wanted to touch her so badly my hands actually ached for the feel of her skin, and for just a moment, that ache was enough to overwhelm logic and common sense, both of which were telling me that I couldn't get involved with Sera.

Not while she was still grieving.

Sera was wounded and fragile, beneath a tough, knife-wielding exterior, and while she certainly needed and deserved comfort, she wasn't in the proper state of mind to make decisions about her personal life. At least, not the kind of decisions intended to last beyond the closure she hoped to find with vigilante justice.

I didn't want her to associate me with such a sad, dangerous part of her life, because when she put that all behind her, she'd want to put me behind her, too. I would remind her of the painful past.

"My biggest regret in the world right now—other than failing Kenley—is how we met." Too late, I realized that sounded like a confession.

It *was* a confession. I was practically admitting that I wanted things from her that I couldn't have. That she couldn't afford to give me, with so much grief in her heart.

Sera dumped cocoa into the sugar and milk mixture and began to stir with the whisk. "You saved my life, remember?"

"No, I nearly got you killed." I forced a smile I couldn't truly feel as I fed her own words back to her. "Remember?"

"That wasn't your…" She bit off the end of her sentence and I got the feeling it had veered from her original intent. When she turned to me again, there was something new behind her eyes. Something sad, and strong, and…resigned. "You didn't fail Kenley. It sounds like she rushed into an unknown situation, and we all know you'd do anything to get her back. And you will get her back. *We* will. Then we'll track down the bastard who took everything from me and gut him like the animal he is."

"You want him gutted?" I shrugged and half sat on the edge of the table. "I'm better with guns than with knives, but that bastard killed three people in cold blood, right in front of you. I'll kill him however you want. And yes, you can watch, if you think that'll help. But I have to tell you, in my experience, that only makes it worse. Violence may balance the scales, but it can't heal wounds. Only time can do that."

"No. Time lets untreated wounds fester." Sera turned back to the stove and tried to ignite the burner, but the knobs were gone again. "And there were four."

"Four what?" I pulled the cookie jar from the top of the fridge and took the lid off, then held it out to her.

"Four people." She selected a knob, then slid it into place on the stove. "He killed four people. There was a baby. Well, there *would* have been a baby. In a few…" Her hand clenched around the stove knob and her words cracked and fell apart. "My sister…"

"She was pregnant?" Something cold, and dark, and nearly uncontrollable unfurled in the pit of my stomach, and my hands clenched into fists at my sides. What kind of sick bastard kills a pregnant woman?

"I don't want to talk about this anymore." Sera lit the burner and adjusted the flame, then stirred the milk in silence while I retreated to my seat at the table, trying to process what I'd just learned. To truly understand the scope of her loss.

I couldn't do it. Even when I'd lost my parents, I'd still had my sisters and Gran.

Sera had been there. She'd seen them die. How the hell had she survived? Had she hidden? That would have been the smart thing to do—surely the only way to preserve her own life. But when had I ever seen her do the cautious thing? When had I seen her try to save herself?

She'd stepped in front of my gun and demanded I hand it over, before she'd had any reason to know I wouldn't shoot her. She'd risked being shot to claim her mother's photo album. She'd attack the man who shot Ian. She'd sprayed bleach in Ned's face to keep him from shooting me, then dented his skull with a fucking toaster.

In the two days I'd known her, I'd seen her step into the path of danger more times than I could count on one hand, but I'd never once seen her hide.

So how the hell had she survived the attack that killed her entire family?

I didn't realize the cocoa was done until she set a mug on the table in front of me, then slid into her chair with a mug of her own. There was a yellow, sugar-coated duck floating in my hot chocolate. I picked the mug up and eyed it, then laughed out loud when I recognized the Marshmallow Peep.

Sera shrugged, and I swear I saw just a hint of a smile. "You're out of marshmallows. That's the best I could do."

Gran had never once given me marshmallows in my cocoa. Much less fluffy little sugar-coated ducks.

Sera's Marshmallow Peep was green, and it left a sparkly spot of sugar on the end of her nose when she sipped from her mug. I wanted to kiss the sugar off her nose, but I was pretty sure that would make her want to stab me again.

"What is that?" She stared at my notebook, open on the table in front of me. "Poetry?" Her eyes narrowed in suspicion. "Do you write poetry?"

"Your skepticism stings." But her interest felt like a ray of sunshine on an overcast day and the moment I saw it, I craved more. "Why is it so unbelievable that I might write poetry?"

"It doesn't really fit with your…image."

"My image?" I closed the notebook and folded my

hands over it, watching her expectantly. "I gotta hear this. What is my image?"

"Well, admittedly, my perspective is colored by my initial impression of you as a homicidal kidnapper who screwed all the doors and windows shut to keep his grandmother prisoner in her own house…"

"That's *not* what I did. This isn't her house, and she's not prisoner." But Sera wasn't listening.

"…but you've kind of got this badass-next-door routine going on, with the blue eyes and the clean-cut thing you have going on here—" she waved one hand vaguely at my face and hair, and suddenly I regretted shaving that morning "—and the guns, and the whole 'you want me to kill him or let him live?' thing."

I scowled and picked up my mug. "That's not me. I'm not clean-cut, and I don't sound like that."

"Yes, you are, and you do. Stop pouting." She tried to hide a grin by sipping from her cocoa. "And if you 'forget' you don't belong in the center bedroom one more time, I'm going to have you declared legally brain dead."

"*I'm* brain dead?" I set my mug down and scowled at her, and she nodded, chuckling now.

"Though that appears to be a selective defect. I haven't seen you forget a single meal, yet you can't seem to remember where you sleep at night."

"This, coming from the woman who tried to give a gun to Ned-the-guard, so he could relieve us of the burden of drawing regular breaths in a body free from extraneous holes."

"That's not what I…" She frowned and abandoned the rest of her sentence. "Let me see this poetry." Sera reached for the notebook, but I pulled it out of her grasp.

"It's not poetry," I admitted reluctantly. I didn't want her to be right about the brain-dead badass thing. "I'm not sure I'd even recognize poetry if I saw it, outside of Dr. Seuss."

She was still smiling, and I considered that a bit of a victory. "So, what is it? A journal?"

"Kind of."

"You're not writing in it." She made a show of studying the tabletop. "I don't see a pen. So you were just sitting here reading your own journal?" When I didn't answer immediately, her brows furrowed. "That's not yours, is it? You're reading someone else's journal. Is it Kori's? What are you, nine?" She reached for the notebook and I tried to pull it away again, but that time I was too slow. Or maybe I didn't believe she'd really take it.

I was wrong, and she was fast.

"Wait, Sera…" I held one hand out to her, then realized I had no idea what to do with it. "I feel like we've made serious strides in the you-not-wanting-to-castrate-me-with-a-kitchen-knife department, and I'd hate to ruin all that by having to actually take that away from you. But I will if I have to. It's not Kori's journal. It's mine. It's just…not about me."

"Why would you keep a journal about someone else? Are you some kind of creepy stalker?" she said, and I wasn't sure whether or not that was a joke. She didn't seem very sure, either. "Is that about the last woman you kidnapped and locked up?"

"Give it back. Please."

When I didn't smile and showed no sign of relenting, she hesitated for one more second, studying my eyes, probably for some hint of violent tendencies. Other than the ones she'd already seen from me. Then she set the notebook on the table and slid it toward me.

But things were different now. Half an hour earlier, she'd trusted me enough to tell me that she'd seen her family murdered, and now that trust was gone. Suspicion swam in her eyes like tears that would never fall. Distrust was obvious in the straight line her lips had been pressed into and in the firm set of her jaw.

I could tell her the truth, or I could lose her confidence. Which might mean losing her as a Jammer. But as reluctant as I was to admit it, the possibility of losing her Skill wasn't what bothered me.

What bothered me was the thought of losing her trust. Of never again seeing her laugh with me, because she couldn't lower her guard long enough to see the humor in what I'd meant to say, when it came out all wrong. I wanted to see her smile again. I wanted to *make* her smile, and as soon as I'd had that thought, I had to shut it down, because somehow I'd slipped right back into the delusion that she might become interested in more than just my trigger finger.

But she wouldn't. Even if she thought she could, she was wrong. I knew that because I'd been in her position, unable to truly move forward with life—or give any new relationship a chance—while I was still mourning Noelle.

Sera wasn't here because she was beautiful, or smart, or brave. She wasn't here because I wanted her here. Or because I wanted to help her. Or because seeing her in the morning made me smile, in spite of the fear and anger practically stagnating in our locked-tight house. Sera was with us because she could somehow help us—because Noelle had known that—and that was all.

The sooner I got that through my baddass-next-door brain, the better off we'd both be.

But I still couldn't stand the thought of her hating me.

"Okay. Sera, wait," I said, and she sat again, reluctantly, and sipped from her mug. "I'll tell you about the journal. But you're gonna think I'm crazy."

"I already think you're crazy." It sounded like she was joking, but her smile was still absent, so I couldn't tell for sure.

"I used to kind of…be with this girl. She was a Seer. And she talked in her sleep."

"Okay." She shrugged. "My ex snored. What does that have to do with your journal?"

I pushed my gun and half-empty mug aside to make room for the notebook on the table between us. "She was a *Seer,* Sera. She could see the future. Bits of it, anyway. And sometimes the things she said in her sleep were… prophesy. Or whatever you call it."

Her brows rose. "How do you know?"

"Because some of them came true. So I started…um… writing them down." I pushed the notebook toward her and when she glanced at me in question, I nodded, giving her permission to peek.

Sera opened the front cover and stared at the name written at the top of the page. Noelle Maddox. "Is that *the* Noelle? Hadley's real mother?"

I nodded.

"Does that mean that you're… That Hadley is…"

"Mine?" I said, and she nodded. "No. There has been some question about her paternity, but I'm not among the possibilities. We weren't together when she got pregnant."

"So, Elle was with you *and* with Olivia's boss? Cavazos?"

"Yeah, but again, not at the same time. It's kind of… confusing."

"No kidding." Sera's finger slid from Noelle's name to the date written on the first line. "That was twelve years ago."

"Yeah. Shortly after the first time we…got together."

"So, you slept with a Seer? And took notes?" She

flipped through the notebook, and her eyes widened. "A lot of notes. Which would imply a lot of…sleeping."

"Yeah." Sometimes Elle and I had had sleepovers even when she and Kori weren't on speaking terms.

I drank from my mug again, trying to decide how I felt about Sera reading from Noelle's journal. Not that she was actually reading it, unless she was some kind of super-freak speed-reader. She seemed more interested in the number of passages.

So I tried to decide how I felt about Sera being interested in the number of Noelle's night-mumblings I'd recorded. And maybe the frequency. Fortunately, she couldn't judge duration or skill unless she really *could* read between the lines.

"Why would you take notes?" She looked up from the notebook with her hand spread across the open page.

"Why *wouldn't* I take notes? It was like looking into the future through a telescope, and I couldn't resist the opportunity, even if the lens was out of focus and I couldn't actually aim it at anything." I fingered the sharp end of the spiral notebook binding. "Since then, I've tried to figure some of them out, but…"

"But it reads like nonsense?" And this time she really was reading. Skimming, at least.

"Yeah. Until something happens, and suddenly one or two of those will make sense. In retrospect, they seem so obvious, but on the front end, it's like reading a foreign language, without a Noelle-to-Kristopher dictionary."

She didn't look up from the page. "Sounds frustrating."

"You have no idea." I took a deep breath, trying to figure out how to say what needed to be said without freaking her out any more than necessary. "You're in there, Sera."

"What?" She looked up from the passage she'd been reading to frown at me.

"You're in there." I took the notebook from her and flipped through the pages, looking for one specific line among hundreds. It was one I knew well, because it was one of few that seemed to give me instructions, rather than random snatches from a conversation I'd never actually been a part of. And finally I found it.

I spun the notebook around on the table, my finger over the date on the entry in question. "See?"

"'Take the girl in the yellow scarf,'" she read. Then she looked up at me with wide, frightened eyes, her fingers hovering around her collarbone, as if she still wore that scarf. "That's me? That's why you kidnapped me? Because of my scarf?"

"I didn't kidnap you," I insisted, and she started to argue, but I spoke over her. "Okay, technically, maybe I kidnapped you, but that's not the point. I didn't take you because of the scarf—that's just how I knew who you were. I took you because you're important."

"Important how?" Her voice sounded hollow. Skeptical. "Important to what? To whom?"

"I don't know," I admitted, and she looked so disappointed I wanted to take it back. But I couldn't claim to have all the answers. "I hope you're supposed to help us get Kenley back, or hide us while *we* get her back, but I doubt even Noelle knew for sure. Either way, though, you're important enough to have been in one of her predictions *years* ago. Important enough for her to tell me to take you." And that was the crux of the matter. The part I hadn't been able to truly vocalize until that moment.

Until I'd found Sera—until I'd seen her scarf and known exactly what to do—I'd never been truly sure that Noelle's messages were meant for me. I'd always kind of thought, in the back of my mind, that I was just the random bastard lucky enough to be in bed with her when she started talking in her sleep. But Sera was proof to the contrary.

Noelle had told me to take her—the girl with the yellow scarf. That prophesy was meant for me. Only for me. None of her other potential bed partners—and I wasn't naive enough to think there hadn't been several—was anywhere near Sera the day she had her yellow scarf on and needed to be removed from a dangerous situation.

Those predictions were intended for my ears. I was *meant* to act on them.

Yet I'd been failing in that respect for years. How many people had been hurt or killed because I was too stupid to interpret the prophesies?

Suddenly the guilt I'd been living with for years, on the theoretical assumption that I could do some good with Noelle's prophesies, felt like the weight of the world. Now that I knew for sure that I'd failed.

"Why would she tell you to take me?" Sera asked. "It's not like you were truly rescuing me—no one was shooting at me until you showed up. This doesn't make any sense."

"Neither does you being in my…Noelle's journal, yet there you are." I pointed to the passage again. "And now *here* you are. Maybe we were meant to meet, exactly like this. Maybe you're supposed to help us get Kenley back, then hide us while she finishes her work. Maybe I'm supposed to help you avenge your family's murder. Hell, maybe we're supposed to adopt a pair of spotted dogs and raise a hundred and one of them, then save them from a homicidal fur lover. I have no idea what Noelle wanted us to do, but I know that I'm going to do it, whatever it is. And I'm going to kill the bastard who killed your family. I swear on my favorite gun." I pushed the .45 toward her in demonstration, but she only frowned at it.

"So, I was never a hostage? You weren't going to trade me for Kenley?"

"Of course not. I'm not a bad guy, Sera. I don't hurt innocent people, I don't find civilian casualties acceptable, and I'm much less reluctant than my sister is to deliver a mercy killing. Which, for the record, I never even considered for you. I didn't bring you here to scare you, or lock you up, or hurt you in any way."

"No. You took me because some ex-lover told you to." Her words felt like a warning. Like a siren spinning up in preparation to blast at full volume. But I couldn't quite see the danger through the fog.

"Well...yeah."

"Why did you kiss me, Kris?"

"I..." I stumbled, caught off guard. There were so many reasons—more of them than I wanted to admit, even to myself. But they were all selfish. Not one of them was fair to her.

"Was that in your book? Did Noelle tell you to kiss me?" She was angry now, and suddenly I could see the approaching storm. She thought I was still taking my cues from a dead woman's dreams. That I'd kissed her not because I'd wanted to, but because I'd thought I was *supposed* to.

"No. That was my own mistake, and I'm not going to blame it on Elle."

"Mistake?" Sera recoiled as though I'd slapped her, and I realized I'd fucked up. *Again.* Surely I was close to setting a record.

"No." I shook my head and reached for her hand beneath the table. "That's not what I meant."

"So it wasn't a mistake?"

I exhaled slowly, trying to focus my thoughts. "I honestly don't know." In fact, I'd never been so conflicted in my life. "If it was a mistake, it was a wonderful mistake. But it wasn't fair to you, and I'm sorry."

She frowned, confused. "It was a surprise, but that doesn't make it unfair."

"It was unfair because you're grieving, Sera. I didn't mean to take advantage of that. I don't *want* to take advantage. I shouldn't have—"

"What if it *was* fair for me?" She squeezed my hand. "What if I *want* you to take advantage?"

"I'm not sure what that means." My brain couldn't process what she was saying, but my body was fully on board.

"You're a good guy. I wasn't sure at first, but I am now, and I get that you don't want to use me. But…people deal with grief in different ways, Kris." She glanced down at the table, and when she met my gaze again, vulnerability shone in hers. "Haven't you ever needed to touch someone? To be touched?"

Panic burned deep in my chest, but something hotter smoldered even lower. She was saying all the things I'd want to hear under normal circumstances. Unburdening me of my conscience. But…

But her eyes reflected something fragile and important. Something like a rose petal or a butterfly wing—too delicate to touch without bruising. And I had the psychological grip of an ogre. A brute's emotional finesse. I wanted what she was offering—I wanted *more* than she was offering—but I'd been where she was, and I could see how vulnerable grief had made her, even if she couldn't see it. I knew how our connection would end for her.

In regret.

I would want more, and she would want out.

I pulled my hand from hers as gently as I could. "I can't. I'm sorry, Sera. That's not what I'm looking for." I didn't want to be something she regretted later. I didn't want to be the Band-Aid she threw away when the wound healed. I wanted more than that. But she wasn't ready for more.

Sera's eyes swam in pain, then when she blinked, all that was gone. She'd closed me out. But when she stood, shoving her chair back with the motion, her cheeks were scarlet.

"Sera. I'm sorry. That didn't come out right." I reached for her hand, but she pulled away from me, and that ache in my chest became a constant, painful throb.

"Don't be sorry. I misinterpreted…things. Good night." She didn't even look back on her way into the living room, and I could only listen to her steps on the stairs, while I held a mug of homemade hot chocolate and grotesquely melted marshmallow Peep, trying to figure out how I'd managed to alienate the one woman in the world I actually wanted to be with. The first in six years.

The first since Noelle.

Damn it!

I shoved the table, and it squealed across four feet of ancient linoleum.

Seconds later, the living room floorboards creaked and I looked up to find Kori in the doorway. "What the hell is wrong with you?" my sister demanded. "She likes you. That couldn't be more obvious."

I poked my melted Peep with one finger. "Where were you hiding?"

"I wasn't hiding. I was using Gran's computer. Mine's frozen again." She pulled out the chair Sera had been sitting in and sank into it. "How was I supposed to know you'd pick tonight to demonstrate how little you've learned about women since your junior year of high school?"

"It's complicated. *She's* complicated."

"Bullshit. Noelle was as complicated as they come, and you kept up with her for years, so why is it you can't master one conversation with Sera?"

"Do you have any *constructive* criticism, or is this just fun and games for you?"

"This is a fucking tragedy, Kris. You like her. Why the hell would you turn her down?"

"I turned her down *because* I like her."

"And, what, now you only sleep with girls you *don't* like? Have I missed some new masochistic trend?"

"Kori, I don't want to be the grief-guy. That guy's disposable. He's not meant to outlast the mourning period. I want to be the guy that lasts, and she's not ready for that guy yet."

"Are you listening to yourself?" She propped one elbow on the table and scowled at me. "Who the hell are you to decide what she's ready for?"

"I've been where she is. I took comfort from girls who had no idea they were disposable."

"Well, then, maybe this is karma kicking you in the nuts. But I doubt it. Sera's not the selfish asshole you were when Elle died."

Sera was the furthest thing in the world from selfish, but... "She just offered me grief sex. How is that different from what I did?"

Kori rolled her eyes and tossed pale hair over her shoulder. "She wasn't talking about sex, you idiot. Well, not *just* sex. She's lonely, Kris. She's *alone*. Her entire family was murdered, and here we are flaunting a house full of siblings, and lovers, and grandmothers, and she's still alone in the crowd. She just asked you for a human connection during the most difficult time of her life, and you slammed the damn door in her face. You fucking humiliated her. If you weren't my brother, I'd kick you in the balls *for* her."

I stared into my cold mug, trying to reconcile what I'd thought I was saying with what Sera and Kori had obviously heard. "I didn't mean to… It came out all wrong."

My sister shook her head in disgust. "You are a world-class idiot. Fortunately for you, the world forgives well-meaning idiots over and over." Kori stood and glanced into my mug on her way into the living room. "That's revolting, by the way," she said with a gesture at the yellow goo floating in my mug.

"It used to be a Marshmallow Peep."

"Well, now it's marshmallow carnage. But to bring my point home, you just turned down the woman who put a marshmallow duck in your hot chocolate. I hope you feel like a real asshole now." With that she headed into the living room, then turned to look at me right before she headed upstairs. "Fix this before it's too late, Kris."

But as I curled up on the couch, under my scratchy blanket, I couldn't shake the feeling that I'd already lost that chance.

Thirteen

Sera

The next day, my third day in the House of Crazy, I avoided Kris as much out of humiliation as out of anger. I stayed in my room until I could actually smell and hear breakfast being served. I ate in the kitchen, while he ate on the couch with his sister. I dodged his glances and stayed out of his physical reach, excusing myself to the restroom twice when I didn't have to go, just to avoid being left alone in a room with him.

I couldn't face him, after making such a fool of myself the night before, and the worst part was that I'd been totally blindsided by his reaction. He'd kissed me. He'd flirted. We'd shared innuendo, and heated glances, and... hot chocolate. He'd seemed more than interested.

I knew we couldn't have anything serious—I had to be gone before he found out about my connection to the Towers, and eventually he *would* find out—but I'd thought maybe I could have him for a little while. A few nights with more than a pillow for company and warmth that didn't come from an overhead vent. The touch of hands that didn't want to kill me and lips that hadn't given the order to fire.

But I'd misread something, somewhere, and in the end, that was probably for the best. I couldn't afford to get attached, and the last thing I needed was another short-term fling, especially considering how the last one had ended.

I shook off that thought before it could reopen old wounds, determined to focus on my current problems. Unfortunately, Kris was prominent among them. I hadn't asked to inherit a criminal enterprise from the father I'd never even met, but if he found out that killing me would break most of Julia's bindings and free his sister from the burden, would he even hesitate to pull the trigger?

Hell, he'd probably decide he was *meant* to kill me— that that's why his dead lover had told him to take me in the first place.

I couldn't afford to trust Kris. I couldn't afford to touch him. I certainly couldn't afford to *like* him. I was on my own again. With any luck, he and his merry band of mafia rebels would help me find and kill my family's murderer soon, and after that I would disappear, hidden by my own Skill, as I had been most of my life.

The hard part would be getting out of that screwed-shut house without a shadow-walking escort…

But in spite of my determination to distance myself, I couldn't help watching Kris through the kitchen doorway during breakfast, while he laughed with his sister like I'd once laughed with mine. Ian and Vanessa were honorary siblings—that much was obvious in the way he made them smile in spite of gunshot wounds and missing loved ones.

And his grandmother…

I'd never seen a grown man so dedicated to his grandmother, even when she smacked him on the back of the head and talked to him like he was still sixteen years old, either because she actually thought that was the case, or because with those blue eyes and that pale hair, he looked like an overgrown teenager when he wasn't scowling or plotting Julia Tower's destruction.

A teenager with a gun, and a dangerous edge behind his easy smile.

Don't look at his smile.

After breakfast—another family affair I existed on the edge of—Kris, Van and Ian sat at the kitchen table brainstorming their next move in the search for Kenley, while Kori disappeared through the hall closet.

I took advantage of their distractions for a chance to circumspectly look for what I'd come to think of as the escape hatch. There had to be one. I remained convinced that he would never leave his Gran—a woman with no Skill or obvious defensive abilities—alone in a house she couldn't leave.

But the house wasn't that big, and all the windows and exterior doors were screwed shut. Frustrated and desperate, I even searched the closet in Gran's room for hidden panels covering a secret exit. Yes, that would be crazy. But screwing the exits shut wasn't exactly sane.

Alas, the closet hid no secrets, so when I emerged, still trapped in the House of Crazy, I took a millionth look at Gran's bedroom window. From the start, it had seemed like the obvious one to leave open, so Gran could escape if a fire started in the middle of the night. But a glance the day I'd arrived had shown me that it, too, was screwed shut.

However this time when I looked, I noticed something I hadn't before. On the sill itself, along with bits of sawdust from where the screws were forced into the wood,

I saw tiny curls of rubbery shavings. I pinched one between my fingers and realized it was dried paint.

Kris had said some of the windows were painted shut, but someone had scraped paint from the opening in Gran's window. Why bother, if it was screwed closed?

Hopeful, I gave the window a tug, and it slid up with little effort and no noise, despite the countersunk screws. And that's when I noticed these screws were different. They were shorter than the others, so they hadn't penetrated the wood. They were just for show.

But why? Who was the show for, if Kris hadn't gone to the Tower estate intending to kidnap and imprison someone?

Half an hour after she left, Kori returned with Olivia— the bloodhound—and a tall, well-built, dark-haired man who could only be Cam, her significant other.

His significance was obvious in the way they stood close together, and sat close together, and kept touching each other for no reason at all, as if any distance put between them caused actual pain.

To my surprise, they'd been in the House of Crazy less than five minutes when they took seats on the couch, facing the arm chair I'd claimed for myself when all the friendship and togetherness started to close in on me.

"Sera, this is Cameron Caballero," Liv said, one hand on his thick left biceps. "Cam, this is Sera."

We shook hands, and when Cam started talking, I realized they'd come to talk to me.

"So, I understand that you have some information for us to start with," he said, and when I looked up, I found Kris watching us from the kitchen doorway. He'd obviously passed along part of what I'd told him, but I couldn't tell how much.

"I can give you a description." I forced the syllables

from my throat with enough volume to suggest confidence. A lie floating on honest words.

They didn't need to know the parts I'd left out.

Cam smiled. "There isn't much Liv and I can do with a description, but if that'll help Van find his name…well, then we'll be in business."

Oh, yeah. Cam was the name Tracker.

"We want anything you can tell us about him," Olivia said, and I hated how soft her voice was, as if any real volume might startle me. As if she was a counselor in a fancy office.

They definitely knew I'd been there. That I'd seen what happened to my family.

I spared a moment for thanks that Kris had had no other information to give them.

"Dark hair," I said, and Liv started scribbling in her notebook with the stubby remains of a pencil. "Kind of long, and very curly. Light eyes. Pale skin. Freckles." I swallowed and closed my eyes, then opened them almost immediately. With my eyes closed, I could still see him. When the room got too quiet, I could still hear him. The sounds he'd made between my sister's screams…

"Anything else?" Cam asked when I'd been silent for at least a minute.

"He's lean, but strong. Tall. Six feet, or more. He doesn't look like…" *A killer.* I didn't know how to finish that without saying the words. "He looks like a college kid. Clean clothes. Hiking boots. And he smiles a lot. Like he's having fun."

Olivia blinked, and something unpleasant flashed behind her eyes.

I knew what they were thinking. My description was too detailed. I'd gotten a good, long look at the monster who'd slaughtered my entire family. I hadn't just glanced at him as I'd fled the house.

They wanted to know how I'd survived, when everyone I'd ever loved had died.

"Okay. That's good," Liv said, but there was nothing good about what I was telling them. "Did you notice anything else? Tattoos or birthmarks? Scars?"

I shook my head, trying to mentally detach myself. To rise above what I'd seen and heard. "His height and hair are his most distinguishing features." My voice sounded cold. Clinical. As if I'd actually been able to divorce myself from the memories long enough to describe him. But that was another lie.

"Did you hear him speak? Did he have an accent?" Cam asked, and I realized that all discussion from the kitchen had ended. Kris stood in the doorway, quiet rage blooming in red splotches on his cheeks and forehead. Vanessa sat in a recliner, clicking away at her laptop, while Kori perched on the arm of her chair, alternately looking at me and at Van's screen.

"No accent. He sounded normal. Educated, but not pretentious. His voice is deeper than you'd expect from such a thin build, but it's soft. Quiet and controlled." Even in the middle of…bad things.

I'd never spoken about him in such detail, but I'd relived that night so many times that I couldn't forget any of it. Ever. No matter how hard I tried.

"Okay. I've got all that down." Olivia met my gaze with a steady one of her own. "But, Sera, it would really help us out if you could tell us where this happened. My range is pretty good, but I still have limits, and we'll need a starting point."

This is it. The moment when I had to decide how much to trust them. I could give them the location, which would lead them to the crime itself and then they'd know who I'd been, before my family died. They'd see the shattered remains of my life laid out across their computer screens in illicitly gained police reports.

Then they would look at me differently. Pity would outweigh any respect I'd gained. But that wouldn't bring them any closer to discovering the secret of my birth.

"Andersen," I said at last. "About an hour north of the state line."

Andersen wasn't my hometown; it was just the latest in a series of relocations meant to keep us from being found, in spite of my mother's insistence that my biological father had no idea I existed. We'd been in Andersen for six years, since my junior year in high school. That was the longest we'd ever lived anywhere, and my family had only stayed there because when I'd gone off to college, I took the target on my back with me.

In retrospect, the town made sense, as had all the ones before. Anderson had just over one hundred thousand residents. It was a big enough place that no one noticed or really cared when someone new moved into the neighborhood, but too small to hold any real interest for any of the major Skilled syndicates. The perfect place to hide in plain sight.

Until a random act of violence—a home invasion with no clear motive—had taken away everyone I'd ever wanted to protect.

The click of computer keys drew me back into the present, where several sets of eyes stared at me. Vanessa was still searching, and if she hadn't found the news articles yet, she would soon. In a town the size of Andersen, the unsolved murder of almost an entire family was still big news.

"Is there anything else you think we should know?" Olivia asked, and I answered on my way up the stairs.

"Only that I want him dead. But first, I want him to suffer."

Kris

When I stepped out of the upstairs bathroom, Van was waiting for me in the doorway to the room she and Kenley had shared. She tossed her head toward the door, silently asking me to come in. Which meant she didn't want someone to know whatever she had to say.

I followed her into her room and pushed the door closed at my back, then sank onto Kenley's side of the unmade bed, where Van's laptop was open on the rumpled comforter. "What's up?"

"I found her."

"Kenley?" My heart thumped almost painfully.

"No. Sera and her family," Van whispered, glancing at the closed door. "I found all of it, and it's not pretty."

"It's the scene of a triple homicide." Quadruple, if you counted the unborn baby, which Sera obviously did. "I wouldn't expect it to be pretty."

Vanessa tucked her feet beneath her on the rumpled comforter and pulled the computer onto her lap. She ran a finger over the mouse pad and the screen glowed to life, zoomed in on a news site I'd never heard of. "I just sent the link to Olivia so she and Cam could get started. But are you sure you want to read this?"

I scooted back to lean against the headboard next to her, angled so that my feet hung over the edge of the mattress. Kenley hated shoes on the bed. "I'm sure I *don't* want to read it." But I had to know. Whatever Sera was—*who*ever she was—this was the event that would shape the rest of her life, and I couldn't know her without knowing what she'd been through. And I wanted to know Sera. Even if she no longer wanted to know me.

"Why don't you just sum it up for me?" I let my head fall back against the padded headboard. "If you don't mind."

Vanessa shrugged and scrolled on her mouse pad, and I avoided looking at the screen. "It's your basic home invasion, made more horrifying because we actually know one of the victims. Middle of the night break-in. One perpetrator, according to the police report. The only description they got out of Sera was 'tall.' Her dad was the only one still awake when it started, playing guitar in the family room. He must have heard something, because he was shot in the kitchen, through his own guitar. The ballistics report says the gunman used a silencer and facts support that. The neighbors didn't hear anything and the mother never woke up. She was shot in her own bed."

Chill bumps popped up on my arms. How much of that had Sera seen? How much had she heard?

"He took his time with her sister. Nadia. Poor thing was only eighteen. The police report says he slapped a strip of duct tape over her mouth while she was still in bed asleep, then dragged her into the living room and… well…took his time."

Vanessa's jaw clenched, and for a second she looked like she'd be sick.

I felt the same way. "Sick *bastard*. Eighteen and pregnant, and he—"

Van frowned at me. "Nadia wasn't pregnant."

"Sera said she was. Maybe the police didn't know, if she wasn't very far along."

Vanessa blinked at me, and suddenly there was caution in her expression. Wariness. There was something she didn't want to tell me.

"Just say it, Van." Though I wasn't sure I really meant that.

"Kris, Nadia wasn't pregnant. She survived the initial attack, but died in the hospital the next day of a stab wound to the abdomen, without regaining consciousness."

As I struggled to think around a thick fog of confusion—the truth was there, but it wasn't sinking in—Van turned her laptop around so I could see it.

The headline ripped me wide open, and horror leaked into my soul.

Pregnant Woman Survives Home Invasion;
Loses Baby

I got through the first three sentences of the article before my eyes closed on their own, as if they'd seen all they could take. I couldn't breathe. That horror had clawed its way up my throat and was blocking my air passage.

Sera had been four and a half months pregnant when she was stabbed in the stomach and left for dead.

Sera. Not Nadia.

The police report said she came out of hiding to defend her sister, fought with the intruder, then crawled to the telephone to call for help after their attacker fled the scene.

That's why she hid.

She wasn't protecting herself. She was protecting her baby.

I shoved the laptop away so suddenly it was teetering on the edge of the mattress when Van grabbed it.

Sera had been pregnant. She saw her parents murdered. She saw her sister brutalized, and when she tried to help Nadia, she'd lost her own unborn child. And nearly died along with her sister.

But even as I thought that over, trying to digest the horror and depth of her loss, the totality of the rage and isolation she must be suffering with every beat of her heart, some small detail nagged at the back of my brain, clamoring for attention.

I opened my eyes and pulled Van's laptop closer to read the first line again. And there it was, in black and white. I hadn't really noticed it my first time through because the crime itself was shocking enough.

She'd kept her last name secret, but it turns out I hadn't known her first name either.

Sera was Sera Brandt. *S-E-R-A.* Short for Serenity.

Holy shit.

It couldn't be. It wasn't possible.

I shoved the laptop at Van again, then stood and crossed the floor in three steps. I pulled the door open so hard and fast the hinges groaned with the pressure, then I raced into the hall and down the stairs, leaving Vanessa staring after me in surprise. In the living room, I grabbed my bag from the end of the couch and pulled out Noelle's notebook, then started flipping through it frantically, still standing.

I was four pages in when I found the first mention.

Find serenity.

Noelle had said it in her sleep, twelve years ago. Then again, five months after that.

Save serenity.

And twice more, over the next two years.

Serenity waits. and *Family, serenity.*

I hadn't once capitalized her name, because I hadn't realized it was a name.

Noelle had been trying to tell me all along, though she probably didn't understand the message at all. Sera hadn't appeared in the notebook to help me—she'd appeared so I could help *her*.

Stunned, I closed the notebook and dropped it into my bag, disgusted with my own ignorance. Horrified by my own failure. What good did it do for me to have glimpses of the future at my fingertips when I couldn't make sense of a damn one of them?

I was supposed to save Sera and her family. I was supposed to find her and stop the bastard who broke into her house and slaughtered her entire family. Including her unborn child. Hunting down their killer was a secondary goal, only necessary if I failed to keep him from committing the prophesied atrocities in the first place.

Which was exactly what I'd done.

I'd given up. I'd put the notebook away and turned my back on every preventable accident and atrocity predicted within it, because I wasn't smart enough to figure out the puzzles.

Because of me, Sera had lost everyone she'd ever loved.

How the hell was I supposed to tell her that?

Fourteen

Sera

When I came downstairs that afternoon, finally drawn from my room by the scent of homemade chili, Kris was at the kitchen table again, alone this time, his nose buried in that journal, his jaw clenched with some intense emotion I couldn't define or understand. I wanted to talk to him, despite my lingering embarrassment. I wanted to know why he was so angry, and whether or not I was the cause.

I wanted to know if he'd found my family online. If he'd read about what had happened to them. To *us*. I wanted to know whether I'd see pity or anger in his gaze when it next met mine, so I could plan my response accordingly. I'd lied to him about what happened, so any anger on his part was probably warranted, and most people would think pity was appropriate, as well, but I couldn't stand to see either. Not from Kris.

So I only watched him for a minute, knowing I should have been relieved by how focused he was on that stupid notebook. Keeping my distance from him would be easier with Noelle standing between us.

But I didn't feel relieved. I felt…alone.

Kris didn't notice me, so I snuck out with a smile and nod to Gran, who was stirring a big pot on the stove.

I hadn't had chili in months. My dad had made it once a week, every winter of my life. He'd spent Saturdays soaking beans and Sundays simmering sauce on the stove, and if I asked nicely and used a clean spoon, he'd let me have an early taste. I'd missed weekend chili when I'd gone off to college, but every time I came home for winter break, I'd find a pot on the stove and a clean spoon waiting for me on the counter.

There would be no more of my dad's chili. That hadn't occurred to me until I saw Gran making hers, and as I fled the kitchen, I fought a sudden, irrational urge to dump her chili into the garbage disposal because it dared to exist when my dad's chili never would again.

In the living room, Van was curled up in the armchair with her laptop, clicking away as if her fingers would never tire. She glanced up at me and smiled, and I found sympathy in her gaze. No—worse—empathy.

She'd found news coverage of my family's deaths, at the very least. I could tell from the new way she looked at me, and if she knew, Kris knew. They might all know. But she didn't call me over or try to ensnare me in some kind of bullshit therapeutic chat, for which I was eminently grateful.

Kori and Ian sat on the couch, talking in hushed tones with a map spread out on the coffee table in front of them. He was shirtless again, with a big white bandage taped over his shoulder. When he twisted to reach for a pen on the end table, I saw a matching bandage on his other side. The bullet had gone all the way through.

When Ian had winced and sucked in a sharp breath three times in less than a minute, Kori stood and tossed her pen onto the end table, mumbling something about stubborn-ass men who made no use of the available resources. She stomped down the hall and into the closet, where—presumably—she disappeared through the shadows, despite his protest.

Several minutes later, the closet door opened again and everyone who had a gun drew it, just in case. Then Kori stepped into the hall again with a woman I'd never seen before, but everyone else seemed to recognize.

"Meg, you really didn't have to come," Ian said, but Kori rolled her eyes and Meg waved away his congenial objection.

"You'd do the same for me or Steve." This was Ian's twin brother's wife. Meghan. The Healer.

I watched, fascinated, as she sat on the center couch cushion and gently peeled off the bandage on the front of Ian's shoulder. "Ready?" Meg asked, and Ian nodded, his jaw already clenched against the pain.

Meg took a small bottle of hand sanitizer from her pocket and rubbed a dollop onto her palms, then pressed her right hand against Ian's bare, still-bloody wound.

He hissed again and Meghan stiffened, and a second later, thin black lines appeared on the back of her hand and across her arm, as though her veins were rotting from the inside out. I'd never seen anything like it, and could only assume that was normal for a Healer when no one else seemed impressed or upset.

A couple of minutes later, Ian's jaw unclenched, and a minute after that, Meg let him go and slouched sideways against the back of the couch. When she'd caught her breath, she inspected the wound, which had closed but was still an angry red color, beneath smears of Ian's blood. "That's better." She nodded, obviously satisfied.

"Not perfect, but good enough that you should be able to use it, if you're careful."

"Thanks, Meghan." Ian squeezed her hand and Kori took his bloody bandages to the bathroom, where she would burn them in the sink to destroy the viable blood sample. Gran brought two smaller clean ones, and Meghan carefully taped them over the wound again.

Then Kori took Meg back to wherever she and Steven were staying while he finished recuperating.

"Liv and Cam got called in," Vanessa said when I settled into Gran's rocker across the room. "They'll be back, though, and hopefully I'll have something for them to go on by then. The police questioned a couple of possible suspects in your case, both parolees with convictions for breaking and entering and burglary. But neither of them match your description, and neither have a history of violence."

"So, no other leads?" I tried not to sound as disappointed as I felt.

"Not yet. But the police have plenty of…physical evidence. All the blood they found belongs to…your family. But it's possible that Liv can find something they missed. She only needs a drop or two to get a feel for the owner, so if he bled on anything, she'll be able to tell us if he's anywhere within her range. The tricky part will be getting our hands on the evidence. Not impossible for a group with our varied talents. But too complicated a project for today."

"Of course." I had to remind myself that I was in no hurry. Kenley was in immediate danger, so her case had to come first. The sooner we found her, the faster they'd be free to help me hunt down and kill the bastard who'd taken my whole life from me.

"How can I help?" I said when Ian looked up at me and smiled. "What are we doing?"

"Van got us a partial list of the Tower syndicate's real-estate holdings, so we're going through the list of warehouses, looking for one that could possibly work for the blood farm."

I stared at all the red circles on their map, trying to make sense of names and places I'd never seen before. "Any luck?"

"Too much luck." Kori walked out of the closet and closed the door, stepping into our conversation as easily as she'd stepped out of the shadows. "Tower owns nearly two dozen warehouses in the city alone, and who knows how many in other areas. I've been to several of them, and the truth is that any one of them could house the blood farm. Julia has the money to set up all of the necessary supplies and equipment anywhere she wants, and it could take us days to search all of these individually."

"And this is just a partial list," Vanessa added, peeking over her laptop screen.

Ian looked grim as he studied his list, then circled another point on the map. "We need some way to narrow them down."

"That's what Kris is working on." Skepticism was thick in Kori's voice. "Did he tell you about the notebook?"

"Yeah. And about Noelle." Did I sound bitter about the fact that she'd had him for so long, but I never would? I must have—Kori's pale brows rose and I swear she almost smiled. "You guys are all messed up. Your relationships are, like…twisted."

Ian laughed, but Kori only nodded. "Sometimes when you're tied too tightly to the people you care about, the strings get tangled. You can either cut them loose or pull them tighter. I'm sure you can figure out which one we chose, based on the knot we're in now."

Yeah. They were tied so tightly together I couldn't tell where one relationship ended and the next began—siblings, lovers, friends, caretakers, defenders and coworkers. They were everything to one another, and I could see that sometimes those bonds chafed, but from where I stood—a single thread dangling alone in the wind— their tangled knot looked pretty damn secure.

"So, do you think he'll find anything in that notebook? Do you think it's even possible?"

Ian and Van looked to Kori for an answer, and I found myself doing the same. Kori shrugged. "It's more than possible. I never knew Noelle to be wrong. But the chances of anyone figuring out what she was talking about in time to be useful are slim to none."

"It's a good thing you didn't put money on that, because I'd own every cent you have right now," Kris said, and I could practically hear the smile in his voice. When I looked up to find him standing in the kitchen doorway, his index finger marking a place in the closed notebook, I could also see the spark of excitement in his eyes.

"You found something?" The rational part of me wanted to be happy for him. That other part wanted to poke him in the eyes to get rid of that spark, put there by a dead girl he'd loved and who might be trying to tell him to kill me, either to put an end to the Tower empire, or because even in her grave, she was a jealous bitch.

My money was on the latter.

Kris nodded eagerly. Kori scooted over and he sat next to her on the couch, then set his journal on the coffee table, open to a page about a third of the way through the notebook. "Ned said they were moving everything to a warehouse, right?" Kris said, and I nodded. I was the only other one who'd heard Ned. "Well, there it is." He underlined a passage several lines from the top with his finger.

We all leaned in for a closer look, and I had to read upside down from my chair on the other side of the coffee table. Fortunately, the line was short, and Kris's script was a neat, masculine cursive, with long narrow letters. Easily legible.

"Blood in the trees," Ian said, echoing the phrase as it played in my head. "What the hell does that mean?"

Kris rolled his eyes and snatched the printout of Tower's real estate holdings from his sister's hands. "That one. The warehouse on Sycamore Grove, in the south fork. See?" But no one saw. "It's the only one with trees in the address."

"Kris, that could mean anything…." Vanessa said, but he spoke over her.

"Look. It's in here again." He flipped more pages to a point farther back in the notebook, marked by his own folded copy of the property list. "'Hidden in the grove.'"

"Kris, there's no rhyme or reason to this." Kori frowned at the notebook. "It looks like those two phrases were spoken months apart." But it was closer to a year, if the glimpse of the dates I'd gotten could be trusted. "How do you know those two are even related?"

"I don't." Kris leaned back on the couch and crossed his arms over his chest, and I did *not* think about how, the day before, I'd seen him without a shirt. And touched his stomach. I didn't think about that at all. "What I do know is that we're looking at a list of more than twenty warehouses, and those are just the ones Vanessa's been able to verify as Tower's. But nothing else on that list sounds like anything I've found in here after reading and rereading the damn thing for nearly two hours. But *two* of these phrases could be pointing at the warehouse on Sycamore Grove."

He flipped back to the first passage and spoke over another objection. "*Blood* in the trees." Then he looked up, eyeing each of us expectantly. "We're looking for a blood farm. A hidden blood farm." He flipped back to the second passage, still marked with his index finger. "*Hidden* in the grove."

"It can't hurt to look." Vanessa shrugged and closed her laptop. "We have to start somewhere, and that's one of only two properties that won't take us into Julia's territory."

Kris sat up straight on the couch, enthusiasm echoing in his very bearing. "Which is more evidence that Elle was right. Julia knows we'd expect her to hide her most valuable assets in her own territory, where it's easier to protect them. Relocating to the south fork is ballsy. But then, so is Julia."

"The south fork?" I glanced around the room in question.

"The south side of town, defined by a fork in the river that divides the city," Ian said. "Tower rules the west side. Cavazos has the east side."

"They've been fighting over the south side for years," Kori added. "But so far, neither has a foothold. The south side is your best bet if you want to avoid syndicate entanglements."

"So, if the blood farm is on Sycamore Grove, Julia's effectively hiding it in plain sight?"

"Well, I doubt she hung up 'Coming Soon' signs or set out a welcome mat." Kris smiled at me, and I looked away, and when he continued, his voice was…different. Disappointed, maybe. But not angry. He wasn't mad that I'd lied to him, but I'd almost rather see his anger than his pity. "But she's definitely hidden it where we'd be least likely to look for it."

"Where *anyone* would be least likely to look." Van glanced from me to him, then back to me, silently questioning the change between us. But it was nothing I could explain to her, or to any of them without further embarrassing myself.

"Why are Seers always so damn obscure?" I flipped through the notebook absently. Casually. "What good are her predictions if they're too vague to be used?"

"She wasn't always vague." Kris took the journal from me and closed it. "Her waking predictions were usually much clearer, like what Hadley told us the other day. But when Elle was asleep, she couldn't elaborate, and when I woke her to ask, she never remembered what she'd been dreaming."

"Okay. So we're going to do this." Van closed her laptop and stood.

"Yes." Kris stood and slid the notebook into his duffel bag on the floor by the couch. "But you're staying here."

"No way." Vanessa clutched her laptop to her chest. "Kenley needs me."

"She needs you to stay alive and unharmed. You have no combat experience, and I don't want to leave Gran alone if I don't have to." Kori glanced at me as she lifted a shoulder holster from the arm of the couch and slid her arms through the straps. "You, too."

Vanessa looked as if she'd argue, if she didn't already know it would do no good.

I knew no such thing.

"I'm going." If Kris was right and the blood farm was at the Sycamore Grove warehouse, then there was every chance in the world that I could cull a couple more indentured servants from Julia's bonds, and a couple of guns made loyal to us—or at least removed from Julia's arsenal—could mean the difference between life and death if Kris and his crew found themselves outnumbered.

Beyond that, I was *not* giving up another chance to test my newly inherited bonds and to free more of the poor bastards bound by them.

Of course, I'd have to do it without anyone seeing, but I was up to the challenge.

"She's right," Kris said, and I turned to find him wearing a double holster, armed with a gun on each side. Could he shoot left-handed? "You'll be safer here." There was no malice in his eyes. He wasn't just trying to cut me out of the action.

"I thought you needed me to jam your psychic signal. I can't do that from here."

"That's a moot point in this scenario," Ian said, and I decided, for the moment at least, that I hated every single one of them. "We can't break Kenley out of a secure building we've never even seen before without being noticed by the enemy. In which case they won't have to track us. They'll be able to see us."

"But couldn't you use an extra hand? Holding an extra gun?"

Kori shrugged a jacket on over her shirt and shoulder holster, then gave me an almost sympathetic smile. "You don't shoot. Guns, at least. And this time I doubt they'll leave bottles of spray cleaner around to tempt you."

I glared at Kris. He didn't have to make me sound like such an…amateur. Even if I was one.

"Liv and Cam can't make it right now, but they'll check in later to see if they're still needed," Kori said, reading from her cell phone screen.

"Fine. Don't give me a gun." I followed them into the hallway, pissed off even further over being forced to beg like a puppy. "I'm not bad with a knife, and I know you have extras."

"Not this time, Sera." Kris held the closet door open while Kori and Ian stepped inside.

"Don't you dare close that door!" I demanded as he stepped in after them. Kris gave me an apologetic look, then closed the door in my face. "You are *not* going without me!" I yelled at the closed door, my hands balled into impotent fists.

Furious, I kicked the door, and something inside me... slipped. It felt like the mental version of bumping into a dresser and knocking one of the drawers open a few inches.

My kick to the door was followed by a louder, deeper thud from inside the closet.

"What the *fuck!*" Kori shouted, and the closet door swung open so fast I had to jump back to keep from getting smacked by it.

"What happened?" Vanessa said from the end of the hall, and I could see Gran behind her, both of them drawn by Kori's shout. Or maybe by my own heartfelt objection.

"I don't know." Kori stuck her head out of the closet and Kris pushed her aside so he could step into the hall. "I tried to travel, and nothing happened. It's like the shadows are *locked*. We ran into the fucking door."

Gran burst into laughter, then headed back into the kitchen, and briefly, I wondered what she'd heard that I hadn't. Did Alzheimer's make unfunny things sound funny?

Van turned from Gran back to Kori, frowning. "Has that ever happened before?"

"No," Kris and Kori said in unison.

"Maybe you're just tired," Ian said, joining the rest of them in the hall.

Kori nodded. "I'm going to try it again." She stepped into the closet alone and closed the door as I backed slowly, silently into the living room. I wasn't sure what I'd done, but I was almost sure I'd done *something*. I'd felt it, right after I kicked the door. Maybe if I removed myself from the situation, things would go back to normal.

I sat on the couch, staring down the hall at Van, Ian and Kris as they watched the closed closet door. A second later, another thud came from within, and this time the string of expletives Kori shouted could have singed the hair off a sailor's butt.

She tried to travel from the closet twice more, getting angrier and angrier with each failure before Kris insisted she give him a shot.

He ran into the closed door so hard he came out with a nosebleed.

I tried not to laugh. I really did.

After that, they turned off the lights in Gran's bedroom—including the infrared bulb—and tried to shadow-walk from there, with no success. Then Ian called up the darkest darkness he could manage, and they both tried to travel through that, to no avail.

That's when Gran stepped into the living room with a bowl of chili in one hand, a full spoon halfway to her mouth. "All three of you owe Sera an apology. Maybe once she gets it she'll take us out of lockdown. Though I wouldn't blame her for keeping you here, considering that's exactly what Kris did to her."

I gaped at Gran, wondering how she knew what I still hadn't figured out. But she only shoveled that first bite of chili into her mouth, then laughed around it on her way back into the kitchen.

When I turned, four sets of eyes were staring at me.

Kori looked beyond pissed off. Kris looked confused and a little wary. Van and Ian looked fascinated.

Kori rubbed the fresh bruise on her forehead, frowning at me expectantly. "What the hell is she talking about?"

I could only shrug. "In the two days I've been here, I've understood very little of what that woman says."

"Gran, how old am I?" Kris stared over my head into the kitchen with a bathroom rag pressed to his dripping nose.

"What kind of dumb-ass doesn't know his own age?" she called back, and wood creaked as she settled into the far chair at the table—I'd already grown to recognize the sound.

"My kind. How old am I?"

"Thirty, last May. Do you need a fucking diaper change, too?"

Vanessa laughed, and Kori rolled her eyes.

"Just checking." Kris's gaze settled on me again. "She's coherent, which means she knows what she's talking about. What the hell did you do?"

"I don't know. I swear. I just…didn't want you to walk through the shadows without me, and the next thing I knew, you were running into closed doors. Repeatedly." My gesture took in the bloody rag he still had pressed to both nostrils.

Evidently I was the only one who could see the humor in the situation. Probably because I was the only one who kinda wanted to see Kris bleed. Just a little.

"Gran, what do you know about this?" Kori stomped past me to stand in the kitchen doorway, where she could see everyone all at once.

"More than any of you, apparently," Gran said, and I shimmied sideways past Kori and into the kitchen, where Gran gave me a conspiratorial wink. As if we were in cahoots about the whole thing. Then she turned back to Kori. "If you want information from me, you better dig up some fucking manners, young lady." Gran took another bite of chili, and I decided then and there that Alzheimer's or not, she was the coolest grandmother ever.

I'd never even met any of mine.

"Gran." Kris sank into the chair across from her. "We're trying to go after Kenley. Remember? We need to get this fixed. Now."

"Please tell us," I added.

This time Gran looked surprised when she met my gaze. "You don't know?" I shook my head and she turned back to her audience, and I could tell by her solemn expression that she now understood the stakes. "Sera's a Blocker."

"No, I'm a Jammer." That was one of very few facts I was sure of.

"What the hell is a Blocker?" Kori asked, and everyone else looked just as clueless.

"It's a myth, that's what it is." Gran dropped her spoon into her bowl and pushed it back as Kori and Van sank into the chairs on either side of Kris, who kept looking at me, then looking away when I noticed. Ian and I stood against the wall, on opposite sides of the doorway, and every gaze in the room was glued to Gran. "I've never actually met one," she continued. "Most people don't believe in them." She shrugged. "But then, most unSkilled don't believe in Skills, either, so who the hell are we to say what's real and what's not?"

No one had an answer, but she wasn't really looking for one.

"Sera's real, and she's a Blocker." Gran leaned back in her chair, easing effortlessly into that instruction-mode only perfected by raising children. My mother had done it well. "My grandmother always told me that blocking was a piggy-back Skill—that it only manifests in someone who already has a primary Skill. I'm guessing she was right, considering that you're a Jammer, too."

I nodded.

"So, she can block other people's Skills?" Kris asked, and I knew he was right the moment I heard the words. That's what I'd done. I'd blocked his ability to travel. I'd kind of mentally bumped both him and Kori and knocked their Skills out of alignment. Or something like that.

Gran nodded. "My grandmother theorized that there were more Blockers out there than anyone really knew. Her idea was that most of them never discover the piggy-back Skill, because they don't know they can do it, and they stop looking for abilities once their primary Skill manifests." Gran shrugged, and her steel-colored hair caught the light. "Maybe she was right. Maybe Sera never would have discovered she could block you if she hadn't *really* wanted to keep you here."

Everyone was looking at me with a certain kind of aggravated respect now, and I would have thoroughly enjoyed that…if I'd intentionally done the thing they respected.

"She can take it back, right? She can just…turn our Skills back on?" Kori looked to me for an answer and when I didn't have one, she turned back to Gran, who could only shrug.

So we tested it out. Kori tried to travel out of the front closet for at least the fifth time in the past quarter hour, to no avail.

"I'm sorry," I said when she emerged angrier than ever. "I don't know how to stop it. I don't even know how I'm doing it. I just…don't want you guys to go without me."

"That's it." When we all turned to look at him, Ian wore a quiet smile, but it appeared to be all for me. "It's just like Kenley and binding. She has to truly *want* to break a binding, in order to remove her will from it, and you have to truly want us to go, for us to be able to leave."

"But I don't want you to go without me." Kris and Kori started to object, but I cut them off. "Arguing isn't going to help. And I'm not going to feel guilty for insisting that you treat me like an equal. I may not be able to shoot the wings off a fly at forty paces, or whatever, but I can do things none of you can do. Useful things. So… either let me join in your reindeer games, or it looks like no one's going to play."

Vanessa chuckled. "You're going to have to take her with you." She shrugged. "At least until she learns how to control the blocking. That's how it works for all Skills, right? They take practice to control?"

Kori nodded reluctantly, and Kris looked almost amused. "I have to admit, that's impressive." He grinned as if he'd forgotten about the night before. About how kissing me was a mistake. "Your psychic temper tantrum put the lockdown on this entire house." He turned to Kori and Ian before I could object to the characterization of something I couldn't yet control as a child's fit. "Maybe we need her with us after all."

Kori didn't look pleased and Ian seemed reluctant to put me in any more danger—they all did, since they'd found out about the smiling man's knife and the weeks I'd spent in the hospital. But when neither of them could think of a logical reason to object, I knew I'd won.

A minute and a half later, Kris and I stepped out of the hall closet and into a small, dark bathroom in the warehouse on Sycamore Grove—the only patch of darkness in the whole building. Kori and Ian stepped out of the deep shadows behind us a few seconds later, and we tiptoed toward the line of light we could see beneath the door.

Kris opened the door carefully, and when no one burst in aiming guns at us, he pushed it the rest of the way open. Then nearly choked on shock.

The rest of us peered around him, and my entire body went cold when I saw what was waiting for us in the hall, facing the door we'd just opened in the only dark spot in the building.

A spot that had been left dark for us on purpose, I realized, as I stared at what Julia Tower had left behind.

Ned-the-guard. Dead, with a neat-ish hole in the center of his forehead. Nude and propped up in a sitting position, with a paper note safety-pinned to the flesh above his heart. His dead eyes stared up at us, and I knew what he was meant to be even before I read the note, which appeared to have been written in blood. Probably his.

Ned was a message from Julia Tower. To me.

I should have known she'd kill him if he was no longer useful to her. And if she knew I had set him free, then she knew I'd figured out exactly who I was and what I could take from her.

Pretense was over. The battle had just begun.

Only one of us could survive.

Fifteen

Kris

"Oh, shit…" I tried to block the dead man from Sera's line of sight, but I could tell by her suddenly rapid breathing that she'd already seen. She tried to push past me, but I refused to move. I'd already lost Kenley by letting her rush into an unknown situation, and I wasn't going to make that mistake again. "Wait!" I whispered when she wouldn't stop shoving. "It's probably an ambush."

"Bullshit." Sera didn't even bother to whisper. "They obviously knew we were coming—this was left here for us. If this were an ambush, they wouldn't want us to know they knew we were coming."

I had to think about that for a second; however, once I'd untangled her sentence, I couldn't argue with it. But caution never hurts.

Kori and I fanned out for a quick search of the four other rooms emptying into the hallway, while Ian and his gun—fortunately, he'd been shot in his left shoulder—stood guard over Sera.

When we were sure the immediate area was deserted, I motioned for Ian to let her out of the men's room. Sera shot an angry glance at me, but I was starting to get used to those. And I refused to feel guilty for trying to keep her safe. Angry-Sera was better than dead-Sera any day of the week.

Although agreeable-Sera would have been a nice change.

She knelt by Ned's body, and when Kori and Ian took up posts on either side, I knelt with her to read the note pinned to the dead man's bare chest.

His blood is on your hands.

"That's Julia's handwriting," Kori said, and I looked up to see her staring at the note as if she'd seen a ghost. "She doesn't usually get her hands dirty, but this time I'd bet my last drop of vodka that the bitch pinned it to him herself."

"But how is his blood on our hands?" Sera said. "We let him live."

Kori snorted. "That's what got him killed."

Sera stood and covered her face with both hands, then ran her fingers through her hair. Her hands were small. They looked softer than Kori's and more feminine, with short rounded nails instead of bitten stubs. I wanted to touch one of them. Then she dropped them, and for a second she was looking right at me—until that seemed to make her uncomfortable and her gaze found the corpse again.

I tried not to be offended that she'd rather look at a dead man than at me.

"Okay." She took a deep breath, obviously collecting her thoughts. Trying to mentally move past the dead body. "My guess is that if your sister was ever here, she's gone now."

"Kenley was here." I was sure of that. "They knew we'd figure it out, after talking to Ned, so they moved her and left him here for us to find. Unless you think Julia left us a rotting welcome gift at every warehouse we might think to search?"

Sera shook her head and I watched her, studying her intense focus. "You think Julia killed Ned because he didn't kill us? Or because she knew it would upset you? Or because he told us they moved the blood farm to a warehouse?" It was a trick question, intended to test her growing understanding of syndicate life. The answer was: D. All of the above. Julia had killed him because she could.

"He's dead because she doesn't know *what* he told us," Sera mumbled, rereading the note for at least the hundredth time, and I shook my head.

"Julia Tower is a Reader. The only way to keep her in the dark is to say nothing, and Ned didn't have that option. He was bound to her."

Sera started to argue—I could see it coming before she even opened her mouth—then seemed to think better of it. "Either way, they obviously knew we were coming. My bet is that this place is deserted."

"Or they want us to *think* this place is deserted, so they can ambush us when we search it." The warehouse was a trap. It had to be. If Julia wanted us dead—and she did—and knew we were coming—which she did—why not take advantage of the opportunity?

"Okay." Kori glanced from Ian to me. Sera looked miffed that she wasn't being consulted about the plan. "This hall has two exits." The only two doors we hadn't checked, because they were locked. "You two go left, we'll go right. Stay together. If it gets dangerous, go home. Immediately."

Ian could make his own shadows for them to travel through, but I'd have to destroy the infrared lighting grid for a chance to travel. "This isn't my first rodeo," I reminded her.

"Well, it is hers." Kori shot a pointed glance at Sera.

"What, the last mostly deserted building doesn't count?" Sera demanded softly. "If I hadn't seen that guard in time, Ian would have been hit in the chest, instead of the shoulder."

My sister scowled. "And if you'd known how to disarm him, Ian wouldn't have been hit at all."

"If I haven't already thanked you…thank you," Ian said.

Kori turned toward the door on her end of the hall and he followed her with a reassuring smile at Sera.

"Is your sister always so bossy?" Sera whispered as we headed toward our locked door.

"Yeah. We let her think she's in charge, because it's easier than arguing with her. But if her way isn't the best way, I do things my way." I shrugged and leaned closer to whisper near her ear, hyperaware that Vanessa's strawberry-scented shampoo made Sera smell like she might actually be edible. And I wanted a taste. "Sometimes I do things my way anyway, just to watch her head explode. Though I usually save that for when the cable goes out and everyone's bored."

At the end of the hall, I tried the doorknob one more time, to make sure nothing had changed. It was still locked. I glanced back just in time to see Ian pull a deep column of darkness out of nowhere for them to step through, then I holstered my gun and took a longer look at the door and lock.

It was an interior commercial door. Aluminum and

hollow, with a standard doorknob lock. Easier to kick open than to shoot.

"Stand back," I said, and Sera backed up to give me some space. Two heel kicks to the left of the knob, and the door swung open with minimal noise and no real mess.

I stepped into the dark interior office beyond and did a quick security check, then motioned for Sera to follow me inside. Though the only visible light came from an open supply closet, I could feel the infrared grid blazing above me, rendering every shadow shallow and useless.

The office held two metal desks, each with the drawers open and emptied. A laptop power cord trailed across the surface of each desk, but the computers themselves were gone, along with whatever information they'd contained.

The wall opposite the door I'd kicked in held a long glass panel overlooking the warehouse itself, a good six feet lower than the rest of the building. A quick glance inside showed that it was empty, too, except for a couple of abandoned medical gurneys and several scraps of tubing, IV bags, and other medical supplies on the concrete floor.

"They left in a hurry." I crossed the room, toward the entrance to the warehouse. "Maybe that means they're still setting up the new place."

"Or that they already had it ready, just in case." Sera followed me down the steel grid stairs into the body of the warehouse. There was a set of bathrooms on the far side of the huge room, both doors standing wide open, but other than that, I saw nowhere for anyone to hide.

"So, what?" She ran one hand down the length an abandoned gurney, and I wanted to tell her to stop—that there was no telling what she could catch. Then I remembered that Tower's victims weren't sick. They were kept unconscious for ease of handling. "They strap these poor people to the bed and drain them?" Sera looked horrified all over again now that she could see a little of what Jake Tower had started and his sister was continuing. "A little at a time, or all at once?"

"Kori didn't mention straps, and these gurneys aren't equipped with them. She says they keep the donors sedated via IV drip and they never take enough blood to kill. Tower was very interested in the renewable aspect of his...resources."

"The bad guys are going green?"

"Only if the color refers to cash. They're trying to milk every dollar they can out of each body before it finally gives out. The Towers are motivated by two things—money and power. The only things they like better than money and power are more money and more power. I think it's some kind of chromosomal abnormality. They lack the genes for compassion and morality."

Sera scowled and her green eyes darkened.

"What now?" I'd thought we were making progress. She was speaking to me again, and as soon as I had a moment alone with her, somewhere other than an enemy warehouse, I was prepared to declare myself an idiot and apologize for the night before. So why was she getting angrier with every word I spoke?

"Nothing." She started across the warehouse toward the bathrooms.

"Sera, wait," I said, and when she finally turned to face me again, her scowl had etched deep lines in her forehead. "Okay, I know you're mad about what I said last night, and I know I deserve it—"

"I'm not mad. You were right." Her gaze met mine with what looked like considerable effort. "I'm not in the best state of mind, and if I'd been thinking clearly, I wouldn't have thrown myself at the first available warm body."

"I was just the first available…" *Ouch.* I tried to pretend it didn't sting to hear that mine was a bed of convenience. That any port in the storm would have done.

"Yeah." She shrugged, but the motion looked stiff and insincere. Or was I imagining that? "So…thanks. You saved us both from a big mistake."

A mistake? My jaw clenched. Was she throwing my own words at me out of anger, or had we really switched positions so quickly?

"Anyway, you're off the hook," she continued, oblivious to my confusion. "I won't be throwing myself at you anymore. I promise."

"Um…okay." I hid disappointment behind what I hoped was a casual smile. "But to prove I have no hard feelings, if you change your mind and decide to throw yourself at me again, this time I promise to catch you."

Her brows rose in surprise. "Are you flirting? Because you should know, that kind of comes off as a mixed signal, after last night."

"Sera, I'm so sorry about last night. I had my wires totally crossed, but today they're all straightened out. I swear."

The crook in her eyebrow said she was intrigued, but the downward tilt of her lips said she was also feeling cautious. I'd never wanted to turn a frown upside down so badly in my life. "I'm not sure what that means, Kris."

"That means I want to be here for you. Whatever you need."

"Thanks, but seriously, you were right. I shouldn't jump into anything right now. I think we'd both regret that."

She was wrong. But… "Hot chocolate, then. With or without the Peeps. Or a shoulder to lean on. A hand to hold. An ear to bend. It doesn't have to be complicated.

Just promise you won't dial me out next time you need something. Okay?"

Her frown finally died, but that caution still swam in her eyes. As if she wasn't sure she could trust me.

I chuckled. "You really make a man work for it, don't you?"

Her eyes narrowed. "Work for what?"

"A smile," I said, and her suspicion disappeared. "All I want is a smile. And you're really making me work for it." Okay, a smile wasn't *all* I wanted. But it's what I wanted *first*. I wanted to be able to make her think, just for a minute, about something other than what she'd lost. How she'd nearly died three times since meeting me. How we were no closer to finding the man who'd stolen everything from her.

I wanted to give her something. And I would start with a smile.

"This isn't the kind of place that inspires smiles," she pointed out. "And this isn't exactly a happy time. There's a dead man in the hall."

"I'm happy he's not you."

"I'm happy about that, too." She glanced at her hands for a second, then met my gaze again, and I could see it in her eyes. I almost had her. "I'm also happy that he's not you."

And finally she smiled.

I felt absurdly triumphant, and I'm sure my own goofy grin reflected that. Even if neither of our smiles would last. And they couldn't, considering where we stood.

With another glance around the warehouse, solemnity returned, and Sera was all business again.

"Why do you think they left these two gurneys?" she asked, but she'd already drawn the same conclusion I had. I could see that in her eyes as she ran one thumb over a dark spot on the edge of the thin white sheet. "These two didn't make it, right?" She looked up at me, and I could only shrug. "They poured bleach over the blood—I can smell it—but it's still damp. We didn't miss them by much. The cleanup crew, anyway,"

I couldn't tear my gaze from that spot of blood. Until I noticed another one. And another, leading to a larger stain where the donor's elbow might have been. Had the donor woken up and struggled? Had something gone wrong with the IV? Had Julia simply cut her losses on a couple of the more fragile donors, who might not be worth the trouble of moving?

"I'm sure Kenley wasn't one of them." The compassion in her voice drew my gaze.

"She wasn't. Julia can't afford to let her die." But she wasn't truly letting Kenni live, either. "Stay put while I check the bathrooms."

Sera's brows rose over what she evidently saw as an order.

"Please," I added as an afterthought, and she gave me another small smile.

"See? That word really can work magic."

I laughed, and as I crossed the floor toward the bathroom, I began composing a mental list of every possible way to use her "magic word" in my own favor. The entries were not all G-rated.

The men's room door was open widest, so I checked that one first, careful not to turn my back on the ladies' room, even with Sera there to shout if someone tried to sneak up on me. The men's room was small and empty, and far from fresh, in spite of the fact that Julia's people obviously kept plenty of bleach on hand.

The ladies' room was just as small and empty, and only marginally cleaner.

With the restrooms clear, I crossed the room to tug on the padlock bolting the exterior door, then gave the rolling bay doors a tug, too. Everything was locked up tight, from the inside.

"Well, the cleanup crew didn't go out this way," I said, but when I turned to glance at Sera, she was gone.

"Damn it!" I drew my gun again and rechecked the bathrooms. "Sera!" I hissed, on my way up the steel grid steps, but the office and its supply closet were both empty. She hadn't gone past me into the warehouse, so the only other option was…

"Sera!" I called again in an angry whisper as I back-tracked into the well-lit hallway. The doors Kori and I had checked were still open, and all of the rooms were still dark, except for…the bathroom we'd traveled into. The door was barely ajar now, and the light inside was brighter than the hallway.

Would it have killed her to tell me if she had to pee? Or to go in the warehouse restroom, where I knew there was no one waiting to decorate the walls with our splattered brains?

I did a cursory scan of the rooms between me and the bathroom to make sure no one was luring me down the hall, only to sneak up behind me, and I was two doors from the lit restroom when I heard Sera's voice. Whispering.

"You don't have orders to kill me, do you? That's why you hesitated," she said, and my trigger finger twitched. Who the hell was she talking to? "That means you know who I am, right?"

Who she was? A Jammer? A Blocker? What did those have to do with why someone—Julia's someone, most likely—had no orders to kill her?

I edged forward slowly and peered into the dark room

on my right, but no answer came from whoever she was talking to—no verbal answer, anyway—and I was starting to wonder if she was talking to herself in the bathroom mirror. I *hoped* she was talking to herself, because if this was a trap, and she'd walked into it, she had no way to defend herself. Not without a spray bottle and a toilet plunger, anyway.

So why didn't she sound as though she needed to be defended?

The room on my right looked empty at a glance, and a glance was all I had time for, if Sera was stalling, waiting for someone with a gun to show up and bail her out.

"And if you know who I am, you *can't* kill me, can you? Not even if she tells you to. You can't even raise a hand against me, right?"

Silence met her latest question and my heart beat harder as I crossed the hall silently to peer into the last room between me and Sera and…whoever was in the bathroom with her, real or imaginary.

"I think I'm starting to figure this out. You can't hurt me, just like you couldn't hurt her. Same game, new dealer, right?"

"Honestly, your guess is as good as mine," a man's voice said, and I stopped in my tracks. Either she'd actually found someone, or the other half of her split personality was decidedly unfeminine.

"You can call me Sera," she said as I pushed that last door open, my pulse rushing so loud in my ears that it threatened to drown out her soft words. How close was she to getting shot? Why wasn't she dead already? Was it true that he couldn't kill her—whoever he was—and if so, why not?

"What else?" Sera said as I stared at a vaguely person-shaped outline in the last shadowy office between me and the bathroom. "Can you lie? That's a stupid question, isn't it? Even if you say no, how do I know you're telling the truth?"

"I can lie, unless you tell me not to," the man said as I aimed my gun at the person-shaped shadow. It didn't move, so I pulled a penlight from my left pocket and flinched when the power button clicked beneath my thumb. But neither Sera nor the man with her heard, and the shadow turned out to be a custodian's uniform hung on the top handle of a filing cabinet.

"Okay, then, let's try this out. Are you here alone?"

"No," he said. "My partner took the other wing."

"Just one man?" Sera paused as I snuck back across the hall, and I had the feeling she was considering. "He doesn't stand a chance."

I'd come to the same conclusion. Kori and Ian could dispatch a lone gunman in their sleep. What I couldn't figure out was why *Sera* was still alive.

"Okay. I suspect our privacy is nearing its end. Tell me where they put Kenley Daniels, and I'll let you go. You have my word."

"Like you let Ned go?" At the mention of the dead man, I glanced at him, still propped up across from the bathroom, less than a foot from me now. "You can see how well that worked out for him."

I could see the speaker by then, through the crack where the bathroom door hadn't quite closed. He was tall and fair-skinned. Reasonably thick, like most of Tower's musclemen. But he had to be Skilled, to have gotten into a warehouse locked from the inside. Had he come through the bathroom, after we'd left it? Was that why she'd turned the lights on? To keep a Traveler from escaping?

But that made no sense, because he still had his gun,

which should have meant he was the one in power. Yet his gun was aimed at the floor, and he showed no more inclination to use it than she showed fear of it.

"That wasn't my fault. I set him free," Sera insisted, and on the wall, the shadow of her hand pushed back the shadow of her hair, hanging over her silhouette.

"Which is exactly what got him killed," the man insisted. "You broke his binding, and she has no use for those she can't control."

She? Julia? How the hell could Sera have broken Ned's binding?

That was the last unanswered question I could take. I shoved the door open and aimed at the man's head. "What the hell are you talking about?"

Sera gasped, and the man swung his gun up in my direction.

"Stop!" Sera shouted, and he took his finger off the trigger. "Put your gun down. In fact, give me the damn thing!"

To my absolute shock, Julia Tower's muscleman clicked the safety switch on, then handed his pistol to her by its grip.

Sera held it with the caution of someone who's never pulled a trigger in her life. But to her credit, she didn't set it in the sink behind her or drop it in the toilet to her left. Though she might have ejected the clip, if she'd known how.

"What the *hell* is going on here?" I demanded, still aiming at the man's head. "How did you break Ned's bindings?"

"Kris, stand down," Sera said. "Mitch isn't going to hurt anyone. Are you?" She glanced at the man with one brow raised, and Mitch shrugged.

"That's up to you."

She frowned. "Well, then…don't hurt anyone."

"Ever?" He stared back at her in challenge and seemed to enjoy her moment of confusion. "Even if someone tries to kill you, you want me to just stand there and let it happen, if the alternative is hurting him?"

"Of course not." Sera glanced at me, then her tense focus slid to my gun before she turned back to Mitch. "Just…don't hurt anyone until I say otherwise. Okay?"

That time a shrug was his only reply.

"Sera, what the *fuck?*" I demanded. "How did you break Ned's bindings? You're a Binder now? How many Skills to you *have?*"

"Just the one. Er…two, I guess. But I'm not a Binder."

"You have two Skills?" Mitch said, and Sera's forehead furrowed in sudden concern.

"You can't tell anyone that. *Ever,*" she said, and he scowled, then rubbed his own forehead, like he was getting a headache. Or thinking about breaching an oath.

"Why is he taking orders from you?" I demanded. "Why hasn't he shot you? How did you break Ned's binding?"

"While we're asking questions, why was this fucker sneaking up on us?" Kori said from behind me, and I spun to find her in the hall, gesturing to Ian, who had an obviously dead man tossed over his good shoulder, dripping blood on the floor at his back. "How did you get in?"

"The lights are on a remote," Mitch said. "When our Tracker hadn't picked up your signal after an hour, we turned this one off and popped in to check. Since you're obviously here, the only reasonable conclusion I can draw is that your psychic signal is being jammed. Any idea how that might happen?" He was looking at Sera, but she only stared back at him, refusing to confirm either of her Skills.

"Mitch. It's been a while." Kori eyed him and I realized they'd once been coworkers. Had she known Ned, too?

"Hey, Kori," Mitch said as if they'd just bumped into each other at the watercooler. "Listen, there's a pool going, and I've got five hundred bucks riding on you gettin' shot in the head, so when the time comes, could you do me a favor and hold still?"

"You placed a bet on how she'd die?" Sera looked horrified, but Kori only shrugged.

"That bet never pays out. You'd think they'd eventually learn."

"I feel like I've missed something." Ian winced as he lowered the body to the ground and propped it up next to Ned. "What's going on?"

"Kori's evidently having a mobster's reunion, and this asshole's taking orders from Sera and blaming her for getting Ned killed. Also, he may know where Kenley is."

"Where is she?" Kori dismissed everything else as unimportant. Sometimes I admired her single-minded focus. Other times, it drove me nuts. I couldn't decide which kind of time this should be.

"I don't know."

"No lies, Mitch," Sera said, and he turned to glare at her.

"I'm not lying. After what happened to Ned, do you think Julia's likely to hand out classified information to every peon with a gun?"

"Speaking of guns, why haven't you used yours?" I glanced pointedly at his pistol, still in Sera's unsure grip. "And *why* are you taking orders from her?"

He deferred to Sera with a single glance and she cleared her throat nervously. "I…um…might have… inherited his binding. Kind of."

"You *kind of* inherited his binding?" Ian's voice echoed my own confusion.

"From Julia?" Kori frowned. "Does that mean she's dead?"

They were all missing the most obvious piece of the puzzle—how Sera could have inherited *anything* from Julia Tower—but she answered before I could ask.

"Not that I know of." Sera cleared her throat again and her hand clenched the edge of the grimy pedestal-style sink she leaned against. "I didn't inherit from Julia. If I understand correctly, the bindings were never really hers in the first place. I inherited from Jake."

"Wait, bindings? Plural?" Ian's hand hovered over the butt of his holstered weapon, as if it was the only thing he was really sure of at the moment. I knew exactly how that felt. "Not just this one?"

"It's…all of them." Sera shrugged again, and her obvious confusion said she didn't understand much more than we did. "Kind of."

"Kind of?" Kori frowned.

"Julia still holds most of them. For the moment."

"How?" I lowered my aim—my arm was aching—but not my guard. "How the hell could you inherit anything from Jake Tower?" But as soon as I'd asked the question, the answer seemed obvious, and for the second it took to sink in, the world seemed to grind to a halt all around me.

"Holy shit!" Kori actually staggered backward and stepped on Ian's foot. "He's your dad. Jake Tower was your fucking *dad*."

"No…" I said, but no one was listening. I'd heard it. I understood it. But I couldn't make *sense* of it. Sera was beautiful, and smart, and she loved and missed her family more than anything else in the world. She couldn't even be related to Jake Tower, much less sired by him, because the Towers were a nest of snakes willing to bite one another's heads off if that's what it took to climb to the top of the heap.

And every time one of us had said something along those lines—that Tower's family tree was rotten to its core—we'd inadvertently been insulting Sera. Implying that she was rotten, as well, by virtue of a shared root system.

No wonder she couldn't trust us with her secrets. I wouldn't be surprised if she hated us.

"He was my father," Sera corrected Kori, and I noted that Mitch didn't look surprised. "He was *never* my dad. I never even met him, but after hearing about him from you guys, I can honestly swear to you that I'm nothing like him. Nothing like him."

Her tense tone and wide eyes seemed to be hinting at something beyond her actual words—something she evidently didn't want Mitch to hear—but it wasn't until she glanced at my gun again that I understood.

She thought I was going to shoot her, if not right then and there, then eventually. She truly thought my hatred of all things Tower extended to her.

I flipped the safety switch on my pistol, and she exhaled softly in relief. But her frame remained stiff and her focus kept flitting between me, Kori and Ian as she spoke. She was on alert.

She didn't trust us.

"I don't think Jake even knew I existed," Sera continued.

"He didn't." Kori looked stunned. Astonished. Her mind had been *blown*. "There's no way in hell that he would have let anyone else raise you if he'd known you existed. Even if there was no emotional attachment whatsoever, you're too valuable an asset to be wandering around out there, unprotected and uninstalled in the Tower machine." She glanced at the ground, then up at Sera again, her eyes even wider now. "This kind of makes sense. Kinda. I mean, it's crazy, but in a totally logical way."

"Not following you, Kor…" I said, and I obviously wasn't the only one.

My sister rolled her eyes at me. "Jake Tower was a Jammer."

Mitch's eyes widened. "That's classified information."

Kori shrugged. "It was. When he was alive and I was bound to him. Neither of which still applies."

"But Tower *hired* Jammers," I pointed out. "Anne said he hired one of the best in the country as his kids' nanny." So they couldn't be tracked and targeted by his enemies, which were numerous.

"Camouflage," Kori said. "That, and a backup system, for when he's not home. His theory was that the less people know about you, the less vulnerable you are. It works the same with names, obviously."

"What's your other skill?" Mitch asked Sera, as if they were the only two in the room. No one answered.

"We need to get out of here. When Julia's Trackers realize they can't pick up Mitch and his partner, they'll be on us like flies on a corpse."

Yet even with Mitch nominally under Sera's control, I didn't trust him, and I certainly wasn't going to take him with us to one of our usual meeting places, so he could later report to Julia, either under orders—if he was somehow faking loyalty to Sera—or for pay. But we couldn't leave him there; we weren't done with him yet.

There was so much Sera still didn't understand…

"Ideas?" Ian glanced at each of us, but Sera didn't know the city, I'd spent very little time there myself, and

Kori seemed reluctant to say whatever she was thinking aloud, where Mitch would hear her. Finally, she leaned toward Ian and stood on her toes to whisper into his ear.

When she dropped onto the balls of her feet again he met her gaze with his brows raised. "Seriously?"

"You got a better idea?"

Before I could ask what the hell they were talking about, Ian shrugged, and Kori turned to me, then motioned for me to bend so she could whisper into my ear. She gave me an address, but it took me a second to realize why Ian was surprised by it. We were going to the east side. Cavazos's territory.

"Can you find the place?" Kori said before I could ask the questions ready to tumble from my tongue.

I nodded. "But what about—"

"Just try to keep it quiet," she interrupted, before I could finish my question. "With Sera there to jam us, no one will know we're there, unless you announce it."

Sera looked bewildered, but obviously understood that we couldn't give her an explanation in front of Mitch.

I pushed my sleeve up and laid her hand on my right arm, so that her fingers touched my skin. I really wanted to hold her hand, but it wasn't the time. Or the place. Or more than remotely likely to happen. Then I clicked off the safety on my gun, and though it felt strange to be touching both Sera and a weapon at the same time, I aimed right-handed at Mitch and pinned him with a scowl. "You so much as twitch on the way and I'll blow a hole right through you."

Before he could answer, I grabbed his wrist, touching as little of his flesh as possible, and nodded at Ian, who turned off the lights. I tugged both Sera and Mitch forward before either of them could object or ask anything, and a couple of steps later our shoes landed on thick carpet.

Even the sound of our breathing was different in this new room, muffled by carpet and furniture I could hardly make out in the darkness.

I let go of Mitch as soon as I was sure we were in the right place, but Sera's hand didn't leave my arm as I tugged her to the side—out of Kori's path—and I made no move to disengage from her hand.

A second later, the quality of the air changed and two new, connected shadows stepped out of the greater darkness, their shoes whispering against the carpet. "Kris?" Kori said.

"Yeah." Sera started to let go of my arm, but I put my free hand over hers and squeezed, a silent comfort in the dark.

"There's a light switch between the door and the window. To your left."

I turned and made out the rectangle of pale light outlining a drape-covered window, then felt on the wall for a switch. My fingers found it and flipped the switch on, and light flooded the room to reveal a small but expensively furnished apartment around us.

"Where are we?" Sera's gaze hardly skirted Mitch as she took in our surroundings.

"One of Ruben Cavazos's apartments on the east side," Kori said. "It was supposed to be his love-shack for Liv, but she never gave it up. To him, anyway."

The rest of us objected all at once.

"Shh!" She glanced at the walls. "You want the neighbors to hear?"

"Kori, this won't work," Ian said, practically tearing the words from my own tongue. "This is suicide."

"Bullshit. It's perfect. Cavazos has no idea we're here,

and Julia would never think to look on the east side. And she can't track us, as long as we have Sera." Her hard gaze took in Mitch's astonished face, then slid to Sera. "Tell him never to mention this."

Sera let go of my arm and caught Mitch's gaze. "Don't ever mention this apartment to anyone. Or tell anyone we were on the east side," she added as an afterthought.

Mitch nodded, his jaw clenched in anger. Or frustration. Or both.

"Okay." I glanced around the apartment, taking in the galley-style kitchen, open dining area and hallway presumably leading to a bedroom and bathroom. "This will work, for the next half hour, at least." It was better than getting caught and slaughtered at Julia's warehouse.

I caught Mitch's attention and pointed at the table, which only had four chairs. "Sit. In the corner, where we can all see you."

He crossed his arms over his chest, silently refusing to move until Sera rolled her eyes and said, "Do it."

Mitch mumbled something angry and profane, but took the seat I'd pointed out. I sat in the chair across from him and pulled another one out next to mine for Sera. Ian took the fourth chair while Kori dug around for something in the kitchen.

"Okay. So you're Jake Tower's biological daughter," Ian said, picking up the discussion almost exactly where we'd left it in the warehouse.

Sera set Mitch's gun on the table, out of his immediate reach and picked at the fingernails of her left hand. "According to Julia, I'm his bastard."

He gave her an infectious grin. "That means little, coming from a world-class bitch."

Sera smiled, but I couldn't really enjoy the sight because my mind had already kicked into overdrive. "That's how you got in to see her," I said, thinking aloud, and Sera practically squirmed with discomfort. "You're family."

"Of the illegitimate, publicly embarrassing sort, yes."

Kori closed one cabinet door and moved on to inspect the contents of the next. "That's the best kind of family."

I ignored the grin she shot me.

"No, the best kind of family is the kind you can count on." Sera frowned. "My mistake was hoping that Lia would help me, just because we share the same blood."

"Your only mistake was not knowing enough about the Towers," I insisted. "And that wasn't your fault. But if you'd known them better, you'd have known they never do anything for free. Even for family."

She nodded pensively. "You'd think I would have picked up on that from the way she and Gwendolyn were arguing when you broke into the house."

"You should have *seen* how pissed off Julia was about that!" Mitch's eyes shone with malicious amusement from his corner and I wasn't sure which of us he was talking to. "You'd have loved it. The bitch threw a full-out temper tantrum when you two disappeared through the closet, breaking shit and yelling at people. The rookies were quaking in their boots."

I'd bet money they weren't the only ones.

"I'm sure she's regretting that now." Kori shot a conspiratorial glance at Ian.

"Why?" I was already irritated that I hadn't figured it out yet.

My sister pulled a half-empty bottle of whiskey from the cabinet next to the refrigerator. "Because the best way to bury a rumor is to shut the fuck up about it."

"That's why you believed me when I told you who I was?" Sera frowned at Mitch, fingering the grip of his gun on the tabletop as I began putting the pieces together for myself.

Mitch nodded. "We all saw how furious the Tower bitch was, and when you told me she wasn't Jake's real heir, it just kinda clicked. Nothing in the world would piss her off worse than having her entire kingdom yanked out from under her."

"That's why she wants you dead," I said, and everyone glanced at me like I'd just figured out why water is wet. "Cut me some slack," I snapped. "The evil machinations of a usurped mafia queen are a little new to me."

"Me, too." Sera stared at the gun beneath her hand, but her gaze seemed to lose focus.

"Oh, shit!" I sat up straight as a devastating piece of the puzzle that was the Tower family tree fell into place.

"What?" Sera said, and they were all staring at me.

"Julia did it. She put the hit out on your family. Only she wasn't trying to kill them—she was trying to kill *you.*"

"What?" Sera sat straight in her chair, confusion warring with disbelief behind her eyes. "How do you know that?"

"Because it makes sense," Kori said, looking impressed by my insight for once, and I could only nod. "Who stands to gain the most from your death?"

"Lia…" Anger took over Sera's features as comprehension set in. "She tried to kill me before I even came to her. And when that didn't work—when she got my family instead—I walked right into her hands!" She closed her eyes and scrubbed her face with both hands. "How could I be so stupid?"

"You're not stupid." I pulled her hand away from her face and held it for one self-indulgent moment. "You just don't think like a mafia queen. Personally, I think that's to your credit."

"But not to my benefit. If I'd understood what I was walking into, I never would have gone in there in the first place."

"So, what? You needed a favor and thought Daddy's side of the family owed you one?" Kori unscrewed the lid from the whiskey and dropped it on the table, and I couldn't tell whether she thought Sera was ballsy or stupid. Or both.

Sera held her gaze. "I wanted justice and she's the only connection I had who could get it for me. At the time."

Mitch snorted. "The Towers aren't in the justice business. They're more revenge kind of people. Vengeance, if you're lucky."

Sera's eyes flashed and I got another glimpse of the hellcat who'd tried to castrate me with a steak knife. "Beggars can't be choosers."

"If you've really inherited a piece of the Tower pie, you'll never have to beg for anything again. Once you get that target off your back." Mitch leaned his chair back on two legs, balancing with one hand pressed against the wall. "Coincidentally, I happen to be in the market for a new job. Need some Skilled muscle?"

"I've got her covered," I snapped, and both Sera and Kori glanced at me in surprise. "We," I clarified, when I'd realized what I'd said, and how they'd probably— rightly—interpret it. "*We've* got her covered."

Mitch shrugged and set his chair down, then launched into a pitch too polished to be spontaneous, eyeing Sera across the table. "What do you want me to do then? Personal chauffeur? No car needed. The dark is my highway, anywhere you want to go. Or maybe you'd like a more *personal* kind of service?" His brows rose and his gaze raked over her with the innuendo, and I wanted to beat him until his blood stained my cuticles and soaked into Cavazos's expensive carpet.

"Ew, no!" Sera said, and I almost laughed at Mitch's insulted expression.

"Like I said, we've got her covered," I insisted, and then they were all staring at me again, and it took me a second to realize what I'd just said. "Not like that. This isn't that kind of…" *Damn it.* I snatched the bottle of whiskey from Kori and started over, while Ian made no effort to hide a grin. "I mean we've already got two Travelers, and Sera doesn't need you. For anything." I tipped the bottle up and took two swigs, hoping they'd all think it was the alcohol that made my cheeks burn.

"Succinctly put," Ian said, and his delivery was so deadpan I almost missed the sarcasm.

"But accurate." Kori took the bottle back and turned to Sera. "So, what do you want to do with him? And make it quick. This is a very temporary hideout."

Sera glanced at Mitch in confusion. "What do you mean? Why do I have to do anything with him?"

My sister frowned at me, then at Ian, and I realized that Sera truly understood even less about syndicate life than I did. "It's like teaching a chimp to play poker," Kori mumbled, then took a swig from the bottle while Sera bristled. "You own him." Kori wiped her lips with the back of one hand.

"I *what?*" If Sera's eyes got any wider, they'd take over her whole face.

"You own him. Metaphorically." I reached down for the leg of her chair and turned her to face me. "Mitch's binding is like a dog's leash. You're holding it. Ergo, you effectively own him."

"Mitch is a dog?"

Kori laughed and nearly choked on another mouthful of liquor. "According to a couple of his exes, yes. But the point is that you can't just drop the leash." She frowned, then amended. "Well, you *can,* but if you just walk away from him, you're responsible for whatever damage he does, or whatever damage is done to him."

"I don't understand." Sera's foot tapped rapidly under the table, as if her nerves knew Morse code.

Kori tilted the bottle up again in my peripheral vision and I turned to grab it, then slid it across the table toward Ian. "Do something with that, will you?"

He shrugged, then took a hit for himself.

Great. If my sister had a superpower, it would be the ability to drive those around her to drink—at super-speeds.

I slid the whiskey lid across the table toward Ian, then turned to Sera. "Okay. Think about it like this—if a dog attacks someone, who do they hold responsible?"

"The owner…" Sera's voice trailed off at the end of the word, and I could practically see comprehension surface behind her eyes. "But that's not fair. He's a person, not a dog." She glanced at Mitch, who was watching our exchange with his arms crossed over his chest, waiting to see how this would play out. "He makes decisions based on thought, not instinct. He has upper-level reasoning—relatively speaking." Mitch scowled, and Ian chuckled. "He has logic and free will!"

"But he doesn't. Not really," Kori insisted. "His will is yours, and if he hurts someone because you didn't tell him not to, whether you're legally responsible or not, I have a feeling you'll have a hard time dealing with the guilt of not having prevented it."

My sister's words struck close to home, and I realized that Sera and I were in a similar position. Sort of.

"Which is why I told him not to hurt anyone," Sera said.

"But that's a problem all its own," I said. "For instance, under that order, he can't defend himself or anyone else without your say so. So if we leave him here, he'll be dead in…what?" I glanced at Ian for a second opinion. "An hour?"

He nodded.

"Maybe less," I added. "Julia's extra pissy since your fortuitous arrival. Which means she's probably trigger-happy. Metaphorically speaking." Had Julia Tower ever even held a gun?

"Don't assume she can't shoot just because you've never seen her do it," Ian warned. "That woman holds her cards close to her chest."

Kori snorted. "Hell, they're practically in her bra."

"But my point is that if she finds him, she'll kill him. Assuming Cavazos doesn't find him first."

Mitch squirmed in his chair.

"Okay." Sera shrugged. "Then I'll just break his binding."

"Hell, no." Mitch stood, as if he actually had somewhere to go. "You may as well pass out guns and paint a target on my back. Didn't you get the memo pinned to Ned's chest?" He ran one hand through his hair. "That's Julia's way of saying she'll kill whoever you set free."

I shrugged. "So run." I turned back to Sera with a frown. "That's where we went wrong with Ned—we left him handcuffed to the fridge, like a sitting duck." Not that ducks had hands. "Of course, if I'd known you'd broken his binding, I would have given the poor guy a running start."

"I couldn't tell you," she insisted, her gaze silently pleading with me to understand. "I thought…" She let her words trail off when she realized Mitch was still listening, but we all knew what she'd thought, and we all understood why. She'd had no reason to trust us not to kill her or use her as a bargaining chip, if and when we found out how valuable she was.

I hated that I'd given her reason to think that.

"It doesn't matter." I made a mental note to reassure her of her safety later, away from stranger's ears. Hopefully in private, where I could tell her other things that still needed to be said.

"Okay." It was a struggle for me to pull my thoughts back on target. "You cut him loose and we'll give him a head start. A Traveler can be hundreds of miles away by the time Julia finds out he's gone."

Mitch started to object again, and I turned on him, rapidly losing my patience. "You won't be a priority. She probably won't even bother looking for you, with us still out here wreaking havoc."

"Bullshit!" Mitch's eyes were wide, his nose crinkled in a bizarre display of fear.

"Sit," Sera said, and he sat reluctantly, then scooted his chair closer to the table and leaned with his elbows on it, watching us all.

"She'll look for me and she'll find me, because her other Travelers can move just as fast as I can. And I *will* be a priority, because Jake taught her how to do business. She *has* to kill me, or everyone else will think Sera can be their savior. Which is exactly why she's killed most of the people your dumb-ass sister set free."

"What?" My stomach sank into my heels, weighing me down. Julia had killed the people Kenley had freed? "Do you know that for a fact? They're dead?"

"Not all of them." He turned to Kori, sitting on the edge of his chair as if he still wanted to stand, and his next words carried special, bitter weight. "A couple of them are still in the basement, *wishing* they were dead. In front of a live studio audience." Then he turned back to Sera. "She's going to hunt down everyone you set free until you stop doing it or she gets to you, just like she got to Kenley. And you're a bigger fool than I can even comprehend if you don't believe that."

Sixteen

Sera

"She killed them?" The words echoed in my head long after they'd left my tongue. They resonated in my bones and churned in my stomach, urging my dinner to stage a revolt.

"Only the lucky ones." Kori took the whiskey bottle back from Ian and sank onto one of the bar stools at the kitchen peninsula.

"You mean we've been making it *worse?*" Kris leaned with his elbows on the table, his arms tense, his brow deeply furrowed. "All that time and effort trying to fix things, and we were really just getting people killed?"

"What the hell were we expecting?" Kori rotated her stool so that she faced us, her grip on the neck of the bottle so tight her fingers had turned white. "That Julia would just pout and shrug, then go on with her life? She can't afford to let us beat her, and she certainly can't afford for people to *know* we beat her. This is our fault."

"No, it isn't," I insisted. "You were doing the only thing you could do. The right thing." The same thing

I'd tried to do for Ned. But then, that hadn't worked out very well, either.

"Right is irrelevant." Kori twisted the lid from the bottle again. "It's just a word. Or do you really believe it's better to be dead than alive but enslaved?" But before I could answer, she stared down at the bottle in her hands and seemed to be reassessing her own question. "We should have just killed them ourselves." She took a long swig. Then one more. "It would have been a mercy."

Anger blazed in my chest like heartburn. "How the hell is death a mercy?" My parents wouldn't have considered their deaths a mercy. Neither would my sister. And losing them was about as far from merciful as an act can be.

"No offense, Sera, but you have *no* idea what you're talking about. That's what makes you dangerous." Kori's gaze pinned me like an insect tacked open for display. I felt as though she could see what was inside me. And she didn't look impressed. "You have more Skills than anyone I've ever met, but you don't know how to use them. You have power Julia Tower would slaughter half the planet to keep for herself, but you don't know how to control it. And you brought all that to our doorstep. Like she needed another reason to hunt us down."

Kris stood and tried to take the bottle from her, but she pulled it out of his reach and swigged again. "Kori, back off. None of this is her fault."

"When has *that* ever mattered?" she demanded, and when Ian stood for the bottle, she actually let him have it. But her frustration didn't fade. "The whole damn thing was Jake's fault, and he lived like a fucking king. Now Julia's taken over where he left off, and if she's suffering guilt or grief, she's hiding it *really* well." She turned to me then, while we all stared at her. "That's what you don't understand, Sera, seeing as how you just fell off the family tree into a pile of money and power. The Tower birthright isn't just fortune and clout. No matter how you use it, it's an obligation. A responsibility you can't shirk. If you abuse it, like Julia, people will die. If you waste it—if you hide out with us and do nothing—people will die, because Julia will kill them."

"Kori, that's enough." Kris glanced at Mitch, to make sure he wasn't trying to pull something while they were all distracted, then turned back to his sister. "Picking a fight with your allies isn't going to help."

"You think I'm hiding?" I could feel my cheeks burn. But wasn't she right? Wasn't I hiding from Julia with them, even as I hid *them* from *Julia?*

Kori pushed Kris out of her way and took two steps toward the table. "I think that if you're not part of the solution, you're part of the problem."

"That's not fair." Kris's jaw clenched in anger at his own sister, and something in my chest tightened. Then warmed. "Sera didn't ask for this. You said it yourself, Kor, she fell into this mess. Not everyone eats and breathes revolution, you know."

He was trying to help. I knew that, and it was *so* sweet, and I was certainly grateful, but somehow his words chafed even worse than his sister's.

I stood and pushed my chair back, but when Mitch tried to stand, I shook my head, and he sank back into his seat with a scowl. "Is that what you all think?" I glanced from face to face, wordlessly demanding the truth. "That I'm some helpless, useless little twit who can't protect herself or her family, or enact her own justice?"

Kris shook his head and Ian frowned, but Kori only pressed her lips together and crossed her arms over her chest.

That *was* what they thought. And why shouldn't they? I'd lived when my entire family died because I'd hidden. I was *still* hiding.

"That's what Julia Tower's counting on," Kris said softly, and Kori and Ian nodded in agreement.

"Well, then, she's wrong. And she's going to figure that out the hard way." Kris smiled, but everyone else flinched when I held Mitch's gun up to get a better look at it. A better feel for it. "If you guys can teach me how to use this and show me what I don't yet know about my own Skills, I think we can bring the fight to her. And along the way, we can release every Tower employee we come across, until there are too many for her to hunt down."

"Won't work," Mitch said, and I ignored him.

"Won't matter," Kori added. "If Julia isn't already binding more to herself directly—making Kenley's bindings obsolete—she will be soon."

"You can't release them all, Sera," Kris insisted. "You can't even let her *think* you're going to release them all, because then she'll have no reason to keep Kenley alive."

For a moment, there was only a fragile quiet, as what he'd said sank in.

"Fuck me." Kori was the first to break the silence, raking one hand through her pale hair. "We're screwed either way."

"No, we're not." I had an idea, but if I was going to live long enough to put it to use, I'd have to get smart. I'd have to let them teach me. Kori was right—I didn't know how to use the bindings I'd inherited, and until I learned the ins and outs of direct orders and loopholes, those bindings would do me no good.

And I was far from sure I wanted to use them anyway.

If I took Julia's employees as my own instead of setting them free, I'd be no better than she was. Right?

I held Kris's gaze for a long moment, hoping he understood my silent plea to stop me if I messed this up, then I turned to Mitch, who still sat in the chair at the corner, considering my words more carefully than I ever had before. "You will never tell anyone anything that you heard here today, except for the fact that I am Jake Tower's biological daughter."

Kris frowned at that, but I'd already thought it through. Julia was killing the people whose bindings she'd lost, but the solution wasn't to *stop* telling people she was a pretender to the throne. The solution was to tell *everyone*. She couldn't afford to kill them all. In fact, my guess was that she couldn't afford to kill many more than she already had, without undermining her own power base.

"Do you understand?"

Mitch nodded slowly, but he still looked angry. And maybe scared. "Releasing me won't help. She'll find me."

"That's up to you." I sat in the chair next to him and set the gun on the table without letting go of it. "The best I can give you is a head start. I release you of all obligation to me and to the Tower syndicate, except for your silence about what you've heard here. If I were you, I'd find a darkroom and start running."

Mitch's eyes widened. He looked at his gun. When I made no move to return it, he glanced at each of us, as if we might take it all back and keep him imprisoned forever. Then he stood and headed through the dining area into living room, and when he glanced back from the hall, he looked almost panicked. As if maybe he'd been enslaved for so long he didn't know what to do with his freedom. Then he stepped into the darkened bathroom.

I couldn't hear him leave through the shadows, but I could practically feel it.

"We should get out of here," Kris said, once we were sure Mitch was gone. Kori put the bottle back where she'd found it, then took Ian's hand. I took Kris's hand and in the second before he walked us into the shadows, I realized that with his hand in my left one and Mitch's gun in my right, I'd never felt so secure in my life.

Seconds later, we all bumped shoulders in the crowded hall closet of what I'd long ago dubbed the House of Crazy.

"Was she there?" Vanessa asked, lowering a small handgun when she saw us step out of the closet in pairs.

"No, but we're going to find her." Kris sounded so sure.

"*I'm* going to find her," I corrected, and they both glanced at me in surprise. "As soon as you teach me how to use this." I held up Mitch's gun. "And the Skills Julia doesn't know I have."

"I'll teach you whatever you want to know," Kris said. "But not until you tell me what you're plotting."

"I'm going to turn myself in." I sounded more confident than I actually felt.

"No." Kris dropped my hand and stomped into the kitchen, dismissing both me and my intentions.

My temper flared and Kori lurched out of my way as I stomped after him. "I'm not asking for your permission— I'm asking for your help. But I'll do it on my own if I have to."

"Are you really that stupid?" Kris turned on me in the middle of the kitchen floor, and I noticed that everyone else had stayed in the living room, though they were too quiet to be doing anything other than eavesdropping.

"I'm not talking about barging in guns ablaze." I

aimed a pointed glance at his holstered .45, presumably the one he'd used to kidnap me. "That really *would* be stupid. What I'm talking about is plucking Julia's inheritance right out from under her, with minimal bloodshed. I'm talking about taking the whole thing at once, instead of piecemeal. And doing it on her turf, which is where I'm likely to find and usurp the most employees at a time."

"You won't catch them all in one place," Kori said from the kitchen doorway, where she and Ian had congregated on the edge of our...discussion. "She has them spread out all over the city."

"But it's a start, right?" I said, and she nodded reluctantly. "And our best chance of finding Kenley before Julia moves her again." Or kills her to cripple my momentum. But that would mean crippling herself as well and surely that would be her last resort.

"Yeah, it's a start," Kori said. "A fuckin' ballsy start."

"No." Kris crossed his arms over his chest. "She'll have you killed the minute she sees you."

"Not if we do this right. Not if most of her people already know who I am when I get there."

"And how are they going to know that?"

"We're going to tell them." I turned to Kori again, then to Van. "Don't either of you still have any connections in the syndicate? You must, right? How else were you finding people for Kenley to free?"

"A few," Kori said.

Van nodded slowly. Then she started to smile. "I have something better than human connections. I have numbers. Email addresses. We could do a sort of viral revolution. They just have to know about you, right? Then their binding automatically transfers to you from Julia?"

She'd caught on fast. So fast I suspected someone had filled her in while Kris and I argued.

"This isn't going to happen," Kris said, but no one was listening to him anymore.

"I think they have to know and *believe*." Whether they wanted to believe or not. "But if Mitch believed, so will some of the others. Maybe lots of them."

"Sera..." Kris was beyond mad. He looked...worried. Scared.

"Kris, I'm not trying to get anyone killed, myself least of all. I don't know how many of Julia's employees know who I am, but I do know one very important thing." Something I was hoping she hadn't yet thought of.

"What's that?" His gaze held mine, and his question sounded...incomplete. Like there was something else he wanted to say.

"Julia was bound to her brother, too, right?" I said, my focus glued to Kris, though my question was for his sister.

"Yes..." Kori said, and I could tell from the sudden cautious glee in her voice that she'd come to the same conclusion I had.

"And she already knows damn well who I am."

"Holy shit." Kris's eyes brightened and a smile spread over his face. "She's bound to you, too. Julia fucking Tower is your employee!"

Yup. Which was why she'd had no choice but to give the order, when I told her to tell her men to put their guns down.

That was just one more reason for Julia to want me dead—but it was also an iron-clad guarantee that she couldn't actually hurt me. Not directly, anyway.

"You ready?" Kori's voice came from the deepest shadows in the far corner of Gran's room, and I nodded from the rolling desk chair I'd been tied to earlier, though I was far from sure of my answer. The truth was that even after a good night's sleep and half a day of practicing, I still hadn't been able to replicate that *slipping* feeling I'd had when I'd somehow prevented Kris, Kori and Ian from traveling without me.

And that was unacceptable.

The only defenses I'd have once I walked willingly into the lion's den were my newly acquired gun—assuming I ever learned to use it—and my ability to block people from using their Skills against me. I needed to be able to lie in front of Julia. I'd done it before—evidently I was blocking, before I'd even known I was blocking—but I needed to be able to do it consistently. On demand.

"Nope!" Kori called from the hall closet, which she'd shadow-walked into, proving—again—that I had yet to master my own Skill.

"This is ridiculous."

"Agreed." She skulked into the room and sank onto the edge of her grandmother's bed. "You're, what? Twenty-one?"

"Twenty-two and a half," I said miserably.

"Whatever. You're way too old for this shit. Most people learn control in their early teens. Elle was already a pro at twelve."

And her daughter was exhibiting significant Skill at age six. Kori didn't say it, but we both knew she was thinking it.

I swiveled back and forth in the chair, trying to exorcize my own nerves. "Did you know her well?"

Kori exhaled from the shadows. "I wondered when you'd ask."

"How did you know I would?"

"Because you look at my brother like he invented sex, and you'd like him to show you how it works."

"I do not." I was suddenly grateful for the dark room, so she couldn't see the fire surely glowing in my cheeks.

Kori actually laughed, and I almost died of shock. "Yes, you do, and you're not the first." She chuckled again. "But you're a smart girl, so I figure that if you're interested in more than one night's worth of sweat from him…"

"I never said I was interested." But she spoke right over me.

"…then you've already figured out your only real competition is a ghost."

I hadn't thought about it in so many words, and I wasn't ready to admit to anything yet, but…yeah. He'd grown up with her. He'd been with her for years, even though they weren't monogamous most of the time, from what I'd gathered. Hell, he kept a written record of everything she'd ever mumbled in her sleep!

"You didn't answer the question," I said when she leaned forward and peered into my eyes, as though she could read in them the things I wasn't saying aloud. "Were you and Noelle close?"

"Best friends. When I found out she was sleeping with my brother, I was beyond pissed off at them both."

"What'd they say?" I had no similar experience to compare that to. Nadia and I had been far enough apart in age that we couldn't even wear the same clothes, much less compete for friends or boyfriends.

"I never told them I knew." A slight shift in the shadows and the squeal of bedsprings told me she'd folded her legs beneath her on the mattress. "They clearly didn't want anyone to know, and I sure as hell didn't want to hear about it, from either perspective. So I left it alone. But I had no idea it went on as long as it did until he showed me the notebook. Three days ago."

I thought about that for a moment. Then I kind of wished I hadn't.

"What was she like?"

Kori leaned forward, her palms propped on the edge of the bed, and I could see her face now, still heavily shrouded in shadow. "Noelle was…a puzzle. I knew that even before I knew I should be putting the pieces together. You're kind of like her, in that respect. But only that one."

I wasn't sure if that was good or bad. "He loved her?"

"Yeah. He did."

"Did she love him?"

Kori hesitated. "Maybe. In her own way. But things with Noelle were…complicated. We didn't know it at the time, but in looking back, I don't think she was ever really a normal kid. Because of her Skill. I don't think she did anything—including my brother—without a reason related to something she'd seen in prophesy."

"So…she used him?" *That bitch.* My own thought surprised me, but I refused to let myself overanalyze it.

"I think she really did care about him, but yes. She used him. For multiple…things. But I'm not sure he actually understands that, even now. I'm also not sure he'd want me to tell you any of this," she said in a conspiratorial whisper.

"Then why are you?" I whispered back, my feet on the floor now, so the chair couldn't spin.

"Because he doesn't always know what's best for him." She paused and seemed to reconsider. "I take that back. He almost *never* knows what's best for him."

"And you do?"

She shrugged. "I know it's no better for him to keep living in the past than it is for Gran."

"And by 'the past,' you mean Noelle?"

Kori frowned. "I mean all of it. Kris is a man on a mission that can never be fulfilled, without a time machine. He can't go back and save Elle from a bullet. He can't go back and save Kenley or me from the Towers, and no matter how many kids he shuttles from one safe harbor to the next, he can never undo what happened to Micah."

"Kids?" *Micah?*

"The kids he works with."

"How do kids fit in with bail bondsmen and private collectors?" Something wasn't adding up…

Kori frowned. "That's what he told you? That he rounds up criminals and collectibles?"

I nodded slowly. "So it's not true?" My chest ached. He'd lied to me.

"Oh, that's true, but it's only half the story. Kris is a smuggler."

"A smuggler?" Pieces were falling into place in my head, but the big picture wouldn't come into focus. "A… *kid* smuggler?" Were those the kids Gran was talking about? "So he *is* a kidnapper?"

Kori shook her head. "No, he's a liberator. And they're not small kids. They're mostly teenagers. Kids who've just discovered their Skill and are at risk of being 'recruited' by the mafia." The bitter scowl that accompanied her air quotes spoke volumes about her own recruitment. "He gets them out of the city and helps place them with families in the suburbs. Families with Jammers. Like you. To keep them safe until they learn how to hide themselves."

Holy crap. "And does Gran…cook for them?" Suddenly the four huge cans of marinara made sense.

"She did, before he had to take away the knives and stove knobs. She's only truly with us about half the time now." Kori shrugged. "Of course, all of that's on hold now while we're here helping Kenley break her bindings."

"He didn't tell me." *Why* didn't he tell me? "Does that mean he doesn't trust me?"

Another shrug. "He's just really careful. It's his life's work, and a lot of people would get hurt—or killed—if the wrong people find out."

People, like the Towers.

"Kenni and I didn't know about it until our bindings were broken. He couldn't tell us, because we'd have had to report it."

I was still mulling that over when she sat up straight and her face receded into the shadows. "I think I know why you can't stop me from traveling into the closet," she said, and girl-chat time was obviously over.

"Why?"

"Because you don't give a shit whether or not I can travel into the closet. When you stopped us earlier, it was because you *really* didn't want us to go without you. Right?"

I nodded. I could see where this was headed. "So, I'm only going to be able to stop people from using Skills I *really* don't want them to use?"

"At first? Yes. But you'll get the hang of it with practice, and for now, the good news is that if someone's Skill threatens you or someone you want to protect, I'm guessing you *really* won't want him to use it. Right?"

"I guess."

"Let's test the theory." She stood and grabbed my hand, then leaned forward to kick the bedroom door closed, cutting off most of the light from the hall. Which left us standing in almost total darkness, thanks to the thick drapes. "I'm guessing the place you want least in the world to be right now is…your parents' den."

My hand clenched around hers and my heart tried to claw its way up my throat.

"That's where it happened, isn't it? That's where you saw him on top of your sister? Where you heard her screaming? Where you realized what he would do when he was done with her? Right?"

"Kris told you?" My voice sounded hollow. Dead.

Kori shook her head, but I didn't so much see that as feel it—movement in the dark. "I read the police report."

Then she knew the rest of it.

"It's none of your business," I whispered, but when I tried to pull my hand from hers, she only tightened her grip.

"I know. I'm sorry for what happened to your family, and for invading your privacy. But if I hadn't done that, I wouldn't know where they lived, and I wouldn't be able to take you there now. He's not there anymore, Sera. I can take you back there, and *he won't be there.*"

"No." I tried to pull my hand from hers again, but she wouldn't let go.

"Good. Stop me if you can. This will be a good test. But if you can't block me, just remember that he won't be there when we get there. No one will be there. You can go back there this one time and put the whole thing behind you."

But that wasn't true. I couldn't go back there. And even if I could stand to be in that room again, being there wouldn't fix anything. Not as long as he still had a pulse.

"I'll be right there with you. No matter what happens, this is a step in the right direction." She tried to pull me forward, but I wouldn't move. I couldn't. So she pulled harder, and I stumbled after her. One step. Two. Three, and we crashed into Gran's dresser.

"Shit!" Kori dropped my hand to clutch—whatever had banged the dresser.

The bedroom door flew open behind us, and I whirled around an instant before the overhead light blinded me. "What's wrong?" Ian demanded as Kris pushed past him into the room.

"She did it." Kori was smiling—*beaming*—like she was proud of me, or maybe proud of herself, but all I could hear was what she'd said before. In the dark.

I can take you there.

All I could see was the tall man with the curly hair. Blood leaking from my sister's stomach to pool on the floor. The tall man's creepy grin as he lurched after me and grabbed my shoulder, his knife already dripping...

"Kori tried..." I said, but I couldn't finish it. "She tried to..." My arm took over when my tongue failed for a second time. My fist crashed into her jaw and Kori stumbled backward into the dresser.

"You ungrateful little bitch!" She bounced back faster than I could believe, brow furrowed in anger, both fists clenched and ready to swing. "I was trying to help you!"

My heart thumped painfully and my fists rose—I was too busy being scared of the tall man to be scared of her.

Kris jumped between us. Ian pulled Kori back with one arm wrapped around her waist.

"What happened?" Kris's gaze bounced from me to his sister.

"I'm fine. Let me go," she said, and Ian let her go, but stayed close. "I was trying to help her. I *did* help her. She blocked me."

They both turned to me for my version. "That crazy bitch tried to shadow-walk me into my parents' house. Where they all died." Where I'd lost everything.

"Kori!" Kris looked furious.

"I wasn't really going to do it." She crossed her arms over her chest and huffed in exasperation. "You know I can't go that far in one shot."

She couldn't?

"I was just going walk her into the hall closet, but she had to *think* I was taking her somewhere she didn't want to go, or she couldn't block me." She turned to Ian. "It's just like what you did for Kenley to help her break my binding. She had to really want it. Same principal, right?"

"That was an emergency, Kori," he said, in that way he had of making quiet words seem more important than shouted ones. "Most people don't respond well to the shock-and-awe approach."

"What the hell were you *thinking?*" Kris demanded, and his arm slid around my waist. Maybe I should have pushed him away, to prove I could stand on my own, but instead I scooted closer, and his arm tightened around me, and I realized he wasn't trying to protect me—he was standing with me.

"I was thinking that she had the balls to do what needs to be done, no matter what that requires." Kori gestured angrily as she spoke. "She's the one who wants to charge into enemy territory, and we can't send her in unprepared. She has to be able to use her Skills."

"Kori…" Kris started, but she cut him off, her anger clashing with his.

"Listen up, all of you." She stepped away from Ian and addressed us as a group—as if she were in charge—and my blood boiled. "None of you know what Julia's capable of. Not like I do."

"She can't hurt me," I insisted, clinging to that very thought.

Kori turned to me, eyes narrowed, studying me. "She can't *physically* hurt you, or order someone else to. But there are many kinds of pain, Sera. What that man did to your sister? What you saw? Julia can and *will* make that happen all over again. Maybe to someone you know— she'll pluck your best friends right off the street, if she can find them. She'll make you watch them tortured, for no reason other than to see you suffer. To make you re- member what you would do anything to forget."

My friends? College felt like a lifetime ago. My friends were a universe away—I hadn't seen even one of them since the funeral. But they weren't beyond the Towers' reach. "Why would she…" My question had no end. I couldn't say it.

"To make you give up your birthright. To illustrate what a heartless bitch she really is. Because she's pre- menstrual. Because she's bored. Because she *can*. She doesn't need a reason to cause pain, but she has plenty of them to choose from."

"We won't let that happen," Kris swore. Then he turned on his sister. "Get out."

"You're sending a lamb to the slaughter, Kris. You all need to *listen* to me."

"And you need to back the fuck off and get out of here!"

Kori blinked, stunned. Then she glanced at me and backed slowly toward the door.

"If Sera goes in there and her plan falls apart—hell, even if it *doesn't* fall apart—they'll use every weapon at their disposal to break her. And her weak spot is pretty fucking obvious." Her hand found the doorknob and one foot landed over the threshold in the hall. "She needs to deal with that shit before she goes in there, or they're going to rip her heart out and serve it on crackers."

With that, she stomped past Ian into the hall and out of sight.

"I'm sorry," he said, when she was gone. "She really does mean well. And she speaks from experience you can't even…" He stopped and studied me for a minute. "Well, maybe you *can* imagine. Her approach was wrong, but her heart's in the right place. She really was trying to help."

I couldn't quite bring myself to accept his apology, in part because it wasn't his to give. But his point lingered. And I suspected he was right—they both were. Not that I was eager to go home again. That house was haunted, if not by ghosts, then by memories. By loss. And if I couldn't face my own memories, how the hell was I supposed to face down Julia Tower?

Seventeen

Kris

"You sure you want to do this now?" I slid the full clip into place in the handle of the .40 Sera had confiscated from Mitch. "You're entitled to a break, you know."

The warm, early fall breeze blew a long dark strand of hair across Sera's forehead. "Screw that." She pulled a rubber band from her pocket and secured her hair in a casual ponytail at the base of her skull, then laid her palm over the gun I'd set in front of her, barrel aimed down our makeshift firing range—a card table in the backyard, fifty feet from a fresh paper target tacked to an old, dead oak tree. "Sitting around thinking about what can't be changed won't help. I need something to do. I need to do *this*."

"No one expects you to get over everything you've been through just like that." I pressed the last 9 mm round into the clip for the gun I'd borrowed from my sister.

"Kori does."

"She doesn't expect you to get over it. She expects

you to deal with it. She's not over all the shit she's been through, either."

"I know." Sera watched as a brown rabbit hopped from a clump of overgrown bushes toward the woods at the edge of the property. I loved that we were far enough from downtown to have rabbits, at least until we scared them off with gunfire. "She has nightmares. Loud ones."

"They're getting better."

Sera turned away from the tree line to frown at me, squinting into the sun. "That's *better?*"

I nodded and picked up an extra clip next to the pistol on the table in front of me. "She hasn't tried to gut anyone in her sleep in, like, a month."

She thought I was kidding. I could tell from her exasperated expression. I decided to let her think that. And to warn her away from Kori and Ian's room after dark.

"So, what happened with Ned the other day?" I said as I pressed the first round into the extra 9 mm clip. "You just freed him, with no clause to make sure he could never hurt you? Why would you do that? Especially after what you've already been through?"

She stared at the table, considering for a second before she answered. "It never occurred to me that he'd want to hurt me. I'd just set him free. I thought he'd be happy!"

"I'm sure he was." I huffed. "He was a happy threat."

"I'm not…wired that way." She shrugged. "I don't look at the rest of the population and see seven billion threats. I can't live in a world where everyone's my enemy. For my own sanity, I need to believe the monster who killed my family is just that. A monster. An aberration."

"He is. But he's not the only one."

"I know, but…" She looked up at me, frowning. "I don't understand how you can stand it, seeing enemies everywhere you look."

"I don't see them everywhere, but I am constantly aware that they exist, and that's particularly true for you. Julia wants you dead, so all her people are your enemies. If Ruben Cavazos finds out who you are and that you're here, he'll want you in custody. That means that nearly everyone you meet in the city is out to kill you or sell you to the highest bidder."

"Even you?" Her eyes asked even more than her words did.

"No. Not me." I took a deep breath, then spit out the truth along with a grin meant to disguise it as a joke. "I want to keep you."

She smiled, just a little, and I had to clear my throat and look away before I tried to kiss her again.

"Okay, show me how to use this thing, or I'm just going to assume it works like they do in the movies."

"Don't. In real life, you have to reload when you run out of ammo, and you're probably not going to be chasing bad guys across busy intersections while leaking blood from three bullet holes in your side. Ian's pretty badass, and one was enough to drop him. But before you learn how to use this—" I picked up her gun, barrel pointed toward the tree line "—you need to know what it is and what it holds."

"It's a Glock 22." She ran one finger over the side of the barrel, and I noticed that her attention to the gun seemed…fond. Not quite eager, but not afraid. "Says so right here."

Okay, she had me there. "Do you know what that means?"

"Glock is the brand name. Twenty-two is the style number. Also says it was made in Austria, but I'm not sure that's relevant."

"Not for today." I wanted to smile, but I resisted. This

wasn't a date; it was a lesson. But that didn't mean I hadn't noticed that her hair smelled like strawberries and her borrowed shirt—Van's this time—was a little snug around her chest. "And what does this Glock 22 fire?"

"Forty-caliber rounds."

"Which means?"

She rolled her eyes over my beginner-level questions. "It means that the bullets this thing shoots are four-tenths of an inch in diameter. If you wanna go bigger, you can get a .45 or a .50, but unless you're shooting elephants or the walking dead, the .50 is probably overkill. On the smaller end, you have the 9 mm, which is measured in millimeters, obviously, instead of inches. That's what that thing fires." She glanced at the pistol I'd borrowed from Kori's collection. "Or, you can get a .38. Or even a .22, like Vanessa's."

I stared at her. I couldn't help it. Fruit-scented toiletries, tight shirts and gun talk—Sera Brant had just outed herself as the perfect woman. "I thought you'd never fired a gun."

"I haven't."

"Then how do you know all that?"

Her brows rose and she looked just cocky enough to be intriguing. "I researched it while you were in the bathroom. Gran's desktop should really be password protected."

It *would* be, if she could remember a password from one day to the next.

"You read fast," I said, and she grinned.

"I learn faster."

"We'll see. Using a gun is a little different from reading about them. Let's start you on the 9 mm. It has less recoil."

"Nuh-uh." She shook her head firmly, her long, dark

ponytail swishing against the back of her shirt. "Kori says you get to keep any gun you take from someone else, and I took this one from Mitch, fair and square. Which means it's mine now. I want to learn on my own gun."

"Fine." Why are girls always so stubborn? "Your clip's loaded, and there's one round in the chamber. How many shots can you fire before you have to reload?"

She stared at the gun on the table, as if she might actually be able to see through the grip. "Um…fifteen in the clip, right? And one in the chamber. So that's sixteen."

"Close. Your clip actually holds seventeen." A cloud passed overhead, and our shadows melted into the grass. "Plus one in the chamber makes eighteen."

"Damn." Sera frowned at the extended clip, and she looked so disappointed by her mistake that I had to stop myself from patting her on the back. "Okay, so what do I do?"

"Pick it up, but don't put your finger on the trigger yet."

Sera picked up her gun, and suddenly every bit of confidence her research had lent her drained, along with the blood from her face.

"Okay, first of all, respect the gun, but don't be scared of it." The only person I'd ever taught to shoot was Kori, back when we were still just kids. And nothing had ever scared Kori, least of all guns and the power they lent her. "Fear undermines your confidence and ruins your concentration. The gun isn't going to do anything you don't make it do."

"Okay, but what about the rules?" Sera still looked nervous. "Aren't there some rules?"

"Several. At the gun range—ours is homemade, but it still counts—you always keep your gun pointed downrange. At the target. If you never aim it at anything else, you can never shoot anything else. And you'll notice that downrange for us also means 'away from the house.' That's very important." Behind our target trees was a small hill, perfect for catching stray bullets before they could hit anything else.

Sera nodded, still holding her gun, elbows locked, lower lip between her teeth.

I took the gun from her and set it down. She needed to relax. "Outside of the gun range, there are two kinds of rules. The first kind is the law, which tells us not to shoot people. Or even threaten to shoot people. Those rules are optional, depending on the situation and how many witnesses are likely to testify against you."

Her eyes widened, and when the cloud retreated, she squinted at me. "You're serious?"

"You're not learning for sport, Sera. You're learning to shoot because you understand that at some point— probably soon—you may have to kill someone. I don't think you'd ever do that unless you had to, but you need to be aware, before you pull the trigger, that witnesses may not always understand that necessity. Sometimes that's reason to hesitate. Sometimes it's not."

She nodded, obviously thinking it over. "And the other kind of rules?"

"Common sense. Draw first, or die. To do that, you have to keep your weapons—not just your gun—accessible at all times. Don't button a jacket over your holster."

"I don't have a holster. Or a jacket." Because she was still borrowing clothes.

"We'll get you both. Next, never let anyone else see your thoughts on your face or in your bearing. If you're obviously scared to fire, your opponent won't take you seriously. In fact, he'll probably just shoot you."

"Okay…"

"The rest of the rules are easy. Never shoot the good guys, unless they become bad guys. Never shoot until you have clear line of sight, unless you have no other choice. If someone fires at you or someone you care about, shoot to kill. Don't hesitate."

"Shoot to kill. Got it." But she didn't look like she had that. Not yet. "Anything else?"

Wind rustled leaves on the trees behind our paper target, as if the woods had advice for her, too, and it might be better than mine. "Yeah. Personal weapons have a hierarchy. Guns trump knives every time, no matter how fast you can throw, slash or stab. Kori will tell you otherwise, but she's wrong." Unproven, at least. "Knives trump fists, unless you know someone who can punch through solid flesh. But Julia Tower's weapon of choice trumps them all."

"What's that?"

"The truth."

Sera frowned. "Are you being melodramatic? Or is that a joke? I don't know you well enough to tell the difference."

I wanted to change that. But it wasn't the time.

"It's neither. Julia has information you want. I know, because she *always* has information someone wants. That's her thing. And it'll be worse for you, because she knows more about the people you come from than you ever will. But if you let her start talking, you're screwed from the start. She can make you cry with the truth faster than I can make her bleed with a bullet."

"Good to know." Though she didn't look like she really believed me, and if that was the case—if no one had ever said anything to her that had ripped her heart right out of her chest—then I envied her.

"You ready to try that now?" I glanced at her gun.

She nodded, and this time she looked more sure.

"Okay. Pick it up, finger off the trigger."

Sera blew a strand of hair out of her face, then picked up her gun. Her grip was nervous, but steady.

"Two hands. Like this." I stepped behind her and lifted her left hand, showing her how to cradle the grip of her gun to steady her aim. I could have demonstrated with Kori's 9 mm, but…I wanted to touch her.

"Don't lock your elbows, or the recoil will throw your arms up. Let them absorb some of the force." I slid my hands over her arms, testing her stance, glad she wore short sleeves, so I could feel her skin.

"Like this?" she whispered. I was so close I could feel her body heat through my clothes. Through hers.

"Just like that." I whispered, too, then took that final step so that her back was pressed against my chest. I had no reason to still be touching her, but she made no objection and I couldn't resist. "Now click off the safety. It's that switch by your thumb."

She started to turn the gun around to look for the switch, but I stopped her with a little pressure against her hand. "Always aim downrange, remember? Just feel for the switch. It's there."

Sera found the switch and pushed it with her thumb. "It's off," she whispered, and that time there was an exhalation on the end, smooth and soft, and I inhaled with her, breathing in the scent of her soap and shampoo, and beneath that, her skin.

"Now line up the notch on the back of the gun with the guide on the front of the barrel," I said, and she made a minute adjustment. "Got it?"

She nodded. "What should I aim for? What…part?"

"The first time? Aim to kill."

Her aim rose. She was going for the target's head, like I'd known she would.

"Now, when you fire, it's going to recoil. Don't drop the gun."

"I won't."

"Take a breath. Then squeeze the trigger."

Sera inhaled again, and that time I held my breath. She squeezed the trigger. The gun fired, the casing ejected over her shoulder and her arms flew up from the recoil. She gasped and would have stumbled back, but I was behind her.

Her grip on the gun loosened in surprise, and I put my hand over hers, so she couldn't drop it.

"Sorry." She was breathless, and I loved the sound. I wanted to hear it again—in another context. "I almost dropped it."

"That's okay." I let her go and stepped back reluctantly, then squinted at the target. "Looks like you got a hit."

"How can you tell?" She set the gun down and shielded her eyes from the sun while she frowned at the target.

"I have good eyes." I picked up the binoculars on the table and handed them to her.

"That's not a hit!" she said, peering through the goggles. "The hole's several inches right of his head."

I chuckled. "You hit the target. Not bad for your first try."

"Is that…" Sera turned to grin at me, and my chest felt suddenly warm. "Did you draw a goofy face on my target guy?"

"You put a marshmallow Peep in my hot chocolate. I thought I'd reciprocate."

She laughed out loud, and I couldn't resist a smile of my own. "Try it again, and this time spread your feet a little. That'll help with your balance."

Sera set the binoculars down and picked up the gun again. She took her time, finding a comfortable grip, taking a wider stance and lining up her target. Then she took a deep breath and squeezed the trigger.

Again, the recoil knocked her aim up, but she didn't let go and there was no gasp of surprise. And this time, before she set the gun on the table, barrel pointed downrange, she remembered to reengage the safety.

"Did I hit him?"

I looked through the binoculars to make sure, because it didn't seem possible. "Yup. Left half of his handlebar mustache." I set the binoculars down and grinned at her. "Nice. Now do it again."

It took her two more tries to get another head shot, but the one she missed went right through the paper man's neck. When she'd hit him in the head five more times, obliterating his nose and forehead, then nicking the corner of his right eye, I gave her a new goal. "Now aim for his heart." Where I'd sketched a drawing of the organ, complete with valves, in Wite-Out, over the black silhouette. "And this time, fire three rounds without stopping.

Sera frowned and took aim with singular concentration, and I knew she wasn't hearing the birds overhead or the tractor mowing the field to our west. Then she fired.

The first bullet went through the paper man's left aorta. A second later, her second bullet hit the other side of his chest. The third bullet, a second and a half after that, hit the poor man's chin.

"Well, he's definitely dead," I said when she reengaged the safety and set the gun down.

"It's harder like that." She swept stray strands of hair from her face. "There's no time to aim between shots."

"That's why you have to get the recoil under control. Try it again. In sets of three."

She did, with similar results. The first shot was a hit, but the second and third went wide.

"Sorry."

"Are you kidding? You fired your first shot twenty minutes ago, and he's more than dead." I smiled, because she looked disappointed with herself. "But here's the hard part. How many rounds do you have left?"

She squinted, staring at the ground in thought.

"Don't try to count the casings!" I said, when I realized what she was really doing.

"I'm not." But that's exactly what she'd been doing. "Two," she said, after another second of thought. "One in the clip, one in the chamber.

"Close. Three," I said, and she frowned. "Two in the clip, and one in the chamber. Now, eject the clip and reload."

"How do I…"

I took the gun from her, letting my fingers brush her hand a little longer than necessary, and ejected the clip in demonstration. Then I slid it back into place and gave her the gun.

Sera checked the safety, then ejected the clip.

I showed her how to load the first round, then I stood back and left her to it.

A minute and a half later, she set the clip down in frustration. She'd only loaded two rounds. "I can't do it. It's too tight."

I shrugged. "If you can't load the clip, you don't get to shoot the gun."

Sera scowled.

"You wanna try Van's .22?"

Her scowl deepened, and she picked up the clip again, determination clear in the line of her jaw.

It took her another ten minutes, but she got it done—

all seventeen rounds. Then she slid the clip into place and fired four rounds with no prompting.

I couldn't find any holes, so I picked up the binoculars. She'd shredded the paper man's groin.

"Classy." I set the binoculars on the table, and she laughed.

"Now try that on a moving target, and I'll be impressed," Kori said, and we turned to find her leaning against the door to the shed we used to Travel into the house.

"You couldn't hit a moving target when you first started," I reminded her.

"Yeah. I was also twelve." Kori glanced from me to Sera, then back to me, her left brow arched in amusement. "Isn't this a little cliché? You wanna teach her to hit a golf ball next?"

"Watch out, or I'll teach her to hit *you*."

"No lessons necessary," Sera mumbled, and I couldn't hide a grin.

Kori laughed out loud. "So, is she ready to be thrown to the wolves?"

"She's getting there." But I wasn't going to throw her to the wolves. Everyone else may have been willing to let Sera march into Tower territory on her own, to find *our* Kenley, but I wasn't. I was going with her. Whether she agreed or not.

"Gran says if you don't come eat, she's going to throw your dinner down the drain."

I huffed. "If by drain, she means her own gullet."

"We'll be in in a minute," Sera said, and Kori must have been feeling generous, because she took the hint and retreated indoors.

"Thank you." Sera ejected the chambered round from her gun, just like I'd shown her.

"No problem. I like guns."

"That's not what I meant. Thanks for helping me, beyond the guns."

I concentrated really hard on putting the unspent .40 rounds back into the box. "I like you, too."

"Now you're just messing with me."

"I'm really not." I met her gaze, letting her see the truth. "And I don't want you to get killed trying to find my sister."

She held up the gun, safety engaged, aiming downrange. "Thanks to you, I just may walk out of there alive."

But the gun was no guarantee. The fact that she didn't seem to understand that scared the living shit out of me. I couldn't lose her. I didn't even *have* her, but I already knew that I couldn't survive losing her, and that was the scariest thought I'd had since the day I'd decided my life was worth living, even without Noelle in it.

Eighteen

Sera

After dinner on my third night in the House of Crazy, Kori and Van started their anti-Julia viral campaign, jokingly referred to as "Off With Her Head." Though I truly hoped no one actually planned to decapitate Julia Tower. A bullet through her brain was enough for me.

Ian held the master list of names and phone numbers they'd compiled—an act worthy of punishment within the syndicate itself, where writing criminal details down was highly…discouraged. Kori and Van each took half of the list and texted every number with a prepared statement, declaring that Julia was actually Tower's regent, not his heir, and naming me as the oldest of my biological father's children.

No one texted back with a response, and I was tempted to see that as the failure of our scheme, but they all assured me that the opposite was true. There would be doubters, of course, but if no one believed the text so many people were getting, there would definitely have been a response.

After that, while all phones remained conspicuously

silent, we went out back to Kris's homemade gun range again, but this time the entire household came with us. We drew faces on our black silhouetted targets with neon markers and Wite-Out pens, then tacked them to trees on the edge of the woods behind the house.

Since there were so many of us shooting at once, Kori brought out a plastic tub full of mismatched sets of headphones she'd evidently taken one at a time from every gun range she'd ever visited. I didn't want to know how she'd gotten out the door without turning them in.

Then I realized she probably hadn't gone out through the door at all.

On the third try, I shot the button nose off the demented teddy bear Kris had drawn on my new target—he was pretty damn good with a marker—and I was feeling pretty good about my new skill, until Kris and Kori pulled down everyone's first target and handed them out.

Neither Daniels sibling had missed a single mark. In fact, Kori had hit the center of her target's forehead so many times that there was only one big hole where his poor paper brains had once been.

Kris went for the heart. And he hit it every single time.

For our second round, I drew shaggy white facial hair on Kris's target man, and when I turned to hand it to him, I found him bent over the card table with a sparkly sliver pen—I have no idea where he got it—drawing on my target as if the rest of the world didn't exist.

I took one look and wanted to hide the one I'd done before he saw it. His soon-to-be-destroyed art was incredible. "Holy shit," I breathed, and Kris chuckled. I recognized Julia's sparkly scowl staring out at me from the face of my target guy with a single glance.

He held the paper up. "I thought you might like the inspiration."

"That's incredible. I'd say it's beautiful, but…it's Julia." My biological aunt was not unattractive in real life, but I would never think of her as pretty, because I would always know what lay behind the blessings genetics had given her. But Kris had drawn her so well I almost hated to shoot her.

"Show off." Kori had already demonstrated the fact that she'd rather decorate her target with 9 mm piercings, and I wasn't sure whether that was because she was obviously violent in nature or because she had no other talents that I could tell.

Ian glanced at the drawing, then at me, then at Kris. Then he gave us both a quiet smile that made me blush.

While Kris nailed up our targets, I headed to the cooler next to the back steps to grab several bottles of water. When I stood with as many as I could carry, I was struck by the sight of them all together, doing what they did best, like any family might. Sure, my family's together-time had been spent singing along with my dad's acoustic guitar rather than shredding paper targets with high-velocity personal projectiles, but the gist was the same. They were together, and beneath the bickering over who'd hit the target's left eye more times in a row and Gran's nagging Kris to quit shooting Kori's target on the sly, you could see that they loved each other. And that more than anything, they wanted Kenley back, to complete their family.

Seeing the pain they shared and how it drew them together made me ache with memories of my own, a pain so deep that for a moment I couldn't breathe. Couldn't move. That ache grew sharper and gained focus, not in my chest, but in my abdomen. Beneath my scar.

My eyes closed and tears rolled down my cheeks before I'd even known they were there. The water bottles fell from my arms to bounce in the dirt and I clutched at my stomach, hating how flat it felt. How empty.

He would have been seven months along now, my baby that never was. He would have been mature enough to live, even if he'd chosen to come into the world at that very moment. But he would never be born. And he would never have a brother or sister, because the wound that ripped him from my life and from my body had ended any chance of me ever having another child.

My knees hit the ground, and my hands followed.

"Sera?" Vanessa called, and when I looked up I saw her at the end of the line of shooters, blurry through my tears. Alone, because she was missing her heart, too. With Kenley gone, did she feel as empty as I felt?

The others loved Kenley, too. They would have done anything to get her back. But in her absence, they still had one another.

Vanessa had nothing, now. Like I had nothing.

"Sera!" Kris set his gun on the table and jogged across the grass toward me, but I was already on my feet wiping tears away by the time he got there. I cursed myself silently and assured him aloud that I was fine. That I'd just tripped. That I hoped the water bottles hadn't burst because of my clumsiness.

He didn't believe a word I said; that was clear. But he only picked up the bottles and tossed each one to a member of his family, willing to let me grieve privately, even though I wasn't actually in private. For which I was more than grateful.

Then he tacked Julia's image up on the tree designated as my target, and as I took aim with a full clip, he leaned in close and whispered in my ear. "I didn't know what your bad guy looks like, so I drew mine. Feel free to blow her sparkly brains out."

With remembered pain still burning in my stomach and fresh loss aching in my chest, I took aim. My first shot hit the left side of her forehead, and after that, my aim only improved. I fired all eighteen rounds into Julia Tower's effigy, and nearly all of them found their mark in her head, her throat and her chest.

By the time I was finished, they were all watching me as the sun—a fat scarlet ball—sank below the tree line to the west.

I didn't realize I was crying again until the echo of my last shot rolled into the distance.

I'd just pulled a clean T-shirt over my head when someone knocked on my bedroom door. "It's open," I called, running my comb through hair still wet from my shower.

Kris opened the door, but stayed in the threshold. "I thought you might want these." He held out two long tubes of paper, which could only be my targets from that evening's shooting session. "And this." His other hand held a roll of Scotch tape.

"Thanks." They were for inspiration. I was proud of learning to defend myself, and potentially protect others.

I took the targets and waved him inside while I set the brush on my dresser. *His* dresser. Then I climbed onto the bed in borrowed socks and stood, leaning against the headboard for balance as I unrolled the first paper.

"We have to get you some clothes of your own. You can't keep wearing Kori's shorts." He tore off a piece of tape for me as I positioned the first of that evening's targets next to the one from that afternoon, already on display above my bed. *His* bed.

I took the tape he offered and secured the top left corner to the wall. "I have to wear something, don't I?"

His brows were arched halfway up his forehead when I reached down for the next piece of tape. "Do you really want me to answer that?"

I didn't reply. I didn't know how to reply.

When I tried to take the strip of tape, his hand closed around mine. "In case you're tempted to misinterpret that as another mixed signal, let me be clear about three very important things. One—I like you. A lot."

A fluttery feeling took over my stomach, like when I'd played on the swings as a kid, and I couldn't make it go away.

"Two—I will never, ever hurt you, for any reason, and I don't give a damn who your father was or how valuable you are to my mortal enemy."

I couldn't breathe. I couldn't blink. I could only stare down at him while he stared back up at me and the rest of the world seemed to fade into the background.

"And three—the biggest mistake I've ever made was letting you walk out of the kitchen the other night without understanding exactly how I feel and why I said what I said." His hand squeezed mine, and tears filled my eyes. "And that's really saying something, because most of my high school extracurriculars weren't exactly legal. If I'd gone to college, I could have majored in Bad Decisions. If there was a title behind my name, it'd sound something like, Kristopher Daniels, Professional Fuckup. But I've never made a mistake as big as letting you walk away from me."

"I…" I had to swallow, then start over, my bare feet buried in a tangle of his sheets. "I'm not sure what to say."

"You don't have to say anything. I just wanted to make sure you understood all of that, so that if you walk away from me again, I'll at least know it wasn't because you didn't know how I feel." He blinked, then let me have the piece of tape now stuck to both of us. "The rest of it is up to you. We'll do whatever you want."

I wasn't sure *what* I wanted from Kris. All I knew was that I liked the way he looked at me. And I liked the way his voice sounded when he said my name. And I loved how the same fingers that could mercilessly aim his gun and squeeze its trigger could also brush hair off my shoulder with the ghost of a touch, or cradle my fingers between his own during that first step into the darkness.

We finished hanging the targets in silence, while I thought about what he'd said, and what that might mean for us, and how the only reason I'd had to walk away from him—the secret of my birthright—was no longer an issue. And when that was done, I stood on the floor at the foot of the bed, staring up at the targets, thinking about how brutally different my life had become in the past three months.

Ninety days earlier, I couldn't have imagined myself like this. Childless. Sterile. A decent shot with a handgun, if unproven in action. Possessing more power, money and authority than I'd ever dreamed possible—yet unsure how to use any of them. Or even whether I should.

"Want to talk about it?" Kris said, but when I turned to look at him, I only saw his profile. He was staring at the targets—evidence of the new me. That she was all I had left.

"Talk about what?"

"About the cooler. Whatever happened."

"No. Thanks, though." I circled the bed and started straightening the sheets and blankets, just to have something to do with my hands.

"Are you okay?" His voice was deep. Gruff. As if he was holding back more than he was actually saying.

I fluffed a pillow and propped it against the head-board. "Are any of us?"

He shrugged, and the gesture looked tired. "Valid point." Kris was quiet then, watching me while I picked up clothes from the floor. When I bent to pull a dirty sock from beneath the bed, he stepped forward and took my hand, tugging gently until I stood, very aware of how close he was. Of how our hands were still touching. "I want to ask you for something." Now he was whisper-ing, and his gaze kept volleying between my eyes and my lips, as if he wanted something from them both. "And you're going to say no, and that's okay. But I have to ask. I need to know."

"Ask," I said, and there was something in his eyes. Something I almost didn't recognize, coming from him. Some fragile kind of vulnerability.

"Can I see it? Please?"

"What?" My heart thumped.

"Your scar."

For a second, I couldn't breathe. "Why?" I whispered, when I could speak again. That wasn't what I'd expected. I wasn't sure *what* I'd expected.

"So I can understand." He was serious. There wasn't a hint of a smile anywhere on his face, but that vulner-ability was as raw as I'd ever seen it. "I want to know who you are, and I can't, until I know what you've been through."

"You already know." Yet knowing wasn't the same as truly understanding. And he'd already shown me his scars—an entire notebook filled with them.

I headed for the door, and he thought I was kicking him out—I could see that in the slump of his shoulders and the regret behind his eyes. But then I closed the door and leaned against it, and he exhaled.

Kris's brows rose in silent question. I nodded, and he crossed the room slowly. His gaze didn't leave mine until he knelt on the floor in front of me and my heart pounded so hard I was sure he could hear it. For one long moment, he stared at the material covering my stomach, and the pervasive anger and underlying sense of loss I'd been living with for months warred with something new inside me. Something fragile and...hopeful.

Then he put his hands on my hips and looked up at me, and I held my breath. Kris looked so different from this angle. From above, his shoulders bunched with tension, his jaw tight. He looked strong, but sad.

He lifted the hem of my borrowed T-shirt slowly and his thumb trailed over my skin beneath the cotton. I held my breath. He was very careful, like my wound might still be open and bleeding literally, as it bled still in my heart.

He inhaled when he saw it, dark pink and smooth to the touch, and when he looked up at me, I saw my own horror reflected on his face.

Tears filled my eyes again when his hand covered my scar, low on the right side of my abdomen, trailing beneath the waist of my shorts. His hand was warm, and I felt it all around the wound, but not in the scar itself. The scar had no feeling, which was odd, because it seemed directly connected to my heart, which hurt all the time.

"I'm so sorry." His hand shifted to cradle my hip, and when his fingers left my stomach, his lips found it. "He will pay," Kris murmured, his breath warm against my skin, the stubble on his chin rough, yet comforting in the way only something so tangibly masculine can be. "No one should touch you out of anything other than adoration, ever again."

My breath caught in my throat, and my hands caught

in his hair, and when Kris stood, he was all I could see. "I adore you, Sera. Will you let me touch you?"

"Yes. Please."

The words carried almost no sound, but he heard them.

Kris blinked at me in surprise, but that was gone in an instant, replaced by desire burning bright in his eyes, tinged with something stronger. Something I desperately wanted to believe in.

I could have this. I could have Kris, and if what I saw in his eyes could be trusted, I wouldn't be getting him just for the night. And I wouldn't be getting him alone. Kris was a package deal. He came with sisters, and friends, and a grandmother. A ready-made family with tempers, and hugs, and dementia, and chili, and arguments, and laughter, even in the worst of times, and a shared mission I already believed in.

They couldn't replace the family I'd lost. But they didn't have to, and they wouldn't *try* to. They would just *be there*.

Kris would be there. If I let him.

Kris kissed me, and I kissed him back. I let everything go, and it was easier than I'd expected, because he wanted the burden. He didn't just want to touch me, he wanted to *know* me. He wanted to know what had made me who I was. So I showed him.

I poured all my grief into that kiss. All my hunger for vengeance. And I fed from the same in him, astonished by the translation of heat from remembered violence to carnal appetite. We kissed until I forgot about the house around us and the people in it. Until I no longer felt the door at my back or the floor beneath my feet. I couldn't feel anything but him, and I couldn't touch enough of him to satisfy hands that had gone empty for too long.

A mouth that had tasted only bitterness and pain for months on end.

But I could sure as hell try.

When kissing was no longer enough, I tugged on the end of his shirt, wordlessly commanding its removal as my mouth demanded even more from his lips. His tongue. Kris pulled away just long enough to tug his shirt over his head, and suddenly I could touch him unhindered by useless cotton.

I tasted him then, clean from a recent shower. His earlobes felt good between my teeth and his hair smelled like guy-shampoo. His neck was rough with stubble, and just a little salty. His chin was strong, and the back of his jawbone fit in the gap between my lips like I was always meant to kiss him there.

My hands found smooth skin over taut muscle. Hard planes and all the right masculine bumps and ridges. He let me play, tasting, testing, learning his body as thoroughly as I could, because I wouldn't get another chance. His hands stayed anchored at my waist, fingers splayed around the curve of my ribs. He was more patient than I.

Until he wasn't.

His eager tug at my shirt demanded reciprocation, so I lifted my arms and let him take it off. I didn't see where it fell, and I didn't give a damn, because then he was touching me, and his touch felt hungry, yet restrained. He took his time, as if every inch of me deserved to be explored with equal attention, and when he dropped to his knees in front of me again, his lips trailing from my navel toward the low waist of my borrowed pj shorts, my head fell back against the door and my hands tangled in his pale hair.

Kris blazed hotter than anything I'd ever felt. His lips were like sparks against my skin, his hands practically on fire, and I burned everywhere he touched me. When his mouth found my scar again, those flames almost overwhelmed me, and I felt my body go still on its own. But then I pushed the memories away. I let him burn them back until I could hardly see them anymore, and when he hesitated at the waist of my shorts, I pulled him up to eye level.

"Is this what you want?" I was suddenly sure I'd misread some signal, or read more into what he was saying than he'd actually meant. Was that why he'd stopped?

"So much," he said, his voice scratchy with desire, and I almost melted with relief. "But if you don't, we don't have to…"

"I do." I wanted to touch all of him. I wanted him to touch all of me. I wanted to forget everything in the world that wasn't relevant to him, and to me, and to the two of us together, for as long as I could have him.

It's sheer luck that we made it to the bed, when the floor was so much closer, but when I felt the mattress touch the backs of my thighs, I sat. Kris joined me seconds later, nude and unspeakably beautiful, and I closed my eyes, afraid to look too long at the miracle I'd found, for fear that it would disappear.

I exhaled at his next touch, then held my breath altogether when his mouth followed a moment later, working its way down from my neck. I kept my eyes squeezed shut and let my hands see for me, sliding over his arms and chest, feeling the curve of his biceps, then traveling over the planes of his back. His mouth trailed down from my breast, over my stomach, and I arched into his touch, drawing another groan from him as he slid the borrowed shorts over my hips. Then came the soft exhalation of surprise when he realized I wore nothing beneath them— I don't borrow underwear.

And that was all the waiting I could take.

I kicked the shorts off and pulled him back up, opening for him, as he settled between my thighs. I slid the arches of my feet up his calves and he leaned closer to whisper into my ear.

"Look at me, Sera. Please," he added.

So finally I opened my eyes, and when I met his gaze, he slid into me, slowly, smoothly, and I couldn't breathe again until I had all of him. And I was terrified by how much I didn't want to let him go.

He lingered there, my legs locked around him, staring into my eyes, and I discovered that now that I was looking, I couldn't turn away from him. Not even when he began to move inside me, and my hips rose to meet him over and over. I couldn't look away until he leaned close to whisper in my ear.

"I promise he will pay, Sera. He will pay with every drop of his blood, and with his very last breath."

I clung to him, as fresh tears rolled down my cheeks and soaked into his pillow. Then I pushed it all away again—the despair, the anger—and lived in that moment with Kris. Our moment, in which nothing else existed. Nothing but him, and me, and the delicious friction building between us, burning hotter with each second, until I couldn't breathe, and couldn't think, and couldn't hold back for another second.

I gasped as that heat spilled over in wave after wave of pleasure, and Kris groaned when his release caught up with mine. And for a moment afterward, neither of us moved. I didn't want to let him go, and he seemed in no hurry to be freed.

Then he kissed the corner of my jaw and his weight and warmth disappeared. I sat up, suddenly sure I'd see him pulling on his clothes to leave the room, but instead he settled onto the mattress next to me. "Don't worry. I'm not going anywhere." Kris pulled the sheet up to cover us both, then slid his arm beneath my pillow, and we lay there listening to each other breathe, while the rest of the world carried on without us.

It was the most peaceful moment I could remember since the night my family died. And I never wanted it to end.

Nineteen

Kris

She was the most beautiful thing I'd ever touched, and the saddest person I'd ever met, and I didn't want to let her go. I couldn't.

Afterward, I lay on my side next to her, one hand splayed across her stomach, trying not to think about her scar and what it meant. What he'd taken from her. What no one would ever be able to give her again.

I hated how helpless—how *useless*—that scar made me feel. I was supposed to prevent that. I was meant to save Sera's baby. Her future. I was meant to spare her the grief she was still mired in, and maybe, if I'd actually done that, we would have come together in a moment of triumph, instead of shared grief.

"Can I ask you a personal question?" I stared down at her profile, no more able to look away from her than I was able to stop touching her.

She turned to look at me, and her eyes were damp. "Only if I get to ask one in return."

"You can ask, even if you don't want to answer my

question. And that's okay, if you don't want to. I don't have any right to ask."

"Just say it." A hint of a smile rode the corners of her mouth, but it was forced. It didn't match the sadness in her eyes. "You're making it worse, with the buildup."

I shouldn't ask. It was none of my business. But I had to know, for purely selfish reasons.

"Who is he?" My thumb twitched over her scar on the last word, surely an unconscious, nervous movement.

Sera frowned, and I saw the moment her confusion cleared. She'd thought I was asking about the killer. Or maybe about the child he'd taken from her. "My baby's father?" she whispered, and all hints of that earlier smile were gone.

"Yeah. But you don't have to…"

"His name is Ben. But he doesn't matter. Really," she said when I started to object. Of course he mattered. He'd lost a child, too. "He didn't want the baby. He didn't want me. We weren't involved, beyond that one time. I don't even know how to get in touch with him anymore, so maybe this was meant to be."

"No," I said, and she looked so relieved I wanted to kiss her. "This wasn't meant to be." I was meant to stop it. I'd failed Sera before I'd even met her.

"My turn," she said, and I let her change the subject because we both needed it. "What was it like, being with Noelle? With a Seer?"

"You really want to know?"

She nodded. "Okay. Um… Going out with Noelle was like going out with Cassandra. *The* Cassandra."

"From Greek mythology?"

"Yeah. The one who could see the future, but couldn't change it." Only what Noelle and I did together couldn't really be called dating. There were no true meals, no movies and no Valentines. We stole moments from the real world, and we stole them shamelessly. We tried to pause time and live in a single second forever. In a heartbeat. In a glance. In that quick breath between desperate kisses. And every single one of those stolen moments happened between one o'clock and three o'clock in the morning. In my bed.

"But it wasn't all sex," I said, and Sera almost looked relieved. "Kori thinks it was, but Elle and I also talked." More accurately, we'd whispered. We'd laughed. We'd teased. And one time, Noelle had cried. "Then, eventually, inevitably, she fell asleep. And that's when things got weird. Every single time."

"She started talking in her sleep?"

"Yeah. And now that I can look back on it with a little perspective—I'm wiser now, in case you didn't know—I think that may have been the point for her all along."

"But it wasn't for you?"

I shook my head. The prophesies weren't the point for me. Not then. Not until after Elle died, and I started wondering why I'd felt compelled to write down everything she said. "For me, *she* was the point. Being with her. I know she didn't love me, but when she came home, she would let me pretend."

"Home from where?"

I shrugged. "Wherever. She always left. But then she always came back, eventually." I'd never talked to anyone else about Elle. Not like this. Not even Kori. Sera was the last person I'd expected to confide in—telling one girlfriend about a previous girlfriend rarely goes well. Not that either of them had officially accepted the title.

But that was the thing about talking to Sera—I always wound up saying more than I'd meant to. She charmed it out of me, as if I was a snake in her basket.

Which sounded kind of dirty, in retrospect.

"Did she ever say what it was like?" Sera still watched me, from inches away. "Seeing the future?"

"I only asked her once. She said it was like sitting in this old tire swing in Gran's backyard. Did you ever swing in one?" I asked, and she nodded. "Remember how you could twist, and twist, and twist, then grab on tight and let the rope unwind? The world would spin around you, and you could only catch glimpses of things flying by? Elle said seeing the future was like that. Scary, and breathless, and never quite enough, but more than anyone could ever truly make sense of."

Sera tried to hide a yawn. "Sounds...disorienting."

"I'm sure it was."

We were quiet after that, and I was starting to think she'd fallen asleep, until she snuggled closer. "Tell me a secret, Kris. You know all of mine."

"What do you want to know?" I would tell her anything.

"I want to know about Micah."

I exhaled slowly, breathing through an ache I could never really ease. "Who told you?"

"Kori told me about the kids. Why didn't you? Don't you trust me?"

"Now? With my life." I squeezed her hand, trying to demonstrate the truth through touch. "But I couldn't afford to trust you at first, and since then, there just hasn't been time, between stealing back your pictures, and looking for Kenley, and getting shot at, and hiding from Julia Tower."

"There's time now," she whispered. "Tell me about Micah."

Another slow breath. Then I launched into a retelling of my biggest shame. "I was nineteen. Gran was getting too old to work, and I thought I was doing the right thing. Helping pay the bills. I took whatever jobs I could find, and I didn't ask questions. It was easier to pocket an envelope full of cash if I didn't ask why the jobs were off the record.

"Micah was the last of those jobs. A thirteen-year-old caught in the middle of a divorce battle. His mother had custody. His dad wanted him back. They told me the mother was abusive. That he'd be better off with his dad, but that Micah couldn't see that yet, so I had to take him while he was sleeping.

"I did." I swallowed a lump the size of a baseball in my throat. "Three days later, I heard Gran cussing at the television. Micah's picture was on the screen. There was a picture of his parents, too. They weren't divorced. The dad wasn't the man who'd hired me.

"The coroner said Micah died of massive hemorrhaging. He was left on the side of the street. Gran said that was bullshit. She said it was a syndicate object lesson. She said that's what they did to kids—to *anyone*—who refused to fall in line. They gave the poor kid conflicting orders and let his body tear itself apart in front of an audience."

"Oh…" Sera's voice carried little sound, but infinite pain.

"It was my fault. I took him from his bed in the middle of the night and gave him to the mafia."

"And now you're trying to make up for it." She didn't tell me it wasn't my fault. She didn't absolve me of the blame, or belittle my responsibility with platitudes.

I shook my head. "I can never make up for it. All I can do is try to stop it from happening to someone else. To *anyone* else."

"That's what you were doing when Kori and Kenley joined the syndicate?"

My exhalation tasted as bitter as it sounded. "Ironic, huh? In trying to save strangers, I let my own sisters fall." I closed my eyes. "I believed Kori when she told me she had it under control. She joined the syndicate to protect Kenley, who was coerced into joining a few days before. Kori made me promise not to tell my grandmother that they'd joined, and she made me promise to stay away from them. She said she could handle it. That they'd serve their five years, then get out, but that if Tower knew she and Kenni were close to me and Gran, he'd use us against her. And vice versa."

"So you stayed away?"

I nodded. "I stayed away. I thought I'd be making things worse by getting involved. Worse for them, and worse for the kids I was working with. And in the beginning, that was probably true. If I'd known what was going on, I would have joined the syndicate instead of Kori, but she didn't even tell me until it was too late, and then there was no one else left to take care of Gran. But if I'd… I don't know. If I'd done things differently, maybe I could have kept Kori out of the basement."

Maybe I could have prevented whatever put that haunted look in her eyes and made her scream at night.

"You couldn't have stopped it." Sera was hardly awake, yet she sounded certain. "You can't stop stuff like that from the outside. Sometimes you can't even stop it from the inside…"

As she fell asleep on my arm, I realized she was talking about herself. She'd tried to save her sister. She'd tried to stop it from the inside, and instead, she'd lost everything.

I wanted to give her something.

I waited nearly an hour until she rolled over on her own because I didn't want to wake her up. But as soon as she was on the other side of the mattress—all but one small foot, resting against my shin—I snuck out of bed and turned off the lamp, then stepped into my jeans and crept downstairs, this new need still only half-formed.

On the bottom step, I groaned when I saw the light shining in the kitchen. *Shit.* I'd hoped to keep this new detail of my relationship with Sera private, at least until I knew how much she wanted everyone else to know.

Also, I'd wanted privacy for my new errand. But that wasn't gonna happen.

Gran never woke up in the middle of the night, unless she was…confused—or someone turned on the TV—and I really didn't feel like pretending I was still a twenty-year-old college dropout. Not with Sera still sleeping without me in the bed that could hopefully now be described as "ours."

"Gran?" The living room floorboards creaked beneath my bare feet.

"It's just me," Ian said, and I was relieved for a second. Until I realized that unlike Gran, he probably wouldn't forget me sneaking out of Sera's room in the middle of the night.

Ian sat alone at the table, tapping on Vanessa's laptop keys with two fingers. I crossed to the cabinet over the sink and took out a bottle of whiskey—the only alcohol in the house—and a short glass, then sat down next to him.

"Kori will skin you alive if you drink the last of her whiskey."

"I'll blame it on you." I unscrewed the lid, and his brows rose. "Fine. I'll pick up more tomorrow. I need to take Sera shopping anyway."

Ian eyed me over the open laptop with a quiet smile. "So…you and Sera?"

I swallowed a groan as I poured two inches into my glass. "Please tell me no one else heard…"

"The walls are thin." Which I knew all too well. "But Van only went up to bed ten minutes ago, and Kori sleeps more soundly than I do—until the nightmares."

"Are they getting any better?" Kori's nightmares made me feel useless, because I couldn't fix her any easier than I could fix Sera.

Ian nodded. "Slowly."

"What's with the computer? You finally joining the twenty-first century?"

"Kicking and screaming." He sighed. "I'd much rather read a newspaper, but they're in short supply around here, so I'm stuck using this thing. Van showed me how to use a search engine, but all I'm getting are pop-up ads and the same ten results, every time I click 'go.'" He turned the computer around and demonstrated.

I laughed. "Click on 'next page' for the rest of the results. There are more than ten thousand of them, but you just keep refreshing that first page full."

Ian took the laptop back and frowned. "Oh. Thanks."

"Shopping for an apartment? Are you leaving us?"

"It's for me and Kori. For after we get Kenley back and things settle down."

"You think she'll want to stay in the city once all this is over?"

"I think she'd be bored in the Outback, and I'm not leaving here without her." He glanced at my show of skepticism and exhaled slowly. "We're going to end it, Kris," he confessed at last. "Not just Julia and the Tower syndicate. Cavazos, too. Kori can't go on with her life knowing that other people are still suffering the same things she went through. This won't be over for her until they all fall down. And if they don't...well, she'll die trying to make it happen. We both will."

"And after we take down Cavazos?" Because they weren't doing it without me.

"Then we'll head to the West Coast and fight the good fight with a view of the ocean." Ian shrugged. "At least that'll keep us busy."

That it would. And they wouldn't be alone.

"So, what's with the nightcap?" Ian closed the laptop with a soft click. "Post-coital regret?"

"Not even kinda." I would never regret a single moment I'd spent with Sera. Except for kidnapping her. "I just need to think."

"Do you find that easier, staring at the bottom of a bottle?"

"Not always." I sipped from my glass, relishing the mild burn.

He pushed the computer toward the middle of the table. "You're more like Kori than you know."

"I'm older," I insisted. "Which means she's more like me."

"You both have big hearts. The only difference is that she hides hers behind guns and a foul mouth, and you hide yours behind guns and a smile. So...where's the smile?"

"I must have left it in bed."

"Sera's?"

I took another sip. "You all seem to be forgetting that it's actually *my* bed."

"Not when she's in it," he said, and I had to concede the point.

I drained my glass, then set it down and studied him critically for a moment. "I need to talk about what just happened with Sera. You game?"

Ian chuckled. "Of course. Should I reciprocate, to cement our friendship?"

I flinched. "Please don't do that."

That time he laughed. "I promise that was an empty threat." He poured another inch into my glass. "So. What's up with you and Sera?"

"Everything. Up there, we just—"

He put one hand flat on the table between us, and the gesture felt very much like a stop sign. "I know what you did. No need to elaborate."

"Not that. Well, there was that, too." I frowned, wondering if I should start over. "But this isn't about sex. Before that, she showed me something. She let me in."

"Still sounds like we're talking about sex…"

"Well, we're not. I owe her, Ian."

Ian frowned and crossed both arms over his chest. "Was she *that* much better than you in bed?"

"Ha, ha," I said when his grin told me he was kidding. "She likes me, Ian. I think she likes me a lot, and I don't want that to change."

"What makes you think it will?"

How could it not, once she found out that I'd failed to stop what happened to her?

"I was supposed to do something, a while back." I took another sip from my glass, then started over from the beginning. A beginning I hadn't even realized our story— mine and Sera's—had until that moment. "For years, I've been wondering about Noelle. About why she picked me. My bed. My ears. My pencil. I've always felt like there must have been a reason, but I couldn't find it. I couldn't make any of the lines make sense, and I couldn't stop anything they warned me about. I couldn't even understand the warnings."

"And now?"

"Now…" I frowned and looked up from the table to meet his gaze. "I know this sounds crazy, but I think it was about Sera all along."

His dark brows rose. "You think Noelle slept with you off and on for six years because of Sera?"

I shrugged. "Well, I hope she had a more personal motivation for the sex part of the equation, but I think she stayed and talked in her sleep with me because of Sera. Her name's all through that journal, Ian. Noelle warned me over and over, and I couldn't see it. I was supposed to stop him. I was supposed to protect her and her family. I was supposed to save her baby, and her body, and her future."

"Are you serious?"

"Yeah." I nodded, just to underline my certainty. "Maybe Elle knew I'd wind up with Sera. Maybe she didn't. But she knew I was supposed to be there three months ago when that bastard shoved a knife through her belly and through her baby." I drained my glass while he stared at me. "The problem is that *I* didn't know."

"I take it Sera doesn't know, either?"

"No. I'm going to tell her. I have to tell her. But first I need to give her something. I need to show her how sorry I am. I need to make her believe that I'll never let something like that happen to her ever again. I want her to know that I can protect her, and that I'm so fucking sorry I wasn't there when she needed me."

"Kris, you didn't even know her."

"But I was *supposed* to know her. I was supposed to protect her." I picked up my glass again, but it was empty. "Ian, I think I love her."

He blinked. "Are you serious?"

"I don't know! I don't know how to tell."

"Okay, so what do you know?"

"I know that she's like a light in the dark, and I'm a

bug drawn to her flame. She's more sad, and beautiful, and determined than anyone I've ever met. She's like...a human superlative. She's the most...everything."

Ian's brows rose, and I knew what he was thinking. "I sound like a sap, don't I? I'm not, though. I'm not blind, or deaf, or stupid. I know she's not perfect. She yells at me, and hell, she tried to stab me. She kicked me out of my own room, and nearly made me break my nose on the closet door. And she lied to us all about being Jake Tower's kid. Sometimes I'm not sure whether I should kill her or kiss her. Is that crazy?"

"You're talking to the man who fell in love with your sister. If 'crazy' were a deal-breaker for me, I wouldn't be here. This whole house is crazy."

I nodded. "This place is crazy, and we're gluttons for punishment, you and I. How we've survived Gran, and Kori, and Sera is beyond me. I wouldn't want to face any one of them in a dark alley on a bad day, and we've got them all under one roof. Kinda makes you think Kenni and Van have the right idea, huh?"

"If you're changing teams in the middle of the game, I'm gonna have to cheer you on from the stands, man. My compass points toward women. One woman in particular."

I laughed. "Glad to hear it, for my sister's sake. And no, I'm not changing teams. Far from it." In fact, the heading on my own internal compass was steadier than I'd seen it in years. Instead of pointing to the entire female gender, it now seemed to be singling out Sera. Only Sera. And... "The thing is that for the first time since Noelle, I'm not scared to do this."

"To do what?" Ian unscrewed the cap from the whiskey bottle and took a short gulp. Bonding with me had driven him to drink, after only a quarter of an hour.

"To be with her. In *every* sense, not just the biblical. Although that was—"

"Stop there…" Ian warned, tilting the bottle up again, but I hardly heard him.

"She's like this living fire, jumping and sparking, and lighting me up even while she casts fierce shadow all around us, and when I'm with her I can totally see how fire could be the source of all life, because that's what she is. She is life. She burns with it. And I want to *kill* everyone who's ever laid a cruel hand on her."

I hadn't realized I was clenching my empty glass until Ian shrugged and pushed the bottle my way. "So do it."

Glass clinked as I poured. "Do what?"

"Kill him. We both know who you're talking about. Find him and kill him."

"I can't." Well, I *could,* but… "She wants to *see* him die. And I don't fucking blame her."

Ian frowned, as if I'd started speaking gibberish. "I didn't mean *now.* I'm just saying that if you want to prove you can protect her, give her what she came here for."

"That's the plan, but I can't do much until I know who the bastard is."

"Just give it a little more time. Before she went to bed, Van was making a list of possible suspects based on Sera's description and details from the crime scene. She's planning to show mug shots to Sera tomorrow. If they can identify him, Cam and Liv will be able to find him." He shrugged. "Then you can do what you do best, which will be giving her what she wants most in the world."

"You think killing is what I do best? Did you learn *nothing* from whatever you heard through the thin walls?"

"Ah. Humor as a defense mechanism. I know that tactic well."

I didn't bother denying it. Nor did I own up to what was really bothering me. I was supposed to stop Sera's bad guy before he killed her family. Killing him as an afterthought wouldn't give her back what she'd lost.

"No use stressing over it now." Ian pushed his chair back from the table. "There's nothing anyone can do until Sera's had a chance to look at the mug shots." He stood and pushed his chair in. "I don't think you have anything to prove to her, though. She likes you. We can all see that. So just don't kidnap her anymore and keep doing… whatever you did upstairs, and you should be golden."

After Ian went to bed, I poured another inch of whiskey and pulled Vanessa's laptop into position in front of me. Ian might not have understood computers, but I understood them well enough to find Van's search history and the files she'd worked on most recently. After three minutes of clicking links and opening documents, I found what I was looking for, though probably only because she'd made no effort to hide it. A series of six mug shots taken from a police database she shouldn't have had access to, compiled and labeled with both a number and a letter designation. Three files later, I found the code key, which provided each paroled—and one escaped—criminal with an arrest record, labeled with those same letter/number combinations.

I stared at the pictures, wondering which—if any—of these men had smiled at Sera as he drove his knife into her. Which of them had shot her parents, then stabbed and violated her little sister? Which man would I have to kill to see that rage in her eyes replaced with a sad peace that would grow a little less sad and a little more peaceful every day?

But their pictures told me nothing, except that all of them had light eyes, pale skin, and dark curls of various lengths.

Their arrest records didn't say much more. All had been

arrested for violent crimes within one hundred miles of her parents' home, including multiple counts of rape, aggravated assault, murder and one other home invasion. Three had been convicted and served time—several years each— before being paroled. One escaped from a local jail, where he was being kept during his appeal. One was acquitted. One never went to trial, thanks to police error. Such was the state of the justice system—I knew men who'd done more time for drug charges and nonviolent robbery than any of the sick fucks the police had questioned in Sera's case.

But none of that told me who to kill. Vanessa's technical sleuthing was no more help than Noelle's incomplete predictions had been. But maybe together…

I stood so fast my chair screeched across the kitchen floor, and for a second, I was afraid I'd woken Gran. But when no sound came from her room, I practically ran into the living room and hauled my duffel bag out from under the coffee table, where I'd been storing all the stuff I'd taken out of my room when Sera moved in.

Elle's notebook was at the bottom. I pulled it out carefully, aware, as always, that the cardboard cover and flimsy paper pages wouldn't last forever.

In the kitchen, I rooted through the junk drawer until I found a pen and a half-used pad of sticky notes, then I sat in front of Van's laptop again, ready—no, *desperate*—to make sense of passages whose meaning had been eluding me for years.

There was no guarantee I'd have any more success this time, but I couldn't help thinking that I was more prepared than ever to unravel Elle's knot of prophesies, considering that this time I already knew not only what and where the crime was, but who the victims were.

All I needed was the perpetrator's identity.

While everyone else slept, I spent the next two and

a half hours reading that notebook all over again, from start to finish, flagging all of the promising passages with a sticky note. There weren't many. Then I reread the suspects' criminal records, wishing that, like Cam, I had a degree in criminal justice. Even an unused one.

But all I had was several years' experience breaking and entering, Traveler-style.

Well, I had that, and I had Google. So I started doing image searches for the criminals Van had listed, as well as all of their aliases, hoping someone, somewhere had posted a picture of one of them with an identifying mark Sera had missed, or in a location or clothing that fit a passage in Elle's notebook.

And finally, somewhere around four in the morning, I found a picture on a social networking site labeled with the second known alias of the fifth man on the list—the one who'd been arrested, but never went to trial. The man in the picture was shirtless, with most of his back turned toward the camera, and on the back of his left shoulder was a small tattoo of a tarantula, crawling up his body.

My heart beat a little faster and I flipped through the notebook, passing up all the passages I'd marked, in search of one I'd had no idea was connected to Sera and her family.

I still wasn't sure they were connected. It could be a coincidence. But one night, about three years after Noelle and I first...got together, she'd started mumbling at about 1:40 in the morning, and I'd written what I could understand.

Spider, caught in the web of lies.

Was the man with the tattoos Noelle's spider? If so, was Noelle's spider also Sera's smiling man? What was the web of lies—could it be Sera's statement to the police?

It took ten more minutes of searching that same alias to find an image showing both the tattoo and the man's face, in profile. But that was enough. It was him. One of the police department's suspects in Sera's case had a tattoo of a spider, and one of Noelle's prophesies was about a spider. If that *was* a coincidence, it was coincidental enough to deserve investigation.

The suspect's legal name was Chance Alexander Curtis. He sounded more like an Ivy League undergrad than a brutal murderer. But then, that fit Sera's description, too.

I closed Van's laptop and stowed Noelle's notebook in the bottom of my duffel again. Then I borrowed the cell phone Ian had left in the kitchen to send a text to Cam.

It's Kris. I need a favor.

His reply came two minutes later, while I was shrugging into my shoulder holster, over a mostly clean T-shirt dug from my bag.

Hell no. It's 4 am & I still owe you a rt hook.

Oh, yeah. I'd punched Cam once, years ago, when I thought he was threatening Olivia. I was wrong, and he'd never let me forget it.

Turn off the light, or I'll wake up Liv.

With my .40 loaded and holstered, I shrugged into a light jacket, then killed the bulb in the hall closet—we still kept it on at night, so no one could sneak in—then stepped into the darkness and out into the living room of Cam and Olivia's apartment.

The second I appeared, something clicked, and light flooded the room from a lamp in the corner. I squinted and found Cam with his fingers still on the switch. Before my eyes had even adjusted to the light, he reached to his left and flipped the switch on another lamp, this one without a shade.

Nothing happened. That lamp held an infrared bulb, to keep the room inaccessible to Travelers—like me— without keeping the house lit up all night. There was one in every room of our hideout house.

"You shouldn't be here." Cam crossed into the tiny galley-style kitchen.

"I know it's late, and—"

"Actually, it's early." He pulled open the fridge and tossed me a soda from inside, then took one for himself.

"—and Liv's asleep—"

"Not anymore," Olivia said, and I turned to find her standing in the hallway in a tank top and short pj shorts.

"You better not be looking at her...anything," Cam growled, and I couldn't roll my eyes fast enough.

"I'm not. We were never a thing." I turned back to her when Cam pretended he hadn't heard me. "Liv, tell him we were never a thing."

"We were never a thing," she said, settling onto a stool at the kitchen peninsula, and I could tell from her mischievous grin that she wouldn't leave it at that. "Except for that time in your basement..."

I popped the top on my soda. "That lasted, like, five minutes—we were just kids—and I never even got past her bra."

Cam glared at me from across the counter, looking less and less like he wanted to do me a favor.

"Seriously," I reiterated. "And it was a teen bra. She didn't even have..."

He growled again, and Olivia looked a little miffed.

"Never mind. That's why I'm here."

Cam frowned. "You're here because Liv was a flat-chested teenager?"

"I wasn't—" Liv started, but neither of us looked at her.

"No. I'm here because I don't want Liv. Like that." I shook my head, struggling to straighten out my thoughts. I was sleep-deprived and too focused on what needed to be done to think through what needed to be said, to make the rest of it possible. "I don't like her like that. I like Sera. I think I *more than like* her. So I need to go kill someone."

"Have you been drinking?" Olivia pressed the power button on their coffeepot and Cam pulled a bag of grounds from the cabinet over his head.

"No. Well, yes, but I'm not drunk. In fact, I'm thinking clearer than I have in years."

"I can tell by how you reek of whiskey and make no sense," Cam said. "And did I mention it's four in the morning?"

"Yeah. I figure that's the best time to catch him unaware." Also, I didn't want to wait. I was kind of eager to put a few bullets in the bastard who'd taken everything from Sera.

"Catch who?"

"Sera's smiling man," Olivia said, and I realized I'd have more luck appealing to her, even though it was Cam's Skill I needed. "She ID'd him?"

"No, I did. With Van's help. Not that she knows she helped yet, but she will."

"Sit," Cam ordered. "Drink your damn soda and calm down. Either you're skipping entire sentences, or I'm only hearing half of them."

"I have a name. Chance Alexander Curtis. I need you to Track him, so I can go get the bastard."

Cam looked suddenly interested, despite the hour and his general disinterest in me as a human being—turns out it's difficult to replace that vital first impression. "No fourth name?"

"Not that I found. I don't think he's Skilled." Most unSkilled people didn't have that second middle name. Their parents didn't know they needed it.

"Why are you doing this at four in the morning?" Liv asked, while the coffeepot gurgled and ticked. "And why are you doing it alone?"

"It's kind of a surprise," I admitted, and her frown looked almost amused.

"Most men surprise their girlfriends with roses," Liv said, and I didn't bother telling them that Sera wasn't my girlfriend. Or the type to want worthless clipped flowers.

"This is what she wants. This is what she *needs,* and I'm going to give it to her." I turned back to Cam. "Can you just tell me where he is? Please? I'll owe you."

"You already owe me."

"Fine. You can punch me in the face, and I won't duck or fire back."

Cam frowned, and I was starting to think that was the only expression he had. "What am I, fifteen?" He drank from his can again, then set it down harder than necessary. "Chance Alexander Curtis?"

I nodded.

"Fine. Give me a minute." He closed his eyes, and I sank onto the stool next to Liv, silently sipping from my can as she opened the laptop on the counter in front of her and began to type.

It took less than a minute.

"Strong signal." Cam opened his eyes and met my gaze from across the peninsula. "East side, about two miles from the river."

"Here in the city?" I'd expected him to be closer to where Sera's family was killed. Closer to where he lived.

"Yeah."

"Got a street name, or a neighborhood?"

"That's not how it works," Cam said. "There's no GPS in my head. Just a signal, coming from a certain direction. I can gauge distance based on the strength of the signal. I could lead you to him...."

"That would take too long. But thanks."

"6141 Holloway, apartment 4C. On the corner of Fourth and Holloway." Olivia turned her laptop to face me. "A man named Glen Curtis has an apartment there, and his social profile says he has a brother named Chase. I bet that's where he's staying."

"How did you find that?"

"Van's been teaching me some tricks I'd rather Ruben not know about..." she said, and I nodded. The last thing I wanted to do was give Ruben Cavazos information he didn't have to work for.

"Thanks." I stood and drained my soda. "Can you get the lights?"

Cam turned off both lamps and Olivia closed her laptop. I stepped out of the thick shadows in their living room and into an alley near the corner of Fourth and Holloway.

There are very few circumstances under which I'd walk down the street in Julia Tower's section of town in broad daylight. Fortunately, 4:47 a.m. wasn't quite broad daylight, and the walk from the alley to Curtis's apartment building only took a couple of minutes.

I jogged up three flights of stairs and made a mental note to stop ignoring cardio in favor of weight training—sometimes, even a Traveler has to run. And if Sera decided she wasn't done with me after one night, cardiovascular stamina would certainly come in handy.

I paused on the landing to catch my breath. And double-check my clip. Fully loaded, with one round in the chamber. Then I found the door to apartment 4C, halfway down the hall.

If I'd ever been there before, or was more than passingly familiar with the area, I could have Traveled right into the apartment itself, assuming the Curtis brothers had left any of their lights off. But since I wasn't, and this was an important job, I'd decided to play it safe and check the place out before popping in unannounced.

From the hall, I could hear no sound coming from 4C, but then, most of the building's residents were probably still sleeping. So I closed my eyes and felt for a dark pocket within.

The whole damn place was dark. So dark I knew the Curtises were either completely unSkilled, or not at home.

I closed my eyes and shadow-walked into the living room. A single step later, my shin smashed into something hard, and I cursed in the darkness. Then cursed silently over my own stupidity.

Something clicked, and a single bright light flared to life, momentarily blinding me. Something moved on my left, but I couldn't focus on it.

I pulled my gun, blinking furiously, but couldn't see to aim. "Who's there?"

"Who do you think?" an unfamiliar voice asked. And as my eyes began to adjust, a man came into focus on the floor, his head slumped forward, sitting in a puddle of his own blood.

Chase Alexander Curtis sat next to him, bound and gagged with duct tape—the dead man could only be his brother. I raised my aim to his chest, and his eyes widened in fear. Desperate, inarticulate sounds came from behind his gag. The smiling man was no longer smiling.

Unfortunately, his terror wasn't directed at me. Curtis was looking over my shoulder.

Chill bumps popped up on my arms and dread churned in my stomach. But before I could turn to see what he was so scared of, pain slammed into my skull, and the room spun around me. I fought the loss of consciousness, but darkness surrounded me from the periphery, a betrayal by the very element I was born to embrace.

The last thing I saw before my eyes closed against my will was the woman's hand that plucked my gun from my grip.

Twenty

Sera

The ringing of a cell phone woke me up, and it took me a second to realize I wasn't hearing my own ringtone. And one more second to remember I no longer had a cell phone. After that, everything else came crashing in, and for a moment, my loss—that fresh remembrance of it—was too thick to breathe through. As it was most mornings.

When I'd pushed it all back again, back into memory, where the pain was manageable, I sat up and turned on the bedside lamp, but Kris's phone stopped ringing before I could answer it. The screen showed one missed call, from Anne.

Kris. He'd been in my bed. Or rather, I was in his.

I twisted, but I knew from the lack of warmth on my left side that he was gone before my gaze ever fell on the empty half of the bed. Still, the memory of the night before surged through me—shared grief, comfort through touch, and a mutual pleasure so perfect that in that instant, nothing else had existed. No pain. No fear. No memories. There'd been nothing but the two of us, and in that moment, I'd been sure we could actually be together. That maybe we were *supposed* to be together.

But now he was gone, and the bed was cold.

I glanced at the alarm clock and groaned over the numbers—it was barely five in the morning—then stretched to turn the lamp off again, when what I really wanted to do was pull on a bare minimum of clothing and tiptoe downstairs to curl up on the couch with Kris. But if he'd gone downstairs, he'd gone downstairs for a reason.

So I burrowed farther into the covers and closed my eyes. But sleep didn't return.

Kris's phone rang again, less than two minutes after the first missed call. I picked it up and scowled when I read Anne's name on the screen again. Why was she calling him in the middle of the night?

What if this was some kind of emergency?

I pressed the accept call button, before I could overthink it and lose my nerve. "Hello? Anne?" I said, and for a moment, there was only silence on the other end. Then someone exhaled into my ear.

"The spider is dead," a child's voice said over the line, and I realized I was talking to Hadley. "The web is a trap."

"What? Hadley? Is something wrong?"

"The spider is dead! The web is a trap!" she shouted, and her high-pitched scream skewered my brain, then bounced around the inside of my skull. "The spider is dead! The web is a trap!"

I held the phone away from my ear to save my hearing, and I had to half shout to be heard over her. "Hadley! Put your mom on the phone." But she was still screaming those same two sentences. "Hadley!"

"Hadley!" Anne's voice echoed mine from the other

end of the line, and a plastic clattering followed as her phone hit the floor, but I could still hear the child scream-ing, and her mother trying to calm her down. "Hadley, what's wrong? Who's on the phone? Did you have a bad dream?"

"Anne!" I shouted, desperate to be heard over them both. I didn't know what spider she was talking about, but I understood both "dead" and "trap."

Something was horribly wrong. And the call had come on Kris's phone.

I was still shouting at Anne, trying to get her attention, when my bedroom door flew open and crashed into the dresser against the wall. "Sera?" Kori had her gun drawn and aimed at the floor. "What happened?"

She stepped inside and Ian came in after her, simi-larly armed, and they automatically scanned separate halves of the room, looking for the threat. When they found none, their gazes returned to me, then slid down from my face. Which is when I remembered that I was naked. And holding Kris's phone.

"It's Hadley." I held the phone out to Kori as I pulled the sheet up to my chest with my free hand. "She's freak-ing out about a spider, or something."

Kori set her gun on the end table, then took the phone and listened as Anne tried to calm Hadley. Ian turned around while I pulled my borrowed pajamas back on, and as I tugged the shirt into place, Kori handed the phone back to me. "They can't hear us, and I can't get to them until Anne turns off the infrared grid."

Her house had state-of-the-art security, which—Kris had explained—Ruben Cavazos had paid for, in order to protect his love child. Noelle's biological daughter.

"Is that Kris's phone?" Van said from the doorway as Kori slipped past her into the hall, and I realized that my shouting into the phone had woken the entire household. "Where is he?"

"Downstairs, I guess." I stood and held the phone a foot away from my ear, and could still hear Hadley screaming.

Kori stepped back into my room a minute later wearing jeans beneath the T-shirt she slept in, with her own phone in her hand.

"Anne still has a home phone," she explained, pressing buttons on her cell.

I listened on Kris's phone, and over the line, as Hadley's screams quieted to a whimper, I heard the home phone ring. Something clattered against wood, and Anne said, "Hello?"

"It's me," Kori said from my room. "Turn off the grid. I'm coming over."

"Just a second." Anne's voice was distant now, over Kris's line. Kori hung up and shoved her phone into her pocket, then headed into the hall. A second later, her footsteps clomped down the stairs so fast I was surprised she didn't trip over her own feet and plummet to her death. An instant after that, the closet door slammed, and I knew she was gone.

"Anne, can you hear me?" I said into Kris's phone, and finally she picked it up.

"Who is this?" she said, and I could hear Hadley crying softly in the background, still mumbling about a spider.

"It's Sera."

"Where's Kris?" she said. "Why are you on his phone?"

"He—" I said, but before I could admit to anything—which I wasn't eager to do—I heard Kori's voice over the line as she stepped into some shadow in Anne's house.

Almost at the same time, more footsteps raced up the stairs, and Vanessa stepped into my room again.

"Kris is gone."

"What?" I said, but she could only shrug. That was the extent of her information. "Anne, I gotta go," I said into the phone, then ended the call and slid Kris's cell into the shallow pocket of my pj shorts. Ian, Van and I all headed for the stairs, and Gran was just trudging into the living room when we got there, her hair standing up in odd places, rubbing one tired, swollen eye.

"What's all the ruckus?" She tried to smooth her hair, but it wouldn't cooperate.

"Hadley's hysterical and Kris is gone," Vanessa said.

"Have you seen him?" I added, and Gran shook her head.

"He'll be back." She looked confused. "It must have been an emergency, or he wouldn't have left in the middle of the night. He's a good boy."

"I know. Would you like some hot tea?" The offer was as much for me as for her. I couldn't get Hadley's screaming out of my head. It wasn't a coincidence that she'd called Kris's phone with what was obviously a prediction I couldn't understand, and now he was missing. Kris and Hadley's spiderweb trap were connected. And that could *not* be good.

"Screw hot tea. I'll make coffee." Gran brushed past me and I followed her into the kitchen, where Vanessa stood at the table, scrolling through something on her laptop.

"Ian, were you going through the police files I downloaded?" There was something ominous in her voice, as if she already knew the answer before she'd asked the question.

"No. Why?"

"This was on the screen when I opened my laptop. It's one of the men from the police's suspect list. In Sera's case."

I edged between them, trying to see the screen.

"Sera, wait," Ian tried to hold me back, but he let go with one angry look from me.

"I was going to show them to you this morning," Van said softly as I closed my eyes and exhaled, trying to prepare myself for what I might see. "But it looks like Kris did some research of his own."

I opened my eyes, and the face on the screen came into focus. My throat closed and the air trapped in my lungs seemed to solidify. I sank into the chair to my left and pulled the laptop closer. My hands shook as I zoomed in, then scrolled to recenter the picture.

It was him. The smiling man. The man who'd killed my entire family and ended any chance I had of having children.

"His name is Chase Curtis," Vanessa said, but I didn't give a shit what his name was. I didn't even have a chance to properly process the fact that we'd identified him, because my gaze was stuck not on his face, but on the back of his bare right shoulder, where the tattoo of a crawling tarantula stared back at me.

The spider.

"Oh, shit. Kris found the spider." I could hardly hear myself because I hadn't taken in enough air to give my words much volume, but they both heard.

"What spider?" Ian said, and Van tapped the tattoo on her screen.

"That's what Hadley was trying to tell us." I scrubbed my face with both hands, but couldn't erase what I'd just seen. Nor could I make any sense of it. "She said,

'The spider is dead. The web is a trap.' And she said it on Kris's phone."

Vanessa exhaled heavily. "He went after Curtis."

"And the web is a trap." I wasn't sure what that meant yet, but I was sure it was true. "Who would set a trap for Kris?"

"It's not a trap for him, it's a trap for you," a familiar voice said, and I looked up to find Anne and Hadley standing in the middle of the living room, the child's face still red and damp from tears. Kori was behind them closing the hall closet door. "And it was set by someone who wants you dead, and knows you're going after the spider."

"Julia," I said, and everyone around me seemed to be nodding. "She set a trap for me, and got Kris instead."

"This is my fault." Ian met my gaze with a heavy one of his own. "I told him to give you what you want most."

"What? Why?"

"Because he's in love with you, and he wants to prove he can protect you." There was more to it than that. I could almost see what he wasn't saying. But before he could elaborate—assuming he would have—Kori turned on me.

"That means this is your fault!" Anger rolled off her voice like smoke from a fire. "And if he's dead, you're going to pay."

I couldn't process all that at once. Hell, I couldn't process *any* of that. "He's in…" I shook that off. I couldn't deal with wondering whether or not she was right, and whether or not loving me had just gotten the best man I'd ever known killed. So I focused on Hadley, who was the only one in the room, other than me, who'd ever seen Chase Curtis.

She was staring at something behind me, as though she'd totally lost touch with reality, her mother's hand still gripped loosely. "Hadley?" I wondered for a second if she'd understood what Kori had just said. Did she know that her biological mother was Kris's other love? Did she know she was the baby Elle had had with someone else—a mafia king, just like my own biological father?

But when I turned to see what she was staring at, I realized her current state had nothing to do with what Kori had said. I doubted she'd even heard it.

She was staring through the kitchen doorway at the picture of Chase Alexander Curtis, still open on Vanessa's laptop.

"The spider is dead," she whispered as if she hadn't already said it a dozen times. "The web is a trap."

"Where?" I dropped onto my knees in front of her and took her free hand in mine. "Where is the spider? Where is the trap? Did you see it?"

Anne knelt next to me, and I thought she'd shove me away from her daughter, or tell me to leave her alone, but she only squeezed Hadley's hand and waited for the answer with us. "Don't hold it in, sweetie. You'll feel better once you have it out of your system," the mother whispered to her daughter. "Once you've told us everything you remember. Noelle always did."

"House," Hadley whispered. "The spider died in a house. By the wall. Kris was there."

"Is he still there?" I asked, and Hadley made an obvious effort to focus on me. "Can you see anything else? Is he still there?"

She shook her head, then looked past me to where Gran stood in the doorway, silent as she took it all in, sipping from a steaming mug of fresh coffee tightly gripped in both hands. "Is it morning? Can I have some chocolate milk?"

"Of course." Gran held one arm out and Hadley dropped

her mother's hand and let Gran fold her into a hug, careful not to slosh coffee on the child. Then she ushered her into the kitchen and pulled a carton of milk from the fridge.

I stood, my hands shaking again. "We have to find him. Olivia?" I glanced at Kori in question. "Cam? Can one of them find him?"

She nodded, already dialing. I put aside the fact that I'd only met her a few days earlier and broke my own rule about respecting other people's personal space—especially those who sleep armed—and stood close enough to hear what was said when Olivia answered her phone.

"Liv? Sorry for the early call. I need you to track Kris."

"He didn't tell you he was coming, did he?" Olivia said, and I began to put it together in my head even before Liv spelled it out for Kori.

"Coming where?"

"Here," Liv said. "He was here less than an hour ago, with a name for Cam to track."

"Chance Curtis?" Kori said, and as I'd known she would, Liv mumbled something in the affirmative. "Can you track him for us? Both of them?"

"How 'bout I just give you the address?"

"I'll certainly take that, but could you also track him for me, to see if he's still there?"

"Sure." Olivia said something I couldn't understand to Cam, then she read Kori an address. Kori scribbled the information on her hand with the purple pen Van handed her, then Olivia was back on the line. "Cam says he's not there anymore. Or else he's being Jammed. Maybe Sera's with him."

"No, she's here with us. I'm going after him."

"Come get us. We'll help," Olivia said.

"No time," Kori said. "But thanks." She hung up and glanced at Ian. "Ready?"

"And willing." Ian shrugged into a jacket, covering a shoulder holster I hadn't even seen him put on.

"I'm coming." I followed them toward the hall. "But I need a holster."

Kori stopped and turned to look at me, and I could feel her assessment like a visual pat-down, only she wasn't looking for weapons. She was looking for competence. "I've never been hit by friendly fire," she said, her voice deeper than usual, and deadly serious. "And I have no plans to start now."

"I'm not going to shoot you," I promised as Van shoved a pair of jeans into my hands. I changed from pj shorts into the jeans in Gran's room in record time, while Kori rummaged in the hall closet for an extra holster. She showed me how to wear it, then slid two full clips into a pocket beneath my right arm and adjusted the straps quickly as I got accustomed to the feel.

I checked my clip, then chambered a round, double-checked the safety and slid the gun into my holster.

"Draw," Kori said, her hand already on the closet door. She was eager to go. We both were.

I drew, but the movement was slow and awkward.

"Again."

I holstered the gun and drew with my right hand, again. And again, the movement felt…strange. Kori made a couple of adjustments in the straps, then handed me a jacket and told me to try it again. I put the jacket on, then drew again. My draw was better that time. Smoother, even with the extra material. However, I still wasn't quite confident that I wouldn't accidentally shoot a hole in the borrowed jacket.

But I didn't let her see that. Lots of people learn through on-the-job training, right? Trial by fire. If they could do it, so could I.

Kori nodded her approval, then waved me into the closet. She and Ian followed, and she closed the door. There was only darkness and silence for a moment, when I assumed she was making a mental search of the address Olivia had given her—fortunately, she was familiar with the building.

"The whole apartment is dark. At least, dark enough to travel into. Get ready."

Her right hand bumped my left, and I took it, my right hovering near the gun, a conspicuous weight at my side. Then she tugged us forward.

Two steps later, the air around us changed as we stepped out of the closet and into Curtis's brother's apartment. Carpet muffled our steps.

The smell hit me with my next breath. Feces. And beneath that, the milder yet more alarming scent of blood.

Kori let go of my hand the instant her first foot landed on carpet. For a moment, she and Ian stood absolutely still, letting their eyes adjust to the slightly lighter room, so I did the same. Fortunately, the only light source was what bled through the blinds from the streetlight outside. We adjusted quickly.

On my left, Kori's head turned as she scanned the room, and I knew Ian was doing the same. So I glanced around, too, and discovered that she'd walked us into the living room—the outline of a couch was a dead giveaway—less than a foot from the closed front door. Where we were least likely to bump into furniture. Where no one could sneak up on us without opening the door at our backs, which would serve as a warning.

Kori thought of everything.

I needed to think of everything, too.

Ian's tall, dark silhouette took several steps toward the wall near the window. "Light?" he asked, and Kori's profile nodded. Something clicked, and soft light flooded the room from a lamp in the corner.

The first thing I noticed was a pile of broken glass next to the end table holding the lamp. Something had been knocked off and shattered on the floor. The second thing I noticed were the bodies. Two of them. Even in the deep shadows cast by the table lamp, I recognized the one on the left. His light eyes were still open, now staring at nothing. But now he had two mouths, one gaping open below his chin, above the blood soaking his clothes.

Curtis wasn't smiling now.

"Sera?" Ian said while Kori headed into the short hallway, gun drawn. She was checking for bad guys, though we all knew the place was deserted. Kris was gone.

"I'm okay," I whispered, though I was anything but. Curtis was dead, but I didn't see it happen. I didn't get to see his life spilled along with his blood. I didn't see recognition of me in his eyes as they lost focus.

He was dead, but he hadn't died paying for his crimes against my family. I knew because Kris hadn't killed him. The spiderweb was a trap. And now Kris was missing.

Somehow, that was worse than how Curtis had died. Without me.

"Kris didn't do this." I stood far enough away from the bodies that I could see what had happened to them, but didn't have to *see*. Kris was right. Death is a horrible thing to see, even on those who deserve it. "He's more of a gun man, right?"

"From what I've seen, yes." Ian stood at my side, his weapon still drawn, but aimed at the floor. "Kori's slit a few throats, but she doesn't enjoy it, and I'd bet money this was done by a man who enjoys his work. Notice the details."

But I didn't want to notice the details.

I wanted to find Kris.

"The apartment's empty," Kori said, stepping back into the living room from the hall. But we all already knew that.

"Why didn't they stay?" I holstered my gun, relieved more by its absence from my hand than by its comforting weight at my side. "If this trap was for me, and Kris showed up instead, they had to know we'd come after him, right? So why are they all gone?"

"Julia's already lost half a dozen perfectly good gunmen to our ragtag little band of outlaws," Ian said. "I doubt she was eager to lose any more. Especially if she's actually lost other employees, thanks to the viral campaign."

That made sense. "So where's Kris? She didn't kill him, right? If so, she would have left him here with the Curtis brothers…" My words sounded like a guess, but felt more like fact. "Maybe Cam can track him again. Or Liv, if we have a sample of his blood." I glanced at Kori with both brows raised. "Do we have a sample of his blood?"

She shook her head. "He's careful to destroy every drop he loses. I think you're right, though. He's alive, but Cam won't be able to track him if Julia still has him, and neither would Liv, even if we had a blood sample. Julia will be Jamming his psychic signature."

"Why does she want him?" I couldn't figure that out. She needed Kenley, but Kris should have held no value to her.

"She doesn't." Ian pulled a piece of paper off the fridge, and the watermelon-shaped magnet that had been holding it in place clattered to the floor. "She wants *you*." He handed me the note. "Careful. It's still wet."

An inarticulate sound of disgust bubbled up from my

throat as I realized that the note I now held had been written in blood. Literally. Chase Curtis's blood, if I had to guess—there was plenty of it available.

But my disgust melted in the face of both fear and rage when I read the still-dripping words.

Let's trade. Sera for Kris. I'll be in touch.

"Is that irony?" I stared at the note, reading it for the third or fourth time. "I think that's irony." I'd thought Kris wanted to trade me for Kenley, but now Julia wanted to trade me for him.

"Okay. So…I'll go. I mean, I was going to go in anyway."

Kori shook her head, her jaw clenched in fury. "Doesn't matter. She's not going to trade him. She'll kill him as soon as she has you."

"No, she won't. I won't let her. She can't hurt me and she has to do whatever I tell her to, right?" Surely the infamous bindings were going to work in our favor, for once….

Ian shook his head that time. "There are too many loopholes. She's bound to you by the same contract that kept her bound to Jake—the same contract she worked around to have him killed. She could do the same to you."

"And that could be as easy as not being there in person when we go for the trade," Kori added. "If she's not there, you can't give her orders. And if her people have orders to kill whoever shows up, she's not specifying that they kill you—thus she's not violating her contract—but you'll still be dead."

Which was exactly how and why she'd had my family killed—hoping to catch me in the crossfire without actually putting a hit out on me.

"Shit." How was it possible that the contracts and system of loyalties were so complicated, but the ways around them were so frustratingly simple?

"Okay. So, if she's not going to give him back, we'll have to *take* him back. Along with Kenley."

"My thoughts exactly." Kori knelt for a better look at Curtis, and my stomach churned. "Sorry you didn't get your revenge killing. I know how bad that sucks. But you're welcome to share mine. Julia Tower's as responsible for what happened to your family as Curtis was, which means we both have a claim on her life." She stood and met my gaze in the dull light from the table lamp. "Help us get Kris and Kenley back, and I'm willing to share the kill."

"You couldn't stop me from either one if you tried. How do you think she'll be in touch? And when?"

"I don't know, but we're not going to wait—" Before she could even finish her sentence, Kori's phone buzzed in her pocket. She frowned and pulled it out, then turned the cell around so Ian and I could see the screen. The text was from Kenley's phone, but we both knew the Binder hadn't sent the message.

Bring Sera to the warehouse at the corner of Bonner and Lexington. I will trade her for your brother.

"It can't be that easy, right?" I said as Kori pocketed her phone without even considering a reply. "I know she's not really going to trade, so what are the chances he's really in that warehouse?"

"Slim to none." Ian scrubbed one hand over his short-cropped hair. "We can try tracking him, but I'd bet my life she has a Jammer sitting right next to Kris. If he's even still alive." The words looked almost as painful for him to say as they were for me to hear, but he didn't shy away from them.

"He's alive," Kori said. "She'll know we'll want proof of that before we agree to anything. And she won't offer Kenley as part of the trade because she knows we'll recognize that as a lie."

"So, we find her and we take them both back." I leaned against the fridge, careful not to touch anything for fear of leaving fingerprints at the scene of a crime. "We know where she's not." The warehouse on the corner of Bonner and Lexington. "That only leaves…the entire rest of the city for us to search." I hoped I didn't look as frustrated as I sounded.

Ian turned to Kori. "I assume she's not at Tower's house. For one thing, that's too obvious. For another, if the viral campaign worked, they may have run her off. We have to assume she still has some loyal employees, otherwise she wouldn't have been able to take Kris. But it's entirely possible that she doesn't have Kenley anymore."

"Then who does?" Kori stepped over the pool of blood surrounding the Curtis brothers and sank onto the arm of their couch. "If she lost enough employees to lose control over Kenley, how long do you think it'll be before whoever's running the blood farm figures out that killing Kenni will free them all permanently? What if that's already happened? *Can* it happen?" She stared at the shadowed carpet, lost in thought. "I can't remember whether or not my oath to Jake prohibited me from killing his Binder— I wouldn't have hurt her anyway."

"I think it's time we make some calls and find out exactly what our viral campaign has done to the Tower infrastructure," I said, and Kori looked up at me, drawn from her thoughts by the possibility. "Worst-case scenario—

we'll find out it failed entirely. Which means Kenley's still alive and Julia has her. And if it hasn't failed, I can get information from anyone whose binding was transferred to me."

Kori nodded, already pulling her phone from her pocket.

"I think I can save you a lot of trouble on that front."

Ian whirled toward the new voice as Kori stood, and they were both already aiming guns at the man-shaped shadow in the short hallway before it even occurred to me to draw my weapon.

"Relax. I'm here to help." Mitch stepped into the dimly lit living room, but no one relaxed. No guns were holstered.

Kori made a show of flipping the safety switch on her gun. "Go out the way you came in, or I *will* blow your brains out the back of your head."

Mitch shrugged, still looking at me as he answered her. "That would make it hard for me to tell you what I know."

"Wait. Let's hear him out." If he really had information, we needed it. Badly.

"He's not bound to you anymore, Sera." Ian glanced at me briefly, but his aim at Mitch never wavered. "He could be lying. He could be here to kill you."

"I could," Mitch confirmed with another shrug. "But that's more work than I'm willing to do without a direct order or the promise of a paycheck, and since I'm a free man now…I'm actually on my way out of town. Which was your suggestion."

"Then why are you here? How'd you know we'd be here?" I moved to stand between Kori and Ian, one hand on my own holstered gun, but the added threat wasn't necessary. Either of them could blow him into several pieces before I could draw, much less aim.

"I'm here because I made a mistake after we parted ways, and I want to fix it. And I didn't know for sure that you'd be here. It was an educated guess."

"Educated?" Ian said.

"Yeah. That mistake I mentioned? After I left you guys on the east side yesterday, I went back to Julia."

"Why?" I couldn't make sense of it. Why would a free man go back to the woman who'd held his chains? And why would that woman let him live when she'd killed everyone else I'd freed?

"Because I've been bound to the Towers since I was nineteen years old. I wasn't highly valued or promoted very quickly, but syndicate life is all I know, and my talents hold no value in any other line of work. When you let me go, I didn't understand what you were giving me. I felt as if I'd been thrown out on my ass with nowhere to go. So I went back to what I knew."

"Why didn't she kill you?" Kori demanded, gaze narrowed in suspicion we all seemed to share.

"Because I didn't tell her what you did. Fortunately, she never actually asked me if my binding was converted. She only asked if I'd gotten a text from any of you, and my answer to that was an honest 'no.'"

"So she thinks you're still bound to her?" Ian didn't lower his aim, but he no longer looked likely to shoot in the next few seconds.

"Yeah. I figured that was the safest bet."

"So you knew we'd be here because you knew how Julia got Kris?"

"I was here when she took him. I knew you'd follow him eventually and my plan was to wait for you here— half an hour would have been my limit, since I'm on my way out of town—and as fortune would have it, here you are. No waiting necessary."

"He's lying," Kori said. "We should kill him."

"Let's hear what he has to say first," I said. "We can always kill him afterward."

Ian glanced at me in surprise, but Kori just looked mollified. "Fine." She gestured at his torso with her free hand. "But first, strip."

Mitch frowned. "Strip?"

"Down to your shorts," Ian added. "The TSA has X-rays. We only have our eyes."

Grumbling beneath his breath about how ungrateful we were, Mitch pulled his shirt over his head, then dropped it on the floor. Next he took off his shoes and tossed them into the corner, on Ian's orders. His pants were the last to go, and when he stood in only a pair of green boxer briefs, Kori made him turn a full circle, so we could see that he was unarmed. And had chicken legs.

"Okay." Ian lowered his aim, but kept his gun at the ready. "Talk fast."

Mitch scowled at Kori, who refused to lower her gun. "You just got a text from Julia, right? From your sister's phone?"

I started to nod, but one glance from Kori stopped me, and I realized that the flow of information would only go one way.

"Fine. Don't answer." Mitch shrugged. "I know you got a text, because I saw her send it. But the information she sent is false. Kris isn't at that warehouse, and neither is she. It's a trap."

"We know," I said, and Kori frowned at me, which is when I realized I'd confirmed that we had received that text.

"How do you know?"

"Julia would never give away her position."

"Well, fortunately for you, I would. She's at the Eight Street warehouse. Your brother and sister are both with her."

My pulse leaped at the thought—could we really get them both back in one shot?—but Kori only frowned. "Why would she keep both her eggs in one basket?"

"Because it's the only basket she has. Your mass texting initiative worked. She only has a handful of employees left. You've practically won already. Why do you think I'm leaving?"

"You're deserting the sinking ship…" Kori's frown became a sneer of contempt. "Like any rat would do."

"Fuck you." But Mitch's profanity just sounded silly, with him still in his underwear. "I've paid my debt." He bent to pick up his clothes, then met my gaze boldly. "Do what you want with the information—I don't give a shit anymore. I'm out of here."

"Don't move." Ian aimed at Mitch's head, and Mitch froze. "Ladies? Verdict?"

Kori glanced at me, and I hid the jolt of glee surging through me over the fact that she was consulting me about a strategic decision. "He did pay his debt." With information that may or may not prove valid.

"Fine." Kori turned back to Mitch and lowered her aim to his feet. "Let the rat scurry into his corner."

Mitch glared at her, but wasted no time retrieving his shoes. Then he backed into the dark hall, and a second later I felt his absence, though I hadn't actually seen him disappear.

"So, now what?" I asked as Ian and Kori holstered their guns.

"Now we rally the troops." Kori pulled her phone from her pocket, ready to dial. "If Julia really is at the Eighth

Street warehouse, she's about to wish she'd preceded her brothers into the afterlife."

I stared at the Curtis brothers while she made her first call, recruiting friends and allies to our purpose, thinking about Julia, and how her death was so long overdue.

Better late than never...

Twenty-One

Kris

My eyes opened, then closed again before the world could come into focus. Two half-blinks later, I managed to keep them open, but then exposure to the bright light brought pain roaring to life all over my body.

The headache was the worst. The pain at the back of my skull was sharp and intense, but another pain mirrored it behind my forehead, dull but persistent. A sure sign that I had a concussion—that my brain had been bounced around by whoever had hit me from behind.

But for another couple of seconds, I couldn't remember actually being hit. Or where that had happened. All I knew was that I was now tied to a chair, my hands behind my back, my wrists already chafed by my bonds.

Having been in a similar position once before, I already knew that panicking would be a very bad idea. My energy would be better spent finding a way to free myself.

"Good morning, sunshine," a familiar voice said, and when I looked up to find Julia Tower watching me from a folding chair four feet away, the rest of my memories slid into place.

A dark apartment.

The Curtis brothers, one dead, one tied up.

Then something had hit me from behind, and as I'd crumpled to the floor, struggling to keep my eyes open, someone had stepped up behind Chase Curtis and pulled a knife across his throat.

He'd died choking on his own blood as I lost consciousness.

I'd failed Sera again.

"Time to wake up now," Julia sang in a falsely cheerful voice, tapping pointy-toed, high-heeled shoes on the stained concrete floor, and I forced my eyes to focus. "You and I are going to have a little chat."

"I have nothing to say to you until you send Kenley home." My voice was hoarse, and my throat was sore, and I wondered briefly if someone had tried to choke me while I was unconscious. Or maybe my throat had dried out from lack of use. How long had I been out?

Julia made a show of sniffing the air, which was completely unnecessary for Reading. "That smells like a lie." Her forehead furrowed, perfectly manicured eyebrows dipping in disappointment with me. "Doesn't matter, though. I didn't expect you to cooperate without the proper motivation. Which is why we've brought your sister in to help motivate you." She gestured with one hand, and movement to my left drew my gaze toward a typically beefy guard as he pulled a curtain back from the wall to reveal a long window.

Beyond the window, Kenley sat in a folding chair, in an otherwise empty room, which had probably once been an office. She was blindfolded, hands bound behind her back just like mine, and her head was slumped as if she was sleepy. But she looked otherwise unhurt.

My relief at seeing her intact was accompanied by a mental asterisk and the certainty that that fact was about to change. Why else would Julia show me my sister?

"When Korinne was still in our company, there was nothing she wouldn't do to protect the baby of the family, and I'm betting the same goes for you." Julia glanced from Kenley to me, her neatly painted lips curled in derision. "The Daniels' family really believes that blood is thicker than water. Doesn't it?"

"That's an odd criticism coming from a woman who had her own brother murdered." I glanced at the guards stationed around the room, hoping for a reaction, but none of them even blinked, that I could tell.

"They already know." Julia crossed her ankles beneath her folding chair. "Most of them don't care. Jake wasn't exactly loved by most of his employees. Those who do object to his timely demise are prohibited from expressing their displeasure by the contracts binding them to me."

I frowned as what she'd said sank in. "She isn't Jake Tower's heir," I called, loud enough to be heard throughout the room. No one reacted.

"They know that, too. These are all *my* men."

"New hires?" I didn't think she'd answer. I was wrong. In fact, she seemed quite forthcoming, which probably meant she was proud of herself.

"Some of them." Julia smoothed her suit jacket over the blue blouse beneath. "Others were on Jake's staff, most of which knows all about Sera's surprise inheritance, thanks to the curse of instant communication."

"So glad to hear the mass texting worked." Surely proof that Sera was smarter than her aunt.

"Not as well as you might think. Thanks to your baby sister's generous blood donation, I've spent the past three days transferring bindings from Sera to me. Starting with the gunmen in this room. None of those newly bound employees were affected in the slightest by your wireless campaign."

"That's not possible." I gave my arms an experimental tug, but the bindings held tight. And they felt sharp, more like a zip tie than a rope. The irony there was that they'd probably gotten the damn thing out of *my* pocket. "Kenni's blood can't be used to bind someone without her will attached to it." And there was no way in hell that Kenley wanted to give Julia Tower any more power than she already had. "You're lying."

"If I were, you would never know it. But as it happens, there's no need for lies. Kenley's will didn't seal the bindings. Mine did." Julia watched me, waiting to see if I could connect the dots on my own.

Kenley's blood, but Julia's will...

Horror washed over me, and the room seemed to spin—the result of my entire world being knocked off-kilter. It shouldn't have been possible. "A transfusion? You gave yourself Kenley's blood?"

"Only a little." Julia shrugged, and the casual gesture looked strange on her. "Honestly, I got lucky. If we'd been incompatible blood types, the transfusion would have been very risky for me. But I had little choice, thanks to you and Jake's bastard daughter."

"You had a choice." I tried to move my legs, and discovered that my ankles were tied to the legs of the chair. "You could have chosen not to be a maniacal bitch."

"Trust me, my way was easier."

"So, what, you took a transfusion of Kenley's blood, then sealed the new contracts yourself?" I said, and she nodded, looking more than a little proud of herself. But I could see what she was trying not to show me. There was a reason we were in a warehouse rather than in the Tower basement. "This is all you got away with, isn't it? Just these men? You didn't have time to reseal most of the bindings. Sera still holds them, doesn't she?"

Julia's scowl could have peeled the paint off a car. "Not for long. You're going to bring her to me."

"Never gonna happen." My legs had less freedom than my arms. By my best guess, they were duct-taped to the chair legs, over my jeans.

"Oh, it will. But first, I need a little information from you, so we'll all be prepared for my darling niece's arrival." Julia recrossed her legs in the opposite direction. "Does Sera have a Skill?"

I stared at her in silence.

"Are you really going to make me repeat the question?"

I shrugged as best I could with my hands tied at my back. "I don't see what good that would do."

"It wouldn't do you any good at all. But I'm sure your sister would appreciate your candor right about now." She made another off-hand gesture, and one of the guards turned and opened the door he stood next to. A moment later, through the glass, I saw the door to Kenley's room open, and he stepped inside.

"You touch her, and I'll kill you," I spat, openly struggling against my bindings now, though I knew I had no shot at breaking them.

Julia gave me a small smile. "You're going to try to kill me anyway, and I have no intention of touching your sister. But Lincoln has been looking forward to it all day. So, you answer my questions, or he's going to give your sister something to cry about."

He wouldn't kill her. Julia couldn't let that happen, without losing every binding Kenley had sealed. But he could hit her. Or cut her. Or burn her. And Julia would let him.

It killed me that I hadn't been able to protect Kori from Jake's fury—I hadn't even known she was in danger until it was nearly over. But Kori was a survivor—a fighter with tough skin and even tougher insides.

Kenley was none of that. I couldn't let them hurt her. But I couldn't betray Sera, either.

"Does Serenity have a Skill?" Julia repeated, watching me while, in the other room, Kenley squirmed in her chair and said something I couldn't hear through the glass.

When I didn't answer, Julia rolled her eyes and dug something from her jacket pocket. Some kind of small remote. She pressed a button, and there was a short buzz of static, then my sister's voice came over the tiny speaker, fuzzy with static.

"—there? I can here you breathing. Say something!" she screeched, and if she'd looked drowsy before, she sounded terrified now.

"Kenni!" I shouted, and Julia frowned at me.

"She can't hear you. Answer the question. Does Sera have a skill?"

I couldn't lie to Julia—a Reader—and get away with it. And I couldn't refuse to answer without getting Kenley hurt. But I knew I'd hesitated too long when Julia picked up her remote and pressed a button, then spoke into it as if it were a handheld radio.

"Kenley, can you hear me?"

Through the window, Kenni's head pivoted toward a corner of the room I couldn't see, where—presumably—the speaker was mounted. "Fuck you, Julia!" she shouted, and I almost laughed out loud, in spite of the circumstances. She'd sounded *so* much like Kori!

"Your family resemblance is showing," Julia warned. "Speaking of family, I have your brother here—"

"Kenni, just hang on. I'll get you out—"

Julia spoke over me. "And you have his stubborn streak to blame for what's coming. Lincoln?" She released the speaker button and Lincoln nodded.

"No!" I shouted, and Julia held the remote up, so I could see that her finger was still off the button. Lincoln couldn't hear me.

A blur of motion through the window caught my gaze, and Lincoln punched my baby sister in the face. Still blindfolded, Kenley never saw the blow coming. She grunted in pain, and my pulse raced so hot and fast that my vision started to blur. Kenley's chair rocked back and forth, and for one interminable second, I was afraid it would tip over and she'd hit her head on the floor, and if that happened, there was nothing I could do for her.

"Stop!" I strained so hard against the zip tie at my back that the plastic bit into my skin, and the sudden warmth told me I was bleeding.

If Kenley fell unconscious, would Julia make it stop? I honestly didn't know. Unconscious people make terrible torture victims, because they can't feel pain, but it was *my* pain Julia was counting on, and I would suffer each of my sister's blows whether or not she was conscious.

Julia held the remote up to her mouth again and pressed the button. "Kenley? How you doing? Hangin' in there?"

Kenley gasped and raised her head. Tears spilled beneath her blindfold and a horrible bruise was already forming at the center of the red patch on her left cheek. She turned her head to the side and spit blood on the

398   *Rachel Vincent*

floor—no reason not to, since Julia already had more than enough of her blood. Then she cleared her throat and sat straighter. "Just fine. Also? Fuck you. And fuck Lincoln, whoever the hell he is. What kind of coward hits a woman while she's blindfolded and tied to a chair?"

Lincoln actually chuckled. "I only work here," he said, examining his knuckles, and I wanted to rip his throat out and watch his blood drain onto the floor. "If I had my way, this would be an entirely different kind of…session."

Kenley bit her lip as silent tears rolled down her face, and my blood *boiled*. I recognized Lincoln now. He was the one who'd slit Chase Alexander Curtis's throat.

"Hmm…" Julia turned back to me. "Someone's been spending a lot of time with her big brother and sister. But I don't think she's as tough as Kori, no matter what she wants us to believe. Do you?"

I didn't answer.

"Tell me about Sera's Skill, or we'll find out just how tough your baby sister is."

She was now assuming Sera had a Skill, and I wasn't sure whether that was a bluff or a conclusion she'd drawn based on the fact that I hadn't claimed otherwise. Julia lifted the radio to her lips again and opened her mouth.

"Yes." I glared at her. "Sera has a Skill." That was the truth. It just wasn't the whole truth.

"Good boy," she said, and I wanted to put my fist through her face. "And what is her Skill?"

But I'd figured out her game. "You already know the answer to that, don't you?" She was testing me.

"I have my suspicions. She's a Jammer, isn't she?"

"Just like her father. Your brother."

Julia nodded. She *had* known. But I was sure she didn't know about Sera's other Skill. No one did, other than the residents of our hideout house. And Julia couldn't make me give her information she didn't know she was missing.

"Sera didn't know, did she?" Julia sat straighter, and her eyes lost focus with the thought. "She was telling the truth when she said she didn't have a Skill, and the only way that's possible is if she didn't *know* she was Skilled. Which makes sense for a Jammer—there's no intent required for her Skill."

I shrugged. I was afraid to say anything, one way or another—Sera had obviously been blocking Julia's Skill when she needed to get away with a lie, just like she'd done with Anne.

"It's too bad, really, because I could use another Jammer—if she weren't trying to usurp my position."

"Sera doesn't give a damn about your position, your money or your power. She didn't ask to inherit the mafia, and she has no desire whatsoever to run it."

Julia frowned at me. "You actually mean that. She spoke to you, didn't she? She *confided* in you." She frowned and glanced at the floor without waiting for my answer. "Why would she do that?" When she looked up, I saw comprehension written all over her coldly attractive features. "You're not just trying to keep her for her Skill. You actually like her. Or is it more than that? Am I making you choose between your sister and your lover?"

"Fuck off."

Julia laughed again. "Oh, you Daniels siblings. You're all guns, and knives, and flying fists on the surface, but on the inside there's nothing but mush. Gooey touchy-feely pulp, rotting you from the inside out. Your emotional fragility is what makes you so easy to manipulate. So let's try another question. What's Sera's *other* Skill?"

For a moment, I could only blink at her. How the hell had she known?

"What other Skill? No one has two Skills."

Julia stared at me with both brows arched high, as if she was waiting for me to take it back. But I couldn't tell her. The only advantage Sera would have, surrounded by Skilled mafia members who wanted her dead was the ability to negate their Skills.

When I said nothing, Julia pressed the button on her radio/remote again and said, "Again, Lincoln. Somewhere else this time."

"Wait!" I shouted, but Julia didn't wait. Neither did Lincoln. He pulled his fist back, and Kenley braced herself for the blow, and I hated myself for the fact that she had to do that. But I hated Julia more.

Lincoln punched my sister in the gut and she hunched over in agony, as far as her bindings would allow. For one long moment, her mouth hung open, silent, because she couldn't suck in enough air to scream. So I shouted for her.

"You cold-hearted sadistic bitch! She can't defend herself. She can't even move. She can't even fucking *see!* What the hell is wrong with you?"

"There's nothing wrong with me. In fact, like my late brother, I am blissfully unencumbered by traits like sympathy and pity, which keep people like you from doing what needs to be done. The only reason I haven't killed you is that I need to know what Sera's capable of. The only reason I haven't killed Kenley is that I need her until I finish transferring the bindings. But I don't need her unbruised. I don't even need her conscious. And I certainly don't need her...untouched."

I could feel the blood drain from my face. *"Don't."*

"Name Sera's second Skill, or I'll tell Lincoln he can do whatever he wants with your sister, as long as her heart keeps beating."

"Why?" This couldn't be happening. It *couldn't*. "Why would you do that to another woman?"

Julia frowned, as though my logic confused her. "You seem to be under the impression that my ovaries came with a lifetime supply of empathy and compassion. I assure you that is not the case. Start talking."

"Sera's your *niece*." Time was the only resource I had, distraction my only weapon. I had to keep her talking, even if that meant pissing her off. So long as she only took that anger out on me. "She shares your *blood,* and you tried to have her killed. You had her whole family slaughtered. And her baby… What kind of psychotic bitch has a *baby* murdered in its mother's *stomach?*"

Julia stood, and I'd never seen her more pissed off. "Flattery won't work, mostly because you're giving me way too much credit." She stalked closer, until she towered over me, staring straight into my eyes from inches away, and I itched to take her down. To put my hands around her throat and squeeze until her skin turned purple and her eyes popped out of her skull. "I had nothing to do with what happened to her family, but I can't say I'm sad about the dead fetus. That's one less Tower in line for my inheritance."

"Would you call that irony when a truth-reader lies through her teeth? I know you had them killed. *Sera* knows you had them killed. And even if you pulled out a gun and shot me through the forehead in the next thirty seconds, I'd die satisfied with the knowledge that when she finds you, Sera is going to rip your heart right out of your chest. And if she's not fast enough, Kori and Ian will fight her for the honor."

"Dramatic. Nice imagery. You have the heart of a poet." She crossed both arms over her suit jacket, the small remote secure in her right hand, and stared calmly

402   *Rachel Vincent*

into my eyes. "But none of that changes the fact that your sister is in a very small room with a very big man, about to suffer what is no doubt her worst nightmare. Start talking, or I swear on the entire Tower syndicate that I will give the order and we'll both listen to her scream."

"The resemblance to your brother is *beyond* creepy," a new voice said, and though it was familiar, I couldn't place the owner, and I didn't even try. Julia turned, surprised, and all I could think about was that whatever this distraction was, it had bought me time. She'd pocketed the remote, and Kenley was still tied to her chair, her clothing intact.

Then I saw Mitch standing behind Julia with one hand on the doorknob, the other holding his shoes. His shirt was on backward, his pants were unbuttoned and his socks were mismatched.

"That was fast." Julia's heels clicked on the concrete as she crossed the warehouse toward him, and I had to divide my attention between what they were saying, and what I was planning—some way out of this mess, for both me and Kenley. "Well?"

"They bought it." Mitch's grin was obscene, in size alone. "I have to say, my acting was superb, but the real clincher was your text. They wouldn't have believed I had legitimate information for them if I hadn't had yours to point out as false."

"That's why I do the thinking, and you do what you're told."

Mitch's grin faltered, but then he rallied with a more intimate smile and reached for her waist. "I'm already half-dressed. Why don't you tell me to do something else?"

Nausea churned in my stomach at the thought of them together. Of Julia intimately involved with anyone. I preferred to think of her as asexual. Which went along with the fact that she was also amoral.

She slapped his hand away. "If you ever touch me without permission again, I'll have you skinned alive and rolled in salt."

Mitch looked hurt for a moment, not by her threat, but by her rejection, and with sudden insight, I understood why he'd come back—he didn't know how to be free. He'd tried to warn us. He'd tried everything he could think of to remain in Sera's employ, and when she'd turned him down—when I'd run him off—he'd obviously come back to Julia. But...

"*You* told her about Sera? About her second Skill? How?" It shouldn't have been possible. The one caveat to his freedom was that he couldn't tell anyone about where we'd been that day or that Sera had a second Skill.

Mitch glanced at me, then at Julia, obviously asking silent permission for something. She waved one hand at me in a "be my guest" gesture and Mitch dropped his shoes on the floor and zipped his pants, then padded across the concrete toward me in sock feet.

"Your baby sister has no idea what a help she was on that front. I 'snuck' in to see her and begged her to break my binding. To free me. She has no idea Sera even exists, and once she'd broken my binding to Jake Tower's bastard, I was free to renew my vows to the true heir." He glanced back at Julia, evidently expecting to be rewarded with a smile or a word of gratitude, but as far as I knew, Julia was unfamiliar with both concepts. I also knew that the fact that he'd had information for her was the only reason she'd taken him back instead of killing him.

"Mitch, do you have a knife?"

"Not on me." He banished disappointment from his

face with visible effort. "I thought Kori and Ian would be less likely to shoot me on sight if I was unarmed."

"Oh, that's right. You were afraid to take a knife to a gunfight." Julia rolled her eyes, then held her hand out to one of the two guards standing against the wall. He pulled a serrated hunting knife from its sheath at his side, then gave it to her, handle first.

My temper surged when she started across the floor toward me, wielding the knife like a conspicuous threat. "What do you know about Kristopher Daniels?" she said, and I realized she was talking to Mitch.

He shrugged. "Only what I've heard. He's a Traveler, like Kori. Better with a gun than she is, but less experienced with knives. No word yet on his hand-to-hand."

Julia stopped two feet in front of me, feet spread in her scary stilettos, hip cocked to the left, knife held ready at her side. "Is he worth keeping, if he could be persuaded to join the cause?"

Persuaded? She meant bound. And the only Binder in the city strong enough to make a nonconsensual binding stick was my little sister.

"It does seem like a shame to waste the resource, if you don't have to." Mitch pulled his shirt off and turned it right side in. "He'll be useful for dealing with his sister, like Kori was. He'll fight you, though."

"Oh, good." Julia held the knife up, and the serrated blade gleamed in the bright lights from overhead. "I love it when they struggle." She turned to Mitch again and gestured with her knife. Your stuff's over there on the table. Bring me a sheet of paper."

I wanted to see what his "stuff"—presumably the weapons he hadn't worn for fear of Kori and Ian—but I knew better than to look away from a psychotic bitch with a knife in her hand.

Something clattered on my left, and a minute later Mitch padded back into sight sliding a gun into his shoulder holster, a blank sheet of paper in one hand. He gave Julia the paper, and she knelt in her pencil skirt and heels to set it on the floor at my feet.

"She won't do it," I said, fighting chills as she ran the tip of the knife lightly down the left side of my neck without breaking my skin. "Kenley won't bind me to you."

"Oh, I think she will, if the alternative is your prolonged death and her own long-term suffering. She'll bind you because she knows that as long as you're alive, there's still a tiny chance you could rescue her, or vice versa." She pressed harder with her knife and my jaw clenched when the point bit into my skin. "Hope is more dangerous than any weapon ever wielded, Kristopher Daniels." My name sounded like profanity, falling from her lips, and I wanted to tear her tongue out as warm blood dripped down my neck. "False hope, even more so. Your sister is going to bind you into a simple servitude contract composed of too few words to form loopholes, because the alternative is nothing she wants to think about." She drew her left index finger up my neck, and it slid too easily over my skin, slick with blood, the key to any man's undoing. "In fact, I think you're going to *tell* her to bind you, because the alternative is something you won't want to see or hear. Something you won't want to know you caused."

"I will tear your throat out the first chance I get."

"There won't be a chance." Julia set down her knife and picked up the paper, then made a show of stamping her fingerfull of my blood at the bottom of the page, where my signature would go, if I were to sign the document that would precede it.

But I wouldn't sign.

And that wouldn't matter—not with Kenley sealing the binding.

Julia wiped the blade of the knife on her dark skirt, then handed it back to her guard. Then she pulled a pen from the purse she'd left on her chair and held the blank sheet of paper against the wall, so she could write on it. She scribbled for mere seconds. Only two lines.

My heart thumped so hard I could practically hear it. I was too far away to read the lines, but I could tell from the brevity that she was right—there weren't enough words to form a decent loophole. It probably said something like, "Kristopher Daniels will protect me with his every breath and obey my every order, whether stated or implied."

Julia Tower was every bit as much of a monster as the one she'd replaced.

"Watch him," she said to Mitch, who now sat in her chair, putting his shoes on. Then she disappeared through the door, into the short hall that would lead her to the room where my sister was being held.

"You saw my family?" I said the minute the door closed behind Julia.

Mitch tightened the knot in his shoelaces, then set his foot on the floor and rested his elbows on his knees. "Just Kori. But her boyfriend and your girlfriend were with her."

Through the window, on the edge of my vision, I saw Julia step into Kenley's room. Lincoln stepped back to make room for her, and when Julia gave him an order I couldn't hear, he pulled the blindfold from Kenni's head.

Her eyes widened when she saw him, and fear glistened like tears in her eyes.

Mitch stood and stalked toward me with an arrogant swagger born of the fact that I was tied up, but he was free—an irony, if I'd ever seen one, considering that he was bound to Julia and I was, at least for the moment, in charge of my own decisions. "You're still bleeding. I'm not going to pass up an opportunity like that."

In the other room, Julia was still talking. She held up the oath she'd drafted, and Kenley glanced at it, then shook her head. Julia gestured angrily at me through the glass, and Kenley responded with what could only be a Kori-inspired string of expletives.

Mitch leaned closer, drawing my attention as he pulled a wadded-up tissue from his pocket. He leaned in to mop up the blood on my neck, and I lurched upright as hard and fast as I could, sacrificing balance for power. My forehead smashed into his and he stumbled backward stunned.

I wobbled on my feet, still tied to the legs of the chair.

The guard by the wall drew his gun as Mitch tripped over his own feet and hit the ground on his ass. "Don't shoot! Julia wants him alive."

The guard hesitated, and I took advantage of that moment to throw my full weight at the ground, using Mitch to cushion my fall. I twisted at the last second, driving my shoulder into his torso. I felt something crack, and Mitch howled over at least two fractured ribs.

When I looked up, the guard was almost on us, his gun in hand, but unaimed. I shoved my legs out straight as hard as I could, and was rewarded when the ties around my ankles slipped over the ends of the chair legs.

Now free from the chair, my hands still tied at my back, I waited until the guard was almost on me, then rolled off of Mitch and twisted to the side. When the guard hesitated to shoot me a second time, I wrapped my feet around his left ankle and bent my knees, pulling as hard as I could. His leg slipped out from under him and he went down on his right hip on the concrete. Hard.

The guard groaned, and I sat up, then spun on my ass. In position, I leaned back and brought both heels of my boots crashing down into his skull. Blood burst from his nose and his eyes closed. His hand went limp and his gun clattered onto the concrete. I slammed my heels into his throat, crushing his windpipe. He gurgled and choked, but did not regain consciousness.

He'd be dead in minutes. I couldn't afford to leave a trained fighter alive at my back.

Mitch backed away from me on his ass, one arm pressed to his side, struggling to get to his feet. He seemed to have forgotten he had a gun, which supported my theory that he'd been a glorified taxi service for Jake Tower, rather than hired muscle. No one with any real training would have forgotten he was armed, even with a couple of broken ribs and a bruised ego.

I couldn't see the window from the floor, but the fact that Julia hadn't sent in more guards said that she and Lincoln hadn't yet noticed what was happening, and my stomach churned over the thought of what would be horrible enough to hold their attention for so long.

My pulse whooshing in my ears, I rolled onto my knees, then stood—a challenge in equilibrium for sure. But the next part was an even bigger challenge. Balancing on one foot, I bent in half and tucked one leg to my chest, then slid my bound wrists beneath my own backside and slid that leg through the loop formed by my arms. I repeated with the other legs and my hands were in front of me, still bound, but now much easier to use.

Bending, I snatched the dead guard's gun and aimed at Mitch, who'd finally made it to his feet. "Lift your gun from your holster with two fingers and drop it on the ground."

"Fuck you."

I took aim at his chest, and he swallowed visibly, then reached for his gun.

"Slowly."

Mitch lifted his gun from his holster with his thumb and forefinger, then bent to set it on the ground.

"Kick it to me."

He did, and I bent to catch it with my foot. "Does Julia have a Jammer?"

He answered without hesitation. "She did. You just kicked him in the face until he quit breathing."

I wanted to shoot him. I wanted to shoot him *so* badly. But he was unarmed. That would be murder.

Julia was a murderer, if by proxy. I was not.

Instead, I crossed the space between us in four steps aiming at his heart. "You don't have to—" he said when I got close enough to see the fear in his eyes, and I slammed the grip of his own gun into his right temple. Hard.

Mitch crumpled to the ground, and I kicked him in the head for good measure. Then I dropped his gun into my holster and knelt to dig his phone from his pocket. I dialed Kori from memory, but my finger froze on the last number when I turned toward the window to find Kenley's room empty.

You can't see the whole room, I reminded myself as I pressed that last button. *She's fine.*

I hadn't fired the guard's gun, so the chances of them having heard the fight were slim.

I held Mitch's phone to my ear, and Kori answered on the third ring. "Who the hell is this?"

"It's me."

"Kris!" Something scratched the phone, and her next

words were muffled. "It's Kris!" Then she was back. "Where are you? Where's Kenley? Are you okay?"

"I'm fine. Julia's around here somewhere, and I don't know how many men she has, but I could use as many extra hands as you have. Kenley's…in trouble. I'm going to find her. But I just killed the Jammer, so you should be able to track me."

"Cam's already on it," she said.

"How's Sera?" I jogged across the warehouse floor toward the panel of switches on one wall. "Is she okay?"

"Scared. Pissed off. Armed and dangerous. She's something else, Kris."

"I know. Tell her I'll see her soon." I hung up, shoved the phone into my pocket, then slammed my hand down on the bay of switches. The lights all went off at once, and the large room was now barely illuminated only by the light shining through the window into Kenley's room. There was plenty of darkness through which Kori could bring in our allies, and just enough light to lead me to the door Julia had disappeared through.

I opened the door and aimed down the short hallway, but it was empty. Three doors opened into the hallway, but they were all closed. The first had a square window cut into it, glowing with light from within.

I peeked inside, and my heart stopped beating. Lincoln had my sister pinned to the wall, out of sight from the window.

When I opened the door, I could hear her sobbing. Begging. I crossed the floor in three steps and pulled him off her by one shoulder. He was huge, but I'd caught him by surprise. One more shove, and I had him against the wall. He shouted something inarticulate and went for his gun, but I was faster. I put the barrel of my .40 against his forehead and pulled the trigger.

Blood and brains flew everywhere. I let him go, and Lincoln's body slid down the wall, then thumped to the floor.

The first sound I heard, while the thunder of gunfire still echoed in my head, was my sister's raspy, shocked breathing. Her shirt was torn open. Her hair was splattered with blood and gray matter. Her eyes were huge. Her face was bruised. But she was fine.

Kenley launched herself at me, and I held my gun to one side while she hugged me, unable to return the gesture with my hands bound. "Are you okay?" I asked, right into her ear, to make sure she could hear me above the ringing in both our ears.

She nodded, and her hair caught on my stubble. "I want to go home, Kris."

"I know. Cut me free, and let's go."

She pulled a knife from Lincoln's belt and cut through my zip tie, then dropped the weapon as though it was on fire.

I glanced into the hallway, and when I found it empty, I led her into the main warehouse, still dark from when I'd left it minutes earlier. I had her hand in mine, my eyes closed, and my focus already on the hall closet in our hideout house, when light flared to life all around us.

"Drop your gun, or Kenley takes a bullet in the leg," Julia said, and I froze, Kenni's hand still trapped in my grip. Heels clicked on the concrete behind me, and a second later Julia stood in front of me, still coldly put-together in her dark suit and stilettos, while my sister and I were accessorized with Lincoln's blood and brains.

Four men fanned out around her, pointing guns at us, and the shuffle of shoes on concrete said there were at least two more at our backs. Shit! Where were Kori and Ian?

"Drop it," Julia repeated, and I clicked the safety on, then tossed my gun toward her. It landed almost halfway between us.

"Kris…" Kenley was terrified. "I'm not going to bind you to her. I'm not going to. I don't care what she does."

"Without a binding, your brother has no value to me. If you won't bind him, I'll have to kill him." Julia gestured to the guard on her left, who raised a 9 mm pistol and pointed it at my chest.

Gunfire exploded and I closed my eyes, waiting for the pain.

The pain never came. I kept breathing. Something thumped heavily to the concrete.

Kenley gasped.

Julia shouted.

I opened my eyes to find the man who'd been aiming at me now lying on the floor with a hole in his forehead. Before I could process that, people started shouting and guards raised their weapons.

Kenley's hands flew up to cover her ears. She dropped into a squat. I dropped with her and wrapped her in my arms, then turned my back to the gunfire.

Three more shots rang out in rapid succession, echoing over one another, half-deafening me.

Three more of Julia's men hit the ground, without firing a shot.

Julia backed away from us, her eyes wide and scared. I let go of Kenley and lurched for my gun, then turned in time to see Ian and Kori each fire one more time, standing just inside the door. Julia's last two men hit the ground, and suddenly Kenni and I were surrounded by bodies.

I stood, gaping at the scene around me, too shocked

to truly process it, beyond the obvious blood spilled and lack of living opponents.

Kori lowered her weapon and ran for Kenley, while Ian held Julia at gunpoint from across the room. My sisters embraced, both bawling, and my own eyes watered at the sight of them together again.

Movement to the right drew my attention and I turned to see Olivia and Cam step in from the hall. "What, you didn't leave any for us?" Liv pouted.

"The rest of the building's clean," Cam said. "If she has any more, they're not here."

I turned to Julia, aiming at her chest. "How many more are there?"

Her mouth opened, but nothing came out.

"How many?"

"It doesn't matter." Another shot rang out from behind me, and Julia stumbled backward. Blood bloomed on her blouse, then spread to the jacket covering it. "They won't be hers when she's dead."

I turned so fast the room spun around me. Sera stood three feet behind me, still aiming at Julia. She lowered her gun and smiled at me, and for the first time since I'd met her, she looked happy.

Three steps later, she was in my arms, and for the first time since I could remember, my world made sense. Before she could do more than hug me back, I whispered in her ear. "I will never let you go again."

Twenty-Two

Sera

The gun was warm in my hand and Kris was warm in my arms, and Julia Tower lay dying on the floor, fifteen feet away. But all I could think about was what he'd said.

I will never let you go again.

"So…you're not mad that I shot your bad guy?"

He pulled back so he could see me, and his blue-gray eyes were bluer than ever. "Are you kidding? I take partial credit for that kill. I taught you to shoot."

"Oh, please. It's not like she hit a moving target from a quarter-mile away." Kori rolled her eyes, but her tone was familiar. She was teasing me like she teased Kris. As if she might actually like me, beneath the criticism. "And anyway, she's not dead yet." Kori nudged Julia's arm with one foot. "Any questions for the bitch, before I put her out of her misery?"

"I have one."

Kori gave me a "be my guest" gesture, and I pulled Kris with me until we were staring down at Julia Tower, who lay gasping on the floor, blood still welling from the hole in her chest.

"Why?" I demanded. Julia's eyelids looked heavy, but she was still in there. For another minute or two, anyway. "Why did my family have to die, just so you could kill me? There must have been another way."

"I didn't—" She coughed and gasped, but her eyes never lost focus. "I didn't kill your family."

"Aren't you supposed to confess your sins before you die?" Kris nudged her thigh with his foot. "Can't you just admit it, and give her some closure?"

"Fuck—" Julia choked again, then swallowed with obvious effort "—you."

Kori aimed and fired her silenced pistol before I even realized what she was doing. Julia shuddered, then went still, and her dead eyes seemed to stare right through me.

I stumbled backward, gaping at Kori in shock. "Why did you do that?"

She holstered her gun and met my gaze. "Because she wasn't going to give you what you want, and I can live with killing her, but I'm not sure you could. I don't want you to have to."

"You don't…" I didn't understand until Kori pulled me away from Kris and wrapped me in a hug that felt like equal parts vise and embrace.

"Consider it a gift. Welcome to the family, Sera." My eyes watered, but before the tears could fall, her grip tightened, and she added. "If you hurt my brother, I will hunt you down and cut your heart out."

"She's kidding." Kris pulled his sister off me. "Tell her you're kidding, Kor."

Kori just gave me a creepy half smile, then walked away to help Ian, Van and Kenley with the bodies.

"She's not kidding." I drew him into a hug and whispered into his ear, "But she'll never have a reason to go after my heart. I'm not going anywhere, Kris. And I would never hurt you."

But the words were hardly out of my mouth when he stepped away, holding me at arm's length, and the look in his eyes scared me.

"You can't know that—" He shook his head and started over, and that unease inside me grew. "I have to tell you something."

"Now?" I glanced around at everyone else, cleaning up without us. We should help.

"Yes, now." He blinked, and his eyes filled with pain. "It's my fault, Sera. What happened to your family. What happened to you…" He reached down and laid a hand on my stomach, over my clothes. "I was supposed to stop it. It was in the notebook, but I couldn't figure it out." He frowned. "No, I stopped trying to figure it out. If I'd tried harder—if I'd *kept* trying—I could have stopped it. They would still be alive. You'd still be whole. You'd be a mother."

"No," I said, and when his eyes shone with tears, my own started to burn. "*No,* Kris, that had nothing to do with you. I don't care what Noelle said, and I don't care what you wrote in that damned notebook. It wasn't your fault for not understanding any more than it was my fault for going off to college and leaving them vulnerable. And I'm not going to let you steal blame from Julia. Let credit go where it's due. *Julia Tower* did this. And now she's paid for it."

"But—"

"No. It's over. She's dead. I'm ready to remember my family the way they lived, Kris. Not the way they died. And if you can't let this go, I won't be able to."

He stared at me like he didn't believe me. Like he wanted to, but couldn't.

"I want to tell you about them. I want to show you the pictures. I want you to know them, but that won't work if you feel guilty for something you didn't do. Let it go, okay? We both have to let it go. Starting now. With *her*." Julia.

With Kris's hand in mine, I stared down at Julia's body, trying to decide what I should be feeling. I'd shot an unarmed woman. I hadn't even hesitated. If Kori's bullet hadn't killed her, mine would have.

What did that say about me? That I was more like the Towers than even Julia had known? That I'd just put an end to their reign of brutality?

Was it even possible to end violence with violence?

"Hey." Kris took my chin and stared into my eyes. "Are you okay?" he said after less than a second. "She deserved much worse, Sera. Kori would have let her suffer first, if she hadn't wanted to take the death off your hands. Do *not* feel guilty for this."

"I don't." And that was part of the problem.

"You saved a lot of people today. Everyone Julia would have gone on to hurt owes you a thank-you."

"I know." And I *did* know. Julia had to die. Someone had to kill her. Someone had to step up and do what needed to be done. The part that bothered me was that I *didn't* feel guilty. I felt…nothing.

Nothing but disappointment. I'd wanted a confession. Without one, her death felt…empty.

"Is it over?" Kenley asked, and I turned to see her staring at Julia with one arm around Vanessa's waist, her free hand holding her torn, blood-splattered shirt closed.

"Almost." I held my hand out, and she let go of Van to take it. "I'm Sera, by the way." She was a slightly shorter, slightly curvier version of Kori, without the obvious hard edges. Except for the fresh bruise on her cheek.

"Kenley." She shook my hand, then shot a questioning glance at her brother.

"Jake's biological daughter." His arm tightened around me. "Sera just inherited…well, nearly everything Jake had."

Her curious gaze found me. "Including the contracts?"

"*Especially* the contracts," Kris said.

"But I'm not going to keep them." I glanced back to see Olivia, Ian and Cam unrolling sheets of black plastic, while Kori came in from the darkened hallway with a gallon jug of bleach in each hand, rolls of duct tape climbing her thin forearms like bracelets. "I don't want any part of this. I'm going to release them. All of them."

"You're serious?" Kenley stared at me in disbelief. "You don't want…the power?"

I shook my head. "All I wanted was justice, and Kris was right—it didn't live up to my expectation." Without a confession, even though Julia's death had no doubt saved countless people from years of suffering, I had no closure.

I would have to recover from their deaths the long way. With time. And Kris, and the new family that had welcomed me into their fold.

"So, you're just going to give it all up?" Kenley was obviously having trouble with the concept. Or with believing me.

"Yeah."

"Not the money!" Kori called, helping Ian heft a dead Tower guard onto a sheet of black plastic. "She's going to keep the money. And if we're all very nice to her, she may use it to help us take down—" she glanced at Cam and Liv, then seemed to be rethinking whatever she'd been about to say "—other hostile organizations. There's no better way to put blood money to use than by taking down the remaining bad guys."

The Cavazos syndicate, obviously. But if Cam and Liv had any real knowledge of that, they'd have to report it. If I understood correctly.

"But we can discuss that later." Kori folded plastic over the dead man and Ian ripped a long piece of duct tape from his roll.

Kenley laid her hand on my arm. "Sera, if you're serious…there's a short cut. It wasn't possible before, because neither Julia nor Jake wanted to break the seal, but if you really want to…I can… Well, I can just remove *your* will from the contracts I sealed for Jake."

"All of them?" I glanced at Kris for confirmation, but he seemed as surprised as I was.

"All of them *at once.*" Kenley gave me a shy smile. "I would have done it years ago, if I could have, but it can't be done unless the instigating party wants to end the agreement."

I stared at her, stunned. "I do. Let's do it." The sooner the better. I hated knowing there was still a target on my back—from Cavazos—and I didn't know how to protect myself from him like Jake and Julia had.

But then, I'd outlived them both. Surely that meant something.

Kenley frowned apologetically and looped her arm through Van's. "I'm pretty tired right now, but…"

"Give us a day to get her fed and rested." Vanessa squeezed Kenley's arm and gave me the brightest smile I'd yet seen from her. "We'll do it in the morning. *Then* this will be over."

"It'll never be over. Not as long as there's anyone out there willing to step into Tower's shoes." Kori's proclamation was followed by another rip of duct tape. "But this is a start."

"She's right." Kris leaned in and kissed me, then whispered into my ear, "This is a damn good start."

We spent most of that day cleaning up the massacre. Wrapping bodies in plastic, bleaching and scrubbing the concrete and getting rid of every sign that Julia and her men had ever been there. And that we had.

If I hadn't already harbored a moral objection to murder, I would have developed a labor-based objection founded solely on the amount of work it took to get rid of the evidence.

By the time we finished, there was a stack of bodies against one wall and more trash bags than three of us could carry. Kenley was beyond exhausted by then, even though she'd spent most of her time with Julia in a chemical coma. Evidently "unconscious" isn't the same as "sleeping." So Kris took her back to the House of Crazy to get cleaned up and rest, where she could keep an eye on Gran and Gran could fuss over her youngest granddaughter.

It took several trips through the shadows to get all the trash out of the warehouse, and once that was done, Kris took me back to the house so I could check on Gran and Kenley and come up with something for dinner. Something that would feed nine.

Gran was glad to see me. Kris had been checking in on her throughout the day, but I wasn't sure how many of those visits she actually remembered, and Kenley had taken a long hot bath, then laid down for a nap.

I promised Gran I'd help with dinner as soon as I'd cleaned up.

When I turned off the downstairs shower, clean, but even more exhausted, I could hear Gran holding a conversation with herself while she cubed cheese for some kind of spicy dip she said Kris had loved since he was a kid. I dried and put on more borrowed clothes, then rung my hair out in my towel. I was wiping the mirror with a clean rag, ready to pull a comb through my tangled hair, when someone answered Gran's question.

The rag fell from my hand into the sink and I froze, listening carefully.

The voice spoke again. It was a woman, but it was definitely not Gran. Or Kenley.

I glanced around the bathroom for several seconds, searching for Kris's phone—which I'd had all day—and my gun before realizing I'd left both in the living room. On the coffee table.

Damn it! I hadn't expected to be threatened in our own House of Crazy. But unarmed or not, I couldn't leave Gran alone with whoever she was talking to, so I opened the door as quietly as I could, then stepped into the hall. I'd gone two steps toward the kitchen, listening as Gran listed ingredients for her dip, before the loose board in front of the hall closet creaked, announcing my approach.

A woman stepped into the living room doorway, and even with her form backlit by the brighter light from the kitchen, I recognized her.

"Sera!" Gran called from behind her, chopping onions at the counter. "Do you know Gwendolyn? She and her friend are friends of my daughter, Nikki. They're going to try some of my dip while they wait for her to get back."

I smiled at Lynn and ran the fingers of my left hand through my wet hair. *Poor Gran.* "Nikki is…"

"I know. Nikki may not be back for a while." Lynn winked at me as her friend stepped into the doorway with her—a tall man who nodded at me, but didn't smile. "This is Sean. He gave me a ride."

Sean was a Traveler. He had to be, because the only way they could have gotten into the locked-up house was through the closet we'd left dark for Kris and the rest of my new family.

"Hi, Sean," I said. He nodded in greeting, but said nothing. "What…um…what are you doing here?"

"We were worried about you." Lynn frowned, studying me. Looking for signs of injury. "My sister-in-law has been ranting about you for days, and that woman is… Well, messing with Julia is never a good idea. When she disappeared yesterday, we worried that she'd gotten to you."

"You were worried about me?" The widow was worried about her husband's bastard daughter?

Lynn shrugged. "You may not be my family—not by blood, anyway—but you're my children's sister. I couldn't face them if I hadn't done everything I could to make sure you were okay."

Wow. Julia, my own flesh and blood, had wanted me dead. But Gwen searched me out on her own, just because it was the right thing to do. *Speaking of which…*

"How did you find me?" Suspicion raised the hairs on my arms. I was untrackable.

"It wasn't easy." Lynn gave a nervous little laugh. "And the solution was kind of…grisly. When Julia disappeared, I searched her office. I found a bag of blood in the cabinet labeled with Kenley Daniels's name, so I used it to have her tracked, on the off-chance that you were with her." She shrugged. "We got no reading on her for the longest time, then, suddenly, she was just…there."

When Kris had taken her back to the house, and out of the influence of my jamming ability.

And that's when I noticed that my gun was no longer on the coffee table.

My pulse raced so fast that my vision started to swim, but I made myself smile. I stopped myself from fidgeting, or glancing nervously at Gran over Lynn's shoulder, or doing anything else to tip them off to my suspicion. Which was ill-formed, at best.

Why were they really here?

"Well, you've found me. And I'm fine, as you can see." I spread my arms in demonstration.

"And Julia?" Lynn watched me carefully as I sank onto the arm of the nearest living room chair, desperate to look casual. "Have you seen her today? She's still…missing."

Oh. Could that be it? Was she trying to find out if we'd taken Julia out of power? Or out of the *world?* I knew from my first encounter with them both that there was no love lost between the widow and her sister-in-law.

"Julia's… You won't have to worry about her for a while," I said. *Or ever.*

"Oh, good!" Lynn looked so relieved I couldn't help smiling with her. Until she pulled my gun from behind her leg and aimed it at me.

My heart clawed its way up my throat, then got stuck there, where I had to speak around it. I stood, my hands out to show that I was unarmed. "Lynn?" Her name came out as a croak—that was all the sound I could force out.

"I'm sorry, Sera. You seem like a sweet girl. But there's no place for sweet girls in this city, and there's certainly no place for them in the Tower syndicate."

"But…I don't want the syndicate. If you'll just listen…" If she'd just let me explain that I was going to set them all free, surely…

"That's good. And if you'd been willing to give it up, I would have let you walk away. But rumor has it you want to *disband* the syndicate. Honestly, you've been difficult from the beginning, and that little stunt you pulled with the texting campaign…" Disgust shone in her eyes. "I can't let you give it all away. This syndicate belongs to my children. It's their father's life's work, and you are *not* going to take that from us."

I heard her, but the part that kept playing over and over in my head was… "The beginning? What does that mean? What's the beginning?"

Nonononono...! But I understood, even before she could say it.

"The hiding, Sera. You've been hiding from me for years. At least, that's what I thought until Julia let it slip that you're a Jammer. Just like Jake."

"You were looking for me? Before Jake died?" The House of Crazy was *full* of guns. Any other time, I'd be tripping over them, but now, when I needed one, there were none to be found.

"At first. For nearly a decade," Lynn admitted. "Then I gave up for a while. I thought maybe you were dead— how else could Tracker after Tracker fail to find you?"

"Did Jake know?"

"Of course not. If he'd known about you, he would have wanted you. To *raise* you. I only knew because Julia told me. To hurt me. On the morning of my wedding, that bitch leaned in like she'd hug me and instead told me that my husband had a lover and a bastard daughter."

She'd known all along? She and Julia had *both* known about me?

"I made him swear an oath, right then and there, that he'd never touch another woman. I had it sealed in blood and everything. He didn't know why, because he didn't know about you. I guess I came off looking like a jealous, paranoid bride, but I wasn't going to take the chance of him fathering any more of *you*."

"My family..." I sank onto the chair arm again, struggling to think through this barrage of information. "Julia didn't..."

"She tried to find you and your family, but she never could. I found your mother's name and info in her stuff. In the documentation from when she'd tried to find them herself. And when I tried, I got lucky. You'd left for college."

Leaving my family vulnerable, without me there to jam their psychic signals…

It was all my fault.

"You had them killed on the *chance* that I'd be there that weekend?"

Julia chuckled and stepped over the threshold into the living room, Sean close at her back, threatening me with his very presence, while Gran chopped ingredients, evidently oblivious. "That was another stroke of luck. My plan was to flush you out by killing them. Who else would you have had to turn to then, other than your real family? I didn't know you were there that night until the man I hired showed up for his money."

That's why he didn't look for me. Curtis hadn't expected more than one daughter.

"So, what now? You're just going to kill me? So your son can inherit?"

Before Lynn could answer, a streak of movement from behind her caught my eye. Sean made a strange, pain-filled sound and when Lynn turned, I saw Gran standing behind him, her hand still around the hilt of the knife she'd buried in his neck.

My heart nearly burst through my rib cage.

Gran let loose a primal scream of rage, then shoved the dying man at Lynn, who instinctively tried to catch him. But he was heavy, and she was wearing heels. She stumbled beneath his weight and went down on one hip. Without dropping my gun.

Gran stepped around her and I grabbed her hand, then hauled her down the hall with me, away from the psychotic bitch with the gun. "Good timing!" I said, following her into her room.

She frowned at me, confusion shining in her eyes. "Nikki's dead, isn't she?"

426 Rachel Vincent

"Yes, Gran. I'm sorry. But thanks to you, so is that bastard in the kitchen." I closed the bedroom door and twisted the doorknob lock. And jammed Gran's rocker beneath the doorknob, for what little good it would do.

Then I lurched across the room toward the window and jerked it open. "Can you make it through?" I asked as Gran stepped into her slippers to protect her feet.

"I'm not that damn old, child!" She bent—she was nimble for a seventy-four-year-old—and I helped her get one leg out of the window, then the other. I lowered her slowly until her feet hit the ground, then handed her the cell phone from her dresser.

"Call Kris!" I said as the first bang of Lynn's fist shook the bedroom door.

"Sera!" Lynn shouted. "Come out now, or I'll go find Kenley."

"You can't kill her." For the same reason Julia couldn't—that would break the bindings she wanted her son to inherit.

"No, but I can *take* her. And if I do, she won't be sleeping on silk sheets. I'm not going to pamper her like Jake did. I watched him for years, Sera. I saw every mistake he made."

"You're going to take her anyway." I said it as soon as I realized it, and I believed it the moment the words left my lips. She needed Kenley alive and in custody just as badly as she needed me dead.

"I will, unless you come out and stop me." Her footsteps retreated, and I recognized the creak of the floorboard in front of the closet—and the soft click as she turned the light on, locking Kris and Kori out.

Shit!

I glanced around Gran's bedroom until I found the lamp with the infrared bulb, which was kept on at all hours. I turned the lamp off, then flipped the regular light switch next to the door, throwing the room into darkness, except for what moonlight shone in from the open window.

Then all I could do was hope that Kris would find the pocket of darkness I'd left for him. And that he'd bring an extra gun.

I'd found the woman responsible for the slaughter of my family—evidently the third time really is a charm—and this one, too, deserved a bullet.

But when Kris failed to materialize more than a minute after I'd given him darkness, Lynn's steps retreated down the hall toward the living room. And the staircase, leading to Kenley's room. Surely Kenley had heard the commotion.

Surely she knew to hide.

But I couldn't take that chance.

When I heard the landing creak with her weight, I eased Gran's door open and tiptoed down the hall, careful to avoid the noisy board in front of the closet. Lynn was halfway up the stairs, but I snuck past her to the body still leaking blood on the carpet where he'd fallen half-out of the kitchen. Surely Sean was armed.

But he was not. Or else Lynn had already relieved him of his weapons.

Crap!

She was almost to the top of the stairs.

"Lynn!" I ducked behind an armchair when she turned, already aiming at me. "Leave Kenley alone." Lynn didn't have a way out of the house anyway, unless she'd already called in another Traveler. How was she planning to get Kenley out?

Her footsteps came closer, down the stairs, but I didn't dare peek for fear of getting shot in the head. I had no idea how good her aim was.

I could only listen as she descended the stairs, squeaked

on the landing, then stepped onto carpet. Her pant legs whispered against each other as she came toward me, and I circled the chair slowly, still squatting, trying to stay out of view.

"You have nowhere to go," she said, but her taunt sounded more like a statement of fact. "You can't get out of this boarded-up house. You have no weapon and you're hiding from an armed woman. And before you decide you can take me, you should know that even if you killed Julia, you weren't her real downfall. Her biggest mistake was underestimating me."

I didn't doubt that for a moment.

She came closer, and my heart thudded in my ears. I circled the chair to my right as she followed on my left, and my thighs burned from holding a squat for so long.

Then Lynn lurched into view on my left, grim smile in place, aiming my own gun at me. "Stand up, Sera. At least face death like an adult, and know that your sacrifice will mean the world to your brother and sister, when they're old enough to understand."

I stood, because my legs were cramping. And because she was right. What kind of dignity was there in being shot on the floor?

"At least your death will be more merciful than your sister's. I promise I'll aim for your head."

"You bitch!" I lunged for her without thinking, aiming low, like my dad had taught me as a kid. My shoulder caught her in the chest, but only because I'd surprised her. She went down on her ass, but it only took her a second to regain both focus and aim.

I froze, and suddenly I couldn't breathe. I was facing my death when I'd only just rediscovered life, and all it had to offer. Kris. Family. Freeing people and taking down bad guys.

"Fine. A graceless death it will be." Lynn frowned up at me from the floor, taking aim two-handed. The world came into crystal-clear focus as the last seconds of my life ticked away, and I saw her finger tighten on the trigger.

Then sound erupted around us, and the side of her head fucking *exploded.*

I stumbled back in shock. My ears rang. My pulse raced. The gun fell from Lynn's hand, and her body hit the floor, half on its side. Bits of her brain dripped down the screwed-shut front door.

My breath came and went so fast the room started to spin around me. Then I saw Kris standing on the landing, still aiming at the dead woman, and the world came back to me. Everything went still, and he seemed to cross the room in slow motion.

"How…" That was all I could manage.

"Kenley let me in through her bedroom." He reached down to pull me up, and then I was in his arms, and I was alive, and he was crying, but he looked so happy. "I thought you were dead. I thought you were both dead."

"Is she okay?" Kenley asked, and over his shoulder I saw her at the foot of the stairs in a thick bathrobe, holding Vanessa's .22 like a kid with a water pistol.

Kris pulled away enough to get a good look at me. "Are you okay?"

I nodded, and tears spilled down my face. "I'm good. I'm *so* good." He wiped my cheeks with both hands, but more tears followed. "She killed my family, Kris. It was her, not Julia."

His brows rose in surprise, then a smile grew on his face, which felt odd, considering the dead woman at his back. "So…I really did kill your bad guy?"

I nodded, still crying. "You did. Thank you." I kissed

him. Then I kissed him some more. And when I finally let
him go, it was only so that I could say the most wonderful sentence ever. "I think we did it. I think we actually
just put the Tower syndicate out of business. For good."

"You rat bastard!" Kori shouted, and I pulled away
from Kris to see her standing halfway down the stairs.
Staring at the stain in the carpet formerly known as
Gwendolyn Tower. "*I* wanted to take out the last of the
Towers! I've fucking earned it!"

Kris laughed. "No one's taking out the last of the
Towers." He pulled me closer. "We're gonna keep her."

"I'm not a Tower," I insisted. But Kevin and Aria were.
I hoped with every cell in my body that it wasn't too late
for nurture to overcome nature for them, as it had for
me. And I fully intended to give it my best shot. With
Kris at my side.

Kori stomped down the rest of the stairs and propped
her hands on her hips, looking down at the corpse. "I'm
not cleaning that shit up. He who spills the brains cleans
the brains. You know the rules."

"I tell you what," Kris said, and his grin was irre-
pressible. "If you clean up this one teeny little corpse for
me now, I'll let you take out Cavazos all on your own.
Bargain of the century, Kor. Act now—this offer won't
last long!"

"Go fuck yourself," Kori grumbled on her way into
the closet, presumably to bring Gran in out from the
cold. "Both of you."

Kris laughed so hard I was afraid he'd choke.

"Don't mind her," Kenley said, clicking the safety on
her little pistol. "That's how she says 'I love you.'"

"Well, in that case, she can go fuck herself, too," I said.
But I secretly hoped she was already gone and hadn't
heard me.

Acknowledgments

This book happened during one of the craziest years of my life. It was born, written and edited while I had three others going in various stages, in the middle of my third move (this one mid-holiday) in four years.

Quite simply put, this book could not have happened without the dedication and patience of many other people, including:

Mary-Theresa Hussey, my editor, who worked on this book (on Kris in particular) during at least two of her own vacations.

My husband, who did all the packing, most of the moving, hauling, shopping, decorating, unpacking, cooking, utility hook-ups and even a bit of the pet-care while I did two crazy rounds of revisions on this book. Your repetition of the phrase, "Go work. I'll handle the rest," did not go unnoticed or unappreciated.

And, of course, all the folks in production at Harlequin MIRA, who hung in there with me, during the delays. I can't tell you how much I appreciate your patience and professionalism. It has been a privilege to write the Unbound series with your unfailing support.

"So, now what?" He tugged me away from the cooling corpse still oozing gray matter onto the carpet. "What will you do now that your mortal enemy's dead, her kingdom in ashes scattered over her corpse?"

"I want to give it all back, Kris." I stared into his eyes and saw my need reflected in his. "The money. The house. It's all stained in blood, and the only way to clean it is to use it for good. For your kids."

"My kids?"

I nodded. "What more could you do for them with Tower's fortune? How much better could you hide them? Protect them?"

"You're serious?" He stared into my eyes, searching for the truth. Demanding it.

"Yeah. But there's a catch."

"And that would be…"

"Me. And Kevin and Aria. We come with the money. You get all of us, or none of us."

I pulled him close for another kiss, and he groaned. "I'm in…" he murmured against my lips. "Kevin and Aria are younger than the kids I'm used to dealing with, but if they're your brother and sister, they can't be all bad." He frowned, reconsidering. "Well, they can't be worse than Kori, anyway. So I'm in for all of it. The only question is…how much of *you* do I get?"

I laughed as his steamy gaze traveled south of my chin. "All of me. But only if you say the magic word."

"Agh!" he growled as I followed him up the steps. "You and that damn word."

But in the end he said it.

In the end, he said it all night long.

* * * * *